REBELLING WITH THE BAD BOY

MOST LIKELY TO ★ BOOK THREE

SARAH SUTTON

REBELLING WITH THE BAD BOY

CHAPTER 1

This wasn't how I wanted to spend my birthday.

I dangled my feet over the bridge and knocked the heels of my sneakers against the side, staring off at the horizon. Lookout Ledge was the tallest point in Brentwood, where one could see the tops of the trees and the small houses below, and I was a giant gazing down at it all. And the houses were *way* down below. Far enough that if I fell, it'd probably be game over. I'd turn into Gemma Settler, the pancake, or end up skewered by a pine tree. Whatever way I went, it'd be messy. I didn't move, though, didn't scramble back over to the safety of the roadway. I looked down, no fear.

I didn't know what time it was, but the sun had started setting a while ago, the sky only a handful of warm colors now. The late August heat was starting to die out, but the back of my neck still felt sticky. Even the comfort of the sunset had left me, too embarrassed to look any longer.

In my hand, I gripped a piece of paper tightly enough for it to wrinkle.

Department of Motor Vehicles – Application for Non-Commercial Learner's Permit

The words were laughing at me.

Like any other sixteen-year-old on their birthday, the only thing I wanted to do was go to the DMV and apply for a driver's permit. Sure, I didn't really have anywhere to go, no friends to meet up with, but there was still a visceral need for that piece of paper. A freedom attached to something I suddenly needed so badly. And I was _sure_ my parents understood. After all, on my brother's sixteenth birthday, taking him to the DMV was the first thing they'd done after he got home from school. Dad took him for the test, Mom celebrated with them when they got home, and we all went driving together.

It'd been perfect, and I was ready for that to happen all over again with me.

Except when my parents got off work, it wasn't a trip to the DMV they'd planned—we drove over to the Oliphant's, where my parents decided to throw a surprise party for me.

"Mom," I'd said when we pulled into the driveway. Even from the other side of the roofline, I could see the bounce house set up, tall enough to loom over Mrs. Oliphant's roofline. A _bounce house_. For a sixteen-year-old. "I thought we were going to the DMV."

"The DMV?" If her voice hadn't been shocked, her

twisted expression made up for it. "Why would we go there?"

"For my learner's permit."

And then Mom had laughed—laughed like I'd told the funniest joke in the whole world. My dad, sitting in the driver's seat, had joined in, turning me into a comedian when I hadn't even given a punchline. "Gemma." Mom had turned around to face me head-on, tears of humor in her eyes. "That's a little silly, isn't it? Of course, you don't need your permit. I mean, you don't *go* anywhere. Not without us. It's a waste of time."

"Besides," Dad added in. "A license opens up a whole can of worms, especially for young ladies like you. Waiting until you're a little older takes away any risks and temptations."

Mom hit his arm. "The riskiest thing she'd do with a license is probably go to the fabric store."

They both laughed in tandem, happily climbing out of the car as if they hadn't left me and my shattered expectations in the backseat.

There had been a crowd waiting for us when we got to the backyard, the chorus of "surprise" ringing in my ears. I didn't have many friends to begin with, but none of their faces popped up in the sea of unfamiliar ones. I had to smile while people congratulated me. I had to pose for pictures with people I barely knew. My parents had only invited *their* friends and their kids, students at Brentwood High I never even talked to. When I cut into the cake, it was *their* favorite—strawberry-flavored when I preferred chocolate. Even down to the balloons, with rosy and pastel pink like they were having a gender reveal. My favorite color was teal.

Those little falling dominoes caused everything in me to jolt, the way one does when waking up from a deep sleep. For the first time, I saw the truth. These past sixteen years, I hadn't been living the life I wanted. I'd been living the perfectly curated one my parents built. And I never thought twice about it.

Until now, and it felt like I'd woken up from the world's most vivid dream.

Sitting on the bridge ledge, I studied the application a bit more, hating the sight of my meticulous handwriting. I'd even dotted my *i*'s with little hearts.

It was like looking at something from a time capsule. The distance between myself this morning before I crawled out of bed and now was immense. It was like I aged ten years in ten hours.

I tightened my fingers on the paper, twisting my lips into a frown even as my eyes filled. *Gemma Marie Settler*, I read in the top box, noting the stupid little heart-dotted *i*. A tear fell and landed directly on my last name, smudging it beyond recognition. Another fell, and then another.

Without warning, something tight wrapped around my chest and constricted to the point that I gasped. My back slammed against something hard, knocking the rest of the wind out of me. Frantically, I glanced down and found two tanned arms binding me, securing me to the chest of whoever now stood behind me.

A scream bubbled up in my throat just as the person

restraining me spoke. "Come off the ledge."

I tried to pitch forward to break free—despite that being a *terrible* idea, given the neck-breaking fall looming before me—but the arms held fast. "Let me go!" I screeched, or attempted to, because with the tears that clogged my throat, my voice came out hoarse. Still gripping the paper, I reached up and slapped the arm, breathing hard. "Let go, or I'll scream!"

Not that anyone would've probably heard me, anyway. This portion of Lookout Ledge was hardly traveled upon, since it had blind curves. I could see the traffic way below me, of course, zooming peacefully without a care of the girl about to be abducted above them.

Images filled my mind of me stuffed into a trunk, carted across state lines, never to be seen again. *On my birthday.*

My breathing started to reach hyperventilation levels, and I scraped my nails into the person's arm, digging as hard as I could to get them to let go.

If anything, it made them cling tighter, pressing me closer. "Don't do it," the unfamiliar deep voice said. The unfamiliar, deep, *male* voice. "I don't know what's going on, but nothing is going to get better if you jump. Whatever it is, it's going to be okay. Okay? So come off the ledge."

My hand on the hot forearm loosened its death grip. I glanced down at the treetops, the wisps of the top branches swaying in the soft wind, the reality of the situation replacing the knee-jerk reaction my brain had conjured up. "You think I'm going to jump off?" I asked incredulously, my voice coming out croaky. So, this *wasn't* an abduction?

"Why else would someone sit on the ledge of a bridge?"

Indignation filled me, overshadowing the alarm for a brief second. "I'm not going to jump."

"Prove it."

This time, I did fight against the stranger's strength to turn, craning my neck to look them in the eye.

A boy around my age stood staring at me, his gray-blue gaze locking onto mine. He had a scowl etched into his brow, like it was a permanent fixture on his face. Thick, black glasses rested on his nose and a blue baseball cap sat snug on his blond head of hair. Despite the heat, he wore a cotton candy-colored sweatshirt, sleeves pushed up to his elbows. He looked both familiar and unfamiliar, as if he looked *like* someone I knew rather than the person themselves.

"Prove it," he said again, voice as level as it'd been before. "Come off."

I blinked away at my hazy vision, and I spotted a scar on his cheek, one that was white and faded with time. "Maybe *you* need to prove you're not a psychopath trying to shove me into the trunk of his car."

The boy raised an eyebrow. "Do you see a car around?"

From the limited view I had, no, I didn't. He must've been walking up the path when he spotted me, which totally threw another axe in my theory. Which meant I had his skin underneath my fingernails for no reason.

I cleared my throat. "You shouldn't grab at people you don't know."

"I had this image in my head that when I came up to say something, I'd startle you enough that you fell."

"Maybe you should've minded your own business."

He seemed less wary about my intentions, despite the tear tracks that had to be on my cheeks. I could feel where the wind dried them on my face, and could see his gaze soften as he spotted them, trailing along my skin like a fingertip. "Couldn't have that on my conscience."

I drew my lower lip between my teeth, his words knocking against my defenses. "You're nosy, then?"

"Not usually." He let go of me entirely then, but stayed close. Close enough that he probably could've grabbed at me if he thought I changed my mind about not hurtling off. Weirdly enough, without the pressure of his arms, my body felt heavier. "But in this instance, yeah. I decided to be nosy."

I pressed my free hand to my chest, feeling my heart slowly returning to its normal state. If I had seen his face before he grabbed me, I probably wouldn't have been nearly as freaked out. He looked pretty harmless, honestly. And something about his presence made me feel a little more put together, less like things were spiraling out of control. The merry-go-round of thoughts slowed to a halt. "I was just clearing my head," I told him. "It's my birthday today. Sweet sixteen."

I saw him glance at the form in my hands, no doubt reading the title. "Were you going to get your permit?"

"I was *going* to," I said, and then sighed, shoulders

slumping forward. "Guess I'll be the only sophomore who doesn't get her permit on her birthday."

"Don't tell me your family forgot."

I halfway wondered if them forgetting would've been better. The thoughts that'd been building and building in my head like water pressing against a dam broke free, and they flooded out my mouth. "They didn't forget, but...I guess it kind of feels like they did, in a way. They threw me a party, but it wasn't really for me. There were so many adults around that it was almost like it was my mom's birthday instead of mine. I didn't even want a party, but did they think of that? Did they think of *me*? Of course not." Looking down at the permit application in my hands, I let out a sigh that rattled in my lungs, cutting off my rambling. "I don't know. In the grand scheme of things, my permit doesn't feel like a huge deal, but I was just..." My voice shrank. "I was just looking forward to it."

If it weren't for the party, though, and for them laughing about my license, I still would've been blissfully unaware of how little they knew me. Blissfully unaware of how little I knew myself.

That thought caused my throat to tighten, like the waterworks were creeping up again. I didn't want to cry, though, especially not in front of a stranger. I turned to him instead, meeting his stare behind his glasses, swallowing down the emotion. "Have you ever felt like the life you're living isn't the life you want to live? Like... you're too tied down to the role given to you?"

The intensity in the boy's eyes almost made me self-conscious at first, on the brink of taking my words back. It felt strange to ask, to vent thoughts that had only sprung into my head hours earlier. I'd never done that before, confessed my feelings to someone. It was like I was now a character who'd suddenly realized she was only saying lines because someone wrote them, not because I wanted to. Not because I believed in them.

And maybe it was because this boy was a perfect stranger, one that I'd probably never see again, that made the words flow much easier. He was probably moments away from berating me for complaining, for acting like a selfish, spoiled brat for not being grateful about even getting a party. I squared my shoulders, bracing myself for that response.

"I have," he confessed after a moment. "I have felt that way. Like I'm tied down to a role."

I hunched my shoulders as I leaned closer to him, like I was about to tell him a secret. "And what did you do about it? Did you fight against it, or did you just give in to it?"

The boy tipped his head toward his sneakers and laughed once, one corner of his mouth lifting in a sideways smile. Something inside me lifted as well, and I had the strangest urge to mimic him, to smile too. Even just a little. I wasn't sure why—the conversation was anything but light. "Is there a point to fighting it if nothing will change?"

My chest fell, because that'd been the opposite of what I'd expected him to say. I expected encouragement, but then again, maybe realism was better. For my situation, as a Settler, maybe it was better.

It's a little silly, isn't it? My mom's words crested in my mind, answering my question, too. *It's a waste of time.*

"You're probably right," I said, steeling myself. With jerky movements, I shredded the paper without mercy, feeling it slice against my fingertips as I worked it down to scraps. My throat ached as I leaned forward, legs scraping along the edge of the bridge, and threw the shreds into the air as hard as I could, like confetti.

Celebrating the death of the Gemma whose rose-colored glasses broke.

The momentum of the throw, though, tipped me off-balance. I gasped as I slipped a little, and even though it was only a second's worth of unsteadiness, the boy didn't miss a beat. His arm shot out and stretched across me like a seatbelt, hand wrapping around my hip and gripping firmly.

And I was suddenly nose to nose with a boy, staring into his gray-blue eyes.

Once again, the slight familiarity of him hit me hard, like a tickle in the back of my brain. The scar on his cheek caught my eye, white and half as long as my pinky finger, indenting his skin. His hand still grasped my hip, fingers splayed over the bone, five points of tingling pressure. Boys had never caught much of my attention before—mostly because I knew my parents forbade dating—but for the first time ever, I found myself hesitant to pull away.

"I'm Gemma," I told the boy, oddly breathless. "With a G."

"Gemma," he repeated, and I watched his mouth as he spoke it. "You should still do it."

For a wild moment, I thought he meant jump off the bridge. "What?"

"You should still fight it." Those long lashes gave a slow blink. "Your role. You should still fight to be the person you want to be, even if it doesn't work out."

There was the bit of encouragement I was looking for, but as he said it, something like panic bolted through me, as if hearing someone tell me what I wanted to hear was how I knew I didn't want to do anything. As if I needed someone to tell me that I *could* to know that I *wouldn't*. Which didn't make any sense. "Have we met before?" I asked, searching his features for some sort of clue.

The boy didn't react. "No."

"Are you sure?"

"Positive. I'd remember."

I drew in a soft breath, lips on the brink of a smile.

My ringing phone cut the silence between us. The boy dropped his hand from my hip and pulled back, straightening, all intensity lost. I fished out my ancient phone from my skirt pocket, sighing at Mom's name. "I should take this," I told him. "My mom is probably wondering where I am. I don't usually go off on my own."

I was reluctant to let him go, though. I still didn't even know his name—he'd never given it. I wanted to ask, but a part of me knew he hadn't given it on purpose. It didn't matter, either. I'd never see him again, and it was best to let him go now before I said something else that I shouldn't.

He took a step back to let me swing my legs around the bridge ledge, watching as I hopped onto the roadway. He gave me a wide berth, putting distance between us, almost like he didn't want to get too close. Or he didn't want me thinking he was too close. "Good luck...with everything."

"Thanks," I said, clutching my still-ringing phone, giving him one last smile.

The boy turned around and gave me the back of his cotton candy-colored sweatshirt, taking a few steps away. I answered the call at the exact second that he turned around, sticking his hands into the pocket of his hoodie. "Oh, and happy birthday, Gemma with a G."

Warmth spread through my chest almost uncomfortably. I wanted to tell him thank you, to call out to him and ask what his name was as he walked away, but Mom's voice interrupted me, high-pitched and echoing into the air even though I didn't have my speakerphone on. "Gemma?" she demanded. "Are you there?"

"Yeah," I said to Mom. I watched him go, waiting for him to turn around, but he never did. He walked far enough down the bridge that it began to slope down with the road, and he disappeared from sight. Whatever role that he felt like he was stuck in, I hoped that he could break out of it. One of us should have the chance to. "I'm on my way home."

CHAPTER 2

In tandem with the lurching hiccup of the copy machine, I tapped my fingers, watching as it pumped papers coated in blue and gold ink out of its side. Or, I was glaring, really, as if my stink-eye itself could keep the ancient thing alive. The main office of Brentwood was quiet, with the two remaining secretaries typing out on their keyboards in sleepy succession. Neither of them had looked at me since I walked in. In fact, as I made my way to the copier, the only greeting I received was "don't break it."

Now, I understood that the words hadn't been a joke at all; this copier was on its last leg. It probably wouldn't be a good thing if a sophomore broke the school's copier the first week of school.

From behind me, one of the secretaries attempted to lower her voice. "Do you think she'll expel him?"

"I doubt it. If she was going to, she would've done it at the *beginning* of the school day, don't you think?"

"Maybe he did something during the day, and she's dealing with it now," the first secretary said.

I didn't turn around to look at them, didn't clue them in to the fact that they really needed to learn how to whisper, and glanced toward the only door *she* could've been behind. *PRINCIPAL OLIPHANT*. During the summer months, she'd been Mrs. Oliphant. Hers had been the house we went to for pool days and barbeques. We'd had family dinners together at least once a week, and two weeks ago, my surprise birthday party had been held at her house. Mom and her became close when Mom was elected school board president a few years ago, and remained close ever since. Despite that, I felt like I only talked to Principal Oliphant a handful of times. Then again, during those dinners/get togethers, it wasn't *me* anyone focused on. I wasn't the child people were most interested in—that was my brother.

From time to time, I could see Principal Oliphant's figure pass back and forth behind the frosted glass as if she were pacing. The volume in her voice would raise high enough that it vibrated into the room, but it was hard to tell what exactly she was saying.

"I'm surprised he's not shipped off to some facility yet," the second secretary replied. Her voice had risen a little when she scoffed, now speaking almost like they'd forgotten I was there. "You heard what he did over the summer, didn't you?"

I flipped open the copier's lid and pulled out the flyer, quickly placing down the next that needed printing. The art teacher, Ms. Stone, had me printing three different sets of art fair flyers, and I was on my final print round.

"Got the cops involved and everything, I heard." One of them huffed—I wasn't sure which. "A student like that belongs at Jefferson High, not *Brentwood*."

I looked over my shoulder at them now and caught the eye of the secretary sitting closest to me. The two women fell silent, and half a second later, the keyboards clacking with a vigor that hadn't been present before. Despite them avoiding my gaze like their life depended on it, I wished I could've asked them who they were talking about. My curiosity had been peaked, and I knew a little gossip lover who'd die to know, too.

When the copier wheezed out its final copy, that's when Principal Oliphant's voice rose loud enough that I could hear it. "You're walking on thin ice as it is...given too many chances. I got the report of what happened over the summer...your last strike."

Yeah, now I was really curious. Who could've been on their last strike two days into the school year?

Despite my nosiness, with the rattling of the copier now silent, I had no excuse to linger in the office. So, with one last glance toward the frosted glass door, I set out for the hallway.

"Finally done, Gemma?" a voice called, and when I turned my head, I found my friend, Morgan Davies, leaning against the wall of the office. Her brown hair was pulled into a loose bun, her bangs swept out from her eyes. She was a sophomore like me, but she looked much older with her slim jawline and bright pink eyeliner. The only thing I wore on my face was the baby fat that seemed to age with me. "I told you I should've done that. You're technologically challenged."

"Am not."

"Are too. You have a *flip phone*."

"It doesn't flip; it *slides*."

And besides, that wasn't really *my* fault. My parents added a phone onto their plan for my brother, who got the latest model, but mine had been a last-minute purchase at the department store. My brother was the one who brought it up first, that since his little sister was in high school, she needed a cell. "*I got a phone when I was Gemma's age,*" he'd argued. "*She should have one, too.*"

Landon had an annoying way of being able to persuade Mom to do anything. Maybe I should've had him ask her if I could get my permit.

"Anyway, technologically challenged or not," I began, lifting the stack of flyers, "I acquired the goods."

Next step: hanging all the posters. Trying to find spots for all of the posters in Brentwood wouldn't be that hard, with two stories to space things out between, but it would take a while.

Morgan raised her arm, showing off where she'd looped the large clear tape around her wrist. "Let's get started. We've got a lot of ground to cover. Remind me how you corralled me into helping again?"

Morgan and I started out as friends when Mrs. Davies, her mother, joined my mom's friend group. With Morgan, it was one of those "friends by association" kind of relationships. That was how all of my friendships were —handpicked by my parents.

Except Mom hated that I talked to Morgan still, ever since she dumped Mrs. Davies from their friend group.

"Do you know someone who would be in trouble already?" I asked her as I handed over a flyer, watching her tear a piece of tape off her roll. We started with the lockers across the hall from the office. Since she was in charge of taping, I made sure to pick out the ones that would look the best against which color we chose. "In enough trouble to stay after school?"

"Hmm, maybe Wes Torres? Trisha Clemms? I could see them being in the office for something." She spoke nonchalantly at first, but then looked at me with wide, interested eyes. Gossip eyes. "Why?"

"There was someone in the office getting chewed out."

"I wonder if they need volunteers in the office. Do you know how much gossip I'd get if I was an aide?"

Especially with those secretaries, who couldn't seem to really keep their mouths shut. "Probably would get better information being an assistant for Brentwood Babble or something."

Brentwood Babble was the school's gossip site. Though it sometimes posted normal stuff like game scores or school events, the posts that people logged on for were the gossip-fueled ones. Especially if it was about the Top Tier, the elite group of the school. I wasn't sure there was a student at Brentwood who had no idea what Babble was; even freshmen knew about it.

"I *wish*. You know, I saw the girl who runs it in the hallway the other day—over the summer, she dyed her hair pink. And now, naturally, *I* need to dye my hair pink."

I handed her over another poster, smiling. "Except your mom would kill you."

"Hey, my family are already outcasted—what more would hurt?"

I knew the dig wasn't intended toward me specifically, but my mother. Morgan slid little comments in like that all the time, ever since the whole debacle last year. Mom was up for reelection as the president of the school board for the Brentwood school district, and Mrs. Davies had let it slip to another woman in the group that she voted for Mom's opponent. That woman blabbed to Mom, who, upon winning her reelection, promptly cut Mrs. Davies from their group.

Back then, I hadn't understood what Mrs. Davies had been thinking, going against Mom like that. I didn't get why she didn't keep it to herself. Now, after everything that had happened on my birthday, her motives were a bit clearer. Maybe Mrs. Davies realized she didn't like the role she played either.

Morgan and I navigated farther down the empty school hallways, our shoes squeaking off the freshly cleaned linoleum. My long skirt swished against my legs with each step, and I looked down to make sure it wasn't dragging too much against the floor. It was a brown plaid patterned one that I made last week, one that Mom picked out for school like she did every morning. I liked it well enough, but I'd caught more than one side-eyed stare today in the halls.

Morgan saw me looking at the skirt. "Why do you wear so many layers when it's hot out still?"

She knew why. She just wanted me to say it. "It's pretty lightweight," I said instead, drawing the side of my skirt out.

"Yeah, but *this* isn't." She reached out and pinched the fabric of my sweater. "You're going to get heatstroke."

Don't take the bait, I told myself calmingly, pinching my lips into a smile.

"How are you getting home after this?" Morgan asked, and once we reached the doors that led to the student parking lot, we backtracked to the opposite wing. "You definitely missed the bus."

"Landon's practice ends at four. He'll take me home."

I knew exactly what Morgan was about to say even before she opened her mouth. "Think maybe Mr. Quarterback will give me a ride home, too?"

"His car only fits two people."

"You can walk home, can't you?" she teased. "I'm just saying, how am I going to start dating my best friend's brother if we never have alone time together?"

This time, I chuckled, and it came out like a snort. "Hate to break it to you, but he's only got eyes for Madison Oliphant."

And of course he would. After all, Principal Oliphant was Mom's best friend, and best friends always dreamed of their children ending up together, right? Landon and Madison would look good together whenever Landon got up the courage to pull the trigger. Then again, it wasn't only Landon's love life Mom had planned out.

"Hey." Morgan pulled my attention to her. "You know, you never told me—why didn't you take the learner's permit test on your birthday? Or even after? It's been two weeks. The second the DMV opens on my birthday, I'm so there."

A ball of something dark turned in my chest, thinking of the way Mom had laughed hard in the car. "My parents want me to wait," I told Morgan now, making a show of shuffling the papers.

I didn't see her eye roll, but her voice made her stance clear. "You don't have to have their permission to get a permit."

"I do, actually. They have to be with me when I take the test. I already checked." Resentment had taken root behind my ribs that day, and I hadn't quite been able to get past it since. Even so, the push to defend my parents shoved me hard, forcing me back into my ingrained behavior. "It's better to listen to them. They know what's best."

Morgan didn't try to hide the twist in her expression. I mentally braced myself for whatever she was about to say. "For a sophomore, you're pretty codependent on your parents, you know that?"

And just like that, we were back where we started. "Just because I don't argue with my parents doesn't mean I'm codependent."

"No, the fact that you do everything they tell you is. And so is the fact that you tell them every single thing.

You don't *have* to tell your parents everything. You don't *have* to obey their every command." Morgan made a show of pointedly looking away from me. "You don't have to let your mom pick out your clothes every morning. You don't *have* to date Jaden Morris if you don't want to."

I squared my jaw, hating when our line of conversation went down this road. And it did often. I'd had the entire summer off from hearing her speeches, but of course as soon as school resumed, so did Morgan's insistence. "I'm not dating Jaden, for one—"

"No, you're *courting*, or whatever freaky thing they did in the eighteen hundreds. Letting your parents arrange your future marriage and what you'll name your babies."

The conversation was devolving at a pace I couldn't keep up with, so instead of fighting back, I simply shrugged. "Takes the pressure off of me for choosing the right name, then."

"Gemma."

I didn't know what she wanted me to say. Sometimes I wondered why Morgan cared so much. She'd built her soap box to stand on after our moms stopped being friends last year. She now took every chance she could to "talk sense into me."

She didn't get it, though. There was no escaping the expectations of me. Living how they wanted me to was easier than anything else.

It was like Bridge Boy had said—what was the point in fighting things if nothing would change?

"I appreciate you worrying about me," I said, pulling

out another poster and analyzing it like I was looking for a typo. "I know it's coming from a good place."

The intensity didn't fully evaporate from her expression, but it did lessen as the silence passed. When she elbowed me, it was a little too hard. "I don't want you being sucked into the hive mind. I want you to think for yourself."

But you know what happens when you don't give in to the hive mind, I wanted to say, thinking of her mother. *You're cut out entirely.* The thought of Mom pushing me away left a panicked buzz in my chest.

We came up to the bathroom doors, and after taping a poster to the girls' room, Morgan passed me her roll of tape and ducked inside. The roll scraped across my skin and hugged tightly against my wrist, looking a whole lot different than the way it spun loosely on hers.

With how jam-packed these halls had been only an hour ago, it was strange to see them so deserted. A "Welcome Back" banner hung from one corner of the ceiling to the other, stretching out with the Bobcats logo. I shuffled the flyers to one arm and smoothed my free hand down the side of my skirt to see where the high and low points were in my hemline. The fabric draped perfectly in the front, but in the back, it dipped low enough to drag along the floor, collecting dust. I didn't realize until now how wonky the hem was. Too thick in some areas, too narrow in others. It made for an uneven hemline.

Mom must not have seen it this morning, but she'd be disappointed when she saw it. She'd probably waste no time in telling me so. I grabbed the fabric of my skirt in the back and lifted it up half an inch, gauging how notice-able it was. Maybe I could fix it before she saw. She didn't get home from work until after five—that was plenty of time, right? I'd have to check my other skirts I'd made, though, to make sure they weren't faulty as well. Before Mom spotted it.

She'd say she taught me better. She'd make me fix it before letting me wear it again, and I could hear her words already. *Us Settlers have to look our best.*

Thinking of Mom's catchphrases weirdly had me thinking of Bridge Boy, and it was the bazillionth time he'd come to mind since I saw him. At first, I marveled at the bizarre quality of the interaction, him grabbing me tightly, afraid I was going to fall off the edge. And then I thought about that stirring feeling that'd come when he wrapped his arm around my waist, bringing our faces mere inches apart. Warmth had bloomed low in my stomach in a way I'd never felt before.

And then, every time, my recounting would end at the resolute way he'd spoken, head tilted at me, gaze seri-ous. *Is there a point to fighting if nothing will change?*

I was too preoccupied with my hemline, with my rollercoaster thoughts, to realize I edged too close to the corner of the hallway.

A figure swung around the corner and had no time to stop before slamming into me. Their shoulder collided with mine like a freight train, and the sharp force sent me spinning, the papers in my loose grip exploding up into the air like giant pieces of confetti. My shoe caught on the fabric of my skirt, and I tripped to my knees amidst the scattered flyers, palms jarring against the ground.

For a long moment, I sat there, blinking and shaking. My wrists ached from the impact, and so did my knees. From my peripheral, the boots belonging to the figure who'd slammed into me stood motionless.

On a numb sort of autopilot, I began shuffling all the papers together, and only stopped when the boots began to walk away.

Walk away. Seriously? "You're not going to help me?" I demanded, the incredulity in my voice crystal clear.

The figure paused in its retreat, turning around.

I cursed myself for letting the words snake out, opening the door for confrontation. Morgan might've, maybe, but I'd been taught better. I tried to pull on the timid smile I knew by heart, frequently used in times of tea parties and banquets, but when I looked up and met the gaze of who owned the bulldozer of a dark shadow, my politeness turned into horror.

Every school had a student whose reputation preceded them. The one that the seniors told freshmen about as a ghost story. Brentwood High had a few rotten apples to dodge, ranging from druggies to potential gang members, but there was one that took the cake. The Grim Reaper.

It would've been funny if the name didn't suit him to a tee. The dark colors he wore made him look like death himself, with a shock of wheat-colored hair that ended near the base of his neck. Even though I was only a sophomore, I'd known about senior bad boy, Hudson Bishop, a lot longer. Hudson had been the other participant in my brother's first fistfight during their freshman year. Landon's eye had been black and blue, and the split in the middle of his lip almost needed stitches. Even though senior-year Landon was the quarterback, ninth grade Landon had no idea how to throw a punch.

Hudson Bishop did. And it wasn't only Landon he'd attacked, but two others from my brother's friend group. After that fight, the Grim Reaper was born.

I ducked my head down until my nose was practically parallel with the ground, squeezing my eyes shut. Landon's beat-up face filled my mind's eye, as well as the other kids rumored to have picked a fight with Hudson and had lost. *Violent*, people would say. *Unhinged. Off his rocker.*

Hudson probably ate sophomores like me for breakfast.

The boots took dooming steps closer, and I curled my head to my chest, instinctively waiting for him to strike me or something. *Morgan, any day now*. Heck, or even a teacher. Someone could've walked down the hallway to save me from being eaten alive, but it was deserted, with no one but me and the scary senior.

The papers on the ground began shuffling again, and I flinched at the sudden sound. Risking the wrath of the beast, I peeked up.

Hudson crouched on the other side of me, his loosely laced boot centimeters from leaving a print on the flyers. Tears in his black jeans exposed the deeply tanned skin at his knee, right at eyelevel. His blond hair hung mostly in his eyes, which were focused on the papers as he compiled them.

"I'm sorry," I whispered, brain already reeling with the certainty that he was gathering the posters to dump them in the trash. My heart was thundering too loudly in my ears, mouth drying at the thought of any sort of conflict with him. Even just talking to him in general. "I —I wasn't watching where I was going."

It took him a second to lift his gaze, and when he did, I froze—turned to stone under the sharp, blue-eyed glare. Eyes much too bright of a blue to be real. They were almost hypnotizing. "*I* ran into you," he murmured, voice low enough to make me shiver. "*I* made you drop your stuff. *I* was going to walk away without helping." Hudson leaned over the papers, bringing the ice of his eyes closer, freezing me further. "Why the hell are *you* apologizing?"

They were words I normally would've shrank back from, especially when paired with the mocking tone he used, but I didn't. His reply wasn't amongst the list of ones I thought he'd choose from. *Get out of my way, grandma* or *Yeah, you'd better be sorry* were options, but not *Why are you apologizing when it's my fault*. Something in my spine prickled.

If I hadn't been thinking about my birthday before, I might not have noticed how familiar his voice was. I might not have noticed that the furrowed brow looked the exact same. I might not have recognized the white scar down his cheek, one that was half the size of my pinky. The outfits and the eyes were so drastically different, and he didn't wear the thick black glasses, but the scar—there was no missing the scar.

The Grim Reaper was the boy from the bridge.

I sputtered with the revelation. "You—you—"

The bathroom door swung inward then, and Morgan stepped out into the hallway while flicking her wrists. "How are they out of paper towels already?" she began in a thoroughly annoyed voice, but like my heart, she did a full-stop when she saw who now occupied the hall with us.

Hudson didn't look up at her as he finished compiling all the fallen flyers, tapping them against the ground once. All the while, I watched him, glad I had enough mental awareness to snap my jaw shut before he looked up. He offered the large stack out to me, but when I finally lifted my hands to take it, he didn't let go. Instead, he studied me for a long, long moment, and I waited for him to react to me, to recognize me the way I did him.

The left corner of his mouth curled upward. "Grow a backbone, Sophomore."

I stared at his twisted smile and the cold gleam of his glare, questioning a bit of my own sanity.

Hudson let go and shoved to his feet, something in his pocket jingling with the movement. Without saying another word, he walked past me, boots squeaking softly on the freshly cleaned linoleum, leaving two sophomores gaping after him.

"That was ten years just shaved off your life," Morgan hissed as she dropped to the ground beside me, bunching the fabric of my skirt in her fist. She craned her neck to watch the senior disappear down the hall. "That was *at least* five years off mine. You encountered the Grim Reaper and lived to talk about it."

I looked down at my now mixed flyers, at the spot where Hudson's hands had been a few moments ago. The depth to his voice still lingered in my ear, matching exactly to the voice from the boy on the bridge. He didn't act like he recognized me, though, even though I was sure I looked the exact same. Even down to the braid that pulled all of my hair back. He had to have known who I was.

Sophomore. He called me a sophomore. So he *did* know.

I looked over my shoulder, but by then, Hudson had disappeared through the double doors leading outside, and my stumbling heartbeat was the only lingering sign he'd been there at all.

CHAPTER 3

When I was little, I always loved it when Mom braided my hair. My dark locks used to be unruly and knot-ridden, and after every night-time bath, it was our ritual of braiding it out of my face. I'd sit on her lavender-printed quilt, tracing the seams in the stitching. Sometimes I'd chatter about my day. Sometimes she'd tell me about hers. More often, though, she'd hum a song that still played through my head in the quiet moments. Those memories were ones I kept in a treasure box, like little pictures I was afraid of warping.

Up until a few weeks ago, I hadn't really minded her doing my hair every morning. Really, I hadn't given much thought to it.

Now at sixteen, though, and never getting to style my own hair, that dark pit in my stomach seemed heavy.

"Why didn't you wear your hair up to bed like you always do?" Mom scolded me Thursday morning as she threaded her fingers through my hair. She was already dressed for the day, her black blazer hanging on the knob of the bathroom door. Her makeup was simple, as always, and the dangling diamond earrings she always wore hung in a swaying pendulum that I stared at in the mirror. She always dressed her best. "You toss and turn like you're possessed, and you've got a rat's nest back here."

"I had a headache last night," I told her, tracing my fingers along the white marble countertop, looking at her concentrated face in the mirror ahead of me. She had her vibrant red locks pulled up into a high bun, a color she shared with Landon. I'd gotten my dark hair from Dad. "I thought maybe taking it out would help. It's just so long."

"So *beautiful*, you mean." She leaned around my shoulder to give me a wide smile. "I can't imagine you without this hair. Even if it is a tangled pain sometimes."

"I can't imagine it either," I said on impulse, but knew that wasn't true.

I'd only had my hair cut once in my life. In the third grade, I'd gotten so sick of all the knots, so I took out my craft scissors and hacked at my hair. Chopping it off had been so freeing, so exciting. So beautiful.

I could still remember Mom's face when she'd seen me, and could still remember how hard she sobbed the rest of the night. Even now, a sick twist of guilt tugged at my stomach from simply thinking about it.

"Be sure you go straight to the library until your brother is done with practice," Mom said as she pulled hair from my temples, weaving it into a large French braid, sectioning it quickly. "I don't like the idea of you roaming around by yourself. There are a lot of...rowdy kids at Brentwood."

The only "rowdy kid" Mom had a grudge against was

none other than Hudson Bishop, and I wondered what she'd say if I told her what happened yesterday. She'd probably have a heart attack.

She wiggled her fingers to break free of a knot, and I bit down on my lip to keep from wincing. "You know," I began slowly, toeing closer to the water I knew would be freezing. "The sooner I get my permit, the sooner I could get my license, and the sooner I—"

"We talked about this." Mom's voice was patient, but in a way that made me feel small. Like she was speaking to a child who was misunderstanding something for the second time. "It doesn't make sense. We don't have a car for you to use, and you're always with us anyway. It isn't like you play sports either, Gemma. What's the point in a permit?"

"Eventually, I do have to get my license. To get my license, I need a permit."

Mom's fingers slipped in my hair again and tugged, hard. Tears sprung to my eyes as she scrambled to salvage the braid, and when she spoke again, her voice was terse. "Not now, Gemma. I thought I was clear about that."

I didn't know what I was expecting, bringing it up again. I didn't even know why I brought it up to begin with. That'd been happening more lately, my subconscious sneaking things out of my mouth. Our once easy conversations felt strained now, and I wanted to lash out, tongue heavy in my mouth with words unsaid. I stared at my reflection in the mirror, one that was wavy from the tears that gathered and pooled but never fell. "I'm sorry."

I conceded immediately, and really, she was right. It was better this way. "You're right."

She patted my shoulder. "One day, okay? It's better to let things be the way they are. Keep our heads down. Right?"

Keep your head down. Part of the mantra that I adopted from years of my parents repeating the phrase over and over again. When Mom first campaigned for school board president, it was exactly what they'd told me so as to not get in the way. Landon was the one they wanted to parade around for his athletic ability, and they never wanted me to get in the way of that.

Over the years, I slowly added another phrase to the mantra, one that they always seemed to insinuate but never said. Even now, it felt like Mom was saying it without saying it. Closing the conversation before we could actually have it. *Keep your mouth shut.*

Landon rapped his fist on the semi-open bathroom door, but didn't wait for a response before he barged in. Suddenly the bathroom was much too small. Even though Landon was the quarterback, he was built more like a defensive lineman, with broad shoulders and thick muscles. His reddish-brown hair stuck up every which way, and his eyes were still puffy from sleep. "I'm late," he gave as a greeting, shuffling through our shared bathroom drawers before he found his stick of deodorant. "The guys and I are doing a morning weight lift, and my alarm didn't go off."

"You're doing a morning workout and an after-school

workout?" The anxiety was clear in Mom's voice. "*Again?*"

But Landon dismissed it with a shake of his head, swiping up his toothbrush next and taking my tube of toothpaste instead of his. "Don't worry, don't worry. I won't pull a muscle."

"The quarterback *can't* pull a muscle. Your arm is one of the most valuable parts of that team."

"My arm and Connor's legs," he said with a smile, and leaned to give Mom a quick side hug. Before he ducked out of the bathroom, he stopped, looking at me in the reflection. "I'll see you after school?"

I nodded, giving in to what Mom had ordered. "I'll wait for you in the library."

And then, without another word, my brother was gone.

Mom finished up the braid quickly, tying it off with a clear elastic, and sending me to my room to get dressed. She had my outfit already laid out for me, and it was a long gray dress that went down a few inches above my ankles, and a big, long-sleeved shirt to wear underneath. It wasn't anything fancy, but to me, the outfits she chose all seemed the same. I wasn't even sure what clothes I owned, honestly. Even the skirts I made myself blended in with the rest.

"Well, don't you look ready to learn," Dad said as I walked out into the living room. He had his briefcase beside him for a day at the office, but he waited for me to leave first. His dark hair was cut short. "Your mother did a great job on your hair, didn't she?"

"She always does," I replied, folding my hands in front of me with a smile.

It was then that the doorbell rang, a delicate melody echoing through the living room. Mom gave a little gasp as she bounded toward the door. "That must be Jaden."

I sucked in a little breath, something like an inward sigh. The only problem was that my little groan sounded a bit too much like Mom's gasp of happiness, and Dad smiled knowingly at me as he got to his feet. "Give your dad a hug before you go."

"Jaden doesn't have to pick me up every day," I said as I went into Dad's arms, inhaling the scent of his cologne. He'd been using the same one my entire life, and it never failed to be as comforting as the hug itself. "It's okay."

"You know we don't want you walking to the bus by yourself," he said, patting me lightly on the back.

I fought another sigh, getting a smile ready for when I leaned back. "Have a good day at work," I said, because that was what I said every day.

"Make me proud," he said, because that was what he said every day. Except I always heard the undercurrent of words he meant but never said. *Don't disappoint us.*

The front door was wide open when I got to it, revealing none other than Jaden Morris.

Jaden grinned when he saw me. His black hair was perfectly styled with the sides closely shaved but the curls coiled on top. "Morning, Gemma. Your hair looks great today."

I was certain the braid looked the same as it always did, but I didn't say that. "Thank you."

Mom was a part of so many clubs that I couldn't remember where she met Jaden's family, but it was one random day that our moms had the less than brilliant thought that Jaden and I were a match made in heaven.

"Jaden, I can't thank you enough for walking with Gemma to the bus stop," Mom said, pressing her hand against her necklace. "I offered to walk her, but I'm sure it's not *cool* to walk with your mom."

"Oh, I don't mind, Mrs. Settler." Jaden sent the grin her way. "Living right down the road has its perks. I may not have my license yet, but it's all okay if I have someone like Gemma to keep me company on the bus."

"Gemma, did you hear that?" Mom tilted her head happily. "He's so sweet, isn't he?"

My cheeks hurt when I smiled. "Very sweet."

I turned to Mom and watched her eyes quickly dart all over me. She reached over and brought my long braid over my shoulder. "You look so pretty with your hair this way," she said lovingly, smoothing her hands over it. "Just like this, just over your shoulder."

This was another part of our morning routine—Mom adjusting my hair one last time. She would always tell me I looked the prettiest with the braid on display. I used to like it when she said that. Now, I felt like a doll as she adjusted my hair, like it was a part of me, but not mine. "Have a good day. Jaden, make sure she stays out of trouble."

"No worries about that one," he said with a teasing tone.

I gave Mom a hug before stepping past Jaden onto the front entryway, heading for the bus stop without looking to make sure he followed.

He did, of course, hustling to get in step with me after shutting the door. "How was your day yesterday?" He glanced at me, hooking his thumbs through his backpack straps. "Mine was okay. I mean, I have Mr. Norman for science, so that sucks, and I still am trying to get used to waking up early again, but it wasn't so bad."

When I thought of yesterday, all of it was overshadowed by the boy who slammed into me in the hallway. The boy who seemed like two different people. Jaden would've flipped if I told him about it, but it was a passing thought. "My day was good. I like school."

That again made Jaden laugh, like I'd told a joke that was moderately funny. "That's cool. I mean, I think the only period I actually like is lunch, but that's great that you enjoy it, Gemma. Hey, maybe some of your enthusiasm can rub off on me. I'll take anything I can get if I have to wake up at six-thirty."

I reached up and flicked my braid back over my shoulder, scratching at where it itched my neck. "Mmm."

The funny thing was that before my birthday, I'd *really* liked Jaden. He was a bit of a talker, but he was the only boy I'd ever been really allowed to spend time with outside my brother. The only boy who cared enough to try, too. I liked the broad way that he smiled, and I loved the vibrancy of his brown eyes. I loved the way he could hold a conversation and that he looked like he could be an actor rather than a kid in chess club. He was always handsome in the way he dressed. I liked the way he treated my parents.

After my birthday, I began really thinking it through —did I really like those things, or was I just going with what my parents said? Because now with the rose-colored glasses off, being with him left me suffocated. Trapped. It was a weird feeling, knowing the people around you were only there because your parents chose them to be, orchestrating every aspect they could. Even a potential love life.

"You okay?" Jaden leaned his head down level with mine, suddenly very close. "You seem lost in thought."

"Just tired," I replied.

"Tell me about it. You know, your mom gave my mom a new tea to try—have you tried the blend with valerian root? My mom said..."

I watched him speak with a buzzing in my ears, and I scratched my neck again.

Thankfully, it didn't take long for Bus 32 to pull up along the curb of the road. The back seats were already filled to the brim with freshmen, sophomores, and the occasional junior who hadn't gotten their license yet. It didn't matter, anyway—I sat in the seat behind the driver.

"Morning, Gemma and Jaden," Mrs. Savion greeted us when we stepped onto the exhaust-smelling bus, flashing me her purple-lipstick grin. She must've been well into her sixties, but her makeup was nothing short of flawless.

"Good morning," I returned as I settled into the seat,

laying my backpack as flat as possible over my lap. Jaden eased down beside me, careful to keep a few inches between our legs. I squeezed against the window, soaking up any amount of coolness from the metal to contrast the humidity.

"It's always a good morning when we see you, Mrs. Savion," Jaden said, buttering her up.

In the large rearview mirror that hung above the windshield, she shot us another smile. "Your mom raised you right, you know. Picture of politeness. Unlike that scoundrel back there—Mr. Kessinger! Get your feet *off* that window!"

One thing that I appreciated about Jaden was that he seemed to need his own private time once we boarded the bus. He'd talk my ear off as we walked to the stop, but as soon as we climbed aboard, he plugged in his head-phones and turned on one of the sitcoms he liked.

Since my sliding phone wasn't equipped for playing music, I fished my MP3 player from my backpack and plugged in my headphones, skipping until I found a song that was satisfying enough to listen to. And then I checked out. Sometimes I closed my eyes, maybe even caught a few extra minutes of sleep like I did yesterday, but today, I stared out the window, letting my mind wander.

Mrs. Savion wound the bus down the bumpy road leading to Vista Villas, one of the only mobile home parks in Brentwood. My eyes lingered on house after house that we passed, spotting kids' toys in the yard or dogs on the porches. The bus stop for Vista Villas was just off the main entrance road, and Bus 32 chugged to a halt, bouncing with each dip in the gravel.

Through the condensation on the glass, I saw him. He'd been sitting on top of a phone company cable box, but when 32 stopped, he stood. He rounded the front of the bus, where for a moment I couldn't see him at all, but he was in full view when he stepped inside.

Hudson.

His hair was wet and slicked off his forehead, and his dark jacket was open at the collar, exposing his throat. He held his black backpack by the handle, and even from a quick glance, I could see that the fabric on the thing was worn and frayed, as if he'd used the same bag all of high school.

The driver held a hand up, stopping him from progressing further, and I quickly pulled out an earphone to hear. "Sit up front, Hudson," Mrs. Savion told him, voice totally lacking the warmth she'd used with Jaden and me. "New rules. If you're going to be on my bus, I have to be able to see you."

"Works for me," he replied in a voice that almost sounded mocking. "I want to be able to see your pretty face, too." And then, after shooting her a grin, he brushed past her outstretched hand, depositing himself into the seat on the opposite side of the aisle from Jaden and me. He dropped his bag beside him, warning off anyone who dared to try and sit there. Not that anyone probably would've. Someone would've sat three to a seat before cuddling up to the Grim Reaper.

Jaden snuck glances over at him, whereas I obviously

gaped, even after the bus chugged into motion. At any second, he could glance over and catch my curiosity, but here I was, bold enough to not turn away. Hudson stared out the window the same way I'd been doing moments ago, but he looked a lot...edgier. Maybe it was the hard line of his jaw, or the cross of his arms, or the firm *stay away* curve to his posture.

Gawking at him now, I was almost positive I imagined the scar on his cheek yesterday. The warmth from the boy on the bridge was completely absent in Hudson; everything about him radiated ice.

"You probably don't want to stare," Jaden whispered in my ear, worry in his voice. "No telling what he'd do."

"Right," I murmured, sitting back into my seat, allowing Jaden's body to block my view. But even though Hudson was out of sight, it took a few more minutes for my pulse, and my thoughts, to settle.

CHAPTER 4

Most of the sophomore lockers were gold, but with the way *BOBCATS* was painted down the hall, mine was one of the few that had blue on it. I was a part of the *A*. I squinted at the folded piece of paper in my hand, trying for the third time to get the combination right. It was the third day of school, and I'd only gotten the stupid thing open a total of six times in between periods. I was convinced the office had copied down my combination down incorrectly.

I squinted, trying to count the right notches. 03-32-23. Couldn't any of those have ended on a five or a zero?

"Gemma?"

I turned to find Principal Oliphant standing behind me, a statue at the edge of the bustling hallway. Her hair was braided out of her face too, but instead of a long braid down her back like me, she wore hers in a bun.

"Lovely to see you," she said while taking a step closer, entering my personal space to step out of the flow of students. "I hope the school year is treating you well so far."

Despite how close she was with my family, I still regarded her warily. Maybe it was *because* she was close with my family. Maybe it was because I knew how brightly people could smile to your face while sneering at you behind your back. "It is."

"Has your brother been faring as well as you?"

"He's even more easygoing than I am."

She laughed on cue, a tinkling sound that only came off as fake if you knew what to look for. Her eyes didn't crinkle. "Well, there's something I wanted to discuss with you. Do you mind if we move this to my office?"

I gave up on my combination, shuffling my last period books from the crook of my arm to the center of my chest, hugging them tightly. "Sure."

She was a fast walker, Principal Oliphant, and she cut through the student body like water, forging ahead as if she was her own stream. Following in her clicking footsteps felt strange, like I was in trouble and not because she just wanted to speak with me.

It didn't occur to me that I could've *actually* been in trouble until Principal Oliphant opened up her private office door, and there sat Hudson on the other side.

He had his long legs stretched in front of him, and like yesterday, he wore a pair of ripped jeans. His arms were folded across his chest in a lazy way, slumping into the chair as if he was trying to fall asleep.

He didn't even jump when Principal Oliphant let the door slam behind her.

"Gemma, please have a seat," she said with a business-like tone, sounding significantly less friendly than she did in the hallway. Or maybe I was imagining it. Maybe I was paranoid. She sat down behind her desk and folded her hands on the top of it, nodding her chin at the empty chair beside Hudson. A chair that was only two inches from his.

I made myself as small as possible in the seat. We were so close that with the way his elbow pointed out, our arms could've touched. I made sure to keep mine tucked against my chest, clutching the textbook tighter.

My brain ran through the possibilities of why we were in here at the same time, but they all went back to yesterday in the hall and the papers flying high. Or even worse—if Hudson *was* Bridge Boy, what if he told Principal Oliphant about how I was sitting on the ledge? What if he told her his wild theory about me jumping off? My mouth ran dry at the thought of *that* conversation.

"Gemma, I understand you stayed after school yesterday to hang posters?"

Posters? This *was* about the posters? *Was that not allowed?* I thought to myself, brain working in overtime. Wait, if it wasn't allowed, they would've called Morgan into the office too. "Yeah, I—I did."

"And I understand this is something you'll be doing consistently for the duration of football season? Staying after school, I should say."

So, not exactly what I'd expected, but still strange. How she'd come to know that information, it was any guess. Maybe Mom had mentioned it. Maybe Landon had mentioned something to Madison, and Madison had told Principal Oliphant. "If that's okay." I glanced at Hudson, but he still hadn't opened his eyes. Maybe he *was* asleep. "I plan to sign in to the library every day, so I swear I won't be wandering around—"

Principal Oliphant chuckled a little, as if my high-pitched panic was amusing. "It's more than okay. In fact, Gemma, I was wondering if I could give you...a task, I suppose you could say, on a few of the days you stay later."

Suspicion immediately replaced the alarm that'd been growing inside me. Well, not entirely. More like eclipsed it for a moment. "A task?"

"We have a peer-to-peer mentor program here at Brentwood," she went on, gaze flicking toward Hudson. "It's usually reserved for seniors being a buddy to under-classmen—sometimes a senior is even paired up with a middle schooler—but I think a unique situation could be beneficial here."

Unique situation... Again, it did nothing to ease the growing confusion. That and the fact that the other third of the conversation still hadn't participated once. Prin-cipal Oliphant didn't seem interested in pressuring him to, either. "How is a senior a buddy to an underclassman?"

"They're like accountability partners. A mentor, of sorts. They do homework together, play games, and talk about life together. The goal is to get the underclassman comfortable with their progression into high school, and to help them feel less alone within the walls. And they always meet on school grounds, of course."

"That sounds...nice."

Principal Oliphant's smile stretched wider. "I'm happy you think so. I was thinking you and Hudson here could be each other's buddies."

And just like that, my alarm was back in full force. A buddy program might've been fun if it were anyone else. But when Hudson slowly lifted his head, like a vampire rising from a coffin, my panic resurged like it was back from the dead, too.

"On a few days you stay after, I'd like you two to meet. Work on homework together, do an assigned task. You can even play a card game if you wanted. Something to keep you occupied for the hour."

My throat was painfully dry, impossible to swallow. "Oh, I don't—I'm—I don't really need a mentor, Principal Oliphant. I have friends. I don't feel alone at Brentwood at all, I swear."

"Actually, Gemma, *you* would be *Hudson's* mentor."

I sucked in air that sounded suspiciously like a horrified gasp, unable to do anything but gape at her. A sophomore being a mentor to a senior? Me, Gemma Settler, a mentor to *Hudson Bishop?*

"That's us rounding back to the unique situation I mentioned." She laughed like it was a joke, but her punchline didn't make me nor the Grim Reaper chuckle. "Gemma, I'm hoping your responsible nature will rub off a little on him. Since you'll be here anyway waiting for your brother, I thought you'd be the perfect accountability buddy."

"I told you." Hudson's first words he'd uttered the

entire time came out low and gravelly, like the three sylla-bles were a threat themselves. "I'm not staying after school."

"And I told you that we're not having a repeat of last year." Principal Oliphant matched his firmness in a way my parents would've applauded. Maybe they all took the same college course. *Being Authoritative 101* and *that* was where they met. "Maybe this will teach you that your actions have consequences, Hudson. This is what I'd like to call preventative care."

He narrowed his eyes at her. "So, you're pairing me with a boring stiff three days a week so I don't go running around kicking puppies?"

I would've been offended if I hadn't been so desperate.

"Let's look at it this way." Principal Oliphant laid her chin on her hand. "I could put you in detention every day of the week. I could expel you entirely—your folder gives me more than enough ammo for that. Super-intendent Filmore is pushing for that. The school board is willing to pull the trigger if something else happens, but you don't seem too concerned about the bullet, huh?"

It felt like I was a civilian stumbling between enemy lines with the way Hudson and Principal Oliphant regarded each other, caught in the crossfire, preparing for impact.

She ducked her head to a folder, flipping up a page. "Tardies, unexcused absences, talking back to teachers—you've been in school three days, and I already have several reports of you displaying intimidating behaviors to other students."

Hudson turned and hooked his elbow on the edge of my chair, nearly touching the back of my head. I stiffened. "*Intimidating behaviors.* That's a new one."

"Brentwood has a strict code against bullying, and you know it. We've been down this road time and time again, and we're reaching the end of the rope."

He bit his lower lip, still smiling. "Did you expel the other kids for tardies and absences, or just me?"

"No other student had an incident like yours over the summer."

And just like that, the smirk vanished, replaced by the icy stare of death.

Principal Oliphant was wholly unaffected. "This is one last ditch effort for you, Hudson, one that I would take." She turned to me with an entirely different tone. "Gemma. What do you think?"

What did I think? I thought Principal Oliphant had a screw loose. What were the benefits she saw in pairing an innocent tenth grader with a senior who probably ate his cereal with freshmen's tears? She was hoping my "responsible nature" would rub off? She was worrying about the effect I would have on Hudson, but did she not stop to consider what would happen putting *me* in this situation?

Whether Hudson was Bridge Boy or not, Landon's swollen, bruised face came back to me in vivid detail, and I could remember Dad telling me to go get a bag of frozen broccoli from the freezer and Landon crying so hard he started hyperventilating. He'd cried so hard that he couldn't even tell our parents what happened. Mom had to get it out of another student's parents.

But, sure, let's pair a sophomore with a boy like that. "Well, I should probably ask my—"

"I spoke with your mother about this already, actually." Principal Oliphant tilted her head from side to side like she was thinking about saying something, ultimately leaning forward. "I told her about the buddy program."

I risked a quick peek to the side. "What about who my buddy is?"

"Well...I didn't name names. I think we both know how she'd react."

Hudson scoffed and tipped his head once more, and I didn't keep my jaw in check as it fell open. Yeah, I knew how she'd react. Mom, who still refused to let me walk to the bus stop alone, would never say yes to letting me hang out with a boy. *Alone.* Not even just any boy—the boy who had beaten her precious Landon to a pulp once upon a time. Mom would be offended if Principal Oliphant even asked. If Mom found out Principal Oliphant was doing this without her permission, Mom would probably have her axed as principal.

Which left the question—why *would* Principal Oliphant even ask?

"For now...let's keep it a secret who your buddy is, okay? Until I can warm your mom up to it. This is important for Hudson. You can really help him stay out of trouble."

Keep it a secret from Mom. *Lie* to Mom. That was

what she was proposing. This was Mrs. Oliphant the family friend now instead of my principal—it was obvious in the way she spoke to me. No school official would ever give the green light to this.

I sputtered for a response, but came up empty, too shocked to coherently piece words together.

She took this as a good sign. "How about we start on Monday? You can meet in our guidance counselor's office after school. After a few days, we'll check in with how you both are faring. Does that sound agreeable?"

Hudson tore his fingers through his blond hair with a sigh, hinting at how disagreeable *he* found it, but he never said anything. Maybe this was him attempting to dodge the bullet Principal Oliphant threatened him with, but it was clear he didn't want to do this. That, like me, he'd rather do anything else.

Everything in me felt like a rubber band on the brink of snapping. I needed to follow my motto of keeping my head down and my mouth shut. I couldn't imagine standing up to Principal Oliphant, but I didn't have to. Once I talked to Mom and told her the truth of who my buddy would be, she'd call things off for me. There'd be blowback for Principal Oliphant—maybe she'd be cut from the friend group like Mrs. Davies—but this was way too crazy of her to ask.

So, despite screaming on the inside, I nodded.

Principal Oliphant dismissed us at the same time, which meant Hudson and I walked out together. He shoved through Principal Oliphant's office and ignored the prying gazes of the secretaries. No doubt *this* would be on their gossip radar the second we walked out of the room. I looked them straight-on, but it didn't matter—they weren't watching me.

The door to the main office banged against the wall as Hudson stalked out. I shuffled my textbook to my other arm to hurry and catch the door before it slammed into my face.

At the last second, Hudson reached back and caught it, his large hand closing on the metal just above my head.

"Thanks," I mumbled, staring at his sharp profile, because he refused to look me in the eye. All hard lines and angry edges, leaving no doubt as to what he was feeling, what he was thinking. He looked very much like the scary senior people gossiped about. Once I was in the hallway, he let the door fall shut and turned away. It was the same as yesterday, his lazy strides starting down the hall. Clearing my throat, I raised my voice. "H-Hudson?"

His boots came to a halt, but he didn't turn. His black jacket was loose over his frame, but even then, I could see his shoulders tense.

"I know this probably isn't something you want to do." *Either*, I tacked on in my head, and though I'd intended to follow that sentence up with another one, he interrupted me.

"Oh, I'm not worried." Hudson turned to show me his twisted smirk, one that looked more pinched than anything. "We both know you're going to tell your mom everything Principal Oliphant said and get us out of it."

My face burned at how easily he could gauge what

my next move would be. As if I were transparent. "You don't know that."

He tipped his head to the side, letting a few blond locks fall into his gaze. "Come on, be honest. That's what you were going to do, wasn't it?"

Heat from my cheeks filled the rest of my body, and I wasn't sure what about this moment made me feel so...*embarrassed*. The fact that he guessed what my next moves were? The fact that I *was* going to run to my mom the first chance I got? The fact that even though I'd been wallowing in all the decisions Mom made for me, I *wanted* her to make this one?

Hudson backtracked toward me, boots hitting the floor hard. He came within a few feet of me, a looming shadow that I had to look up at. "You don't want to do this with me. That expression on your face the second you laid eyes on me makes that clear. And yet you let Principal Oliphant force you into submission because... what? She's Mommy's BFF? Are you really that easily manipulated?"

My heart raced frantically in my chest, telling me to get away while I still had room to do so. Yeah, wow, Hudson intimidating? Never would've guessed. "Principal Oliphant said you needed help—"

"I don't need you." There was no hesitation, no holding back. "In fact, I don't *want* you. So go ahead, run along and get us both out of it. Save yourself while you still can."

I stared up at him, torn between feeling annoyed and freaked out at the same time, once again noting the scar on his cheek. The sight of something so small, so faint, so familiar, broke through the terror of the moment, pulling me from the corner he'd shoved me into. Before he could fully turn around, my hand shot out and grabbed the pocket of his jacket, fingers curling around the narrow zipper.

Hudson tilted his head down at my hand as if wondering how dare I touch him, and then only lifted his electric eyes. "Let go."

"You're the boy from the bridge," I said with more confidence than I felt, refusing to look away, to let myself waver. I still held fast to his jacket. "Aren't you?"

Hudson didn't even blink. Instead, he took a step closer, forcing me back, back, until my spine hit the lockers lining the wall. I let go of his pocket to clutch my books in front of me, using them as a pitiful shield. He was a head taller than me, but seemed so much larger, like he could crush me under his boot if he wanted.

Hudson ducked his fingers underneath my braid and eased it slowly behind my shoulder, his fingertips brushing the skin of my neck in the process. My heart sped up uncomfortably, telling me to run, but my legs wouldn't move.

"You know, I *am* disappointed. I thought you'd have taken what I said to heart, but looks like you're too comfortable playing the role of the dutiful daughter. Which is fine. You can be spineless for the rest of your life." He reached out and patted my upper arm, and though his touch wasn't firm, I jumped so hard that I nearly dropped my books. "Works out better for me, anyway. Get us out of this *buddy* thing, would you?"

And with that, the Grim Reaper turned on his heel and resumed his procession down the hallway, taking a left and dipping from sight.

I leaned against the lockers, breathing as if I'd run a marathon. The weight and sharpness of his parting words felt like a blow to the stomach, knocking all the air from me. No one in my entire life had spoken to me with so much malice. What had I been expecting? "Oh, yeah, I am the boy from the bridge, good to see you again"?

The same sort of tingling feeling that I'd gotten yesterday when Hudson had picked up my papers rose in my chest again now. The same feeling that'd come when he reached his arm around my waist at the bridge, holding me steady. A feeling that I didn't fully understand.

Despite him being the boy from the bridge, this version of him definitely seemed like a bear I shouldn't poke. Our little post-meeting chat had one thought running around my head—I wasn't sure I ever wanted to speak to Hudson Bishop again.

CHAPTER 5

Over the weekend, I had so many chances to bring the mentoring up to Mom. While we waited for the game to start Friday night. While we drove to brunch with Mrs. Jasper and her family Saturday afternoon. While we sat in front of the television for our Sunday night Netflix binge. So many opportunities and chances, but each time I opened my mouth, I couldn't find the words.

Or, really, other words filled my head, ones that stirred my stomach like a sickness.

You don't have to tell your parents everything. Morgan's annoyance streamed perfectly clear.

Hudson's condescension, impossible to miss. *We both know you're going to tell Mommy everything Principal Oliphant said and get us out of it.*

And, of course, his line that had been playing on a loop in my brain ever since he first muttered it.

Grow a backbone, Sophomore.

Each time I started to tell Mom about the truth of the mentoring, those words had me shutting up. In the end, they made my decision for me. I'd show him, *and* I'd show Morgan. I could stand up for myself on my own. I could grow a backbone. I could show them I could make my own decisions. Monday after school, I'd walk straight into the office and tell Principal Oliphant that I wasn't doing this, without anyone's help. Without anyone's persuasion. All me.

And the morning had been off to a good start. My alarm had gone off at six-fifteen and I'd woken up refreshed, which was strange for a Monday. Mom hadn't tugged on my hair too hard when she braided it, and Landon even saved the last banana for me this morning. He'd left for school early to lift weights again, so the house was extra quiet until I left for the bus stop.

Jaden walked with me, and even he wasn't as chatty this morning. As we waited for the bus, he looked like he was about to nod off standing up. I didn't look up when Hudson climbed on, both of us ignoring the other's existence.

The morning was normal, until lunch.

My lunch table was filled with people whose names I wasn't entirely sure of. Most everyone at my table was a freshman or a new transfer. Brentwood High was big enough that it needed two cafeterias, A and B, and mostly freshmen and sophomores ate in Cafeteria A since it was the closest to our classes. Cafeteria B was fuller than A, though, since the Top Tier and other populars at Brentwood High ate there.

My table was peacefully eating until an array of chimes and rings lit up the cafeteria, startling me enough to nearly drop my water bottle as I brought it to my lips. One of the alarms had come from Morgan, who sat beside me, and she pulled her phone from her pocket.

"Oh my gosh," she breathed, eyes bugging wide. "The Most Likely To list is out!"

And just like that, everyone at the table dove for their own phones.

"Wait, what's the Most Likely To list?" a girl across from us asked. I was pretty sure her name was Rosie. She was new this year, and another sophomore. Her brown wavy hair was pulled back into a high ponytail, exposing her array of earrings along her cartilage. "I haven't heard of it."

A boy who sat on the other side of her with a buzzcut, Hector, nudged her shoulder. "It's a list the popular people make every year. They put students' names down to gossip about. It's *super* embarrassing to get on. Like, if you're voted Most Likely To: End Up Alone or something."

Rosie put her hand over her mouth. "That's horrible! And they do this every year?"

"Every year," he confirmed with a nod, though his eyes were lit up with excitement. "Jaden needs to hurry up from the bathroom. He loves the MLTs."

"Isn't that, like...bullying?" Rosie glanced around the table, but since everyone else's head was turned toward their phones, I was the only one she locked eyes with.

Morgan nodded, though, scrolling on her screen. "I guess kind of, but no one takes it that seriously. I'm excited to see if I know anyone on it."

"Freshies and sophomores aren't usually on it," Hector added, leaning close so Rosie could look at the list. "What with them being too new and all, no one would recognize them. It's more shocking when people know the names on it, you know?"

I smiled along with the conversation, hoping I looked at least somewhat on the same page as them even if I didn't feel like it. It was kind of how I felt when Mom lugged me around to her afternoon brunches or when Dad had me at his side, chatting with a few of the football dads at a game. Head down, mouth shut. I didn't want to talk about the list anyway, or all the people who might've been on it, because unlike them, I thought the list was stupid. This was only my second year experiencing the flood of excitement it generated, but I always felt bad for anyone who'd been put on it. I had been hoping they wouldn't do one this year.

"Gemma," Morgan said in a soft voice, one filled with caution. When I looked over, she had her phone pressed to her chest. "Don't freak out, okay?"

Well, that was a sure-fire way to get someone to freak out. My pulse skipped. "What?"

She didn't tell me; she showed me.

It took my eyes a second to adjust to what I was looking at, a whole slew of names on a webpage that seemed to blend together. I scrolled down them, but jerked to a sharp halt at the sight of one familiar name with a tag that made my stomach sink.

Most Likely To: Stay A Prude

Gemma Settler

"Oof." Hector hissed from his side of the table. "That's kind of rough. But hey, think of it this way, at least it isn't the opposite."

"What is the actual definition of a prude, anyway?" I asked as I stared at the label. "It sounds like something someone would've said in the eighties."

"Don't know," Morgan said, continuing to scroll down the list. "Look it up."

Rosie piped up. "It's someone who's shocked by nudity and sex."

Color burst across my cheeks in an immediate response and my jaw dropped. *That* was what it meant? I blinked, starting and stopping a sentence several times before finally getting it out. "I—I'm not shocked by any of that. When have I ever acted *shocked* about that stuff?"

"You did cover your eyes during that one *Titanic* scene," Morgan pointed out.

I ignored her. "Where is their proof, anyway?" I went on, voice sounding higher and higher as I spoke. "Who's to say I'm shocked by those things? Maybe I like those things!"

Hector looked up from his phone with renewed interest.

Morgan gave me a slightly sympathetic shoulder raise. "Maybe it's because you're, like...covered up."

"Covered up?"

Morgan set her phone down and finally gave me her full attention. "Remember how in eighth grade, Dakota

Murphy asked when you were joining a convent because of your skirts and long hair?

I did remember it, because it was the first time I'd snapped at someone. He'd made the comment at lunch, and everyone around him had laughed, but my reply had been, "I'll go when you actually come up with an original insult." I could remember it clear as day because I'd cried my eyes out in a bathroom stall while afraid for the rest of the day that I'd get called down to the office for bullying.

"I was put on the list because of my outfits?" I looked down at my skirt and oversized sweater, suddenly self-conscious. Mom was the one who laid out this outfit, and all of my other clothes. Was I really on blast because of her?

"I think it's part of it," Morgan admitted, but wouldn't look me in the eye. "I think it's the image you put off, Gemma. Even in the summer, you wear clothes that cover you up. You don't go out much, and you're pretty shy, too. You're just...under your parents' wing."

Hector pointed a finger at me. "You're like a good girl. Like a goody-two-shoes."

Each of their bullet points hit me like actual gunshots, and I curled my fingers into fists to keep from flinching. Shy. I didn't feel shy. I wasn't a dictionary, but *shy* always seemed like such a negative thing. Like being a prude. I was quiet, sure, and kept to myself, but *shy*... It sounded worse.

A good girl. Why, when attached to the Most Likely To label, did it sound like a bad thing?

"You need to get out of your shell more." Morgan

reached over and patted my knee. "It's like I said the other day, Gemma. I really think you should try to do more things for yourself."

Much like it hadn't felt supportive then, her suggestion didn't feel supportive now. "You mean stop being codependent on my parents?"

The look she gave me was like *well, I mean...* "I just think you need to let your hair down a little. That's all, okay? No more, no less."

Rosie and Hector both looked at me, gauging my reaction, but I couldn't hold their gazes for long. I stared at my packed lunch in front of me, the one with little star-shaped sandwiches with no crusts. Mom had even cut my grapes in half. It never seemed childish before, but now as I stared at the bread, I couldn't help but feel like a toddler she packed lunch for.

Prude. Codependent. Shy. Words that didn't feel like me, but apparently, they were. In the eyes of everyone else, that was who I was. I wanted nothing more than to prove them wrong, but I had no idea how. How did you prove to someone that you weren't a prude? And besides, who was I going to prove it to, anyway? Morgan? The Top Tier?

Grow a backbone, Sophomore.

I spiraled so deep into my thoughts that the rest of the lunch period passed by in a blur, and the bell rang before I had a chance to even touch my star-shaped sandwiches. Without remorse, I dumped them into the trash, wishing I could dump my stupid label along with them.

Hector had been right—being on the list was embarrassing. I'd always thought that I flew under the radar at Brentwood High, or at least as far under the radar as one could with Landon Settler as their brother. But as the day passed, I caught more and more people staring at me, whispering, giggling, and I'd never felt more self-conscious in my life.

At the end of the school day, I found a piece of paper taped to the front of my locker, and the words were written in big, fat letters for all to see.

MOST LIKELY TO: STAY A PRUDE

Gemma Settler

It looked like boyish handwriting, all blocky and uneven, and I tried to imagine who would've been behind the scrawl. My fingers curled into fists.

I'm not a prude, I thought as I stared at the words. *I'm not shy. I'm not codependent.*

But, a small voice would whisper in response, *you do everything with your parents.*

Which...yeah. I've lived my whole life in a box my parents made. Let my parents dictate what I did and who I did it with. Let them control every aspect of my life, even down to Mom picking out my outfits in the morning. The textbook definition of the perfect daughter.

My whole life, I'd been raised thinking that it was a good thing—and now I was a laughingstock because of it.

I didn't want to be a prude. I didn't want to be shy. I didn't want to be codependent, or any of those other negative things that labeled me like the nutrition facts on a can of soup. The label fit the girl who settled under her parents' rules without question. It fit the girl who let her mother dress her and do her hair every morning. It fit the girl who wasn't allowed to get her driver's permit and didn't push back about it.

I didn't want to be her anymore. I wanted to be a new Gemma.

Suddenly, a hand with two rings on its middle finger came up and tore the paper from my locker. I turned toward the rapid sound of crinkling paper to find Hudson materializing behind me, crumpling it into a ball.

His sudden presence was more surprising than anything else, mostly because my brain was trying to make sense of the sight of him. He was dressed in the doom-and-gloom attire, and his expression was neutral, as if he hadn't just moved. The only indication that he had was the paper ball in his hand.

"What are you doing here?" I asked, impressed by how steady my voice sounded.

"I came to see if you told Principal Oliphant that this was off yet." He raised a blond eyebrow, hooking his thumb around his backpack strap. "We were supposed to meet today, remember? For the buddy thing?"

Right. The mentoring. The thing that'd been occupying my thoughts all weekend. Funny—since lunch, I'd forgotten all about the speech I prepared for Principal Oliphant. Ironically, the Grim Reaper hadn't been my most pressing concern.

The sophomore hallway at this point was mostly cleared out, so the last few students caught my attention. A girl with glasses and a neon orange backpack hurried down the hallway, her gaze fixed ahead of her, lips pressed in a line. Was she on the list? What about the boy across the hall, rubbing his hand down his cheek with a sigh? Was he on the list?

Prude. Shy. Embarrassed.

Grow a backbone, Sophomore.

And that was when I made the first impulsive decision of my life.

"No," I told Hudson, turning to hold his glare. It was weird how much brighter his eyes seemed now than they had a few weeks ago. The brilliant blue looked like someone had photo-edited the irises, so electric against his dark lashes. "We *are* meeting. Right now."

Hello, New Gemma.

I saw his features twist into a scowl before I turned around and unlocked my locker, gathering my things at supersonic speed. "Why?"

My heart fluttered in my throat like a little butterfly had gotten trapped there, and I swallowed against the pressure. "Because," I said as I slammed my locker shut, and then, without another word, I turned on my heel.

And I didn't get one step down the hallway before Hudson grabbed my arm, hauling me back. His grip wasn't painful, but it was too tight to break free from. "I told you." His voice was low and sharp. "I don't need a mentor."

"Last I heard, you didn't have a choice."

I'd be a little proud of myself for sounding so bold if I wasn't about to pass out.

He let out a disbelieving chuckle and looked down

the hallway, debating. It was clear on his face. *Do I change her mind with civility or with violence?* There was no running away with his hold on my arm. I held perfectly still, hoping that whatever he decided to do, it wouldn't be painful.

Hudson dropped my arm, flicking his eyes to the side. "Lead the way, then, Sophomore."

I booked it away from him before he had a second to change his mind. As I walked down the hallway, trying to shake the whole encounter off—and *not* think about how easily his hand wrapped around my arm—I knew one thing was for sure. If I was going to do this, I couldn't let him terrify me that much. I couldn't let him win. If I was agreeing to this buddy thing, I had to hold out until the end.

The steady *clomp-clomp* of his gait following behind me already hinted that the score was Gemma 1, Grim Reaper 0.

Hudson was wrong—I wasn't going to let Principal Oliphant force me into a decision, and I wasn't going to beg for my mom to get me out of this. I was going to face this head-on. I was going to do something crazy. Like Morgan said, I was going to live a little.

The office for the guidance counselor was in the same hallway as the main office, but a few doors down. Ms. Murphy's door was propped open when we came to it, and the petite brunette woman was sitting behind her desk. Her office itself was small—more like a large closet than an office—but she'd done wonders decorating it with pastel pinks and bright yellows. There was a foldable card table set up in the corner of the room, offering enough space for two chairs pulled up to it.

She looked up when we walked into the doorway, her face splitting into a smile. "Gemma, Hudson," she greeted, pushing to her feet. "Oh, I'm so happy you're here."

I'd never personally met with Ms. Murphy, but it made sense that she'd be expecting us. Knowing she'd be here too took away some of my nerves. "Hi."

"I went ahead and set up the table for you two to do your homework at," she said, gesturing at the card table. "The library would've been much more comfortable, but...well."

"You're afraid of unleashing me on the public," Hudson answered from behind me, his voice sounding way too close over my shoulder. He propped his elbow on the doorframe above my ear, leaning closer. "Because me in a library full of burnable books is a safety hazard, right?"

"We're minimizing your opportunities to cause trouble," Ms. Murphy replied, but her voice was warm and soft, not the scolding tone Principal Oliphant had wielded last week. She looked at me. "Plus, this gives you both a quieter space to work."

I wasn't sure if she knew Principal Oliphant was trying to keep this a secret or not, but she was definitely on board.

This time, Hudson replied by sighing. The breath tickled the back of my neck, causing me to shiver.

Ms. Murphy moved from behind her desk and

smoothed her hand down her navy blazer, picking up a folder from the table. "Well, I'll leave you two to it. The door will lock behind me, so no one should stumble in."

Whoa, wait, wait—did I hear her right? "You're leaving?" I demanded, feeling the urge to spread my arms out in the doorway and forbid her from taking a step. "With the door locked?"

"It won't lock from the inside." She patted my shoulder, edging past me. "I'll see you two in an hour."

I turned around to gape at her, realizing just how close Hudson stood. Which was *way* too close. Close enough that I could see each of his individual lashes when I looked up. Hudson gave her a two-finger salute as Ms. Murphy walked away from us, and then swiveled that electric gaze down onto mine. "Are you going to move?" he asked.

I took a very large step away from him, cornering myself in the small room. Despite all the cheery colors, I felt one thousand percent claustrophobic.

Especially when Hudson came deeper into the room, shutting the heavy door behind him with a terrifying *thud.* It was him and me now. Only him and me. No one was going to be coming in, and he was fully blocking all chances of my exit.

A slow, wicked smile stretched across his mouth. "Regretting it?"

Yes. Very.

And then I mentally shook my head and told myself to get a grip. Showing fear wasn't going to get me anywhere. *Just pretend he's Bridge Boy.*

Stiffening my spine, I turned around and made my way to the card table, pulling out a rickety chair and sitting down. Hudson sat across from me, lounging into the seat much like he had in Principal Oliphant's office. With his arms crossed and his body slouched, he looked like he was trying to fall asleep. "So, *buddy*," he said with a heavy dose of sarcasm. "What are we doing?"

I unzipped the front pocket of my backpack and withdrew the rectangular box of playing cards, setting them on the table between us. I kept them in my bag to play solitaire on the days I had to stay after for Landon. I wished I'd had cooler cards, though—they were my well-loved *Winnie the Pooh* deck I'd played with when I was six. "We'll play a game."

Hudson stared at the box as if he was waiting for it to move on its own. "When Principal Oliphant mentioned playing games, I think she was kidding."

"I don't know many card games," I admitted as if he hadn't spoken, dumping the cards out. "But I do know Go Fish. Do you?"

Hudson gave one slow blink.

I pressed my palms to the pile of cards and started mixing them in circular motions around the tabletop, careful not to accidentally flip any. Careful not to let my shakiness show. "We each get a set number of cards and we try to pair them up. Whoever has the most pairs—"

"I know how to play."

My attention remained on shuffling. Under my breath, I murmured, "Well, you didn't say anything, so—"

Hudson's hands came down over mine, slender

fingers stilling my own in their chaotic shuffling. It made me think of his hands grasping my shoulders that day on the bridge, his arm shooting around my waist.

I yanked away, focusing my now-wide eyes on him.

He collected the cards, much like he'd done with my posters the day in the hallway. He tapped them on the table and then split the deck into two stacks, arching the cards. They shuffled together with a soft *shh* sound, and then Hudson bent the cards in the opposite direction, letting them cascade into one neat pile.

The awe had to be showing on my face, because a corner of Hudson's lips tugged up. "It makes sense that you only know how to play a kid's game with the way you shuffle."

I struggled to think of a response as he dealt us each seven cards.

"So, you couldn't do it, huh?" Hudson asked as he studied his cards, boredom leaking from his expression. He laid down a pair of twos from his hand. "Couldn't stand up for yourself and tell Principal Oliphant no deal?"

"Maybe I wanted to be paired up with you." I hoped my voice didn't sound so high. "Maybe I wanted to do something...dangerous."

Hudson's lips stretched even further, but the smile was not a warm one. "Of course, because there's nothing more dangerous than playing Go Fish in the guidance counselor's office."

"It's all in who you're playing with," I replied, laying down my last pair. If I'd been playing with Jaden, my expression would probably look the same as Hudson's had a moment ago. Bored. Wishing we could do anything else. But sitting here across from Brentwood's bad boy now, I was on the edge of my seat.

Hudson looked over his deck of cards, those blue eyes fixing me in place. "You go first."

I cleared my throat. "Do you have any fours?"

He picked a card out of his hand and passed it over between his index and middle fingers. It gave me a brief, closer glance at the rings on his left hand and the intricate designs carved into the silver metal. There were little white scars over his knuckles too, like the skin had been broken once upon a time.

Like broken over someone's jaw. I forced my face not to twist. "Any eights?"

Hudson shook his head. "Go fish."

The reality of the moment didn't really hit me until he spoke those words. It was a sort of surreal "am I dreaming" moment, looking at the boy drenched in black cloth sitting across from me, holding my *Winnie the Pooh* cards between thin fingers. The Grim Reaper, playing Go Fish.

I definitely would've allowed someone to pinch me.

Hudson asked for a three, and I frowned at the three of hearts in my hand. "So..." I said as I passed it over. "Why are you on thin ice not even a week into the school year?"

"It's this nice little reason called none of your business," he snapped. "Do you have a queen?"

Begrudgingly, I handed that to him, too. The ice in

his tone had clearly been a warning, one I wanted to back down from, but I still managed another sentence. "You had tardies and everything last year, but how does that translate into this year? What happened over the summer?"

This time, Hudson ignored me completely. "Any ones?"

So, I took a page from his book and ignored him, too. "If I'm your buddy, I should know a little bit about you, don't you think?"

"Let's get one thing straight." Hudson laid his cards face-down on the table, hard enough for the surface to shake. He leaned forward, lowering his voice. "This mentor buddy thing or whatever the hell Principal Oliphant called it? It's a load, okay? It doesn't mean anything. I don't need to know about you, and you don't need to know about me. You're suffering this on your own accord; I don't owe you anything. So let's just shut up and play cards. Okay, Sophomore?"

Oo-kay. I struck a nerve, but strangely, his intensity didn't have me cowering in fear like I would've thought. I didn't understand why a prying sophomore like me could've pushed a button like that so easily, but he reacted like *he* was the one backed into a corner.

A buzzing sensation kept my spine straight. My timidness from earlier was gone now, replaced with the adrenaline of confronting Goliath with nothing more than a slingshot. I wouldn't let him beat me down. "You know, you were a lot nicer before. Over summer break."

Hudson looked at me carefully, but his expression

was still nothing close to friendly. He almost looked *angry*, in a muted sort of way. Like my existence annoyed him. One thing that I quickly learned about Hudson was his affinity for staring. A glare fit for the Grim Reaper. "That's why you're here, then? Because we met on the bridge?"

"So what if it is?"

"I think that it's obvious, but I was only nice and chatty because I thought you were going to jump off. If you're expecting the same guy, you'll be sorely disappointed."

"Which role is it that you feel tied down to? That version of you or this one?"

From the way his jaw clenched now, he hadn't planned for that conversation to ever come up again, much like I hadn't. If I knew who really grabbed my shoulders that day, would I have even mentioned my thoughts to begin with? Would I have brought up my birthday? The only difference was that I didn't regret it—like he clearly did.

"Don't," he warned.

I almost felt like smiling, like instead of cards, we were suddenly playing chess, and I'd called check. "Don't what?"

"Don't act like you have me all figured out just because I said something to a sad, pathetic girl on her birthday." The line between his eyebrows was vivid, and his fingers clutched his cards furiously. "And if that's your reason for being here, because you want to uncover some secret, you should get lost now. Before you *really* start to test my patience."

I rocked in my seat and looked down at my cards, needing a reprieve from the hatred he radiated. That was *not* how I was expecting this to go. Then again, when he'd first said he felt forced into a role, I never expected *this* role—the one of the villain. *Is there a point to fighting it if nothing will change?*

"Maybe I'm here for me," I told him. "Maybe this is me growing a backbone and facing something that scares me."

"You're only saying that because of your Most Likely To label," he shot back. "They'll be the sort of kids who peak in high school and go downhill from there. This is the happiest they'll ever be, and they have their entire life ahead of them. And you're going to let what they think bother you?"

I regarded him quietly for a moment. "Are you on the Most Likely Tos?"

"No, I just have an unhealthy hatred for the Top Tier, can't you tell?" He'd said the words with a sneer, but when he looked down at his cards, his discomfort was clear. "Got any eights?"

I passed the card over, looking at the few pairs I had. My gaze lingered on the king of hearts. For this deck, it was Pooh with a crown on his head and a scepter in his hand, but he wasn't smiling. He was as serious as Hudson was. "I may be suffering through this, or I might not be, and I might be here because of the bridge or I might not be, but you're right—it *is* my choice."

All of his sharp words were designed to inflict the most damage, cutting anything within reach like glass. But the longer I looked at him, the longer he looked at me, the more they felt *hollow*—like the words *were* slivers of glass, but shards from something that had already been broken. A weapon of defense rather than offense. That strange warmth from before danced across my skin, not from anger or embarrassment—it was the feeling one got at the top of a rollercoaster, seconds before the drop.

"You'll regret it, Sophomore," he said at last, unflinching.

"It's Gemma," I told him. "With a G."

Hudson's harsh gaze didn't falter, nor did the crease from his forehead fully smooth out, but that corner of his mouth tugged up again. "*Gemma.*" He enunciated the two syllables slowly, lips curving around the letters. "With a G." He sat back into his seat and picked up his cards, but his posture wasn't as lazy as it'd been before. He propped an elbow on the table's surface, like now he was fully into the game. "Got any sevens?"

CHAPTER 6

That night, instead of eating at home, my parents decided to eat at a seafood restaurant in Clinton. Mom invited the Morris family to come along with us, which meant I was wedged ever so perfectly at the rounded table between Landon and Jaden. Being beside Landon wasn't too bad, but he did nothing to help intercept Jaden, who hadn't taken a breath since we got to the restaurant.

"I've never been here before," he said now, leaning closer to me to drop his voice. Our parents were laughing about something related to the school board, but instead of listening to them—or at least *pretending* to listen, like I'd been doing—Jaden wanted to start his own conversation. "The atmosphere is really cool. Le Petit Bateau? French, right? I like it. Is the food any good?"

"If you like seafood," I replied, picking up my glass of water and taking a long drink.

"Last time I had it, it made me sick," Jaden admitted, putting his hand on his stomach now. "I guess my stomach can't process it very well, or whatever. But I'm sure this will be different. After all, it's Settler approved, right?"

I glanced at Landon. "You think so, too, right, Landon?" *Help me, brother, make this a three-way conversation.*

My brother glanced down at us, his carefully composed expression breaking into something more amused. He looked like he was laughing on the inside. If my parents weren't in plain view, I could've hit him. "Mmm-hm."

And he didn't say anything else. I definitely could've hit him.

"Gemma." Jaden leaned closer and dropped his voice, dark eyes glimmering. "Did you tell your parents about the list?"

He'd whispered it, but I still looked at my parents anyway, drawing in a breath. Thankfully, they were immersed in a conversation about football. "No, and I'm not going to."

"Oh, well, I—"

"This is Landon's favorite place to come," I told Jaden, cutting him off and lifting my voice a bit louder. "At least, when the *Oliphants* come along."

If he wasn't going to help me with Jaden, I was going to tease the heck out of him for *his* crush. Whenever we went out to eat together, he always sat beside Madison, and their small talk always seemed way less painful. She actually made him laugh, which was a rarity for him. He was totally crushing.

Landon looked at me now with a little bit of a

frown, but the damage had been done. Mom actually did a full-stop in whatever she was saying to Mrs. Morris and turned to look across the table. "Oh, Landon, have you asked Madison to the homecoming dance yet?"

Landon drew in a breath, the tips of his cheeks getting red. It was a curse of his—whenever he was even the slightest bit embarrassed or angry, his cheeks reddened like a tomato. Another trait he got from Mom. "Homecoming is still almost a full month away, Mom."

"So? You have to ask her sooner than later—think of all the boys who will snatch her up before you!"

No one would've caught the dirty look Landon gave me unless they actually knew him. Nothing about his features changed—his lips were still relaxed, his forehead was still smooth—but the depths of his blue eyes promised payback.

"Jaden," Landon began, leaning around me to peer at the junior. "Have *you* asked anyone to homecoming yet?"

Underneath the table, I jammed the heel of my shoe onto the toe of his, but the giant didn't even flinch.

The entirety of our table turned toward Jaden. His teeth glinted when he smiled, and he sat up straighter in his seat, clearing his throat like he was about to give a grand speech. "Well, actually, I was thinking—"

"All right, who had the garlic shrimp scampi?" Our server swept into the moment like the most beautiful reprieve, grinning around unwittingly. She looked high school-age with her hair pulled out of her face into a cute bun in the back, and even from across the table, I could see the bright glint of a nose ring. "Ah, it was *you*, wasn't it, sir? Mr. Extra Garlic Sauce?"

"That's correct," Dad said with a laugh. "The wife probably won't kiss me for the rest of the night, but it's worth it."

"Should've gotten extra, *extra* garlic," Mom teased back, which caused Mr. and Mrs. Morris to chuckle—whether out of actual humor or discomfort, it wasn't clear.

I eyed the nametag pinned on the server's apron, and in an elegant scrawl, it read *Lacey*. "Crab legs for you, my dear," she said as she set the plate in front of me, careful not to brush against my arm.

The server quickly divvied out the rest of the dishes. Landon watched her closely, no doubt waiting for his own food. Jaden reached for my plate of crab legs, but I jerked it closer to my chest. "Oh, I can do it."

"I don't mind helping," he replied, placing his hand on the other side of the ceramic, his thumb nearly landing in the ramekin of butter.

I kept my grip strong. "It's fine. Really."

"Don't worry, I can get all the crab meat out for you." Jaden winked and tugged the dish closer to him.

I refused to budge, but I should've. The server was in the process of placing Jaden's plate in front of him—a plate of sushi, which seemed suspicious for a guy who got sick off seafood—and his elbow collided with her side. He let go of the plate, but since I was in the process of pulling it back, I ended up yanking it too hard.

The crab legs slid to one side of the plate, and though

they didn't fall off, they did knock the ramekin of melted butter over, and it spilled into my lap.

Jaden started profusely apologizing, and Lacey joined in, though Landon quickly assured her that she did nothing wrong—all the while I sat there silently, staring at the butter that quickly soaked into my most recently created skirt. The grease stain was already setting in.

"Oh, Gemma," Mom said from across the table, pursing her lips in a disappointed way. "Why do you always have to make things more difficult?"

"*I* make things difficult," I muttered under my breath as I scrubbed at the butter splotch with stain remover in front of the washing machine. I wasn't sure I was making much of a difference—the bottle said to apply the remover within five minutes of the stain, and I'd gotten to it over an hour later—but taking out all the recent frustrations on the fabric felt good. "Right. *Me.* Not grabby hands Jaden, who couldn't crack a crab leg to save his life."

Despite the butter debacle, Mom insisted that I let him attempt to crack my crab legs for me. *Attempt* being the operative word—it took him five minutes to get one leg cracked, and even then, the meat came out all shredded and mangled. Still edible, of course, but harder to dip into the new butter dish Lacey dropped off. And yet *I* made things difficult.

Then again, what *had* I been thinking? I should've let

Jaden take the stupid dish to begin with. Standing my ground over stupid crab legs? What happened to keep your mouth shut and your head down, Gemma?

Grow a backbone, Sophomore.

I threw the skirt into the wash and twisted the dial to *delicate*, angrily praying for a miracle.

When I walked down the hall, I knocked on Landon's open door, already dressed in my pajamas. I had an immediate view of my brother when I stepped up to the threshold. He had his head bent over his desk, feathering his pencil across the piece of paper in front of him. Through his reddish-brown hair, I could see a white earbud stuck in his ear. Totally lost in his own world.

I flicked the light switch once, startling him enough to jerk his head up. "Oh, hey," he greeted, pulling out the earbud and angling his scrap piece of paper over the picture. "What's up?"

"Can I talk to you about something?"

"Ominous." Landon set down the pencil and turned his chair toward me. He, too, was already dressed in his pajama pants, though his eyes were wide awake. "But sure."

My brother's bedroom was the same size as mine, but since he had a larger bed—a queen instead of a twin—the space felt more cramped as I made my way inside, sitting down on the blue duvet. There wasn't anything overly personal about his bedroom, but then again, he wasn't in it too often. Between school and practice and working on homework in the kitchen, he only ever was in his bedroom to sleep.

To sleep, and to draw. From here, I could see that his fingertips were smudged with graphite. "The sketch coming along okay?"

He double-checked to make sure the image was obscured. "Oh. Well. I'm just goofing off." He dusted his hands together, but it did nothing to rub away the smears on his skin. "What did you want to talk about? The whole thing with Jaden today?"

My shoulders slumped. "How come you don't help me out a little?"

"I thought you *liked* Jaden's attention. What was up tonight?"

Before, I *would've* liked the attention, or at the very least, I wouldn't have minded it. Now, though... "There's attention, and there's *too much* attention."

"I get it. Next time I'll intervene before he tries buttering you up like you're a crab leg."

I scrunched my nose at him, but quickly sobered as the real reason why I came in here resurfaced. I smoothed my palms over my knees as I cast a quick glance at his door, but I knew where Mom and Dad were. Dad was currently parked in front of the TV, enjoying his Monday night football, and Mom was probably already in her bubble bath.

Landon beat me to it. "Is it about the list?"

"I was wondering when you were going to say something," I said, eyes falling on the sketch on his desk. Landon tried not to draw too much, since he knew our parents didn't love it for him—"you should be training or watching plays on YouTube," they'd say—and he only really drew when he got the urge to. I wished I could've seen what he was working on. "Listen, I've already heard the speech about the list, so you don't need to give it again."

"Who gave you the speech?"

The people who made it are pathetic. They'll be the sort of kids who peak in high school and go downhill from there. This is the happiest they'll ever be, and they have their entire life ahead of them. "Morgan."

Landon looked down at his hands and dusted them, though it only proved to smear the graphite residue more. "Well, she's right. It's *not* a big deal. Don't feel bad about being on it. You're probably only on it because of me."

I frowned. "Because of you?"

"When you're a senior in the Top Tier, you have to vote someone onto the Most Likely Tos or else you're put on it. They probably made up a label for you for extra retaliation. Think about it—being a prude is a new label."

Would his friends really do that? The Top Tier consisted of so many types of people, self-centered and funny types alike. Connor Bray and Reed Manning definitely weren't the type to put their friend and his sister on blast like that, but Jade Dyer and Ashton Shaw? I could see it.

And then something else occurred to me. "Are *you* on it, then? For not voting someone?"

He smiled a little. "A little self-focused, were we? You didn't even notice your own brother got a label?"

"I *was* a little preoccupied."

"I'm Most Likely To: Never Get A Girlfriend." He

turned to his covered-up drawing, tapping his fingers against it. "It doesn't bother me, though. So don't let it bother you, either."

Landon was much different at home than he was at school. At home, the way he spoke seemed much more relaxed, less on edge. At school, he was the picture of stiffness. Quiet. Reserved. Like he was afraid of slipping up or making a mistake. We were similar in that regard, and it made me think of Morgan's comment. *Shy.*

"Do you think I am too reserved, though?" I asked him, even though it was weird to say aloud to my brother. He shook his head, but before he had a chance to say anything, I asked, "Do you think I'm too codependent on Mom and Dad?"

"Morgan again?" Landon sighed a little. "I think it makes sense, in a way, to spend so much time with Mom and Dad. It's not like you've got sports or a job to distract you, you know? Don't let the stupidity of the Most Likely To list get to you. And don't let *Morgan* get to you. You know how she is." He lowered his voice. "And don't try to remedy your casting, or whatever the phrase is to prove the list wrong. Got it?"

I wanted to ask him how he expected me to prove Most Likely To: Stay A Prude wrong, but thought better of it at the last second. My imagination was creative enough to think of what his responses would be. It was, however, the perfect segue into the conversation I'd initially come into his room to talk about, one that I still hesitated on bringing up even after going back and forth all day. I tried to prepare myself for all of his reactions, but there was truly no telling what he'd say. "What do you know about Hudson Bishop?"

In the Settler household, there was really only one name not to mention. To my parents, and my mother especially, it was practically a curse word. To Landon, it made him turn as white as a sheet. I knew it was a topic I'd have to tip-toe carefully around to avoid setting off a landmine. "Why?"

"There are rumors going around, and Morgan lives for the gossip mill. I was wondering if you knew anything so I could tell her."

"That's what Brentwood Babble is for."

"She said she looked but there'd been no search results for him." *She* meaning *me*, of course. I'd used the school computer to reference Babble and had found zero search results for *Hudson Bishop*. There weren't even any for *Grim Reaper*. "I guess whoever runs it is afraid to get on his bad side, huh?"

Landon rocked back into his chair. "I don't know much about him. He keeps to himself. I don't think anyone really knows enough about him to give good gossip."

Everything I'd heard about Hudson was more legends and scary stories than actual gossip, but it was interesting that Landon didn't know anything. "I figured you'd be a good person to ask, since you have personal experience."

"I wouldn't say that I do."

"You wouldn't call getting jumped personal experience?"

He shifted to try and hide his reaction, but I saw him flinch. "It happened so long ago that even if I did know anything about him, I'm sure he's changed now. I do know that he's not someone you want to go around gossiping about. Morgan tends to run her mouth, and he's not someone to do that with. So just... You should still steer clear, okay? For your own sake."

I thought of the icy look Hudson gave me in the counselor's office, the threatening way he'd leaned forward over the table. All the malicious things he'd said, the intimidating way he said them. But those thoughts were quickly overshadowed by his hands closing over mine to shuffle the cards, or him bending to scoop up my flyers in the hallway.

Contradictory—that was the word. It all was contradictory.

Landon waved his hand at me. "Are you listening? Dodge him, okay? If only to put your big brother at ease."

"Dodge who?"

Both Landon and I started at the sound of Dad's gruff baritone, turning to find him standing in the doorway of the room. He still wore his clothes from dinner, which consisted of an office-appropriate dress shirt and a pair of khaki-colored pants.

"Who are you talking about?" Dad repeated, venturing farther into Landon's bedroom.

"Boys in general," Landon answered, giving one of his practiced, perfect smiles. One that put all parents at ease, especially our high-strung ones. "I'd be too on edge if she wanted to start dating."

Dad rolled his eyes a little at the prospect. "Boys nowadays don't have their heads on straight. You're too young for that, Gemma. You shouldn't be thinking about it. Unless, of course, we're talking about Jaden."

I pressed my knees together, cursing Landon in my head. But Dad's swift dismissal and eye roll had me feeling a little breathless. No, not breathless—suffocated. "I'm sixteen, Dad."

"I didn't have my first girlfriend until college, and it was your mother." Dad stopped halfway into Landon's bedroom and gestured to where my brother sat. "Look at Landon. He's well on his way to getting a football scholarship because he's more dedicated to sports than girls. *He's* got his head on straight."

Landon looked at his covered artwork.

I saw Dad's gaze fall to Landon's smudged hands, but he didn't say anything to him. "Gemma, how was your buddy program? You met with the student today, right?"

Now could've been the time to spill the beans. The time to back out of the whole peer-to-peer thing and get out from being stuck with Hudson.

But despite Landon's warnings—and the alarms blaring in my head—I smiled at Dad, shaking my head. "You wouldn't know her, but I think it'll be good. I think I'll be able to be a good influence."

CHAPTER 7

Turned out, Jaden should've chosen a safer entrée last night. Mrs. Morris called our house early Tuesday morning, apologizing that Jaden wouldn't be able to walk me to the bus this morning—he was "sicker than a dog."

I would've preferred him walking me to the bus over my mom, though, who followed through on her threat and did exactly that. Thankfully, she changed out of her house robe for the journey, and into a pair of linen PJ bottoms that almost could've passed as normal pants. "Poor Jaden," Mom murmured as we walked, wrapping her arms around herself. "Be sure you text him later telling him to feel better, okay? I'm sure that'll lift his spirits."

My phone suddenly felt so heavy in my backpack pocket. "Okay."

"I've got a feeling he's going to ask you to home-coming soon. We need to go get you a dress for the dance. Maybe this weekend, after my hair appointment, we can go."

I knew how it would go. We would both browse dresses, but I'd never actually pull any off the rack—Mom would pick the ones for me to try on. "Okay."

"Are you not feeling well either?" Mom paused to press her hand against my forehead in the middle of the sidewalk. "You don't feel warm—"

I pulled my head back, glancing around in case anyone on the street was around to watch. "Just tired."

I didn't look at her to see whether or not she was suspicious, but instead walked all the way to the bus stop. Thankfully, Mrs. Savion pulled up within minutes. Mom waved at me as I climbed aboard, like I was a second grader rather than a sophomore.

The bus seemed livelier than normal, which meant Mrs. Savion was beginning to grow hoarse from calling out at those who refused to keep their butts in their seats. She threatened them with making them late, and then with detention for not listening. I plugged my headphones in and tried to ignore the sounds.

We turned into Vista Villas a little earlier than normal, and I braced myself on the seat as we bounced along. I tried to be nonchalant looking out the window, but I kept my eyes peeled, waiting for Hudson's figure to come into view.

And then he did. Once again, he leaned against the cable box, head tipped down as if studying his shoes. His blond hair was half obscured by the black hood he'd drawn over his head. As the bus rumbled to a stop, I realized he wasn't alone. A little girl stood at his side with her blonde hair pulled up into two braided pigtails, a rainbow backpack strapped across her back.

Hudson didn't straighten from the cable box, didn't act as if he was going to get on the bus, so Mrs. Savion opened up her window. I yanked my earbud out in time to hear her ask, "Aren't you getting on?"

His voice was faint over the voices of the students in the back and the roar of the bus's engine, but I caught the reply. "Go ahead without me. Her bus is late today."

I pressed my face closer to the glass, close enough to fog it up. The girl looked no older than eight, so he couldn't leave her alone to wait for her bus. But he couldn't miss *his*. If he didn't get on the bus, how would he get to school on time? It had to be at least a thirty-minute walk—he wouldn't make it before the bell.

If he was tardy, would Principal Oliphant count that as breaking the "thin ice" he walked on?

Mrs. Savion shut her window and put the bus into gear, and through my window, Hudson looked up and met my gaze before the bus rolled past him. It wasn't the glare of the Grim Reaper, though, but the open expression of the boy on the bridge. He hadn't had time to pull the mask on.

"Wait!" I reached forward and touched Mrs. Savion's shoulder, grasping the denim. "We can't leave him."

"I have a schedule to keep, Gemma," she said in a voice that she'd never used with me before, but when she looked up in the rearview mirror, her expression softened a fraction. "I'll tell Principal Oliphant about the late bus."

I looked out the window, finding the little girl holding

Hudson's hand and swinging it back and forth. He looked down at her, and if I hadn't known any better, giving her a reassuring smile. A *smile*.

I only had a split second to ask myself why I cared. A split second to acknowledge that if Hudson lost his last chance, that meant I'd no longer have to meet with him after school. He made it perfectly clear yesterday that that was what he wanted. I would've been home free of the scary senior and could've laughed the whole situation off.

In that split second, I couldn't turn away from how genuine Hudson's smile looked.

Two thoughts warred in my mind. *Don't do anything to prove the list wrong.*

And the second, the louder of the two: *Live a little.*

Without thinking twice, I snatched my backpack and stumbled into the aisleway. Mrs. Savion slammed on the brakes, rocking me forward. I would've faceplanted if I hadn't caught the leather seat at the last second. "Gemma," she said, eyes widening. "What are you doing?"

My heart pounded fiercely in my throat, making the air that I drew in taste thinner and thinner. "Open the door, please."

"Gemma, I can't let you—"

I didn't wait for her to finish. Something foreign possessed me in that moment, reaching my arm out and wrapping my hand around her door handle, yanking it open. My legs shuffled down the steps until I hopped out onto the dirt road, free.

Mrs. Savion gave her head a little shake, muttered

something under her breath, but ultimately pulled the doors shut.

It was probably the craziest decision I'd made to date, getting off the bus and joining the Grim Reaper, but there I was, standing in the plume of dust the bus kicked up while looking at the bad boy in question from across the road.

He hadn't noticed I'd gotten off yet. Instead, he rubbed his fingers into his left eye, slumping against the phone box. "Are you going to get in trouble?" the little girl asked him, swinging her backpack to and fro.

"Of course not," he replied easily, but didn't open his eyes. Gosh, even his voice sounded different, lacking all the steel and edge. I could hear Bridge Boy. "Don't worry about it, okay?"

The girl hummed a little under her breath and turned around, and that was when she spotted me. Her eyebrows slammed down in a frown, regarding me almost territorially. She tugged on Hudson's arm, and he lowered his hand from his eyes to glance up.

It was a funny sort of thing, watching his expression go from troubled to exasperated in a nanosecond, all due to the sophomore in a long skirt and white sneakers standing on the side of the road.

Hudson grabbed the girl's hand and hauled her across the street, stomping toward me with a ferocity that had me thinking about Landon's broken face. Gone was the expression of Bridge Boy. His hood cast shadows across his face, but the anger was clear. "What the *hell* do you think you're doing?"

Yeah, right then, I knew I made a huge mistake.

Despite the discomfort blooming in my stomach, I forced my posture straighter. "I'm waiting for her bus with you." The girl had to be none other than his sister, because even though she was little, they had nearly the same features. Same small nose, same high cheekbones, and same wheat-colored hair. Their eyes were also the same—not in color, but in fierceness, because she regarded me the way a wild animal might. "I'm Gemma," I told her.

"No, you're insane." Hudson came closer, stopping a few feet from me. "Are you serious? You're going to make this my problem now, too?"

I folded my arms across my chest, trying to stop myself from backing down under his stare. It was hard, though, because every inch of me demanded to chase the bus down with my arms flailing. "What kind of mentor would I be if I left you in this situation alone?"

"Mentor?" the little girl whispered to Hudson in confusion, but he ignored her.

"Did you not hear me yesterday?" he demanded. "You're *not* a mentor, and you're not my buddy—you're an unlucky underclassman forced to be my babysitter. One Principal Oliphant knew she could get to do whatever she wanted. You're easily manipulated, you have no backbone, and, *apparently*, you make god-awful decisions."

Just words, I told myself, but dang, did he really know how to hurl insults where they hurt. Then again, me standing here was clear proof of my bad decision-making skills. "We'll be late together. If we're both late, maybe Principal Oliphant will let us off with a warning."

"Oh, yeah? Where's *that* logic coming from?"

I couldn't, for the life of me, figure out why he was so angry. I mean, sure, I hadn't expected him to drop to his knees and thank me for being on his side, but I hadn't expected so much hatred to exude from him. Then again, this *was* the Grim Reaper. Angry. Scary. Mean. If I'd thought that through, I probably wouldn't have disembarked. I would've listened to Mrs. Savion's warning stare and sat down. But the bus was gone, and the dust had just begun to settle, so I wasn't going anywhere.

And really, what *had* I been thinking? Getting off the bus *had* been stupid. Because it wasn't like there was anyone to call to come pick us up. We were stranded with a half-hour walk ahead of us.

A new fear entered my mind. Once his sister was picked up, I'd be alone with him. Outside of school grounds. Without a witness. I thought of the route to the school and all the places he could stash my body.

The Brentwood Elementary bus rolled up then, with Hudson glowering at me and my thoughts running rampant. The driver, a stout man with graying hair, opened the door for Hudson's sister to climb on.

"Have a good day, Paisley," Hudson called to her, and she looked back and waved at him. She didn't look at me.

Hudson let out a harsh sigh as the bus door wheezed to a close, and I could hear the gravel crunch underneath his boots as he turned away. My heart thundered in my chest at the prospect of trailing after him, but at the last second, inspiration hit me like lightning.

The bus was already moving forward, but I hurried to catch up. "Wait! Wait, sir!" I slapped my palm against the glass of the bus door. The driver, thankfully, ground the bus to a halt, wasting no time in opening back up. I gasped for a breath, tucking a piece of hair that had come loose from the braid behind my ear. "We're students at Brentwood High. Do you think you could drop us off at Walnut Street?"

Walnut was a street the bus would have to pass to get to the elementary school, and from there, it'd be probably a five-minute walk to the high school. A two-minute sprint, even. Depending on how much left he had of his route, we'd be cutting it close, but we'd never make it before the bell without him.

But the bus driver set his gaze straight ahead, gruff and unwavering. "I can't pick up anyone who's not on my route."

I fished out my student I.D. from my backpack, breathing hard as I showed it to him. It was last year's, since this year's hadn't been issued yet, but I still looked relatively the same. Same braid, same baby cheeks. "We're students at Brentwood High, I swear. We missed our bus because we were waiting with...ah, Paisley. I'm a sophomore and he's a senior. If you call the school—call Principal Oliphant—they can confirm it. Gemma Settler and Hudson Bishop." *Please, make an exception this once. Please, please, please.*

The driver leaned around me to peer at Hudson, and

I prayed that Hudson's ripped clothes and dark expression wouldn't make the driver's decision for him.

On impulse, I blurted, "My mother's the school board president. Naomi Settler?"

"Settler?" The driver scrunched his brow, like he was trying to remember the name from somewhere. Then something like a lightbulb went off behind his eyes. "Is your dad Clayton Settler?"

I nodded, hoping that was a good thing.

The bus driver smiled, and it transformed his face entirely. "I went to school with Clayton Settler! Small world, small world. I knew he had a son, but didn't realize he had a daughter, too. My, you do look just like him, don't you? Wait—that's probably not a good thing to say, is it? That a girl looks like her father?"

The relief that swept through me was so potent that I actually felt my knees shake. "Would you be able to drop us off at Walnut? Please? Would that be okay? We...we can't be late."

"Yeah, of course! Sit up in the front where I can see you, okay?"

I pivoted and walked the few steps to grab ahold of Hudson's wrist, right underneath where his long sleeve ended. Even though I was mildly freaking out about touching him, I yanked him forward. "You're seriously a lifesaver."

"Glad I can help. You'll have to tell your dad old Jimmy Heisner says hello."

There was one fully empty seat in the front, and I fell into the worn-down leather, tugging Hudson down after me. The seat was smaller than the one Jaden and I normally sat on, and Hudson's arm jarred against my shoulder, his thigh pressing up against mine. Both of us stiffened on contact, but there was no room to shy away.

"Now." I breathed as the bus blessedly accelerated, turning to peer at Hudson. My pulse had yet to die down, the relief making me dizzy. "I'd say I *fixed* your problem, wouldn't you?"

Hudson was reluctant to look over, but when he did, he simply blinked at me, those long lashes sweeping down and up slowly. The longer he stared, the higher my lips twitched into a smile, triumph surging at the sight of some of his prickly quills lowering. "Whatever...Gemma."

CHAPTER 8

"I'm sorry, you *what?*"

I flinched at Morgan's high-pitched tone, glancing around rapidly to see if anyone was eavesdropping. "Can you be a little quieter? I don't really want this getting around."

"You don't—I don't—*Gemma.*" Her brown eyes couldn't have gotten any wider if she tried. "You're meeting the Grim Reaper in *private* and you don't want anyone to *know?*"

"It's not like that." We stood in front of my open locker at the end of the school day, when the hallways were the busiest. "Don't make it weird."

"Oh, right, *me* make it weird." She took a step closer to me, and even though she was shorter than me, her fierce gaze was instantly intimidating. I inched backward, closer to my locker. "No, Gemma, what's *weird* is that you met with death himself yesterday and didn't tell me. Did you at least say something to Jaden?"

I pretended to be super absorbed in my English textbook. "No."

Even though I confessed to her about Hudson, I didn't tell Morgan about getting off the bus this morning. I knew I should've. There was no guessing what her reaction would be, but she surely wouldn't understand the decision. I didn't understand it in the moment. I hadn't understood it while Hudson's body rocked into mine with every bump in the road, and I hadn't understood it when the driver dropped us off at Walnut Street. We'd run the rest of the way. His legs were definitely longer than mine, but somehow, our strides matched. Side by side, no doubt looking like maniacs trying to book it before the bell.

I'd done it despite everything. Landon's warnings, Morgan's worries, and all the rumors.

I was clearly out of my mind, but we both made it. Hudson had stopped for a brief second when I got to my classroom's door, and then, with an expression I had no time to read, he hurried off toward his homeroom.

"Isn't it better to have more people know? I mean… just in case?" She narrowed her gaze at me, leaning closer. "*Please* tell me you told your parents."

"I thought you said that I shouldn't tell them everything."

"Jeez, Gemma, not when it comes to Mr. Death himself! He could take your soul. Or suck your blood. Or—"

"He's not a vampire, Morgan."

She let out a sharp sigh, one that I knew was accompanied by an eye roll. "Who are you, and what have you done with Gemma Settler?"

My hand grabbing my backpack strap froze, fingers curled around the nylon. It wasn't that I wasn't acting like myself, but I wasn't acting like the version that everyone expected. Like the shy prude everyone thought I was. The codependent daughter. But it didn't feel like I was acting fake or anything—it sort of felt like I was digging up someone I'd always been, just buried underneath.

As terrified as meeting with Hudson made me, it didn't stop a small smile from springing to my lips.

Something hard bumped into my back with enough force to shove me forward into my locker, and I caught myself before face-panting into the metal. At first, I assumed Morgan had been the one to give the shove, at least until she shouted. "Hey! Watch it!"

"You were in my way," the male voice responded without a care in the world, and when I looked over my shoulder, I found a boy looking well past high school age standing there. He was taller than Morgan, barely, but menacing enough that height didn't seem to really matter. Though his reputation didn't precede him the way Hudson's did, he fell into the other bad seeds at Brentwood High. Wes Torres. It wasn't quite clear if he fit into the druggie or gang category, but he was definitely a jerk to steer clear of, along with the girl who lingered over his shoulder. He had an affinity for picking on underclassmen, and apparently, we were next in line. "You should respect your elders, fresh-meat."

"Hey, look at the goody-two-shoes Settler," the girl over his shoulder called to me, narrowing her cat-liner eyes at me. "Since the girl who runs Babble included everyone's pictures for the Most Likely Tos, we can finally put a face to your name. Nice skirt, grandma. I guess that prude label fits you perfectly."

Wes looked newly interested in the two of us and took a step closer. No, his attention wasn't on the two of us—it was on me. "You're the golden boy's little sister, then? Part of that prissy family? I mean, I thought I knew he had a sister running around, but never knew what she looked like."

I dropped my gaze to my feet, too freaked out to look him in the eye.

"You know, if I squeeze hard enough, I could probably get you to fit in that locker. Maybe we can even get two-for-one." He looked at Morgan.

"You shouldn't," Morgan said. "H-Her brother is the quarterback. And her mom is the school board president."

"You shouldn't," the girl added, "because who knows what kind of rumors that family would spread about you?"

Wes advanced farther, and his sneakers came into the view I had of the ground. Too close. "It's people like you that really piss me off, you know," he said in a low voice, sending a shiver up my spine. "More than the other nameless freshmen. *You.*"

I had no idea what he was talking about, but I didn't move an inch. Didn't throw out a comeback. My body had already locked down—there was no fight or flight. Only freezing. *Keep your head down, Gemma.*

"You all think you're so much better than anyone

else," he went on. "Making up rumors, ruining people's lives. So, this? This isn't bullying. It's payback."

Morgan piped up beside me, sounding like a mouse. "She—she has nothing to do with the Most Likely To list!"

"The list," he scoffed, barely sparing her a glance. "You think I'm talking about the stupid list?"

Wes slammed his hand on the locker beside and drew in close, close enough for his hot breath to waft across my face. I flinched back, my shoulder slipping half into the locker, the side of the metal cutting into my spine. I waited for him to grab me, to seal me inside the open locker, when the scene before me seemed to freeze, like everyone held their breath. Morgan's sneakers squeaked as she backed up, but I still didn't lift my gaze from my own white shoes. There was dust and dirt smeared into the canvas from climbing out of the bus this morning. As I studied them, Wes's, too, took a sharp step backward, his looming presence receding.

I didn't want to look up, but I couldn't help it.

Hudson Bishop stood like a shadow beside me, his hands in his front pockets. His blond hair fell in a side part that exposed a section of skin on his forehead, showcasing plenty of his flat, bored expression. For a brief second, I thought he stood there to assist in closing me into my locker, but the guy in front of me just took another step back.

"Pick another underclassman," Hudson said, voice monotone. "Because if anyone's going to mess with this one, it's me."

Yeah, see, that wasn't *quite* a comforting sentiment.

"I was just helping you out," Wes said, lifting his hands lazily as if someone pointed a gun at him. He didn't look Hudson directly in the eye, though. "Just doing your dirty work for you."

Hudson didn't even blink.

Wes took another step back, the sneer smeared on his face faltering. "Have at it," he said. "You do have dibs on that family, don't you?"

Hudson didn't reply, but Wes didn't really wait for him to. He walked away, the girl trailing behind him with a glare.

I let out a big breath, the relief loosening my lungs. Morgan shifted her wide eyes from Wes's retreat to Hudson to me, leaning forward to mutter, "That was kind of cool."

I shoved her away, because Hudson definitely stood within earshot, and his attention focusing on her proved it. There wasn't a trace of amusement—if anything, it was like he was debating to follow through on the boy's threat to seal me in the metal box. My heart had squeezed upon seeing him, but now raced in double-time. "This—this is Morgan."

Hudson absolutely didn't care. He looked down the hallway, but the seniors had already walked down the sophomore wing. "Were you really going to let Wes put you in that locker?"

"*I* wouldn't have let him," Morgan answered, raising her tiny fists. "He's probably double my weight, but I could've taken him."

Her boldness was back now that the two students had walked away, which made her sentiment that much weaker. Hudson still wanted an answer, but I wasn't sure what to tell him. I didn't know what I would've done if Wes grabbed me. So instead of answering, I turned to Morgan. "I'll text you."

She dropped her voice lower, eyes widening. "Remember—your elbows and your knees can be your best friend for self-defense."

Hudson's flat gaze fell on her, and if she turned around, no doubt she'd have a heart attack at drawing his attention. I shut my locker door and gave her a nod, and when I walked away, it felt a little bit like I was walking to my own funeral.

I only got a few feet away before Hudson caught my arm again, grinding me to a halt in the middle of the hall-way. Not many students remained, and those who did didn't look at us directly, almost like they were afraid to do so. "Answer me," he demanded.

"You *really* like grabbing me," I muttered as I looked at his hand, swallowing the butterfly fluttering in my throat.

"You really wouldn't have stood up for yourself?"

"I've always been told not to fight back. To turn the other cheek." It was something my parents said often, though mostly metaphorically. *Never throw a punch. Never be the one someone can point a finger at. Turn the other cheek.* "He wouldn't have gotten away with it, and if I just put up with it, I wouldn't have gotten in trouble, too."

"Is that what your parents who forgot your birthday said?"

For some reason, him acknowledging the bridge made me feel lighter. It was stupid to feel that way, given his tone, but it felt like we were moving in the right direction. "They didn't forget, they just...made it about them."

"Because that's so much better. Remember what I said about a backbone?"

"I have one. I just know when to use it." Or, really, it was more like using it caused more problems than it was worth. Standing up for myself, being defiant—it brought nothing but complications. Especially at home. It would earn me a week's worth of cold shoulders and a hefty dose of emotional blackmail. It was better to do what people said.

"Like this morning?" The blue of his eyes did nothing to dampen my pulse, especially not when I looked straight into them. "Was that you thinking it was an appropriate time to use your backbone?"

"It's like I said yesterday." I shook his hand off my arm, and it was surprisingly easy to do. His grip had been light. "I want to live a little."

"Except it terrifies the hell out of you."

Ha, true. "Maybe I want to do things that scare me."

The words, initially, were all talk. Who wanted to do things that scared them? Hanging out with Hudson Bishop in a public place was scary enough. Except the longer the thought lingered, the more real it felt. Before yesterday, when was the last time I willingly chose to do something scary? Something *thrilling*? When was the last time I'd done anything without my parents' approval?

The answer was easy: never. Maybe that was why, even though I *was* terrified, I still stood across from the Grim Reaper anyway.

Hudson didn't look confused as he studied me. "No," he said finally. "You don't. You just don't want to be tied to the role you've been playing."

"It's not me. I'm not what everyone thinks I am. The label...that's not *me*."

"Don't do anything because of what others think. Trust me, it never works the way you want it to. Do something because *you* want to."

And with that, Hudson started walking toward Ms. Murphy's office. I hurried to catch up, wanting to explain that these feelings stemmed from *before* the list, but in a weird way, I thought he knew. As if he knew from the day at the bridge. *Is there a point to fighting it if nothing will change?*

Today, Principal Oliphant had a task for us—to help apply barcodes to new books for the library. Mrs. Juniper, the librarian, had dropped off a cart full of books that needed barcodes applied. There were probably one hundred books on the cart, and it was definitely going to take us the full hour.

"I'm surprised they're trusting us with something like this," Hudson said as he peeled off a barcode from the sticker sheet, slapping it on the interior of the book cover. "What if we put the barcode on the wrong book?"

That had been my fear when we'd first started, which

was why I double—no, triple—checked the title on the book before applying the barcode.

"We could cause anarchy," he went on, carrying through in his assembly line. Peel sticker off, slap it on the cover, set the book aside, and do it again. It almost seemed *too* flippant. "The fall of the Brentwood High library would be within reach."

I paused in applying my next barcode, narrowing my eyes at him. "You *are* putting them on correctly, right?"

"Of course."

I didn't look away from him. He tucked some of his hair behind his ear, though a few of the front pieces fell into his line of vision. He sat in the same seat as yesterday, but today, something was different. My brain fumbled to try and figure out the minuscule change.

With his head bent down, Hudson looked over with only his eyes. "Apparently, I'm going to do all the work, huh?"

I dropped my gaze to my barcodes, resuming my progress as if no time had passed, pretending like I wasn't embarrassed for getting caught staring.

The curiosity of everything that was *him* began eating at me. Like why he was on thin ice, why he got his nickname, why he was always alone. Why he felt he was forced into a role—what role that was. Prying into his business was a definite no-no—I learned my lesson yesterday—but it was so tempting.

"So, what's up with the skirts?" he asked me after a few minutes, not beating around the bush and not bothering to find a more polite way to ask the question. "Is it something with religion?"

"I didn't realize there was a religion based on wearing long skirts."

Hudson cleared his throat a little, suspiciously sounding like he was fighting a laugh. "I guess I meant, is it a conservative thing?"

I looked down at my lap. This skirt wasn't as long as the dress I wore yesterday—it came down to my mid-calf, exposing my pale ankles. "My mom picks them out. Sometimes she gets me material so I can make my own. They're more comfortable than jeans."

Even though I confessed to Mom buying them, there was absolutely no way that I was telling him that she was the one who laid out my outfits every morning. I could practically hear all the insulting jokes he'd crack.

I peeled off another label and took my time centering it on the book, smoothing out the air bubbles. "This morning. That was your sister, wasn't it?"

His teeth grazed his lower lip. "Yeah. Paisley. Seven, and as mean as they come."

The little blonde girl with the rainbow backpack this morning hadn't really struck me as mean—at least not when she was giggling with her brother. However, the glare she turned to me did seem a little vicious. There wasn't a trace of spite in Hudson's expression at all as he spoke about her—in his voice and on his features, there was nothing but affection. "I've always wanted a little sister."

"You can have mine." Once he finished the book he

worked on, he paused, still staring at the spine. He seemed to debate something before ultimately turning his attention to me. "Her bus driver is late a lot. He was late a lot last year."

I blinked. "O-Oh."

"That's why I had so many tardies." He waited for the realization to dawn on me. "Because I missed the bus waiting for her."

"Does Principal Oliphant know—"

"I know exactly what she'll say," he interrupted, grabbing another barcode. "She'll say there are only so many free passes she can give with that."

"What about your parents—"

He cut me off again. "My dad leaves for work before the buses go." Hudson all but ripped another barcode off the sticker sheet, not lingering on that line. "And I had a lot of absences last year because Paisley was sick a lot. She couldn't be home by herself."

"What about your mom?"

"She died when Paisley was three," he said without hesitation, without flinching. "It's just us."

Why he was suddenly confessing all this to me, I didn't know, but I held still, giving him my full attention. Much like earlier, how it felt like he was letting a bit of his guard down, it seemed that way now. It wasn't fair that he was on thin ice because he had to take care of his sister, though, and it made me newly angered toward the way Principal Oliphant had painted it. Like he was *willingly* skipping school, not forced into it. Then again, had he ever told her the truth?

Hudson leaned his head onto his hand, strands of his hair feathering between his fingers. Underneath the sharp lighting of Ms. Murphy's room, the color shimmered more golden than wheat. "Speaking of siblings, when Principal Oliphant said your brother played football, I didn't realize it was Landon."

It felt like a weird switch of topic, given what we'd been talking about, but I let him change it. "Pieced that together, did you?"

"And your mom is the school board president."

"Yeah."

"Makes sense why Principal Oliphant wants this to be a secret from her, then," Hudson said, corner of his mouth flicking up. "Since she's the one trying to get me expelled."

I drew my lower lip between my teeth, an uncomfortable feeling sinking through me. "I'm sorry."

Hudson raised an eyebrow. "Do you have a habit of apologizing for things that aren't your fault?"

I dropped my gaze back to the barcode sheet, resuming the labeling without another word. It didn't cause the feeling in my stomach to disappear, though, weighing me to the chair.

"You know, I didn't..." Hudson began and then stopped, clamping down on the words before they could escape. His expression was as complicated as I'd ever seen it, but there wasn't a trace of the barbed wire I was used to. "I didn't thank you for this morning. You probably saved me from Principal Oliphant kicking me out. I was a jerk, but...thanks."

I could still hear the savagery of his words spoken just twenty-four hours ago, could see his expression in my mind. *You're suffering this on your own accord; I don't owe you anything.* That was what was different now—everything about him yesterday had been like a wild animal backed into a corner. Today, the ferocity was absent, revealing a more subdued person underneath.

"How about this." I drew in a breath and tried to speak without faltering, though my brain already braced for his reaction. "This buddy thing. This...*good influence* thing that Principal Oliphant wants. Let's try it for the rest of the month. If you're still uncomfortable with it all, I'll tell Principal Oliphant I don't want to do it anymore. You just...have to trust me."

It was a strange thing to say—*trust me.* I wasn't sure I'd ever said it to anyone before. It was always me relying on someone else. Mom, Dad, Landon—that bubble was strong enough without me, and they never viewed me as someone to rely on, and until that moment, I didn't realize how badly I wanted to be that person for someone. How badly I wanted to be needed by someone. How badly I wanted to *be* someone to someone.

It was a blink-and-you-miss-it sort of thought, because a second later, I was freaking out for thinking that that someone could be Hudson Bishop.

"You should make a list," he said. "Make a list of things you've never done before but secretly want to do. Things that always scared you. It can be like your rebellion list."

"Rebellion," I echoed, and at first, the word sounded

wrong. Rebel against what? My parents? The more I thought about it, the more I realized that they'd never really *forbidden* me to do anything. I just never went against what they wanted. "What would I do with a list?"

"We could check them off." He looked mildly nauseous as he said the next line. "For our...*buddy* thing. I was the one who told you to fight to be who you want. Makes sense I should help you with it, I guess."

That was his response to what I'd said. *Trust me.* This was his reply. *Okay.*

With my pulse jumping a mile, I stuck my hand out to him, like we were making a business deal in the quiet room, surrounded by books. "Deal."

Hudson regarded me for a moment before reaching across the table. Instead of clasping my hand, he wound his pinky around my littlest finger. It was such an easy, confident move, that I held perfectly still. When he squeezed it, my heart seemed to clench in response, that rollercoaster feeling resurfacing in my stomach. With one of his half-smiles, the scar on his cheek bending with the movement, he said, "Deal."

CHAPTER 9

I stared at the paper in front of me as if the words would begin forming themselves.

A rebellion list. Where was I even supposed to start with that? My pen sat beside the lined paper, but I was too chicken to pick it up. Too chicken to write any of this down and make it real. The thought of such a thing seemed so much easier in Ms. Murphy's office, when I wasn't tasked to do it in the moment. In Hudson's presence, I could at least pretend I was more confident than I was. Now, with my parents down the hall, I wanted to bail on the thought of rebellion entirely.

I told Hudson I would make a list. No, I *pinky promised* him. That was basically contractually binding, and there was no way I was double crossing the Grim Reaper.

With a shaking hand, I picked up the pen, but right as I poised it to the paper, Mom's voice came from behind me. "Hey, sweetie."

I dropped the pen like it burned, turning in my chair to face her. She had a few of my shirts on hangers dangling from one of her fingers, freshly ironed from the laundry. "Hi."

"Doing some homework?" She came close enough to peer at my desk and at my empty sheet of paper.

What was it that Landon always said when he was caught drawing? "Just...goofing off."

Mom hummed a little under her breath as she hooked the hangers in my closet, smoothing the shirts between her fingertips. She eyed my clothes lovingly. I sat with my hands in my lap, because even though it was an innocent sheet of paper before me, I was on edge with it in her presence.

She turned to face me. She'd scrubbed her makeup off since being home from work, and her rosy cheeks were in full bloom. "I feel like we haven't gotten to chat lately," she said as she made her way over to my bed, sitting on top of the made duvet. "Today was your second day of the mentoring, right? How is it going so far? Are you two getting along okay?"

Before, I would've answered in an instant, telling her the truth and leaving nothing out. There was never a reason to lie to her, and it never would've even occurred to me. When I was little, my parents always told me that my lies will always find me out. No matter how small, they'd always know. Now, as a teenager, I could see the fear tactic for what it was, but years of dreading the anger and disappointment of my parents had me hesitating.

I stared at her a moment, contemplating how to answer. "I think it's going okay. I think I'm really getting through to...them."

I mean, he was at least calling me by my name now and not "sophomore." Sounded like we were making progress to me.

Mom nodded approvingly, leaning her palms back on my bed. "When Talia told me she had a student that needed some help, one-on-one, your dad and I were both happy you could help. It's a good opportunity, isn't it? She thinks you're responsible enough. And a great use of your time after school. You know, I hated the idea of you sitting around for an hour. Now, this works much better, don't you think?"

"You didn't check with me," I said before thinking about my response.

"I already knew what you'd say."

I was struck with the consistency of Mom. It wasn't like Mom making choices for me was anything new—she'd always done this. I was just only now noticing.

My gaze flicked to the sheet of paper on my desk. The promise of rebellion. The promise of freedom. "Thank you...for signing me up to do this. I think it could be good for both of us."

"I think I'll lay out your sage skirt tomorrow," Mom said, standing to her feet and making her way to my closet. She'd grown restless with the conversation. "The one that comes just above your ankles. That color looks so beautiful on you."

"Mom."

"Yes, sweetie?"

It was like the words were already written on the

paper—that was how clear they stood out to me. "Can I pick out my own clothes tomorrow?"

She was silent. My whole life, she'd purchased clothes *she* liked for me. She laid out clothes *she* thought would look nice. The most I ever got to pick out were my socks.

I held still under her scrutiny while a war waged inside me. Was it worth it to even ask? It wasn't like I had an entire new wardrobe I could pick from—I'd still wear the outfits Mom put me in once upon a time. But still. It was only a sliver of my autonomy, and I was taking it back.

"I suppose so," she answered finally, but her confusion was clear. "Do you not like me picking out your clothes, Gemma?"

To appease the lines between her brow, I tried to smile. "I just want to do it from now on."

Mom walked up to me and coasted her hand down the side of my head, stopping once she got to my ear. Her eyes were so cloudy, like she was fighting the urge to cry, and guilt stirred hotly in my stomach. *Is it really so wrong to let her pick out your clothes?* the guilt whispered.

But then the dark feeling pushed back against it, the one that surfaced on my birthday. *Is it worth fighting if nothing will change?* Hudson's words were so clear that it was almost like he spoke them now.

If I don't fight, I thought stubbornly, *then it definitely won't change.*

"You *are* getting old enough to," she said, tucking a few hairs behind my ear. The melancholy expression hadn't vanished. "When I was your age, I was wearing things my mom near had a heart attack over. Don't you be like that, okay?"

I wasn't sure what she expected me to wear—or what it was that *she* wore—but I nodded.

Mom stood before me another moment, still tucking my hair back. I sat motionless as she did so, feeling a bit like a porcelain doll she'd drawn off the shelf to admire. She dressed me. She brushed my hair. She decided what she wanted me to do for the day. The longer the thought lingered, the more the dark feeling closed in.

Eventually, she dropped her hand. "Well, I'll let you get back to work. Remember, lights out at nine-thirty. Don't forget to brush your teeth, okay?"

I nodded, and then she was gone, easing out into the hallway. My room felt both lighter and emptier with her gone, a weird warring feeling, much like the guilt and darkness that stirred inside me. It felt wrong to think about rebellion, but it also felt wrong to go on the way things were. I couldn't live like a toy for the rest of my life.

Turning back to the paper, the first thing I did was scrawl a title at the top. *Rebellious Things Gemma Has Never Done Before.* I wrote down *pick out my own clothes* on the list before drawing a fat line through it, pulling in a slow breath. My first rebellion bullet point checked off. Maybe it wouldn't be as difficult as it seemed.

What did I want, more than anything? What were things that made my heart squeeze when I turned them down? Things that caught my eye, got me curious? After so long of pushing all of it down, it was hard to think of any at first.

And then it wasn't difficult at all, because as soon as I crossed off the one bullet point, another danced into my head, and then another. Too many for my pen to keep up with, but I scribbled them down anyway, waiting until I was fully finished to stop and remember that I wasn't just writing down a list of activities.

I was writing down a list of activities that I had to do with the Grim Reaper.

During the class period before lunch on Wednesday, Morgan sat tracing the end of her pencil along my back while Mr. Broker talked about the history of Europe. He was going straight up until the bell today with no regrets, flipping through his PowerPoint slides with an excited smile. I listened patiently, even though my stomach was growling like there was a monster in there.

Morgan gave me a hard poke before she whispered directly in my ear. "Have you gotten your dress for the homecoming dance yet?"

I shook my head ever so slightly.

"We should go this weekend." She tapped my shoulder again. "Did Jaden get a tie yet?"

This time, I shrugged my shoulders.

She went back to tracing patterns into my sweater, giving

a little humph as she did so. I knew she wanted me to be more excited than I was—that was the one thing her and Mom had in common. I wasn't sure what I was supposed to be excited about anymore, though. Wearing a pretty dress? Waiting for Jaden to ask me as his date? None of it seemed like it mattered too much. They could be excited enough for me.

The bell cut off Mr. Broker in the middle of reading his PowerPoint, and students began standing from their desks without waiting for a formal dismissal. Our teacher simply sighed. "Ah. Well. We'll finish it tomorrow. Have a great lunch!"

"We could go to the mall this weekend," Morgan said in her normal voice, watching as I packed up my bag. "In fact, we probably *should* go to the mall soon before all the good dresses sell out."

"My mom wants to come with me," I told her, zipping up my backpack and hooking it over my shoulder. I kept it with me for third period since my locker was all the way on the other side of the school, and this way I had easy access to my lunchbox. "She wants to see all the options."

"You mean she wants to pick it out for you."

I didn't respond to that because we both knew she was right.

Jaden joined us when we got close to Cafeteria A, and he nudged his shoulder against mine. "How's your morning been so far?"

"It's been okay."

"Just okay?" Jaden ducked his head to meet my gaze.

"Then again, it *is* school. It's not going to be anything really exciting, is it?"

Morgan chuckled a little, lowering her voice. "Depends on who you run into."

I knew who she meant, but Jaden frowned, left in the dark.

It was almost as if Morgan summoned him, because not even a second later, Hudson appeared. He walked down the hallway from Cafeteria B holding a blue tray of food. He sauntered through the path students made for him easily, almost as if he didn't even notice that they were there. He looked zoned out, thoughts elsewhere. Jaden and Morgan were chatting, but I was too focused on Hudson, on how he drew nearer and nearer. He was about to walk past us.

Except before he got to us, he took a left down a hallway, away from both cafeterias.

I turned to Morgan, acting like something just occurred to me. "I, uh—I have to talk to Principal Oliphant about something."

"About what?" she asked, frowning. "Does it have to be now?"

We got to the hallway that Hudson ducked down, and thankfully he was still walking down it, still in sight. I nodded to the two of them. "It does. I'll, uh—I'll catch you guys later?"

They both looked confused, but Jaden at least waved goodbye before I turned, and thankfully, they didn't look farther down the hallway to see what had caught my eye.

I turned on my heel and zeroed in on the black shoulders striding away.

Where is he going? I didn't know why I was so curious, but I couldn't help it. Hudson didn't really strike me as the kind of guy to eat in the cafeteria, surrounded by everyone else, but where was he going? A part of me wanted to raise my voice and grab his attention, but instead, I picked up the hem of my skirt and hurried after him.

He took a right down the main corridor, disappearing. By the time I got to the corner, the hallway was empty.

I turned in a circle, as if expecting to find him standing behind me. He wasn't, of course. I now stood in the hallway alone. The main office door had glass, so from a quick peek, I found that he wasn't in there. The only other door that would open to non-staff was Ms. Murphy's office, but she didn't have a window for me to peer through.

I sighed a little, hooking my thumbs around my backpack straps, ready to start my walk back to Cafeteria A.

And that was when Ms. Murphy came out of her office, a smile on her face. "You're too funny. Don't forget to shut the door when you leave, okay?"

The reply was faint, but I recognized it easily. "Aye-aye."

Once she shut the door, Ms. Murphy turned, and that was when she spotted me. "Oh, Gemma. Are you here to see me? I was about to go on my lunch break."

"I was just walking through," I told her as nonchalantly as I could. It probably wasn't a big deal, me seeking Hudson out even though this wasn't our buddy time, but I didn't want to admit that I *was* seeking him out. "Enjoy your lunch."

"You too, dear." She patted my shoulder as she brushed past me, heading for the teachers' lounge, leaving me alone once more in the hallway.

For some reason, my heart picked up its pace as I stepped up to her door, studying her name plaque. There wasn't a single sound from the other side of the door, but I'd heard him. He was in there.

Placing my hand on the doorknob, I gave it a twist, but it didn't turn. *Locked.*

Right. It automatically locked when the door was shut. I drew in another breath, one that steeled me, and knocked.

A noise came from inside the room, sounding like a chair pushing back. And then, right before the door opened, a voice sounded. "Jeez, that was fast—" Hudson pulled the door open and found me standing on the other side, his expression going from amused to shocked in a fraction of an instant. "Gemma?"

"Were you expecting someone else?"

Hudson leaned his arm against the jamb, regarding me in the way that always made me want to squirm. "Yeah. I was."

I grazed my teeth along my lower lip and looked underneath his arm at the small space beyond. The table we'd been sitting at for the past few sessions was pushed up against the far wall of the room, and on top of it sat Hudson's blue lunch tray. "Are you eating in here?"

"Ah, look at your deductive reasoning skills."

I fought the urge to roll my eyes, and without waiting for him to move, I ducked underneath his arm. "I'll eat with you." There was another chair brought up to the table, making it clear that he *was* expecting company. Who would've agreed to eat with the Grim Reaper alone, though? "Got anything you want to swap? Jaden and I do that sometimes."

Hudson hadn't moved from the doorway, but simply watched me take my pastel pink lunchbox out of my backpack. I started unpacking it across from his tray, hoping that my trembling fingers weren't obvious.

With a sigh that could've passed for a groan, Hudson closed the door, but didn't come closer. "Can't we meet after school?"

This is just his prickly side, I reminded myself. *Don't let it get to you.* "I'll split my brownie with you."

His eyes narrowed. "Is it the kind with the little chocolate chips on top?"

"Of course." I held the cellophane package up as proof.

Hook, line, and sinker. The way to Hudson Bishop's heart, apparently, was dessert. Without a word, he walked over to the table and sank into his chair, offering his palm out.

I broke the brownie in half and gave him the bigger one. It was clear that Hudson would rather eat lunch with whoever was coming, and he was annoyed I'd butted in. I couldn't help but wonder if the person he'd been expecting was a girl or a boy...a romantic interest or not. I shouldn't be curious. Definitely shouldn't.

"So, who was coming to eat with you?" I asked, trying to seem nonchalant. "A friend?"

Hudson picked up one of his grilled cheese slices. "I do have them, you know."

"You do?" I couldn't have sounded more shocked if I'd tried, and in response to his raised eyebrow, I hunched my shoulders up toward my ears. "I mean, right. Of course you do."

I truly hadn't known Hudson had friends. Wait, did that mean his friend knew the Bridge Boy side of him?

As I thought long and hard, Hudson interrupted me. "Is that the name of the guy who sits by you on the bus every day? Jaden?"

I nodded. "Jaden Morris."

"A friend?"

He mimicked what I'd said, but the question still rang oddly in my ears. Maybe it was because Morgan had just asked about Jaden and homecoming, but my spine prickled. "Why do you ask?"

Hudson let out a little breath through his nose. "Trying to make conversation, since you're apparently not leaving. You were the one who said we should get to know each other."

"And then *you* said to buzz off." With words that were much harsher.

He set his spoon down and folded his arms on top of the table, the sudden weight making it wobble a little.

"Then *you* told me to be all in with this buddy thing. We're like friends now, aren't we? Friends tell each other things about themselves, right?"

I *had* said that. And maybe that was why I'd been so curious about where he was going to eat lunch to begin with. Right now, though, with the way he was looking at me, I was ready to rescind my offer. *Friends.* Was that even possible? "Let's start with you, then," I breathed out, straightening my spine. My stomach still growled, but I was fighting to win his attention, to get him to relax. "What do you do for fun?"

"My cousin and I are fixing up this old van," he answered without missing a beat. "One of those vans people go traveling around the country in."

"Is that what you want to do? Travel in a van?" I wasn't sure I'd want to be stuck in a car for a cross-country road trip, but the thought of traveling was fun. The farthest the Settlers ever went on vacation was to the beachfront an hour away, mostly because it was rare to find a time where my parents' vacations lined up with our school schedule and Landon's sports schedule.

"Not really," Hudson replied, turning back to his tray. Aside from his soup, his grilled cheese, and the brownie, the only other thing he had was his mini water. "It's more her dream than mine. But it gives me something to do, I guess."

I hummed a little under my breath and picked up my brownie, about to take a bite.

At least until Hudson stopped me. "You're not going to save the brownie for dessert?"

"It's my favorite thing. Why wouldn't I eat it first?"

He looked at me like I was crazy. "If it's your favorite thing, why not save it for last?"

With his attention fully on me, I gracefully shoved the entire brownie into my mouth, attempting to smile as I chewed.

"All in one bite, too," he said in a voice that was dripping with disappointment, shaking his head sadly.

I laughed a little, savoring the chocolatey taste. I had to admit, even though he was as deadpan as could be, teasing with him was fun. Trying to get him to open up was fun. I knew there was another side to him—I knew Bridge Boy was in there. I just had to keep digging to get him out.

We were quiet for a bit as we ate, me munching on my chicken tenders while he nursed his soup and grilled cheese. It was weird to be eating in such quiet, since I was so used to the noisy lunchroom. Despite the fact that it was the Grim Reaper sitting across from me, this was the most relaxing lunch I'd had in a long time.

Hudson glanced at the door for the third time in under a minute, giving a little frown. "Where is the person you were supposed to have lunch with?"

"Apparently, she's not coming."

I hesitated in biting my chicken tender. So, it *was* a she. Now the only question remaining was whether or not this was supposed to be a romantic lunch period. Hopefully not, because Ms. Murphy's room didn't provide much in the way of amorous ambiance. "Why do you eat in here, anyway? Why not in the lunchroom?"

"I have to eat in here this year," he said. "I guess they're afraid I'll do something crazy, like start a food fight or shove a freshman in the trash can."

The words themselves sounded like a joke, but there was nothing about his tone or his expression that hinted at it. It didn't seem fair that he was targeted like this—being forced to sit up front on the bus, being forced to eat his lunch in solitary. It was like they were purposefully ostracizing him.

"Did the school board decide that? To separate you?"

"From what I've gathered, it's Principal O's decision. She says she's on my side, but..." Hudson trailed off, giving his shoulders a lazy shrug.

"You don't think she is?"

Hudson dipped his grilled cheese in his soup again. "I think she cares a whole lot more about what her friends on the board think than me."

I didn't know how she felt about the board, but I did know that she at least seemed to care more about him than she cared about Mom. Otherwise, Principal Oliphant would never lie to her for Hudson.

I cleared my throat, trying to change to a brighter subject. "You know, I was thinking about the Most Likely To list."

"What about it?"

"I think it's kind of lame that you're not on it. If I was 'Stay A Prude,' you'd think they could've come up with a creative one for you. Most Likely To: Sleep In A Coffin."

A corner of his mouth tugged up. "Most Likely To: Sacrifice A Freshman on An Altar."

I burst out laughing, pressing my hand over my mouth to keep it from being too loud. He shook his head as he scooped up another spoonful of tomato soup, but I caught his hidden smile. "That's a little long, though."

"Maybe," he agreed. "In reality, it'd be something like 'Get Arrested' or 'Be Expelled.'"

My amusement sobered a little when I remembered what Landon had said Monday night. But it wasn't like Hudson was wrong. Even from remembering some of the labels, either of those options would've fit in nicely. It would've been perfect for the MLTs. Which begged the question... "They must be afraid of you if they didn't put you on the list."

The sort of ice I'd grown accustomed to Hudson peeked through then, freezing his smile. "Good."

The topic had subdued him in a way that was only noticeable if someone paid attention, and here I was, practically unblinking. Hudson said he desperately hated the Top Tier, which included Landon. Why? It seemed that with Hudson, that was a constantly recurring question, one that wouldn't leave my mind.

I glanced up at the clock on Ms. Murphy's wall, frowning when I saw there were only five minutes left. The period definitely passed much quicker in here, and I found myself wishing it'd slow down.

"So," Hudson said, wiping his fingers on his napkin. "Speaking of the list. Did you work on your rebellion homework?"

I picked up my backpack and fished it from the front

pocket. "I did it last night, and I tried to think of a lot, but I only have eight things."

"Eight works," he answered, folding his fingers on the tabletop. To give him credit, he looked genuinely interested. His way of giving this friendship thing a try too. He leaned forward, trying to see the paper. "Read them to me."

"Did you make a list, too?"

"This isn't my self-discovery journey." He blinked expectantly at me, leaning his head against his hand. "Rattle them off."

For no good reason, my cheeks heated, almost like we sat out in the sun. His undivided attention made me nervous, especially opening up about something like this. "No judging."

He held a hand up. "Scout's honor."

"That only works if you were a Boy Scout."

"Did I say I wasn't?"

The image of a blond Hudson as a Boy Scout nearly made me smile, but I remained focused on the task at hand. "They're not in order," I said, already taking on a defensive tone. I cleared my throat to get rid of it. "Paint my nails. Cut my hair. Pull an all-nighter. Sneak out."

"Aren't these a little...tame?" Hudson raised his eyebrows. "Couldn't you think of anything more fun?"

"These are fun," I argued, regarding my bullet points. "I told you not to judge."

He lifted his hands in defense. "I'm just saying, I guess I didn't realize how repressed you are. Poor thing."

Okay, now I was really getting ready to smack him. "I'm not repressed."

"I bet you go to bed at nine."

"No," I replied immediately, making a face at him.

He arched an eyebrow. "Nine-thirty."

I tried to hold my annoyed face in place, to not give the truth away, but dang it—he got it.

Hudson reclined in his seat with a triumphant smirk. "You have the bedtime of a toddler, Gemma."

I decided that I was going to ignore him now, readjusting my paper with a deep breath in. "The next one is to try coffee. Watch a scary movie. Skip a class. Say a swear word."

Hudson laughed suddenly, a short chuckle that lasted only a second, but filled to the brim with humor. "You're telling me you've never said a swear word? Like, not even on accident? Like you stubbed your toe, and you said..."

"Ow?"

He leaned back as far as he could in the small chair, regarding me with a fascination that made me want to smile and duck my head at the same time. "You're seriously something else. Well, that's an easy one to check off right now." He gestured to me, giving me the floor. "Go ahead."

I glanced around at Ms. Murphy's small room. "Not now. What if she has her room tapped or something?"

"We're not in a spy movie. And besides, there's no time like the present." Hudson laid his arms on the table. "I'll start you off. *Ffff—*"

My hands shot out, almost like they wanted to seal

Hudson's mouth shut for him, but I managed to stop before actually touching him. Between my parted, desperate fingers, I could see a hint of his lips curling up. "Not that one," I whispered. My pulse started pounding rapidly in my throat, as if I was about to do something worse than say a word. One measly word. That was it. No one was around to hear—I could say one and then cross it off my list. I drew in a quick breath through my nose, let it out even quicker through my mouth, and then met Hudson's gaze. "*Crap.*" And then I laughed.

Hudson's teeth caught on his lower lip, almost as if he were fighting a smile. His voice was incredulous. "*That's your swear word?*"

I couldn't stop laughing, as if the word itself unlocked a new sense of humor. "Dang it," I went on happily, but then that wasn't enough. "*Damn it.*" This time, I slapped a palm over my mouth, but it didn't stop the humor.

"Easy, now, let's not get too crazy." Hudson's teasing only made me laugh again.

I'd feel really stupid about this later—and probably even regret saying the word at all—but in that moment, there was something so funny about this scene. The Grim Reaper sitting across from me, his lunch tray in front of him, laughing with the school's goody-two-shoes as she said her first swear word.

It was the first time that something between us just *clicked,* like the two of us were working on a puzzle and I'd been able to connect another piece.

At that moment, he was just Bridge Boy. There was nothing scary about him at all.

With a happy sigh, I crossed *Say A Swear Word* off my list. "Are you sure you don't want to make a list of your own?" I asked Hudson. "Join this path of self-discovery with me?"

"Maybe when we get to the end of your list."

"When will we get to the end of it?" I took another bite of my chicken tender, thinking. "I can't really watch a scary movie while at school."

"After school, then." He said the words so quickly, so easily, that I wondered if he'd been thinking them all along. "Take our buddy sessions on a field trip. Principal Oliphant didn't say anything about that."

It took my brain, still caught on the list nonsense, several seconds to process what he said. Go off campus? *Together?* Staying on Brentwood property meant there'd always be someone around, whether it be faculty or students at sports practice. Going off campus, though, meant I'd officially, *officially* be alone with Hudson. With the Grim Reaper. The boy my brother explicitly told me *not* to even think about.

"Or not," he said after my hesitation became painfully loud.

"Sure." The word was impulsive, sudden, nearly drowned out by the two mantras in my head. *Grow a backbone* and *live a little.* "That would be perfect."

And maybe I shouldn't have agreed. Maybe it was a bad idea. But what was the point in creating a rebellion list if I didn't cross things off? I wouldn't do any of that on my own, either. I needed to live a little.

I needed Hudson Bishop.

CHAPTER 10

Thursday, during third period History, Principal Oliphant called me down to her office.

I settled into a chair across from her desk a little nervously, but I fought to keep from fidgeting. The last time I'd been in her office was when she paired Hudson and me together, and though I'd—mostly—gotten past my fearfulness when it came to him, this small space gave me flashbacks.

She had on her signature smile, but today, it didn't exactly calm me. Until she spoke, I wasn't sure anything could calm me. "This is kind of a dual meeting," she said once she sat down, leaning into her seat. "I want to talk a bit about Hudson and a bit about the Most Likely To list."

My pulse had hiccupped at the first topic at hand, so by the time she mentioned the list, it was already racing. "The Most Likely Tos?"

The list had flitted from my mind after the first few days. Especially in the last twenty-four hours, I hadn't thought of it once. How could I, when I'd actually been focused on the rebellion list Hudson had urged me to craft?

"I wanted to check in and see how you were feeling about it," she said. "I'm meeting with every student, and you're one of the first. Since I wanted to touch base on the peer program we've set up, I thought it was a good opportunity to chat about both."

Chatting with my principal about how I was voted Most Likely To: Stay A Prude was a level of embarrassment I didn't think I'd be able to reach, but here we were. "Um, it's okay. I mean, I'm okay. About the list."

"Do your parents know about it?"

"If they did, I'm sure Mom would've talked to you about it by now," I said, and then blinked a little at how blunt the words sounded. "I mean, no, they don't know. It'll just make them upset, and I don't think it's that big of a deal."

Principal Oliphant nodded slowly, tapping her fingers against her chin. "We've already had plenty of calls about the list. I think you're right, though. It's good that we can anticipate your parents' reactions to avoid unnecessary stress."

I pinched my fingers in my lap. "Is that what you did with the mentorship? You anticipated Mom not being on board with me mentoring Hudson, so you told her I was mentoring a girl?"

Her reaction came as a slow inhale through her nose and then a long sigh out of it, the sort of manufactured politeness fracturing in her eyes. "In a way, yes, I suppose so."

"And you knew I wouldn't tell her?"

"I *hoped*. I hoped that knowing Hudson's situation, you'd agree."

"That's why you chose me, then," I said, a weird sensation buzzing in my chest. "Because you thought you could easily manipulate me."

Principal Oliphant's eyebrows drew together in an expression that almost looked offended. "No other student would've given Hudson a chance. Not with the horror stories everyone has in their heads. You were the only one I could think of who could see past it all. I thought that partnering Hudson with a student who was his opposite would be a good idea. You, admittedly, were the first person I thought of, but I never thought you were easily manipulatable, Gemma."

I pinched my fingers tighter, unsure whether or not to believe her.

"The school board has had it out for Hudson ever since his freshman year," she explained. "Since the fight with your brother, Brentwood High has a no-bullying policy, and he managed to escape on the loophole that it didn't happen on school grounds."

"Why do they care so much?" I demanded, leaning forward in my seat. "It happened years ago, so I don't get—"

"Because it happened to Landon Settler," she said simply, never wavering in holding my gaze. "I'm sure you know how influential your parents are to Brentwood.

How well liked your mother has been ever since she was elected as school board president. It's a pack mentality, Gemma, and everyone is on one side. Including the rest of the school board."

She was right. It was no secret Mom had friends all over Brentwood, especially in the school district. We weren't a rich family like the Brays, but Mom did have a certain charm about her that could lure people. *Pack mentality*. It made sense. "Not you, though," I said. "You're standing up for Hudson."

"I don't agree with the grudge they're holding against a student. If I let the school board's vendetta get in the way of him moving forward, what kind of principal am I?" She rubbed her fingers into her temple. "The buddy program isn't a magic fix-all, of course. They'll still look for any opening chance they get. I only hoped that it could...well. I hoped that it could get Hudson to take it all more seriously."

Was he, though? I liked to think so—I liked to think I was making a little headway in getting him to open up a bit more—but I wasn't sure.

"Which, now that we're on topic, I wanted to check in earlier in the week, but with the list, time got away from me. How have the peer meetings with Hudson been? He hasn't been giving you trouble, has he?"

Trouble. I thought of his harsh words in Ms. Murphy's office our first day, and then the stony glare he gave me when I stood on the opposite side of the dusty road. Those images were quickly replaced by other ones —Hudson twining his pinky around mine, him leaning his head against his hand and threading his fingers through his hair. "Things are good."

"I was curious because Ms. Murphy said you ate lunch with him yesterday."

She spoke the words like a hidden scolding. The air conditioning in her office hummed in the quiet, words chilling in the air. Ms. Murphy knew I went into her room yesterday? Wait, *did* she have a recording her room?

"Gemma, it's okay. In fact, in a normal buddy situation, I'd encourage it. But it's like I said." She glanced at the ceiling as if the words were written on the tiles. "The school board has their vendetta. I'd hate for you to get caught in the crossfire."

The way she spoke made me wonder how much she knew about Hudson. I was certain she knew more than me—it wasn't like Hudson and I swapped juicy secrets—but I couldn't figure out why she was being so doom and gloom. "You said something happened over the summer to make the school board more upset with Hudson, didn't you?"

"I can't discuss too much about his life with you, but since you're his mentor, you should know a few things." Principal Oliphant leaned her elbows onto her desk. "He was arrested this past summer."

Curiosity and horror pretty much summed up what I was feeling. "For what?"

"Assault."

Assault could mean a lot of things, my mind tried to reason, and then I wanted to kick myself for trying to do that at all. Assault was assault. Arrested was arrested.

There was no manipulating the words to fit into what I wanted them to—the square block would only ever fit into the square hole.

Landon's beaten, bruised face popped into my head.

"You can see how, with that new development, now the school board is determined." She let out a little breath. "So, let's keep your meetings after school, okay? Superintendent Filmore comes into this wing during his lunch break, and if he saw you, he *would* tell your mother —I wouldn't doubt it. Do you understand?"

I curled my hands into little fists as I thought about the whole situation. It was clear that Principal Oliphant was taking precautions, but the way she was trying to isolate Hudson for his own good still made me frown. But ultimately, she was right. She had me snared. If there was one thing my parents couldn't find out about, it was Hudson Bishop. "Yeah," I eventually said. "I understand."

"Okay, tell me." Morgan pressed herself up against my side Thursday after school, the smell of her post-gym class perfume tickling my nose. "Who is it?"

"Who is what?" I asked, tugging my history book from the top shelf.

"Who is your brother dating?"

The textbook slipped from my fingertips and clattered onto the floor, slamming onto my toes in the process. The shock of Morgan's words masked the pain. "What?"

She lowered her voice further. "It was a rumor going around last period, that he's got a girlfriend. One of the juniors was talking all about it."

"He's not dating anyone." I bent down and picked up the book, wincing at the fresh ding in the right corner. "Think about it, Morgan. Who would he date anyway?" I, too, lowered my voice now. "Madison?"

"Doesn't he like her? You said he drew a picture of her."

It was a doodle from his sophomore year, one he hadn't moved off his desk when I'd ventured into his room. "Yeah, but liking her from afar is way different than gathering the courage to ask her out." The drawing was nothing impressive, not compared to his previous sketches, but it was clear that this was purposefully messy. There were four characters in the small drawing: a boy who was clearly Connor Bray, the star player on the football team, Jade Dyer, Connor's girlfriend, and then a boy and a girl. The boy was Landon, obviously, and I'd assumed the girl was Madison. "And besides, if they *were* together, there wouldn't be a rumor. It'd be blasted every-where. Babble would have a field day."

"That's true," Morgan said thoughtfully, shoulders slumping a little at the reality, but she peered up at me. "But it *is* going around. You should ask him. And...you know. Tell me."

"I'll ask him," I promised, but it was a begrudging sort of agreement. It was something I'd always wanted to fight against—being used to gain information about Landon since I was his sister. "I should get going."

"How long do you have to be around the Grim Reaper again?"

When Morgan backed up, she backed straight into Hudson, who replied, "Until she dies, of course."

The sound Morgan let out was torn between a screech and a gasp, and she flung away from him as if she'd catch death itself by having contact with him.

Morgan grabbed my arm, and I didn't miss how she edged herself slightly behind me, almost into my locker. "W-We were just talking," she said, voice like a mouse.

"About me?" Hudson watched her squirm for a moment longer before looking over. "Please tell me we don't have more barcodes today."

"I have homework to do today, so thankfully, no barcodes."

He flicked his hair from his eyes and waited for me to finish gathering my things and shut my locker door. Morgan squeezed my arm again. Though her gaze still cut to Hudson's like she expected him to lunge at any second, she was hesitant to let the topic go. "Text me when you find out."

I swallowed a sigh. "I will, I will."

A part of me expected Hudson to ask what we'd been talking about—if the roles had been reversed, I was sure my curiosity would've been piqued—but of course he kept silent as we walked down the hall. The history worksheet I had was nothing too substantial—a paper I'd no doubt be able to finish with twenty minutes of focus—and I wondered if Hudson had any homework.

As we turned into the main hallway, my steps faltered. It was easy to spot members of the Top Tier in the Brentwood High hallways due to the way other students reacted around them. Sort of like how everyone edged away from Hudson, afraid to get too close, the students *flocked* to the members of the highest tier, almost like some of their popular-ness would rub off. It was the way people got invested in celebrities—curious about their lives, wishing they could be a part of that crowd, too.

There was a little bubble of people surrounding two football players, Connor Bray and Ashton Shaw. Landon had quite a few friends from the football team, but it was safe to say that Connor Bray was his best friend—possibly only tied with Reed Manning. Landon told me once that even though he was the quarterback, he was glad that Connor was the one who got all the attention and love. Which made sense, given how reserved Landon was. And it also made sense why everyone ogled Connor—the guy was almost stupidly handsome.

I didn't know much about Ashton, since Landon never talked about him or brought him over. The only thing I knew was that he'd been in the fight with Hudson and my brother in their freshman year. Landon wasn't close with him anymore.

But both boys were on the football team with my brother, and they'd no doubt report on seeing me walking down the hallway with the Grim Reaper in tow.

Hudson stopped walking, too, when he spotted the football players, and when I looked over at him, a muscle in his jaw tensed. His eyes darted from boy to boy, shoulders stiffening as if he was bracing himself. Just when I was going to suggest we go the long way around to avoid them, Hudson started forward toward Ms. Murphy's office, toward the boys, leaving me behind.

Even from here, I could hear Connor speaking to one of the underclassmen who'd crowded near him while he shifted through his locker, but Ashton wasn't as engaged. He was the only one who looked at Hudson as the boy approached, thick eyebrows pulling together in a frown.

"Look who it is," Ashton said, cutting off what the underclassman had been saying, drawing everyone's attention. "The Grim Reaper. Whose funeral are you off to?"

"Yours," Hudson replied, not even glancing over at the glaring boy.

I took a step forward, my heart picking up its pace.

Ashton wasn't satisfied with Hudson's lack of interest, because when Hudson was about to walk past him, Aston snatched the handle of Hudson's backpack and pulled him to a stop. The students who'd been around the Top Tier boys shuffled back, the awestruck excitement draining from their faces, leaving nervousness behind.

"That a threat?" Ashton asked, seeming much too entertained by the situation he was creating. "Because I don't think you want to threaten me, freak."

"Knock it off, Ash," Connor ordered, grabbing his

backpack out of his locker and slamming the door shut. He turned to the two boys warily. "Let's go. Coach will kill me if I'm late again."

Listen to him, I willed to Ashton, taking another step forward while clutching my backpack straps tighter. Right down the hall were the doors to the offices, which meant the door to Principal Oliphant. If I raced past them, I could get her before anything escalated.

"Go ahead," Hudson said to the football player, unbothered with Ashton's hand still wrapped around his backpack handle, holding him in place. It was like Hudson couldn't help but provoke him. "We both know how it turned out last time."

"If you haven't noticed, I'm a whole lot bigger than I was freshman year." Ashton tugged Hudson closer by his backpack, staring down into the Grim Reaper's eyes. "Bigger than *you*."

He was right, of course. He had a few inches in height on Hudson, inches on the muscles he held the Grim Reaper in place with. He pummeled guys on the football field for *fun*.

But instead of backing down, Hudson lifted his chin to the side, offering his jaw to Ashton, almost like he was saying *try it*. He would've seemed completely unaffected if it hadn't been for his right hand, which had clenched into a fist as Ashton spoke.

For a long moment, no one breathed.

Ashton didn't move, though. Didn't pull his arm back, didn't do anything besides clutch Hudson's strap.

I only had a side view of Hudson, but I could see the

wide, amused smile when it spread across his mouth. It made my heart stop. Hudson reached over his chest and pried Ashton's hand free. "Don't worry," Hudson said, readjusting his bag, glancing around at the few students who still gathered. "Not that many people saw your ego get knocked down a peg. I wouldn't sweat it."

And then, without another word, he turned and continued down the hallway toward Ms. Murphy's office. He walked with the same lazy gait he always had, not glancing back once.

Connor smacked the back of Ashton's head, too hard to be playful. "You're asking for it," he muttered, letting out a breath. "If you had hit him, I would've told Landon."

Ashton muttered something under his breath, something that sounded like a curse word. Connor would've told Landon?

They started in my direction, with their fan club dispersing behind them, and that was when Connor spotted me. "Hey, Gemma," he greeted, cutting a look at Ashton, who didn't even meet my eye. "I'd stay and chat, but Coach'll skin me alive if I'm not on the field in five."

"You should go, then," I said, forcing a smile that felt so totally phony. I hoped he didn't notice. "Good luck at practice."

The two boys hustled past me then, leaving the tense atmosphere behind them. Stiffening my spine, I headed toward Ms. Murphy's office.

Hudson sat rigid in his seat at the foldable table when I walked into the doorway, his fists clenched underneath the table. In that second, there was no snark in his expression, no dark humor, and no malice. Everything that he'd been wearing a moment ago no longer showed on his face. For a brief second, his gaze was transparent on the table, almost like he was unsettled. Beneath the table, his fists shook.

And then he spotted me, and it was like everything shifted. He went from Bridge Boy to the Grim Reaper in a snap. His tight posture slackened, and he propped his elbow on the table, trying for nonchalance. "There you are. Enjoy the show?"

I felt off-kilter staring at him, unsure how to respond. I pulled the door shut behind me, sealing us inside Ms. Murphy's small office. "Why did Ashton do that? Pull you aside like that?"

"It's funny," Hudson said with a smirk, sitting back in his seat. "*He's* funny. Putting on a show for his followers but too much of a coward to follow through. I must've made quite the impression freshman year."

"That, or your fist did."

Hudson's smile deepened.

"Then again," I said as I sat down across from him, still unable to shake the uneasy feeling. "If he grabbed you in the first place, how much of an impression could it have made?"

"He just wants me to be afraid of him like he's afraid of me." Hudson reached up and scratched the spot underneath his eye, right where his scar was. "I guess he gets credit for trying."

If I hadn't seen Hudson's split-second reaction a

moment ago, with his shaking hands and stiff spine, I never would've thought that the football player affected him. I wondered if Hudson *was* afraid of Ashton, but he didn't want to show it.

I almost told him about Connor's response to it all, about how he was going to tell Landon, but thought better of it at the last second. "Principal Oliphant called me to the office today," I said instead, pulling up my backpack and taking out the textbook.

He seemed less than interested in the topic. "What'd she want?"

I debated on my answer, deciding to give a half-truth. "She wanted to talk about the Most Likely To list. She said she was going down the list and talking to students about it."

To a bit of my surprise, Hudson pulled out a math textbook from his backpack and set it on the table as well, flipping open to a page bookmarked by a folded lined piece of paper. His handwriting was neat on the page, half-finished. "That's what they do, huh? Try to cover up the aftermath instead of planning to stop it? So much for their zero-tolerance bullying policy. It's only zero-tolerance as long as it isn't one of their own, huh?"

The Most Likely To list hadn't been around that long, at least to my knowledge. I thought I remembered hearing that it started when Landon was a freshman, but there was no solid evidence. The school's gossip site hadn't started until Landon's sophomore year, and there had been a list out then. "How can they stop it if they can't find out who runs it?"

"I'm sure if they went after that the way they go after me, it wouldn't be hard to figure it out." Hudson's voice took on the edge it always seemed to gain whenever he talked about the Top Tier. "That was all she wanted?"

I didn't hesitate before nodding.

We worked on homework in silence after that, with no sound but the fluttering of textbook pages between us. It was impossible to focus with my thoughts dancing the way they did, especially with Hudson beside me. I read and reread the same passage probably four times before I set my pencil down, rubbing my knuckles.

"There's an away game tomorrow," I said haltingly, saying the first thing that came to mind. "Are you going?"

He didn't look up, his pencil scratching across the page. "Do I seem like the type to go to football games?"

"I could see you in full Bobcats spirit gear."

"Unfortunately, I look incredibly tacky in blue and gold."

I cracked the world's tiniest smile. "What a shame."

Something in my expression caught Hudson's attention, because he leaned further across the table, lowering his chin. "Tell me honestly. What else did the principal say?"

I'd hate for you to get caught in the crossfire. Whether it would hurt Hudson or not, I didn't know, but I couldn't bring myself to say it to him. "She found out we had lunch together yesterday. She said that's usually when Superintendent Filmore takes his lunches, and if he saw us together, he'd tell my parents." I dropped my gaze to my textbook. "And my parents can't find out."

He blew out a breath accompanied by an eye roll. "Nosy, isn't she?"

"It just means we have to meet after the program." I was convinced, then, that the person who spoke *wasn't* me. Normal Gemma wouldn't propose meeting outside of school—outside of the peer program. Normal Gemma wouldn't even dream of seeing him without school as an excuse. "I mean, if you want."

"We have to finish checking things off your list," he replied without hesitation. "So, yeah, I'm down."

I'm down. The words themselves seemed flippant, but the way he said them felt like anything but. That excited thrill came back, and I didn't try to bottle it up.

CHAPTER 11

That night, Landon went out bowling with friends while Mom, Dad, and I stayed in. After dinner, we all sat in the living room and watched some sports-centered movie Dad put in. I sat on the couch with a skirt draped over my lap, a needle and thread between my fingers. It was a bit too dark to see clearly, but I still worked on sewing the zipper on the back anyway. It kept my fingers busy while my mind was elsewhere.

Mom sat on the other side of the couch of me while Dad was propped up in his recliner, and every so often, she'd glance over at me. "It's looking a bit uneven there, can you tell?"

Before, I'd always apologize on impulse, wishing I could sink into the couch. Now, though, I didn't look up. "I see."

"Practice makes perfect," she chirped, settling deeper against the cushions. "You're not too far in. You could seam rip it and try again."

I didn't answer this time, sliding the needle into the

fabric of my skirt and tugging it taut. Careful not to put too much pressure on the stitch, I wound it around again. "Mom," I said slowly, hoping my voice sounded nonchalant. The blood was pounding so heavily in my ears that it was hard to hear. "I was wondering... Can my buddy and I go see a movie after school? At the theater in Jefferson?"

"Your buddy? You mean your mentee?"

"Yeah." I shifted the material of my skirt closer, hoping the concentration could disguise my nerves. "They don't, uh...they don't have a lot of friends to hang out with, and I thought that'd be a fun little field trip for us."

Mom parted her lips with a sigh. "How would you even get to a movie theater?"

I hadn't thought that far, but my mind picked up its pace quickly. "I can see if Morgan can come with us. Her mom could drive us."

"Morgan? Morgan Davies?" Her voice curled up on a question, but also with something that sounded like distaste. "Are you still hanging out with her?"

"It's not like *she* didn't vote for you for re-election."

Dad paused the movie with a huff. "Was that a bit of attitude there, Gemma?"

My needle slid between my fingers, and it slipped through the fabric to pierce my finger. *Had* that been attitude? For a moment, I floundered in what my response should be, or even how to form my facial expression. It hadn't felt like attitude when I said it, but then I realized —that wasn't how I would normally have responded. I would've heard Mom's tone and altered course. I would've yielded to that. Instead, I responded to it.

"Sorry." I threaded the needle into the fabric to hold it in place and looked up between them. I hunched my shoulders a little. "Yes, I have still been hanging with Morgan at school. I...I thought it could be fun, doing something with my mentee."

"Landon has a game tomorrow," Dad pointed out. "Are you planning on missing it?"

"Of course not." Missing a game in the Settler household was not allowed. I hadn't been allowed to stay home on a Friday night since summer break. "Morgan's mom should be able to drop me off before you leave for the game.

It was a strategic move, using Morgan as my alibi. Since our moms were fighting, I knew Mom wouldn't call Mrs. Davies up to make sure it was okay, and nor would she call to check in. Even if Morgan did see my mom at the game tomorrow night, she'd avoid us like the plague—Morgan might've liked me, but she was loyal to her mom. There was little chance it could go wrong.

Even still, I sat with my lie lingering in the air, wondering if it would suffocate me before my parents responded.

"I guess it would be okay," Mom said, refocusing on the paused TV with her lips still lingering in a small frown. It almost looked pouty. "I'll be at the office late finishing up paperwork for a case, so I suppose it could be okay. But make sure you're home by six-thirty before your father leaves, okay? You can't miss kickoff."

For a moment, I stared at Mom, and it was a good thing she didn't look over, because she would've seen my expression in its full, shellshocked glory. She'd said yes. She'd actually said yes. She hadn't seen right through me. I wondered if it was because I was that good at lying or they just never expected me to tell one. The refreshing pour of relief nearly had me slumping against the pillows, and I nodded eagerly, picking up my skirt and unsheathing the needle. "I'll be home by then, I promise."

My hands shook so badly that I pricked myself a few more times with the needle, but it didn't erase the near giddiness that swelled within me.

I hugged my books tight to my chest as I walked down the upperclassmen hallway. It was much less chaotic than the underclassmen hallways after school, mostly because seniors hightailed it from the school building as soon as the bell rang, so I was able to move without much jostling.

A part of me hadn't expected to find him here, the idea of lockers too mundane for the Grim Reaper, but there he was, standing in front of a bright yellow door that didn't suit him at all.

Hudson stood with perfect posture as he loaded textbooks into his tattered backpack, head bent, focus on nothing else around him. Like before in the halls, there was a bubble of space surrounding him, as if it was too dangerous to get close. As people passed by him, they'd only shoot quick glances before hurrying away, not wanting to get caught staring. Through it all, Hudson didn't notice.

Or he was just pretending not to notice.

I held my textbooks tighter, crossing the distance between us slowly. It was like a moment from a dream, where the hallway felt longer and longer even though I kept walking, my brain's way of telling me that this was my chance. This was my out. I could turn around and hurry to the bus. I could even text Landon and tell him to wait for me, since he didn't have practice on game days. It wasn't too late to not go through with it.

Until Hudson lifted his head from his locker. He'd been oblivious to everyone else passing, but it was like he had a detector for sophomores named Gemma, because he zeroed in on me in an instant. The only indicator that he even recognized me was the small line that formed between his brows.

"Hey," I said as I got close enough, stopping a few lockers' lengths between him and me.

"Hey," he returned slowly. "I thought we didn't meet on Fridays."

"We don't." I reached up and flicked my braid over my shoulder, itching my neck. "At least...not for the mentorship."

Now one of Hudson's eyebrows peaked. "Your list?"

"It's the perfect opportunity. I was thinking we could go see a scary movie. There's one playing at the theater over in Jefferson. I mean, if you don't have anything else to do. If you wanted to."

He leaned his arm against his locker door so that it

brought himself closer to me. "What more would I have to do than to hang with Gemma Settler?"

Something about the teasing had me unable to fight a small smile, one that caused his to stretch wider. A split-second thought fluttered through my mind. *Hudson Bishop is smiling at me.* This time last week, I wasn't even sure he *could* smile. Now, though, there was no missing it. No missing how it was directed at me.

For no reason at all, I felt like smiling back.

Before I had a chance to say anything more, my gaze caught down the hallway past him and his open locker door to where two people had just turned the corner. One person wearing a blue and gold football jersey and one wearing cheerleading gear.

Landon and Madison.

Everything in me jolted.

Without thinking, I stepped into the space between Hudson's body and his open locker, hiding behind the open door, using him as a wall between my brother and me. I grabbed a fistful of Hudson's black sweatshirt and tugged him to me, and with the way his arm was still propped on the locker door, it brought us *close.* Closer than I'd ever been with a boy before. The toes of his boots brushed my sneakers, and my nose nearly grazed the front of his chest.

Landon's voice slowly came within earshot as he walked down the hall. "...know it's sudden. But relation-ships always are, aren't they?"

Hudson was close enough that I could feel his body stiffen, his gaze drifting from me to the side, as if he was listening in, too. I clutched his sweatshirt tighter, knuckles grazing his chest in the process, willing him not to turn. If he turned now, it would be game over—over before we'd even begun.

I drew in a deep breath, and it was the wrong move. The warm scent of him from both his locker and his skin hit me like a wave, everywhere all at once, filling my head. He smelled a whole lot better than any boy I'd come into contact with before, and something about it caused my stomach to turn hollow.

"When they make *sense*," came Madison's reply, closer. "You and her, though..."

And then I could see Landon directly over Hudson's shoulder. It was like he walked in slow-mo past us. He was fully looking at Madison, head turned in the opposite direction, ignoring the fact that Hudson stood only a few feet away. Unaware that I was tucked up against him. My forehead brushed Hudson's chest as I ducked down farther. *Please don't turn, please don't turn.*

"Ah, well." Landon's discomfort was clear in his voice, even as it grew farther away. "What happened at lunch wasn't her fault."

I risked a glance over to see the back of his jersey. *SETTLER 10.* He didn't glance at me at all before continuing down the hall with Madison at his side, both of them heading for the parking lot. I let out a harsh breath of relief, but then remembered exactly the position I had myself in, and tipped my head up.

Hudson's electric blue eyes peered down at me in such a way that the charge sprang from them to me.

Warmth spread over my skin, starting in my cheeks and sliding down my throat, but whatever emotion it was tied to, it wasn't embarrassment. Whatever it was, it caused my heart to beat faster.

Hudson then looked at my fist still wrapped around his sweatshirt and then back up at me, and I dropped it with a small gasp. I took a jerky step away and instantly hit my head against the shelf in his locker, effectively shattering that weirdness between us. "Ow," I grumbled as I rubbed the spot. And then I looked up at him, giving him a pained smile. "I mean *crap*."

Hudson tried to smother his laugh, but it came out as a snort. "Not to rain on your parade," Hudson said, taking a step back to give me breathing room. Room I desperately needed. "But if we go to the movies, how are you proposing we get to the movie theater?"

"I was thinking about it," I began, tightening my grip on my books. "And I wondered if you had any ideas."

Asking Morgan's mom to drive us had been a good enough excuse to give my parents, but there were too many flaws in that plan. Would Morgan let the Grim Reaper ride in the backseat of her mom's minivan? Probably not. Would Mrs. Davies be okay with him riding in the backseat? Probably not, and despite their feud, I could see her calling Mom to tell her.

Hudson considered, and I held my breath, ready for him to say no. The sort of buzzing feeling in me simmered, like someone had taken the anticipation of everything and turned it down low.

He pulled his cell from his pocket and unlocked it

with a click, quickly scrolling down his contacts. When he found the one he was looking for, he pressed his phone to his ear. I could hear the faint ring from where I stood, and could hear when the ringing stopped. "Derrick," Hudson said in greeting, eyes flicking to me. "You busy?"

The faint murmur on the line was too low to pick up, and I suddenly felt rude for listening in. I turned toward the inside of Hudson's locker instead. The interior was immaculate with the spines of his textbooks even and aligned perfectly. His backpack, though worn, hung neatly from the hook inside. There were two pencils on the top shelf sitting on top of a spiral-bound notebook, everything new and clean-looking.

"You up for a movie?" Hudson asked presumedly Derrick, reaching around me to grab his backpack off the hook. "I mean, sure, *you* can go see *Super Sonic Racoons*, but we're seeing something else."

There was no missing what Derrick said back. It was practically a shout. "*We?*"

Hudson cradled his phone between his ear and his shoulder, threading his arms through his backpack straps. After he waited for me to get out of the way, he kicked his locker door shut. "Get pants on and pick us up from the school."

This time, it was my turn to snort.

After stopping by my locker to grab my bag, we waited inside the doors for Derrick to show, and knowing that Landon was officially out of the building took a bit of my edge off. The buses would've left by now, which meant Jaden was gone too, and Morgan's dad was usually waiting for her in the curb lineup by the time school got out.

Hudson leaned against the hallway corridor across from me, probably eight feet away. "So," he began. "You want to check off watching a scary movie first, huh?"

"If that's okay."

"Stop that."

I blinked at his flat tone and the suddenness of it. "Stop what?"

"'If that's okay.'" He tilted his head in that way of his, causing me to see a bit more of his expression as his hair fell away. "'If you want to.' If it's something *you* want to do, be firm about it."

Again, I blinked, thinking back on our past conversations with each other. My past conversations in general. "I didn't realize I was doing that."

We regarded each other for another moment, neither of us speaking. It was different from the way that he and Principal Oliphant had their stare-downs. It was different from even before between us. There was something quiet to the stare, something that caused me to grow more and more comfortable rather than on edge. "So," he tried again. "You want to check off the scary movie from your list?"

This time, my voice was absolute. "Yes."

Hudson glanced out the double doors before straightening. "Then let's go."

Once we were outside, it was clear to see which car had drawn Hudson's attention. A rough, scratched sedan pulled up in the opposite direction along the curb, with the driver's side closest to the sidewalk. There were several dents in the body work, a taillight with duct tape over it, and a black plastic piece replacing a section of the front metal bumper. The guy in the driver's seat had his arm hanging out of the window, cut-off T-shirt exposing his dark skin and all the muscles attached to that bicep. His head was buzzed, leaving only a thin layer of spiky black hair. He looked over once we stepped out of the school building, lowering his sunglasses, lips pulling into a wide smirk. "Hudson Bishop!"

Hudson didn't falter in his steps, sauntering up to the car with a chuckle. "You didn't take as long as I thought you would've."

"Hey, I figured if you were calling in a favor, I should oblige in a timely fashion." The guy's gaze dipped past Hudson, and he lowered his sunglasses even further. "Especially if it's for a lady."

I clenched my backpack strap tighter.

"This is Derrick," Hudson told me, gesturing toward the guy. "Good friend. He looks worse than he is. His car, though...it's as bad as it looks."

"Hey, don't hate on Betsy," Derrick replied, but with a smile. "She's been in a few accidents, but she's still kicking." Then he tipped two fingers at me in a salute. "Nice to meet you...Gemma, right?"

It occurred to me that Hudson never mentioned my name on the phone call. Meaning that he must've told Derrick about me before. "With a G."

"Well, Gemma with a G. Your chariot awaits."

Hudson opened up the backseat door and stood

behind it, gesturing me to climb in, but I still didn't move forward. He really expected me to get into a stranger's car? Was all his support about creating a rebellion list meant to lull me into a false sense of security or something? Was I going to end up stuffed in a trunk a mile down the road?

Derrick didn't seem scary, not with his easy smile and snorting laugh. The only thing about him that was scary was how badly his car was crunched, hinting at some not-so-stellar driving skills.

Seeing my hesitation—and no doubt guessing what dark turn my thoughts took—Hudson walked over to me, pulling something small and metallic out of his pocket. "Don't tell anyone I had this." He deposited it into my palm. "The button here pops the blade out, so, for the love of God, don't cut yourself."

It took me several seconds to realize he'd given me a pocketknife. An actual pocketknife. It was an iridescent sort of purple, folded up and scrunched. As I flipped it again, I found two initials engraved into the purple. *H.B.*

"You really think I have it in me to stab you?" I demanded, jaw dropping a little.

"It's supposed to make you feel safer." Hudson rounded the open door and slid into the backseat. He turned toward me once he got settled into the middle, and with raised eyebrows, he patted the seat beside him. "You told me to trust you. Can't you trust me, too, Gem?"

And then he lifted his pinky, calling back on our promise.

Gem. It became impossible to swallow. I wasn't sure

if it was the word or the way he said it, with the tilt to his lips that should've made me take a step back. I didn't, though, because the thrill had returned. I was once more at the top of the rollercoaster, and if I took a step forward, I'd feel the drop. The sensation swelled behind my ribcage, building the longer our gazes were connected, promising an exciting ride.

Trust Hudson Bishop. I never would've before, but I wanted to now.

I picked up the hem of my skirt and climbed into the backseat, clutching my backpack to my chest like a shield. Or an extra airbag, since the car looked old enough that it might not have had any. Hudson reached across me and tugged the door shut, the back of his blond head right in front of mine, and it was the first time I could smell the citrusy scent of his shampoo.

"I feel like one of those rich people drivers," Derrick mused, pushing his sunglasses up on his nose, adjusting in his seat until he sat straight up. "All I need is one of those cool hats."

"He's a little off his rocker," Hudson whispered, tipping his head ever so slightly toward the driver's seat. "But he's the only one of my friends who has a car."

"Ah, it's nice to be used," Derrick mused while tapping his fingers on the steering wheel. "I guess if I have to be used for anything, this isn't too bad."

"Drive responsibly," Hudson told Derrick. "Seriously."

"Precious cargo," Derrick replied, and in the rearview mirror, he slid his glasses back down to give me a wink.

Hudson hadn't moved from the middle seat, so his shoulder was flush against mine. When Derrick pulled out of the school lot, taking a sharp left, my body leaned against his ever so slightly. I should've pulled away, should've pressed myself to the door to avoid touching him, but I didn't move.

"I can't believe you carry a pocketknife," I muttered, looking at the thing closer. It was a little dinged up around the edges, but mostly looked in good condition. I slid the knife into the front pocket of my backpack, and Hudson was right—its presence gave me a bit of peace, even if it was tucked away. "You must not take Principal Oliphant's threat seriously, then."

"I do." When he inhaled, he ran his teeth along his bottom lip. My attention caught there momentarily. "You never know when you might need it, is all."

"Except Milady is right," Derrick said from the front, eyes glancing in the mirror. "You probably won't ever need it at school, unless you're *trying* to get kicked out."

Hudson just rolled his eyes.

The drive to Jefferson didn't take very long, not with the music playing over the speakers to keep us company. Hudson looked up the showtimes on his phone, and I peeked over as he did so.

"I think all these are rated R," Hudson said. "There's one PG-13 one, but I don't technically think it's horror."

Derrick's gaze flicked up to meet mine in the rearview. "How old are you again?"

"Sixteen."

"Ah, bummer. If it's any consolation, Hudson can

only barely get in at seventeen. But you'll have to stick with a PG-13 flick."

I nodded slowly, knowing that it was probably best to work up to anything rated R. "That's okay."

Hudson didn't reply, but kept scrolling down the showtimes of the movies. Derrick didn't slow down as much as he should've as he pulled into the theater's parking lot, but otherwise, his driving wasn't *that* bad. Better than I expected. We unloaded from the car quickly, joining the after-school rush into the building. A lot of the kids were ones I didn't recognize, most likely from Jefferson High since their high school was right down the road. We waited in line not speaking, the three of us shuffling forward.

When we got to the ticket counter, Hudson took the lead. "Three tickets for *Super Sonic Racoons*, please," he said with the politest voice I'd heard from him before, but I looked up at him in confusion. He didn't correct himself.

The lady who stood on the other side of the counter glanced between us. She no doubt took in the all-black outfit Hudson wore, Derrick's shaved head, and wondered why in the world we'd be seeing a kids' movie.

Derrick, who stood on Hudson's left, grinned. "Have you seen it yet?" he asked her.

"Uh...no."

"It's part of a trilogy," he carried on in his same excited tone. "Before, there was *Super Sonic Dogs*, and then there was *Super Sonic Cats*, obviously, and now this one. SSC wasn't as cool as the first—wasn't as much of a hit at the box office, either—but I heard *SSR* is really good. That they really nailed their animation in this one."

I caught Hudson's eye as he lazily looked down at me, spinning a finger around his ear.

The ticket lady seemed thoroughly confused—that, or freaked out—and she took Hudson's cash without a word, passing over three tickets. Using the allowance money I'd accrued my whole life, I bought us all popcorn and drinks, and then we moved toward the left wing of the building.

We were supposed to go to Theater 8, but when we got to Theater 4, Hudson's hand curved around my elbow. The touch was light, but I flinched at the suddenness of it, turning to face him.

"What do you say?" he asked.

I didn't realize what he meant at first, until I looked up at the marquee that read *Mirror Man 2*. "But...that's not the movie we bought tickets for."

He raised his eyebrows expectantly. "Didn't you say you wanted to live a little?"

Derrick frowned and brought his popcorn closer. "Wait, so we're not going to see *Super Sonic Racoons?*"

"It's up to you, then," Hudson said as if Derrick didn't speak, his voice neutral, adding zero pressure. "We can go sit and watch *Super Sonic Racoons*. We can even go and see about exchanging our tickets for the PG-13 film. Or we could watch *Mirror Man 2*."

"I mean, it's not *illegal*," Derrick said, bending his head down and scooping up popcorn with his mouth. "It might just, you know, get us kicked out. Which is fine, since this theater totally serves stale popcorn, anyway."

In some ways, I wanted to take baby steps. Telling Mom and Dad I was going to Morgan's when I wasn't was a baby step. Going to the movies in general was a baby step. But these baby steps weren't on my rebellion list. Watching a horror movie was. When would I get another chance to check it off?

Live a little. It was a rebellious sort of whisper. The voice that pushed to agree when Hudson asked to go off-campus the first time. The voice that had me getting off the bus Monday. The voice that ultimately had me taking a step forward now, toward Theater 4.

The rebellious whisper was like a voice singing a song, one that I wanted to learn the words to.

Mirror Man 2 was already in its opening credits when we crept into the dark theater, and there were a lot of people already sitting with their popcorn in front of them. We moved up toward the top few rows, with Hudson sitting in the middle.

I tipped my head toward him, making sure not to lean too close. "Do you know what this movie is about?"

"No clue," he whispered back, eyes darting across the screen. "I haven't seen the first."

It turned out that the movie was about a demon that only appeared in mirrors and could reach through them to kill people and take their souls to hell. The concept itself wasn't that scary, but the movie really did rely on jump scares to cause an audience reaction. Even though I'd never watched a scary movie before in my life, it was easy to tell when they were coming, especially when the creepy violin music would get louder and louder.

At some point, I glanced over to see how much popcorn Hudson had eaten, but found him staring intensely at the bucket. I waited for him to turn back to the movie, but he didn't, almost like he was ignoring it entirely.

My jaw dropped a little as I leaned in, trying to keep the amusement from my voice. "Are you scared?"

Hudson jumped at my sudden voice so close to his ear. "Are you kidding? Of course not."

"Why aren't you watching?"

"Why aren't *you* watching?" he returned, sounding defensive. He slumped deeper into his seat, trying to appear as comfortable as possible despite his frown. "You shouldn't be so focused on me."

Derrick leaned over, too. His whisper was barely audible, but I could read his lips in the dimness. "Hudson *hates* horror movies."

Hudson made no attempt at denying it. He stared stonily at the screen like we weren't even there, but the tightness in how he clutched the popcorn tub hinted at his true feelings. "The Grim Reaper is afraid of scary movies," I whispered to myself, knowing he could hear. And then I leaned in closer once again. "You can use my shoulder to hide behind if you need to."

When he turned, our faces were suddenly only inches apart, and I was consumed in the blue ice of his eyes, their odd, electrifying color. They were bright even in the darkness of the theater. Some of my amusement sobered up as the rollercoaster feeling returned.

"Very funny," he whispered back.

A loud bang came from the movie, causing someone in the back of the theater to let out a sharp yell, and the sudden sound made Hudson jolt in his seat. It broke the weird hypnosis that had been there a second ago, splitting my gaze from his.

When crafting my rebellion list, I wasn't even sure initially why I'd written down *watch a horror movie*. It wasn't like the desire was ever there. I wasn't sure I'd ever seen a trailer for one and thought *man, I wish I could watch that*. Maybe it was because there was a forbidden tie to it. Maybe I wanted to watch it because I knew I wasn't allowed to. I could be more independent and my parents would never have to know. That was the true nature of the rebellion list to begin with—to do what was not allowed. To find out what I did like. To find myself.

To live a little.

So even as the music began its creepy, violin-filled build, I couldn't help but smile a little at the screen, heart pounding with the adrenaline of the moment.

CHAPTER 12

Jaden was relentless Saturday afternoon.

I sat in the corner of the beauty salon with my legs drawn to my chest, trying to make myself as small as possible in the overflowing space. Stylists flitted about, chattering with their clients. Mom sat in a seat closest to me, laughing happily as her hairdresser, Kim, applied dye to her roots. I'd never seen the salon so busy. Normally when I accompanied Mom to her hair sessions every six weeks, it was dead enough that there was an empty chair I could sit in, but not today. Every black seat was full, and the scent of hairspray and dye was fresh in the air.

I stared at a stray clump of hair and dust bunnies on the floor, wishing I could get swept away along with them.

It was the one and only time I openly welcomed Jaden as a distraction.

JADEN

I'm just saying, I really enjoyed you
sitting by me at the game last night. I'm
probably one of the only guys at
Brentwood who is clueless when it
comes to football, so I really appreciated
you explaining it yesterday. I really did.
Maybe...well, maybe we could sit by
each other again next Friday?

He was long-winded even in text. I could practically hear his rambling voice in my head.

And "me sitting by him" was really only him sitting down beside me after Mrs. Morris claimed the spot in front of us on the bleachers. My dad and his talked about the game the entire time, and our moms talked about Landon's performance, which left me to entertain Jaden. As always.

GEMMA

I thought you don't usually come to
football games.

His reply came so fast that I could've sworn he'd already known what my reply would be and had the sentence prepped.

JADEN

If it means I can sit by you, I wouldn't
mind.

I hated myself for walking into that one.

"I'm so glad I got that pass Landon threw on video last night," Mom was saying to Kim as she applied more dye. Mom always said that her fiery hair dulled with age, so every month and a half, she came to the salon for a refresh. "It'll be great to send to college scouts."

The moment in question was Landon throwing the football twenty-five yards at last night's away game, and Connor caught it perfectly, launching across the endzone. They were a well-oiled machine last night, one that succeeded in defeating the Vikings.

"You've got two beautiful children, Naomi," Kim said, and in tandem, they both cast glances to where I crouched beside a potted plant. "Gemma, you're growing up into the most stunning young woman."

I smiled and ducked my head, wishing they'd go back to talking about Landon.

"Her hair's getting long," Kim went on, and waggled her pointy eyebrows. "How about it, Gemma? Should we put you in the chair next?"

"Oh, heavens, no," Mom said with a breathless chuckle, pressing a hand to her chest. "Cut that beautiful mane she's got? Oh, I could never. She cut it once, but she hated it."

I watched Mom as she lied, but the way she said it so easily, I wondered if it *had* been a lie in her mind. Because it wasn't me who hated it—it was her.

My phone buzzed again, and I slid it open to read the next text.

JADEN

What are you doing today?

I'm at the hair salon with Mom. We'll be
here for a little while longer yet

"Ah, a young girl has to have a little fun now and then," Kim insisted. She picked up the small bowl that'd been sitting on the rolling table beside her, stirring her brush around in it. "I'm going to mix it up a smidge more, and I'll be back to apply the rest, okay?"

Mom lifted her hand out to me, and I was quick to comply. Pushing up from the dusty floors, I walked over until I could lay my hand in hers. "I look kind of silly, don't I?" she asked with a teasing grin, eyes flitting up as if she attempted to look at her head. "Do I look like someone dumped spaghetti sauce on my head?"

"Only a little," I replied, but matched her smile. "You always look so beautiful afterward, so it's worth it."

"It's a lot of upkeep to look beautiful." She tugged on my hand until I angled toward the mirror in front of her, and we both looked at our reflections. My braid was loose today, looser than Mom normally weaved it, which allowed a few of my baby hairs to fall out and frame my face. Beside Mom, with her glamorous makeup, I looked plain. Half of her head was wet with hair dye, but she radiated an energy that I lacked. "But you—you're beautiful, all naturally. You'd never want to dye your hair like this, would you?"

A narrow part of my brain wondered if it was a test. "No."

And it wasn't a lie. I wouldn't want to dye my hair. But the long braid that hung down my back, that my mom picked each morning and styled how she pleased—I wanted nothing more than to cut it all off.

"I talked to Talia at the game last night," Mom said, turning to peer up at me. "She said that your peer partnership is going well. Are you finding it mutually beneficial?"

I tried to figure out when Principal Oliphant would've run into Mom. "It's been nice to have someone to spend time with after school."

"But you *are* getting things accomplished, right? I'd hate to think you're goofing off."

Mom really would've flipped, then, if she knew what I'd really been doing yesterday. Sitting through a murder horror flick while trying not to laugh at Hudson jumping with every scare. I nearly grinned now imagining it, but stifled it at the last second. "We worked on homework last time."

"Well, good. Make sure it's more than just a social hour, okay?"

I nodded.

Kim had returned with her bowl, forcing me to drop Mom's hand and take a step backward. "Gemma," Mom said before I could get too far, lowering her voice. A gleam popped into her eye. "Some of the football moms and I were chatting last night, and I heard something interesting. Did Landon get a girlfriend and not tell us?"

Kim gave a little gasp while I blinked in surprise, mostly because it'd been a topic I'd forgotten about. Morgan had pushed it and pushed it Thursday after school, but she hadn't asked about it at all on Friday. It'd totally slipped my mind to ask him. "What did the moms say?"

"That there's a post on something called Babble?" She shook her head. "I'm not sure, but it talked about Landon having a girlfriend."

Since my phone wasn't a smart phone, I wouldn't have been able to access the internet with it. I almost asked Mom to borrow her phone to look up the post. I caught myself, though, knowing that if Landon kept it a secret, it was for a reason. "Babble is a gossip site one of the students runs. Like a tabloid but for our high school. I'm sure it's only a rumor."

"He's never brought a girl home to meet you, has he?" Kim asked.

"Never. Oh, and I've been waiting, too!" Mom tsked her tongue, like she expected as much. "It would be a match made in heaven if it was Madison Oliphant—she's the co-captain of the cheer squad, Kim. Cutest little thing. Gemma, it would be so good to spend some quality time with her, don't you think?"

I didn't have a thought about Madison one way or the other—she rarely talked to me at our family dinners—but even though Landon was crushing on her, I couldn't exactly picture them dating. I couldn't imagine Landon dating anyone.

The conversation had opened up a segue that taunted me, and there was no ignoring the thought. "So, dating in high school is okay?"

"For Landon, yes. For you...well, you're still young." A gleam suddenly popped into Mom's eye, and ignoring

Kim wielding the hair dye brush, she turned her head toward me. "Are you asking because you're interested in *Jaden?*"

"No!" The word tore out of me, loud enough for it to seem to echo throughout the hair salon. I drew in a shaking breath, trying to ignore the flare of surprise on Mom's face. "I mean, not...I don't know."

Just like how I couldn't imagine Landon dating, I couldn't really see myself doing it either. Dressing up, going on dates, making idle small talk with people to get to know them. It didn't sound like anything interesting at all. Inexplicably, I thought of Hudson's body close to mine in front of his locker yesterday, my hand fisted around his shirt.

When I glanced into the mirror, I had a straight view of the chair directly behind the one Mom sat in. A little girl was on one of the black stools. Her hair was long, sectioned off into three ponytails, and her mother was taking photographs of it. In the reflection of the mirror, I could see tears on the mother's cheeks, but she still smiled.

The hairstylist picked up silver scissors from the tray beside him, flashing them to the little girl with a smile. He must've asked a question, because the little girl gave an exaggerated nod, gapped grin and all.

The dark feeling that coiled in the pit of my gut returned at the sight. In that moment, I knew exactly what the emotion was—resentment. It flared and festered until it left me angry inside, coming face to face with the realization that my life wasn't mine. I couldn't even style my hair the way I wanted to. It was the reason for the rebellion list to begin with, but watching the little girl get her hair cut—watching her mother approve of it—slapped the truth of it all into my face.

Mom let out a sharp gasp, one that spiked my heartrate in an instant, but when I turned, there was no blood. Instead, she stared toward the front entrance, beaming. "Speak of the devil!"

I turned too, and for a wild, random moment, I thought I'd see Hudson walking into the hair salon. Instead, it was Jaden.

He had his skateboard underneath his arm, looking vastly out of place in the salon filled with women. I had to see him every day at school, and now apparently, my weekends weren't safe either. Since we were a straight shot from the door, his gaze found where I stood by Mom —and I'm sure her bloodcurdling gasp only helped.

"I was in the area," he said before either of us could get a word in. "My mom comes here to get her hair done —and plus it's like the only good salon in Brentwood—so I figured this was where your mom comes too. Mrs. Settler, you're looking—"

"A little crazy, right?" she teased, grinning. "We're going to the mall after my appointment. *Someone* needs their homecoming dress."

Jaden turned to me with a happy expression. "You'll have to text me a picture of what you get."

"Of course she will!" Mom's demeanor had completely changed with Jaden's presence, animated to the point that Kim had a hard time putting the dye on

Mom's hair. "Gemma, this is perfect, isn't it? I easily have an hour left, and now you won't have to sit and watch anymore. Now you have someone you can spend the time with."

I sometimes wondered if Jaden and Mom were on the same wavelength. Then again, they both probably had the same motive in mind—woo Gemma Settler. I half wondered if they'd even planned this.

"I don't mind sitting," I tried to object, but Mom wouldn't let it slide.

She winked at me. "Why don't you go get something sweet from the gas station down the road? I'll allow it since it's the weekend and Jaden's here to walk with you."

The decision, as always, was made for me. Jaden moved to set his skateboard down by Mom, who fished out a couple of bills from her wallet before he urged her that he would cover the snacks. After he effectively flattered her, he waved an arm toward the door, urging me to go first.

"You look nice," Jaden said once we were away from prying ears. "I don't normally see that much of your leg. Was that a weird thing to say?"

For mid-September, it was warmer than usual, so I opted for a skirt that fell just below my knees. It was nicer than I usually wore, the lace pattern making it seem fancier than the ones I wore to school. Knowing my luck, Morgan would've spilled juice on it at lunch or something.

However, if I'd known I was going to see Jaden, I would've worn something much plainer. "Uh, thanks."

"It's kind of funny that we keep running into each other."

"Funny."

"I'm glad I caught you, too. I was at the videogame store over on Main when I got your text, and thought 'man, this must be fate.' I hope you don't mind that I stopped by."

With the gas station in view, I nearly stopped walking. I wished Jaden and I could've been friends instead of *this*. That we could've laughed at our parents' poshness and the way they tried to push us together. That we could've met up and talked if only to get their version of "fate" off our backs.

"Next time...do you mind asking me first? I'm—well, I'm not very good with surprises."

His expression grew thoughtful. "Well, I *did* ask first. I asked your dad."

"My *dad*?" Now I did stop walking, a foot from the gas station door, whirling to stare up at him. "What?"

"I asked him if we could spend some time together today, and he said you were here with your mom. He gave me permission to swing by and see you."

The fact that my dad was in on it made the whole situation even weirder. Not my mom, my *dad*. After the whole *too young to date* conversation, he still let Jaden come by? "So, your whole 'my mom gets her hair done here' was a lie?"

"No!" His eyes grew wide. "Of course not. I'd never lie to you, Gemma. Honest. I just wanted to see you, hang out a little."

I inhaled slowly, wondering what kind of response would work in this situation. Maybe it was time to have The Chat with him, but even as I began to imagine it, the spool of issues began to unravel in my brain. If I told Jaden I didn't have feelings for him, would he tell his parents? If so, would they tell mine? Most definitely. And then they'd ask me why I didn't have feelings for him, and I'd have to come up with an answer.

That was impossible, though. Everything tied back to them.

"I am happy," I said finally, the words weighing me down like a rock sinking in water. "The hair dye fumes were starting to go to my head."

With his confidence renewed, Jaden grinned.

The gas station's air conditioning blasted into us as soon as we crossed the threshold, instantly freezing my skin. I ducked my head and kept it down, feeling Jaden loom closer behind me. His hand brushed my elbow, and even though my long sleeve was a barrier from his skin touching mine, I pulled back.

Without saying anything, Jaden sauntered toward the back of the gas station to where the sodas were, probably expecting me to follow, but I instead headed down the candy aisle, taking the moment to breathe.

Somewhere in the store, I could hear a bundle of people laughing. They went down the aisle on the other side of me, and I could see the tops of their heads as they walked down it. Their whispers were indistinguishable, but their amusement wasn't. In that moment, I wanted nothing more than to join them, to have something to laugh about that hard. Instead, I stared at the chocolate nuggets, wondering how long I could avoid Jaden.

When I let my eyes lift, peeking over the top of the aisle to see the fridges, I didn't spot Jaden.

I saw Hudson.

At first, I didn't realize it was him. Instead of his usual dark attire, he wore a sweatshirt that was a happy yellow, the hood up over his head and covering most of his hair, which looked tangled and unbrushed after a night of sleep. He didn't have his glasses on, but he was still Bridge Boy.

Hudson and Derrick dropped me off a few streets from my house yesterday around six, and I came home to Dad packing up his cooler for the game. Derrick and I had talked about the movie the whole drive back to Brentwood, discussing the scenes we liked and the scenes we thought were campy, while Hudson listened in. We parted on good terms, and I told him I'd see him Monday.

So it was majorly bizarre to see him now.

He had his head ducked as he studied something on the shelf, but when I rose up onto my tiptoes, I could see a wide grin spread across his features. As big as I'd ever seen him smile. He was a part of the laughing group, which consisted of four people. His head was bent, wheat hair falling across his eyes, and he used a ringless hand to shove it back.

The sudden sight of him caused my chest to tighten.

Before he had a chance to look, I dipped down, coming face-to-face with a Hershey's bar. The feeling I got from seeing him outside of school wasn't the same as the one I'd felt when Jaden walked into the salon. No, the air felt *much* thinner, harder to breathe.

I could pick his laugh out easily amongst the group now that I knew it was Hudson, and that was even stranger. Hearing Hudson *laugh*. It was lighter than I thought it'd be, a genuine happiness leaking from the soft sound. Much like I hadn't believed he'd been able to smile, I really wouldn't have believed that he'd been able to *laugh*. But here I was, listening to it as plain as day.

Snatching up a bag of chocolate nuggets, I hurried toward the cash register, already fixing in my mind that I'd text Jaden that I had to go back to the salon. He could come and get his skateboard and do whatever he wanted.

I set the nuggets on the counter, meeting the gaze of the middle-aged woman behind it, already pulling out what few dollars I had left in my wallet.

A yellow-clad arm brushed against my side as someone placed a soda on the counter, depositing a granola bar alongside it. I stiffened from the contact, knowing exactly who I'd find when I turned.

And sure enough, I came face to face with Hudson.

And by face to face, I meant *face to face*. His nose was probably six inches from mine, the vibrancy of his eyes swallowing me. His yellow hood was still up, and it made his hair paler. He was close enough that I could practically *feel* where his chest was behind me, though we weren't touching.

His gaze skidded past me, and he tipped his head toward the counter. "Last chance if you want me to buy it, dude."

In a second, three bags of barbeque chips piled up next to the candy, and I turned to find one of the laughing friends being the culprit. Derrick was instantly recognizable from his shaved head and bare biceps, and when he looked at me, realization flared in his gaze. "Milady! Twice in twenty-four hours? We've been blessed."

"Hey." I blinked at him, still a little dazed from the sight.

"Simon and Tee are still looking," Derrick said, batting his eyes. "But you could buy *my* chips if you wanted."

Hudson rolled his eyes, casting his gaze to the woman behind her counter. Upon seeing him, though, her once-friendly expression hardened into something more distrustful, as if Hudson's reputation extended even beyond the confines of Brentwood High. He blinked as if he didn't notice. "How much?"

"You don't have to—" I began to interject, but Hudson leaned his hand against the countertop beside my hip, pressing closer than before.

"I usually buy for my *friends*," he murmured in a low voice I was sure no one else could hear, lingering on the word long enough for it to mean something else.

Whatever the emotion was, it swelled in my chest as the lady began scanning the items. "What," I began, raising an eyebrow, "you only wear happy colors on the weekends?"

"Dark colors aren't happy colors?"

I shook my head.

"I'll let you in on a secret." He ducked down to my

level, coming in close to whisper. Four inches between our noses now. "I only wear happy colors when I don't think others will see."

"People can't know the Grim Reaper's happy?"

"Ruins the image."

My mind snapped to us on the bridge, me sitting on the stone and him leaning against the edge. "Have you ever thought about changing the image?"

Something warm stirred in his expression, and he looked on the verge of smiling again.

The world suddenly blurred as I was jerked back away from Hudson. My shoes caught on the sticky tile, and I would've fallen if Jaden hadn't hauled me up against his side, tucking me there without a second's notice. It jarred my shoulder painfully. "I'm sorry," Jaden said, and with his arm around my waist, his intentions were clear. "She didn't mean to cut in line. You guys can go first."

I angled my head to peer up at Jaden, who might've been able to pass for calm if his eyes weren't wide with fear. Which made sense. To Jaden, this wasn't just Hudson Bishop—this was the Grim Reaper with one of his four horsemen. Even if he *was* wearing a happy color.

Hudson regarded the shorter boy without a trace of expression on his face. It was funny how it'd transformed from when he spoke with me, like this was a different person entirely. "She didn't cut," he replied calmly, tilting his head. "If anything, *I* cut in front of her."

"That's okay," Jaden insisted, waving his free hand

wildly as if it would deescalate the conversation. "She was going to wait for me anyway."

"Was she?" Hudson glanced at Derrick, who looked as if he wanted to open his bag of chips to munch on as he watched. After a second, Hudson raised his eyebrows at me. "Were you?"

The challenge in Hudson's voice was clear—so clear that I didn't need to see the mocking eyebrows or the glint to his blue eyes. I could've been blindfolded and known what he was implying. He was waiting to see if I'd allow myself to be tucked away like that. For my choices and intentions to be decided for me. Was I really going to wait for Jaden? No. Hudson knew that.

As nervous as Morgan was about Hudson, I could trust her not to spill the beans. I couldn't trust Jaden, who was practically a snitch for my parents. I couldn't introduce the two boys to each other as nonchalantly as I'd introduced my other friend. It wouldn't end well. My own house of cards I'd begun to build trembled in this wind, but I wasn't ready for it to collapse yet.

So, I simply nodded.

Hudson picked the chocolate nuggets off the counter and offered them out to me. His eyebrows hadn't lowered, but his smile had. "My mistake, Sophomore," he replied as I took the candy back.

Jaden seemed to dig his fingers in firmer at the word, not picking up on anything except the way Hudson said it. I could see past the tone of his voice though, because the intention of it stung more. *Grow a backbone, Sophomore.*

I held my breath, waiting for him to back away, but he didn't. Instead, he swiped his stuff to the side of the counter and turned to us. He reached out and laid a hand heavily on Jaden's shoulder, causing the boy beside me to stiffen like a board. A slow smirk crawled across Hudson's lips, his signature mocking smile. "You can go on ahead of me. Jaden, right?"

Jaden looked like his life flashed before his eyes at the sound of the Grim Reaper saying his name. I didn't understand why Hudson was purposefully making a game out of getting Jaden to squirm. I didn't understand why he was putting on such a show, putting on his Grim Reaper mask.

"Someone check out," the cashier interjected, finally seeing an opening. She glanced around our little circle with annoyance. "Or am I going to have to listen to your high school drama some more?"

Derrick snorted, not even trying to cover up the sound. Hudson threw a few bills onto the counter, nodding his chin at us. "Add what they have to my tab." To Derrick, he said, "I'll see what's taking Tee so long." And then finally, he regarded Jaden and me one last time, and the amusement in his expression was gone now. There was only his mocking malice. "See you two around."

Jaden didn't linger to say anything else. With his fingers digging into my waist, he tugged me toward the door. I took one last glance at Hudson, who didn't turn around as he went to the aisle his friends were in. Derrick turned to look at me, but wisely didn't react. Instead, our gazes held until the door shut between us.

Jaden let out a sharp breath of relief once we were out into the air, like we'd both narrowly avoided our early demise. He clutched his soda with white knuckles. "Oh my gosh, are you okay? Did he say anything to you before I came up?"

I pulled away from him, drawing in a deep breath. "No."

"Gemma, he knows my name! How does he know my name?" He sounded on the brink of hyperventilating. "Oh my gosh, am I on his radar now?"

Of course, that was what Jaden first thought of, being on Hudson's radar. I rubbed my waist, hating that I could still feel the pressure of his fingers.

"*Gemma.*" Jaden tried to catch my eye where it was trained on the gas station door. "This is the Grim Reaper we're talking about—he knows about us now. He—"

"He's a person," I cut Jaden off without even thinking twice, voice rising for possibly the first time ever with him. The shock of it reflected on his face. "He's a person who wears dark colors and has a scary nickname, Jaden. That's all. We're not 'on his radar'—he was talking to us because he wanted to. You should get to know someone more before you decide you know everything about them."

The words had come like a rubber band snapping, full-force and hard-hitting and then losing all momentum. My chest ached like I'd finished a sprint, and I let out a harsh breath.

Jaden blinked in astonishment, probably not knowing such a harsh tone could come from Gemma Settler. "But he attacked your brother."

Now it was my turn to jolt with surprise. There were times when that fact would weave in and out of my mind, but I couldn't even picture Hudson lifting a hand against my brother. Sure, he could be snarky and harsh sometimes, but how could a boy who closed his eyes in scary movies beat my brother and his friends up? How could the thick glasses-wearing boy from the bridge do anything like that? It was so contradictory that my brain couldn't even conjure the image.

I glanced toward the gas station doors before walking away, leaving Jaden kicking up gravel to catch up. "I guess the Most Likely Tos made me touchy," I said softly, because even though my thoughts were still stuffed with confusion, I needed to clear the air. The last thing I needed was Jaden saying something to Mom. "I just don't like the idea of judging someone I don't know."

"How about this?" Jaden leaned closer, brushing my arm with his. "I promise to not be so judgey. I think you're right—I think we can all can give someone the benefit of the doubt."

I tilted my head up to look at him, taking in the way his deep brown gaze settled on me. I searched for any sign of suspicion, but there was none. Like always with him, his expression was nothing but open. "Sounds like a plan," I told him, and we both walked away from the gas station with our items bought by the Grim Reaper, not looking back.

CHAPTER 13

Mom took Jaden and me out for lunch after her hair appointment, which meant we didn't get home until five-ish. When we did, we found Landon and Dad on the couch. Landon had his eyes shut with his head tipped back onto the couch cushion, while Dad had a hot rod magazine in his hands, reading glasses on his nose. Upon our shuffle into the living room, only Dad startled. "You've been gone a while."

"That's the first thing you say?" Mom demanded, fluffing her hair to show it off. Kim had styled the freshly touched up red with a few curls, and they'd relaxed into small waves on the drive home. "What do you think of my hair?"

Dad lowered his glasses, squinting. "Did you cut it?"

In Dad's defense, the change wasn't all that noticeable. Still, her shoulders slumped. "Men." With a sigh, Mom ventured into the living room and peered at Landon's sleeping figure, lowering her voice. "Napping?"

Dad nodded. "That game last night must've worn him out."

"When did he get home?" He rode separately from us last night. Instead of riding in the backseat of Dad's SUV, filling the entire cab with his post-football stench, he rode back to Brentwood with the rest of the team on the bus to get his car from the school. I'd gone to bed before he got home.

"He went out this morning, too," Mom told me, moving toward the kitchen. "A busy little bee, that boy. I'll make us some sandwiches, and then we can wake him. I'd hate for him to throw his whole sleep schedule off."

"Where did he go this morning?" I asked, but she'd already moved away.

Dad was the one who shrugged. "He didn't say, but he came home a little bit ago."

I eyed his sleeping figure, the steady rise and fall of his chest. They didn't know what time he got home last night, and he went somewhere this morning. Those two things alone screamed of the freedom he had, so much more freedom than I had. I wasn't even sure *why*. Because he was older? Because he was a boy? Because he was the star of the family?

I shifted where I stood in the hallway, rubbing my fingers across the tight band of my skirt. "I'm going to change into lounge clothes," I told Dad, who gave me a thumbs up and flipped a page in his hot rod magazine.

When I passed by Landon's open bedroom door, I wavered for only a brief second to peer inside—but then stopped dead when I spotted his phone on his desk. It was a beacon of shiny blackness. Normally, I wouldn't have given his phone a second glance. Sure, he got one that had actual internet access whereas mine didn't even have the ability to load songs, but it wasn't like I ever wanted to play any of his apps or surf the web.

Until I remembered what Mom had said.

There's a post on something called Babble? I'm not sure, but it talked about Landon having a girlfriend.

I gave into the beckoning pull of the small black rectangle, curiosity compelling me forward.

Landon didn't have a passcode, so it was easy to crack into the device. I only let myself marvel at the touch-screen momentarily before opening the web browser.

It was no secret that whoever designed the Brent-wood Babble website deserved a reward. It was a much better layout than whoever had done the Most Likely To list, because when Morgan had showed me the labels, my eyes cringed. Babble, though, was sleek and efficient, and I found the blog post I was looking for within seconds.

UPDATE ON DATE NIGHT!

Last night, I posted about how a fancy group of Top Tier all-stars graced their presence at Allen's Alley, but I've got some updates for you. Let's start off with a certain Landon Settler and his new girl! That's right, I've got the confirmation first for you—the quarterback has said so himself that he's officially off the market. Which also

means he's the first to remedy his Most Likely To casting! Most Likely To: Never Get A Girlfriend? Nice try, MLT's!

Hopefully we get some pics of them together soon—Lacey and Landon = Lacedon! <3

The blog post went on further about the others who'd gone bowling Thursday night, but I stopped reading. *Lacey*. So *not* Madison. I couldn't believe that Landon got a girlfriend and didn't tell me. When had they started dating? In fact, where did he meet her anyway? Why hadn't he told any of us? Was that who he was out with last night? What about Madison? *Lacey*.

Bigger question: why did the name sound familiar?

I closed the browser and set his phone down, but I didn't retreat from his bedroom right away. A piece of paper caught my eye, mostly obscured underneath other sheets, but there was enough graphite smudged at the corner that I found myself curious. Normally, I never snooped on Landon's drawings. Normally, he kept them hidden well. Unable to stop myself, I nudged the papers aside, taking a peek.

It wasn't finished, but the drawing was obviously of a girl. She had her hair braided into two pigtails, ones that only just barely hung past her shoulders. She was smiling widely, so wide that her eyes were squinched shut, and the closer I looked, I realized there was a stud in her nose.

She looked familiar, but there was no written indication of who this girl was. Was this his girlfriend?

A part of me wanted to go into the living room, wake him up, and haul him here for answers. At the very least, I thought about ambushing him the moment he woke up. But the longer I stood in his room, the more I knew I couldn't. I *wouldn't*. For whatever reason, Landon was keeping this Lacey—whoever she was—a secret. In the same way I kept Hudson one. And despite how things went down at the gas station today, I had at least the rest of the month to keep my secret.

Besides, what if this was Landon's reprieve, his way to get out from underneath our parents' thumb? I wasn't going to take it from him, much like I wouldn't want him taking mine.

So, despite my burning curiosity, I walked out of his bedroom, resigning myself to wait until he brought it up first.

I had a pit in my stomach the entire day Monday, and it started with the fact that when Mrs. Savion pulled into Vista Villas, Hudson wasn't at the bus stop. She waited for a moment, but he didn't magically appear, rushing to climb on. When she shut the doors and put the bus back into drive, flicking off the loading sign, I had a bad feeling. However, this time, I had kept my butt in the seat.

Was he sick? Was Paisley sick? Was he skipping? Did

this absence count against his "walking on thin ice" threat?

"Lacey," Morgan murmured, tapping her fingers against her chin. "Do you know a Lacey?"

"I don't think so," I replied, taking a bite of one of my apple slices. We'd gotten to the lunch table before Rosie and Hector today, though Jaden sat on my other side, munching noisily on his carrot sticks. "I mean, there are, like, ten at Brentwood, but I don't *know* any."

Jaden lifted his head. "Lacey. Sounds a little familiar, but I don't know why."

Weirdly enough, the name sounded familiar to me, too. As much as I wracked my brain about it, I couldn't remember *any* girl hanging around Landon enough, let alone a girl named Lacey.

"Too bad we don't have a yearbook or something." Morgan narrowed her eyes at me. "You didn't ask him about it?"

"He's been tight-lipped about it for some reason. It's weird."

Morgan peered around the cafeteria, as if she could pluck the mystery girl from one of the tables. "I'm guessing she's either a senior or a junior, then. Do you think she goes to this school?"

If Lacey went to a different school—like Jefferson—I was sure Babble would've mentioned that. *That* would've been juicy, the quarterback dating someone from the rival school. Or, at least, I thought it sounded juicy. And then again, if she went to a different school, would the article have mentioned her name? *Lacey.* Like the readers were supposed to know it.

Stop, Gemma, I told myself, biting down on another apple slice. *You promised yourself not to be curious.*

Jaden leaned across the table, changing the topic. "Morgan, did Gemma tell you what happened on Saturday?"

"No." She drew the word out suspiciously, glancing between us. "What didn't she tell me?"

At first, I had no idea what Jaden could've meant. And then— "It was nothing," I insisted, turning to stare Jaden down with *drop-it* eyes. "Jaden and I went to the gas station together."

"And ran into Hudson Bishop," he interjected, voice hissing out the name as if it were a curse word. "Like, he was *all* up in Gemma's space. Oh my gosh, I thought she was a goner. Gemma, your life probably flashed before your eyes."

So much for not judging anymore, I grumbled in my head.

Morgan looked from him to me again, though this time, her expression was more wary than suspicious. I gave *her* the meaningful look this time, begging with my eyes. *Don't mention the buddy program,* I thought at her, desperate. *Please don't mention it.*

She looked down at her lunch tray, stabbing her broccoli salad. "In her space, huh? How so?"

"He was like—" Jaden stopped to display with his hands, bringing his palms nearly touching. "—this close to her face."

"He was not!" I insisted, smacking him on the arm. "You're exaggerating. And it wasn't that big of a deal. So, let's just...drop it."

Talking about Hudson had me thinking about him, and thinking about him had me worrying. It was something that'd been nagging at me all day. No, not specifically that—his *absence* had been nagging at me, and the possible repercussions of it. If there even were any. No matter how hard I tried, though, I couldn't shake the anxiety each time my thoughts wandered to what would happen after school.

A sudden inspiration hit me then, one that my brain instantly shied away from. I couldn't. I *couldn't*. And yet...

"I thought of something," I told Jaden and Morgan, grinning. "If Landon's girlfriend goes to school here, she's probably sitting with him at lunch."

Morgan's eyes widened. "You're a genius."

Hector dropped his lunch tray onto the table and sat down on the other side of Morgan, glancing around. "Why is she a genius?"

Because I'm going to kill two birds with one stone.

The distance between the cafeterias wasn't very far, since the kitchen was between them. Cafeteria A was more crowded than Cafeteria B, so it took me a few moments to spot Landon. The Top Tier table was at the center of the room, a straight shot from the doorway. Landon sat with his face toward me, though his eyes were downcast at his lunch tray. Narrowing my gaze, I scouted the spots next to him.

Madison sat on his left, with her hair pulled into a ponytail so high that my hairline ached in solidarity. The seat on the other side of him was empty, like he was waiting for someone to fill it.

Dang—so no Lacey.

At that moment, Landon's eyes lifted and found mine where I loitered in the doorway, recognition causing his eyes to light up. My heart leapt as I tipped my head toward the hallway, hoping the meaning was obvious. *Time for phase two.*

In about the time it would've taken for him to cross the room, Landon came out into the hallway. "What are you doing down here?" he asked.

I didn't realize how sweaty my palms would get from the impromptu plan. "I just...uh—I came to tell you...something."

He raised his eyebrows as if to say *let's hear it.*

I knew it was a bad idea. It was why my first reaction was to dismiss the idea entirely, to pretend I'd never thought of it in the first place. But even as I did that, the devil on my shoulder brought it to the forefront of my brain, and that devil seemed to have inhumanly bright blue eyes. "I'm going to go get ice cream with Morgan after school."

"I thought you met with your buddy after school."

"They were sick today." I narrowly avoided using the wrong pronoun. "I'll have her mom drop me off at home, so you don't have to worry about me."

He shifted on his feet. "Did you clear it with Mom or Dad?"

"Do I have to clear everything with them?"

That was the wrong thing to say, and I instantly knew it. It was too defensive, too abrasive. I wasn't even sure where the words came from anyway, just that when they absorbed into the air, I knew it was a mistake. Especially when Landon's auburn eyebrows pulled together. His confusion spun my thoughts into high gear, stumbling to figure out how to right the wrong.

"Remember how you said you wouldn't go all rebellious?" Landon asked, folding his arms across his chest in the signature big brother way.

"I'm not allowed to get rebellious because of the list," I began, holding his stare, "but you're allowed to go get a girlfriend because of it?"

The words were exactly what I'd been hoping for—they effortlessly defused the ticking bomb. Landon's cheeks flushed pink the way mine would've if the tables had been turned, but he glanced at the cafeteria doors. "Let's talk about this later."

"Later," I agreed, taking a step backward. "Like I said, I'll have Morgan's mom drop me off."

"Be home before Dad or Mom gets home," he warned, and then his gaze softened as he flicked his head toward the empty hallway. "Go finish your lunch. Have a good rest of your day."

I wasn't sure if I'd have a good rest of my day, but I knew one thing for sure—I'd spend the next three hours plotting out something I never should've considered in the first place. It was too late, though. I'd made up my mind, and I wouldn't let myself change it.

CHAPTER 14

The buses rumbled and pumped out exhaust fumes as student after student loaded into them, and I stared at bus 32 from where I stood behind a pillar. The doors were open, and the seats were filling up fast. The timing on all this had to be perfect. All of the scenarios I'd run in my head had all come down to one fatal flaw: Jaden rode this bus home, and he'd see me.

As soon as I thought his name, he got to the open doors of the bus with a few other upperclassmen, chatting as they climbed aboard. Through the dusty windows, I could see him make his way down the aisle, passing our seat up front. Which was good—if he sat up front, there'd be no possibility of avoiding him. He picked a seat three rows from the back, on the opposite side of the aisle that I couldn't see.

I held the column tighter, nails scraping into the concrete. Could I do this?

I brought my braid around over my shoulder to remove the tie, shaking out my hair as quickly as possible. The locks had a soft wave to them, scalp sighing in relief at the loosened grip. I'd worry about tying it later—now, I needed it as my disguise.

Mrs. Savion reached across to buckle her seatbelt, and I could hear the other buses begin to pull out in succession. Last chance.

Grow a backbone, Sophomore.

A girl in my grade hurried up to bus 32, and without thinking, I ran up behind her, ducking my head. I tried as best as I could to mirror her movements, to fully use her as a shield in case Jaden was watching us climb on. She had to feel me breathing down her neck, but as soon as I got to my seat—which was empty, since everyone always wanted to sit in the back—I dropped into it. I waited several seconds, prepared for his face to appear over the back of the seat, but Jaden never came. He didn't see me.

And that wasn't even the hard part.

"Gemma," Mrs. Savion said with surprise, looking at me in the rearview mirror. "You're riding today?"

"Going to a friend's house," I replied, leaning close so I could keep my voice down. "It's a place you normally stop at, so you don't have to add anything to your route."

Mrs. Savion pursed her lips to the side. "I can't let you get off early without parental consent."

I presented a piece of notebook paper, and my heart leapt into my throat as she unfolded it. A necessary evil. A necessary lie. Because the signature at the bottom saying I was allowed to get off at a different stop wasn't my mother's. It was my forgery.

Mrs. Savion probably only looked at it for a few

seconds, but it felt like forever before she handed the note back. "Okay, dear. You can hop off when we get there."

Another step, checked. Again, not even the hard part.

I closed my eyes for the whole ride, my knees bumping with the rough road and with nerves. What I'd been thinking about all day was about to come to fruition, and my thoughts were in a civil war about what to do. One side begged to take the risk while the other demanded to play it safe.

But then again, being on the bus in the first place—wasn't that a declaration in and of itself?

With my eyes still closed, I pictured Hudson with his glasses and his cotton candy-colored sweatshirt, blue eyes that seemed so much gentler than other times. And like all of the other times I went down memory lane, I traced the thought back to when his arm snaked around my waist, holding me still in a moment of unsteadiness. From that moment on, I felt tied to him, like there was no escaping the mystery that was Hudson Bishop.

I held my breath as Mrs. Savion turned onto Vista Villas' road, squeezing my backpack strap so tightly in my hand that my fingers almost felt numb.

Mrs. Savion stopped the bus, flipping on the red flashing lights. My breath came in rapid gasps. The sound of feet thudding in the bus startled me, and so did the kids that walked past. There were more students getting off in this neighborhood than those who rode in the morning—in the morning, it was only Hudson who climbed on, but now, four students were hopping off.

I got to my feet. *Five.*

I tried to blend in with the group getting off, hoping my loose, long hair took away any ease of identifying me.

Hoping in vain, apparently. I heard Jaden's voice call from the back of the bus. "Gemma?"

Without reacting, I leapt off the platform, sneakers landing in the dusty roadway, heart racing. With a parting smile, Mrs. Savion closed the doors behind me, sealing Jaden inside and me outside. Even though the bus started rolling forward, I kept my back to it, my head ducked as if that would help me disappear.

Just when I let out a sigh of relief, Jaden's voice came again.

"Gemma! Gemma, what are you doing?"

I slowly pivoted to find Jaden's head hanging out an open window, the incredulity on his face crystal clear. Scrunched eyebrows, dropped jaw, disbelief on every inch. I didn't have to answer, though. The bus rumbled away, and Jaden was yanked inside, leaving me staring at the dirt-covered back end as Mrs. Savion drove away.

My phone began buzzing in my backpack, but I already knew who it was. I couldn't fully ignore it, though. I declined Jaden's call and sent him a text instead.

GEMMA

> I'm going to a friend's. Don't worry. See u tomorrow.

And then I shoved my phone in my backpack pocket.

I turned toward the collection of narrow homes lining the road, letting out a little breath. The sun was out and bright, but it wasn't as hot today as it had been. The breeze was cold enough that I tugged my sleeves down over my fingers, as if the wind itself was saying, *you should've stayed on the bus.*

Wait. This stop where Hudson climbed on the bus every morning—it wasn't like it was in front of his house. It was the Vista Villas bus stop. It was at the corner of two of the dead-end streets, which meant his house could've been down any of them. Any one of these houses could've been his.

Which meant I had no idea where he lived.

I *really* should've stayed on the bus.

Out of everything I'd planned for, this hadn't been one of them. I walked over to the cable box Hudson always leaned against, listening to the electrical hum trapped inside the metal container. I totally screwed up. Totally, totally screwed up, and now I was probably an hour's walk away from home.

Right when I was ready to give up and start the long trek home, another bus rumbled down the sharp bend of the road, a plume of dust puffing behind it. Probably going faster than it should've. I edged away from the road, but it slowed as it approached, and that was when I could read the side. *Brentwood Elementary.*

A few little kids hopped off the bus, crossing the road to my side, and I recognized one of them. Her blonde hair was loose around her face, her rainbow backpack straps caught in the crooks of her elbows. She walked with her head down, and all of the other children hurried on ahead of her.

"Paisley?" I called, and her footsteps faltered. She whirled to look at me, and her zoned-out gaze became wickedly sharp for a seven-year-old. "Your name is Paisley, right?"

She moved with the grace of a third grader, jostling her backpack in front of her and reaching into the pocket. A second later, she had something pointed at me. Something that glinted in the sunlight. "Leave me alone."

I stood there, gaping like a fish, for the longest second. The glinting object was a knife. An actual knife.

I lifted my hands like she pointed a gun at me. "I'm—I'm here to see your brother. You remember me, don't you? I got off the bus last Monday? I'm Hudson's...friend."

Her blade was almost a copy of the one Hudson had given me last week, but a bit smaller. She wielded the army knife's handle tightly, but her hand was small enough that I could see the purple metal of the base. I wasn't sure why it made me smile, the fact that Hudson and his little sister had matching pocketknives, but it did.

"Hudson doesn't have any girl friends," she threw back.

I tossed my loose hair over my shoulder, the strands tickling my neck. "Is your brother home? He was home sick from school today, so I wanted to check on him."

"He wasn't sick." Paisley lowered the knife, as if after a moment of giving me the stink-eye, she determined I wasn't that big of a threat. "He didn't get up this morning."

"Why not?"

"He didn't go to sleep until, like, super late. Daddy said he needed a rest day."

I felt my forehead crease as I frowned. Why would he have been awake that late on a school night?

Paisley reached up and pushed her hair from her eyes, but still clutched the knife. "I'll take you to him, if you want. But don't try anything funny."

The only funny thing here was how intimidated I was by a third grader. I followed along behind her shuffling steps, keeping my hands where she could see them. "I like your rainbow backpack."

"I like your old lady skirt."

I glanced down at the beige midi skirt I had on today, wondering if that was an intentional dig. The gapped smirk she had when she looked over her shoulder told me it probably was. "I need new clothes," I told her with a small frown. Even though I'd asked Mom for permission to wear what I chose, my options were still limited to a wardrobe she'd collected. It was still limited to my long skirts. I hadn't had a chance to get anything new yet. "My mom buys all my clothes for me. Can you tell?"

"Yeah." She gave my skirt a look of disgust that was kind of cute with her gapped teeth. "You should find someone to take you shopping. Someone who's not your mom."

"I agree."

"You're my brother's mentor, right?" Paisley slowed up her pace to let me walk beside her, and she craned her neck. "I remember you said that word."

"That's me. Our principal has Hudson and me together for a few projects at school."

She pursed her lips in a way that looked comical on her. "Is it because Hudson's a bad kid?"

"He's not a bad kid," I said at once. "It's just so we can be friends."

She squinted up at me, and I was struck by how much she resembled her brother in that moment. They both had the same intensity about them, even down to the way their eyes glittered. "Do you like him?"

"Yeah, he's—well, he's pretty cool—"

"Do you *like*, like him?"

"No!" The answer came out as a sharp shriek, and it echoed down the road. "I mean—I mean, I like him as a person, but I don't—I don't *like, like*—"

"Uh-huh," she murmured, giving me the gapped grin. Despite feeling thoroughly embarrassed, it felt like I passed a test.

Paisley stopped at a bright yellow house along the side of the road, shrugging off her backpack and letting it drag on the cobblestone walkway that led to the narrow porch. The house was small, longer than it was wide. She led me up the steps, holding the screen door out for me. "Wait here," she ordered, kicking off her little sneakers as we stepped inside. "Hudson! I'm home!"

"Already? Your bus isn't supposed to get here for ten more minutes! Did you at least walk with the other kids, Pais?"

As she bounded off toward a hallway, she left me taking in the mobile home behind her. I had a straight shot view of the couch against the far wall, and there was a pillow on one of the seats that looked like it belonged on a bed. Almost like someone had taken a nap there. There was a small table in the middle of the room with a few chairs around it, and a bouquet of flowers on the top of it. From the small snapshot view, it looked homey.

I could hear Hudson's voice from the hallway Paisley disappeared down. "Why do you have this out? Wait, did you take this to school?"

"You said it was for protection."

"Not at *school*, Paisley! Good God, have you been taking this with you every day? No, I'm not giving it back—privileges revoked. You're really trying to get me in trouble with Dad, aren't you?" His voice got closer. "I swear to God, if you'd been caught with it, I'd never have heard the end—"

Hudson appeared at the mouth of the hallway, stopping dead in his tracks as we locked eyes. Behind his black-framed glasses, he blinked once, twice, almost like he expected me to disappear. For a blissful moment, he only seemed surprised, stunned.

And then when he took a step closer, that emotion morphed into something else, something perfectly clear: anger. "What are you doing here?"

He was barefoot, and the gray sweatpants he had on looked well worn and well loved. His black tank was snug enough to hug his sides, showcasing his lean frame but highlighting the muscles in his arms. He wasn't as muscular as Landon or the other football players, but he was definitely fit.

Not that I was noticing.

"Gemma." Hudson's voice snapped my attention back to the moment, back to his livid face. Each word was an enunciated curse. "What are you doing here?"

"You weren't at school today," I said lamely. In all the scenarios in my head, Hudson's irritation hadn't been in any of them. "I thought I'd check on you."

Paisley ducked out from behind Hudson and eyed the two of us, clearly picking up on the tension. "I'm going to ride my bike," she told him. "See you later, Gemma." She added the last bit with a small wave.

I had my arms tucked close to my body and couldn't bring myself to wave back, but I did give her an uncertain smile. She let the screen door slam shut behind her, the cracking sound pinching my nerves.

"This isn't okay," Hudson said in a voice that didn't sound like him. Even though he wore his glasses, he was the Grim Reaper version, all low and sharp and harsh. It sent a chill through me, and if my feet weren't firmly planted, I might've backed up a step. "There's a thing called privacy, Gemma, and you're really butting into mine."

"I thought we were friends. Don't friends check on each other?"

"Oh, we're *friends* now," he retorted, and though my words had been awkward and nervous, his reply came out strong. "Only when no one can see, right? Because heaven forbid your good girl image get ruined by Brentwood's bad boy."

I frowned up at him. "What are you talking about?"

"I'm talking about Saturday. Afraid your boyfriend'll think you're being swayed by the Grim Reaper?"

A moment ago, I'd wanted to retreat out onto the porch to give myself space from his severity. Now, even though the space was narrow, I stepped closer, squaring my jaw. "It hurt your feelings, didn't it? Me not acknowledging you. Acknowledging our friendship. That's why you're being like this."

Hudson leaned down to bring his eyes level with mine, and they were darker than normal, pinning me in place. One corner of his mouth tugged up, the smile as bitter as could be. "What feelings?"

"You were the one to ruin the conversation first. You were the one who got all mocking and mean with him. Was that you not *fighting your role*?" Despite the way he rolled his eyes, I knew that was it. Him leaning into the image that was tied to him. There hadn't even been any hesitation. "You could fight a little. You could care a little."

"Why? I should care because you want me to?" He took a step toward me, the floorboards creaking beneath his weight. His eyes were a flame of blue. "Is that what this is? You're trying to *change* me? You're trying to take a rock and wash all the dirt off? Guess what, Gemma—I *like* the dirt."

I began shaking my head even as he spoke. "You don't."

He stopped within a few feet from me, leaning forward as though we were sharing a secret. "Wanna bet?"

"You don't scare me," I told him, because I knew that was the reaction he was looking for.

Hudson took a step closer, entering dangerous territory with a foot of space between us. "No?" The word was a soft lilt, almost teasing. Another step forward, and six inches disappeared. "What about now?"

If I was bolder, I would've demanded to know how his nearness could be so scary. Except I was a coward, and six inches was *way* too close. "No." Voice still steady. Good.

Hudson didn't stop there, though. Instead of taking another step, he leaned his forearm onto the wall above my head. His other arm reached out so that his palm pressed against the wall, boxing me into the cage that was the Grim Reaper. The warm citrus scent of him was strong, enough for my head to swim with it. When he spoke, the words were practically a whisper. "What about now?"

I tilted my head to look up at him, brought nearly nose to nose with Grim Reaper, who didn't even flinch. His eyes were so electric blue that I could never stop being startled by them, rendering me speechless each time. His rosy lips were twisted up into a half smirk, one filled with condescension to the brim. I swallowed the uneasiness that came with being in his sights, forcing myself not to waver. If I did, it was game over. "No."

"You're lying."

"I'm not." My heart was thumping fast, and my body was hot, like I was standing under the glare of the sun instead. My veins hummed with the moment, almost energized. "You're forgetting that I've seen who you are. I heard you laughing with your friends. I saw you smile. *That's* who you are, not some bully. You're trying to convince me otherwise, but it's not going to work. You're not going to scare me off."

The electricity in his gaze faltered, but even though it dulled, I knew it could still sting. His words whispered against my neck as he repeated them, causing my skin to shiver. "Wanna bet?"

My lips curved into a small smile on their own accord, because this was what he did. Hudson pushed and pushed and pushed, but then he'd give openings like this—a chance for me to cling onto. "Sure, I'll bet you on it."

Hudson shook his head a little, and even with his glasses on, he was the perfect appearance of antagonistic. There was no warmth to draw from. "You're delusional."

The thrill began to recede as I felt my cheeks warm, and this time—for the first time—it *did* feel like embarrassment. There was no thrill present now, not with the way he looked at me. Like I was a solicitor knocking on his door. Unwanted. Annoying.

I drew in a breath as I regarded him, squaring my shoulders. "I didn't act like that on Saturday because of my *good girl image*. But I did do it for myself. If Jaden knew that we were friends, he would've told my parents. If my parents knew, that'd be it. It'd be over. After sixteen years of never stepping out of place, of keeping my head down and my mouth shut, scrounging as much freedom as I could, I'd lose it all. I'd go right back to doing everything everyone tells me to." I scoffed out a laugh, the sound bubbling up even though this situation wasn't even remotely funny. "Come on, Hudson. I've never even said a swear word."

Hudson's gaze turned transparent for a fraction of a moment, expression turning into something uncertain.

"I thought you could relate to that, I guess. I thought we were both in the same boat. So, yeah. I pretended like I didn't know you. But despite being *delusional*," I repeated the word with the same amount of severity he'd used, "I am sorry it hurt your feelings."

The mocking expression slid off of Hudson's lips, leaving a frown line between his eyebrows. He dropped his hands from the wall but didn't take a step back. Still, though, I knew it was my cue to leave. If I knew anything about Hudson, it was that he'd never reply when something was as serious as this.

Without another word, I pushed open the screen door, walking outside. I hurried the rest of the way down the steps and shouldered my backpack higher up, stalking out from underneath the carport and toward the main road. I refused to look around to see if he watched me go.

I got to the main road in time to see the handlebars of Paisley's bike jerk sharply as she tried to turn around, and the tires slid crookedly on the gravel, giving way and depositing her onto the street.

"Paisley!" I called to her, running the short distance to the crash. "Are you okay?"

"I'm fine," she huffed, dusting her palms together. "I turned too fast."

The knees of her leggings were scratched but not totally torn, and otherwise, she looked okay. "Here, let's get you up." I offered my one hand while I grabbed the handlebars of her bike with the other, righting both of them. Paisley dusted off her legs. "You really should be wearing a helmet, you know."

She narrowed her eyes at me. "You sound like Hudson."

If I hadn't just come from her stone-faced, scolding brother, I might've laughed.

"Don't let him get to you," she went on. "He's always grumpy. He doesn't like it when people get too much in his business."

Yeah, no kidding. "That's okay. I shouldn't have stopped over without permission."

"Hudson doesn't have a lot of friends. I hope...I hope he didn't scare you off."

"I don't scare easy," I told her, trying to give her a reassuring smile. It felt like the kind that I usually gave Mom's friends—practiced but phony. "I'll see you later."

"Hopefully next time I see you, you don't have an old lady skirt."

This time, I did laugh, and gave her a small wave before I started the long walk to the main road.

I walked along the side of the road, not quite into the shoulder—shards of glass shimmered in the dirt and gravel along the edge. The list of people I could call were few, and really, it only narrowed down to Morgan. She was the one least likely to kill me for being here. Landon would kill me for lying, and Mom would have a whole list of reasons to choose from. Leaving school property when she strictly told me not to, getting off the bus early, forging her signature on a note. Whatever way I cut it, I was dead meat. The other option was to walk the whole way home, an option that was risky because I'd have to walk along the main road. Any one of my parents' friends could see me. My *parents* could see me on their way home from work.

I curled my hand into a fist, wanting to kick myself for being so absolutely stupid. I should never have gotten myself into this situation. Of course Hudson and I weren't friends. He'd made it very clear before—he didn't need me, and that thought settled heavily on my stomach. Why had I been so worried about him missing school? Why had my interest piqued at what he'd been doing the night before?

Maybe more importantly, why did I care what he thought about me? Why did the fact that he was upset with me make me feel sick?

No, I knew why. It was because without Hudson, I couldn't do the rebellion list. He was a staple in it, like a prerequisite to a class. I couldn't be rebellious on my own —I didn't have it in me. I needed him to push me. I needed someone to experience it all with.

It was a fun run while it lasted, my thoughts murmured sadly, and I kicked a clump of mud as I walked along the road, nearing the bend that led to the entrance of the mobile home park.

"Gemma!"

I turned around to see Hudson walking toward me,

brows pinched together, expression not all that forgiving. I sighed a little. "What? I'm not really in the mood for round two."

Hudson's frown deepened, and he opened his mouth to say something when a loud barreling sound of an engine drew my attention to the bend in the road. I almost expected it to be another bus. The truck that rounded the corner, though, was much shinier, going a speed too fast for the gravel road. Except it didn't look like it had any intention of stopping or swerving out of the way, like they didn't see me.

And since I wasn't walking along the shoulder, I was right in its path.

Hudson's body slammed against mine from behind, and his hand wrapped around my upper arm to tug me to the side, off the roadway, out of the path of the monster-sized truck. The toe of my shoe caught on the hem of my skirt, and that, combined with the uneven ground, sent me stumbling into Hudson's arms. They wrapped around me as the two of us lost our balance, falling into the shoulder before rolling into the grassy ditch together, finally coming to a stop.

With my world still spinning, I lifted my head, staring directly into Hudson's eyes.

The way I was sprawled across him was somewhat reminiscent of the way two people in love laid together, limbs tangled, breaths mixing. Except neither of us breathed. We were chest to chest, with one of my hands pressed against his bare shoulder while the other was spread into the grass at his side, propping myself up. My loose hair hung around us in a curtain, rays of sun peeking through the strands. Hudson was still as a statue underneath me, but his arms were unrelenting at my waist, wrapped in a vise I couldn't push up from even if I had the wherewithal to do so.

Ever so slightly, I flexed my fingers against his skin, feeling the smooth muscle underneath.

This was the first time our bodies had really collided since the bridge, but we had never been like *this*. Chest to chest, legs to legs. My heart gave a surprised *tha-thump*, one that seemed to bring my body to vibrant alertness.

As I stared down at him, feeling my heart race in my chest, I had one thought. *He is the prettiest boy I've ever seen.*

And it was at that moment that I wasn't sure if it was my heart racing or his.

"Are you okay?" he whispered.

"Yeah," I whispered back, because something about the distance between his mouth and mine made talking normal too loud. "Are you?"

"I probably have a grass stain along the back of my head, but I think so."

I wanted to laugh, but I just continued to stare.

Hudson's hands loosened their band around my waist, moving to settle at my hips. With all ten of his fingers pressing firmly into my sides, he eased me off of him and into a sitting position on the grassy bank. It was my heart racing fast, I knew then, because it sped up even more at the touch, and dipped in disappointment when he drew away. Swallowing hard, I looked away.

"People drive like idiots on this road," he said, dusting off his sweatpants with one hand while rubbing his head with the other. "I...should've told you that."

"Yeah, a heads-up would've been nice," I said with a breathy chuckle, wincing. "Is that why you followed me? To tell me to mind the *NASCAR* racers?"

"I was going to apologize for being a jerk," he said, the blue in his eyes much different than they'd been five minutes ago. All of the irritation was gone, replaced with vivid concern. "Are you really okay?"

Even though he'd taken most of the fall, I took mental stock of everything. There was a big grass stain along the hem of my skirt from where I stepped on the fabric and mashed it into the ground, one that would take a lot of pre-treatment to get out. Not as bad as the butter incident with Jaden, though, thankfully. My palm had a pretty bad scrape across it from where I'd braced myself in the fall. It stung something fierce, and I couldn't tell if any glass slivers from the shoulder had embedded into my skin.

Hudson reached out and cupped my hand with his, peering closely. "It's not bad, but we should still clean it. I have stuff at my house."

At that moment, I didn't question the one-eighty Hudson had turned, how he went from so angry upon seeing me to concerned. I didn't think about how he'd been snapping mere minutes ago to gently holding my hand now. In fact, that dazed thought from a moment ago still lingered now, becoming a distant whisper. *He is the prettiest boy I've ever seen.* "Okay."

CHAPTER 15

I sat on Hudson's porch while he gathered the first aid supplies, turning my sneaker over to see the array of scuffs and stains on the white canvas. What would my parents say when they saw it? Better question: how would I explain the cut on my hand? Or my grass-stained skirt? I didn't even know what time it was—would I even make it home before they did?

The screen door opened with a vicious creak, and Hudson edged past me on the narrow steps and crouched on the bottom one, looking up. His blond hair had fallen a bit into his eyes, but he didn't push it back. "How's the pain?"

I stared down at my stinging skin. "A three."

"Trooper," he said appreciatively, and set down a *My Little Pony* metal lunchbox on the stair. He caught my amused look. "Don't ask me why the supplies are in this."

I didn't ask. I watched as Hudson navigated through the collection of household medical supplies, peering at the little bottles of antiseptic. He reached up and nudged his glasses higher up his nose with his knuckle, reading. "You're wearing your glasses," I said.

"Uh, yeah, I've been wearing them this whole time. You didn't notice?"

"How do you see at school if you don't wear them?"

Deciding that the bottle was what he needed, he uncapped it. "I wear contacts."

I lowered my head to look at him straight on, noting the dullness in his eyes, finally knowing why they looked less blue. "No way," I murmured. "Do you wear *colored contacts?*"

Hudson gave a full-body cringe, physically recoiling away from my words. He started spreading the antiseptic wipe on my hand, worsening the sting. "It was an accident."

"How does one accidentally get colored contacts?"

"My cousin went with me to the eye appointment. I gave her the clipboard while I tried on glasses, and she checked a box on the paperwork for blue contacts." Hudson used the tip of his finger to knock away some of the dirt on my palm, and then continued his gentle ministrations. "I guess she thought it would be funny."

I reached out and laid my hand on his arm, and it was shockingly warm to the touch. "Look at me."

Hudson didn't hesitate in lifting his gaze. I wasn't sure what was more startling—not seeing him with the blue eyes I'd grown so accustomed to, or finding the gray-blue ones peering back at me. They were the color of the sky when dawn broke, with only the slightest shade of blue starbursting through them. These eyes fit him in a way I didn't think mattered until it did.

"My life is a lie," I told him in a deadpan voice.

"Don't tell Babble. The Grim Reaper could never have such boring eyes."

"They're not boring." Without thinking about it, I reached out and pushed his wheat-colored hair back off his forehead, giving me a clear, unobstructed view. "They're pretty."

I should've pulled back, but I hesitated. I'd never touched a boy like this before, in such a tender way, and I found myself wanting to linger in the moment. He was holing perfectly still, like he patiently waited for me to stop invading his personal space. His expression was empty, and ultimately that had me dropping my hand. I couldn't tell if he liked it or if it thoroughly freaked him out.

Even after I dropped my hand into my lap, Hudson didn't move. "Did you hit your head too?"

I touched my temple, but there wasn't an ache there. It was him who hit his head, not me. "I didn't mean to make you uncomfortable. Coming here, I mean."

Hudson pulled a sticky bandage from the metal lunchbox, peering at it to judge the size. "I'm...I'm just not used to having someone care." He unpacked the large bandage that would fit over the plane of the cut, and with careful precision, he smoothed it over my skin. After that, he set my hand into my lap. "Not like you do."

"I shouldn't have pretended not to know you in the gas station." I tried to put myself into Hudson's shoes, wondering how I'd feel if he pretended not to know *me*. "I should've thought about how it'd feel to you."

He let out a soft breath, resting his forearms on his thighs. "It's funny." He didn't look at me as he spoke, but at my bandaged hand. "I wouldn't have thought it'd bother me, either."

"But it did."

"I'm used to people turning away from me, ignoring me when I walk past. I'm used to all that now, but I..." Hudson met my stare. "I didn't realize it would hurt if you turned away, too."

A physical ache clenched my chest, stealing the air from my lungs. I thought about what Paisley said. Her words rang differently in my ear now that there was distance between the broody boy and me. *He doesn't like it when people get too close.* Was that why there was a Grim Reaper mask to begin with? So people wouldn't get too close?

Hudson moved to stand up, but I caught his arm. "Do you really like the dirt?"

He stilled, no doubt recalling what he'd said word for word, much like I was. *You're trying to take a rock and wash all the dirt off? Guess what, Gemma—I like the dirt.* He looked uncomfortable with the question, like he wished he could rewind time and take the words back. "I don't know." He pressed his palm against the step I sat on, using it as leverage to push himself up. He stopped halfway, hovering in front of me, and his eyes on me were like a physical touch. It nearly made me shiver again. "Your hair."

"What about it?" I sucked in a breath. "Is there blood?" Had I really hit my head and not noticed?

Hudson's lips twitched into a bare smile. "It's undone. I've never seen it loose before."

I reached around to thread my fingers through it, plucking out bits of grass and debris in the process. "My parents don't like it when it's loose." The words came out before I could think about them, and something about it made me feel guilty. Like I was talking about them behind their backs. "I'll have to braid it again before I get home."

"I can do it."

I was sure I heard him wrong. "You know how to braid hair?"

"You saw Paisley's hair the other day, right?"

I thought of the dual braided pigtails I saw her in the first time, fighting a smile at the thought of Hudson navigating his way through it.

Hudson came around to sit on the step behind me, and after an awkward pause, his feet came down on a step on either side of me. I could see his knees from the corners of my eyes, but I refused to look over. He didn't touch me, but I knew that if I leaned back, I'd be leaning into the pocket of space his legs created. My skin grew hot.

"I was ten when Paisley was born," he explained as he picked up my hair and swept it behind me. The action nearly caused me to shiver. "My mom was so excited to be having a girl that she actually bought one of those cheap wigs off the internet to practice braiding hair. She taught me, too. I'm not sure why—it was like she knew I'd need to know how to braid hair one day."

I pinched the fabric of my dress, trying to diffuse the rigidness of my spine. "What happened to her?"

"She was in a car accident, about three years after Paisley was born. A guy blew a red light at an intersection." Despite the heavy topic, his fingers were infinitely gentle in my hair, comforting. "She hung on for a little while—only a few days—but eventually passed."

"So, you were thirteen?"

"I just turned fourteen. I finished the last two months of my eighth-grade year at home, and then started at Brentwood High freshman year."

Freshman year. The year he got into his fight with Landon. My heartbeat stirred in my chest, creating an uncomfortable buzz behind my ribcage. Was it a coincidence? Or did the two things correlate?

"You have a lot of hair," Hudson mused. He combed his fingers down the strands, careful around the back of my head, but just the touch was enough to feel heavenly. Ten times more heavenly than when Mom did it.

"Too much," I replied, trying to breathe normally when his fingers touched the base of my neck. For a flash of a second, it was cold skin on hot. "That's on my list, you know. Cut my hair."

He didn't answer, continuing his weaving.

"I cut my hair once," I told him, staring at the collection of homes along the road. Somewhere in the distance, I could hear a lawn mower, and for some reason, the sound was comforting. "In elementary school. It was probably as long as it is now, and I took the kitchen scissors and cut it all off."

"What made you grow it long again?"

"My mom hated it. She'd cry every time she saw me. She said I looked like a boy and that I looked better with long hair."

Hudson's fingers paused, stilling in my hair. "I can see why cutting your hair is on your rebellion list."

"Do you think I would look okay with short hair?" I asked him, but then, that wasn't exactly the right question. "Would I look pretty with short hair?"

Hudson's right leg grazed the side of my arm as it slid closer, and he reached around me to gather any remaining loose strands near my temples. His fingertips brushed against my skin in the process, a whisper of a touch.

My cheeks grew hot the longer the question sat unanswered between us, almost like he hadn't heard me. "Would I look more mature?"

He worked on French braiding the back of my head, expertly keeping pressure on the section to keep it from loosening while he gathered more hair. His touch was so soft that it tickled, instead of where Mom's always pulled. I wanted to pick up the remote and put this moment into slow-motion, live it for as long as possible. "I think you should do whatever you want to."

"That didn't answer my question."

Hudson's fingertips brushed along the side of my throat as he built one section up. When he spoke, it was a low murmur. "Long hair or short, I think you'll still be pretty, Gemma."

You'll still be pretty, he'd said. Still be. Present tense.

My insides felt like they were having a party.

I felt him begin to quickly braid the end of my hair, finished with the sectioning. He was almost done. "Why did you miss school today?"

"I was out late last night."

"With someone?" I asked, trying to sound as nonchalant as possible.

He hesitated like he wasn't going to answer at first, and I felt my insides brace as if waiting for a blow. "With my dad," he replied. "My cousin's been living with us these past few months because she's having issues with her mom—my dad's sister—and she kind of...well, she didn't tell us where she was going, so we were looking for her. Dad called the office at school, though. My absence was excused, so no worries there."

"Did you end up finding her?"

"Yeah. All's okay." He didn't elaborate, but I understood why. It wasn't his story to tell, but his cousin's. "Gemma?"

He finished tying the braid, so I turned around to face him, trailing my fingers along the bumps in my hair. "Yeah?"

"Have your parents always been so strict?"

Just like how it felt every time Morgan brought up the subject, my first instinct was to wave it all away. *My parents aren't strict*, I'd always tell her, to which her response would always be, *If you do everything they say without questioning it, you wouldn't know, would you?*

"I think they're just used to me going along with what they want for me. They're used to me never questioning their decisions. I think some of the blame is on me, too, for never pushing back."

"No one's blaming anyone," he said, leaning his elbow onto his knee and coming closer. "But if you can get in a lot of trouble just by spending time with me, maybe we should reconsider everything."

"No." I laid my hand on Hudson's knee, pinning his leg down to keep him from standing up. "I don't want to let them make this decision for me, too. I don't want to care about the consequences."

He stared at my splayed fingers on his sweatpants for a long moment before lifting his gaze to mine. "The thing about consequences is that you never really know what they're going to be."

"I won't regret it." The declaration rang true in my ears, certain as anything. This was going to be my choice, the first I'd ever made for myself. I refused to regret it. "You won't either, right?"

Hudson dipped his pinky underneath my hand and curled it around mine, squeezing the promise between us. "Never."

The mood was entirely different from when I'd first seen him, and it left me feeling bolstered in the decision. There was relief, too—relief that he didn't give up on me, that he would still be there. But he wouldn't be like everyone else. He wasn't there to see what I could do for him—he was there to see what he could do for me. And I wasn't sure I'd ever really be able to let it go.

My last period class was Chemistry, which was really a junior class, but a few sophomores who were advanced got in. I was one of them, and my table partner, Rosie, was the other. Even though we also sat with each other at lunch, silence between us could still ring awkwardly, like we were two complete strangers. She normally kept her head ducked during the hour, as if she was trying really hard to not make eye contact with anyone. Or maybe it was someone in particular.

Hopefully it wasn't me. Clearing my throat during the last ten minutes while we were working on a worksheet, I leaned over an inch. "Hey, Rosie?"

She looked up, setting down her pencil. "Yeah?"

I opened my mouth, but before I could say anything, the loud beep of the intercom kicked on, followed by a voice of one of the secretaries. "*Attention all JV and varsity football players: practice for today is canceled due to the rain.*"

Some boys in the back let out a loud whoop of excitement, and I turned to find a few of them out of their seats, grinning. There was a boy looking in my direction, but then I realized—he wasn't looking at me. His attention was on the seat beside me.

"Did you have a question, Gemma?" Rosie asked as she scanned her worksheet, unaware of the gaze on her.

"I'm crap at explaining science, but I can try to help if you're stuck."

I slowly pivoted toward the front. "It's not about science. It's about...fashion."

Rosie tucked her fringe behind her ear, attention piquing. "Fashion?"

"I've been wanting to upgrade my style, and you have the best fashion sense of anyone I know."

It was true, too. The way she layered her cardigans and sweaters always looked so cute that I was jealous. Even today, all she wore was a pink tank with a white cardigan over her shoulders, but it was still really pretty. It was like she was always fashionable without trying. I watched Rosie's face light up with the compliment, and I knew that was all I needed to break the awkward ice between us—to find common ground with her.

"I think I want to get rid of my skirts," I went on, glancing down at the light blue floral one I wore now. "But it's so hard to find a pair of jeans that fit my waist and my thighs."

"I like your skirts. I think they suit you." Rosie reached over and smoothed a wrinkle near my knee, tilting her head as she analyzed it. "Long skirts can some-times make people look shorter, but since you're tall, you can pull it off. Normally, if you wear a loose, flowing skirt, you'll want a tighter top. You wear loose, oversized shirts with it, so it sort of swamps you. Cropped sweaters or shirts would even work great, honestly, because it balances everything out and you can flash your tummy a little while you're at it." Rosie winked at me.

I turned to my Chemistry worksheet with a little laugh. "I feel like I should be taking notes."

"It's not that hard. I learned everything I know from magazines, honestly. Without *Seventeen*, I'd probably still be wearing polka-dots and stripes at the same time." Rosie went back to analyzing my outfit, taking note of the top I wore before going to my skirt. "There are some prints that might look better as shorter skirts, though. Like this one."

"How short?"

Rosie hit the side of her hand at the middle of my thigh. "Long enough for school, of course, but short enough to show off some of those long legs. Plus, your oversized shirts and sweaters would look better with a shorter skirt. Your bare skin would balance it out."

I had a sort of epiphany moment then. Cropping my skirts. Why had it never occurred to me? When I made my skirts, I always hemmed them long—the shortest I'd ever go was above my ankle. Why had I never thought to go shorter? I looked down at my legs, hidden beneath the fabric, and did the same as Rosie did. I cut the side of my hand on my leg, trying to picture what it'd look like with all the skin from there down exposed.

Would Mom ever let me do it, though?

Would she ever have to know? a soft voice in my head whispered.

The bell rang as I contemplated it, and Rosie was slow to collect her things. "I have a few cropped sweaters and stuff that I don't wear anymore. My sisters usually get all my hand-me-downs, but I can bring a few in for you, if you want."

Instinctively, I wanted to tell her to not worry about it, that I didn't want to inconvenience her, but I stopped myself. "That would be great, honestly."

Rosie lingered at the blacktop table while I walked out of the science room, heart drumming excitedly with all the possibilities. I had so many skirts I could crop and re-hem, and it wouldn't even take me that long. Already, I could picture ones that would look best shorter, ones with busier prints like Rosie suggested. I also smiled at the idea of breaking the ice with her, and hoped that would make for more conversations in the future. She would technically count as my first friend outside of Mom's premade social circle, and it felt like a huge win.

As I was turning the corner to leave the west wing and head toward the senior lockers, I collided with someone tall and hard, nearly ricocheting off their chest. I would've, too, if their hand hadn't shot out, grabbing my forearm to steady me. When I looked up, recognition flared. "Connor."

"Gemma," Connor greeted warmly, eyes wide and breath quick. Almost like he'd been running. He had an Algebra II textbook tucked underneath his arm, and he hurried to press it against his chest. "Sorry, I should know better than to tear around the corner."

"It's okay," I said, rubbing my shoulder. "I can see why you're a football player, though. You nearly knocked me over."

He laughed good-naturedly, patting me on the upper

arm before he made a move to brush past me. I wasn't sure where he was going, since the west wing only had classrooms, but I wasn't going to ask. At the last second, though, I stopped him. "Connor. Can I ask you a quick question?"

"Sure. I can try to give you a quick answer."

"Do you know the fight my brother was in freshman year?" I watched the wariness enter his eyes, but he ultimately nodded. "Who all was involved? Do you know?"

"Any reason why you're randomly curious?"

"Gossip purposes, of course."

He laughed a little, gaze turning thoughtful as he tapped his Algebra II textbook. "So, I think it was your brother, Ashton Shaw, Kyle Filmore. And then Hudson, of course."

I blinked. "*Just* Hudson? Like, he didn't have any help?"

"I think so."

Why would Hudson have gone up to them, three against one? Sure, Landon was much lankier as a freshman than he was now, but still. Three against one?

"Do you know why it happened? Like...what started it?"

Connor shook his head apologetically. "The guys don't really talk about it, you know? Since they got their asses handed to them. I only know what rumors people spread, so I don't even know if that's really what happened or not. You haven't asked your brother?"

"He wouldn't tell me." Not that I asked, but I already knew what his answer would be. "He thinks I'm a dainty, fragile girl who faints at the thought of violence."

Connor's grin was wide. "That's Landon for you. He plays the big brother role well, doesn't he?"

"He's pretty good at it," I allowed, and then took a step back. "Well, I should get going. Have a good rest of your day."

Connor tipped his head in goodbye and continued on his way with his textbook, heading toward the west staircase.

I started walking toward my locker, thinking. That conversation didn't leave me feeling any more enlightened than before about Hudson's fight with my brother, only more confused. I guessed the only way to find out the truth was to go to the source—either Landon or Hudson—but I couldn't even imagine broaching the topic with either of them. Landon would be way too suspicious, since that'd be the second time I was asking him about Hudson, and Hudson... I was too afraid of his answer.

So, what? my thoughts demanded. *You're going to stick your head in the sand about it and pretend it didn't happen?*

It sounded like a good idea, didn't it?

The area around my locker was empty when I got to it, for once, without Morgan or Jaden hanging around. I fished around in my small backpack pocket for my phone, brushing past mechanical pencils and something cold and metal before I found it. A text from Landon was waiting for me when I pressed the button.

LANDON

You heard practice was canceled, right?
Do you still have your mentoring?

I wasn't really sure why he texted me instead of coming to ask me in person, but it made me roll my eyes.

GEMMA

Yes, I do. Can you come in an hour and pick me up?

LANDON

sounds good. Happy mentoring

I slid the keyboard into my phone, stuffing it into my backpack pocket. As I did, though, this time I felt the piece of paper I'd left in there. I knew exactly what it was when I touched it, but I pulled it out and unfolded it anyway.

Gemma's Rebellion List

The last thing we'd checked off almost a week ago was to go see a scary movie, so it felt like the perfect time to cross out another. I scanned the list for the perfect one. *Skip a class, paint my nails, try coffee...*

I drew my lower lip into my mouth as I locked onto one of my bullet points, knowing it was perfect. In my head, I began to sift through pieces of a plan, trying to fit them together into the perfect puzzle.

That was how Hudson found me, his backpack over his shoulder. "What are you concentrating so hard on?" he asked, looking down at the paper I held in my hand. "Thinking about adding to it?"

"What are you doing tonight?" I asked without hesitation, folding the sheet up and putting it back into my bag.

"Tonight?"

"I think it's time to check the next thing off." I leaned in close to whisper the words, and even though they were quiet, the thrill that went through me wasn't. It warmed my skin, the anticipation of it all. "I think it's time to sneak out."

CHAPTER 16

I bent over the sewing machine in my room, trying to line up the hem on my skirt. I'd pinned it all the way around, but with how shaky my hands were, it wouldn't have surprised me if I screwed it up somehow. As soon as I'd gotten home from school, I'd taken Rosie's advice and picked out the busiest print skirt in my collection and had taken scissors to it. Mom would've had a heart attack if she saw the amount I cut off, but it'd almost felt like how it did when I chopped my hair—exciting, freeing. Best of all, working on this kept my thoughts busy.

Now, though, with a cut-up skirt on my sewing machine and my plans for tonight looming closer and closer, I was busy contemplating how much I really wanted to die at sixteen.

Sneak out. How had I planned to do that, again? It wasn't like I could waltz out the front door. There was no way I could leave my bedroom window open—it faced the street, and I could just imagine nosy Mrs. Jasper calling Dad, asking about it. I wanted to throw my hands up and say *well, what a bummer*, and tuck myself in like I *hadn't* planned anything, but I had no way to contact Hudson and call it all off. We never exchanged numbers.

I pressed a button on my cell phone to look at the time. Nine-oh-eight. He'd be waiting soon.

My foot let up on the pedal and I clicked the machine off, rocking into my seat. It wasn't like I was going to be out all night—this wasn't the all-nighter we were pulling. I knew what I had to do; it was just putting the plan into motion that had me uneasy. I looked down at the puckered skin of my palm. The scrape from the gravel wasn't deep, but it left the skin tender, and I'd been able to take the bandage off the first night after the anti-septic seeped in. It was a wincing reminder, like Hudson had said, that actions had consequences.

And I had a feeling that this action's consequence would be major if it was ever found out.

I finished the rest of the hem at nine-twelve and left my room to lock myself in the bathroom. My reflection showcased my wide, wild eyes. This was a bad idea, and the risk versus reward had me asking myself if this was really worth it.

Except the more I tried to convince myself to stay home, the more unsettled I felt.

As I stared my reflection down in the mirror, the background of the bathroom became clearer, and my gaze focused on something behind me. It was covered by thick curtains, but it was an obvious beacon—the window. It was a window that faced our fenced-in backyard, where no Nosy Mrs. Jasper could see an open window, where

Mom or Dad wouldn't notice if it was cracked, just an inch.

My escape route.

My bare feet squeaked on the wooden floor as I turned the corner to my bedroom, and they squeaked again when I ground to a halt over the threshold. "Where's the fire?" Mom asked from where she leaned against my bedpost.

I frantically looked toward my sewing machine, but the fabric of the skirt was so bunched up that it was impossible to tell how long it was. Or, really, how *short* it was.

Breathe. My heart didn't seem like it wanted to quiet down. I forced myself to not look at the clock. "I saw a spider." *Lie.* It was such a bald-faced one that I couldn't believe Mom didn't call me out for it. Small words or big, lies were lies. That was what she should've said.

But she didn't. "Are you going to bed early?"

It was a little before my normal bedtime, but not by much. I looked down at my pajamas. "I, ah, don't feel good. I was thinking about turning in early."

Okay, spoken with a bit more hesitation than I'd initially planned for. I added a fake cough for good measure.

"Landon said he wasn't feeling good either," she said as I came closer, and she reached out for me, laying the backs of her fingers on my cheek. "Hmm, you do feel a little feverish."

Wait, Landon beat me to that excuse? Was Mom suspicious because *both* of us were sick? Was he actually sick? I fisted the edge of my nightgown, swallowing hard. "Maybe it's just being overtired. The back-to-school season...it's starting to hit me."

"Maybe we should all go to bed early, huh? It's the middle of the week, and it'd be a great time to recharge our batteries." She nodded her chin gently toward my covers, and I followed her instruction, climbing in. "I think you should braid your hair for bed. It's such a tangled mess in the morning."

"I'll try not to toss and turn so much," I promised her, the scent of lavender tickling my nose. "Did you wash my sheets?"

"I did." Mom beamed and sat on the side of my bed. I could feel where her body pressed into the mattress. It was how she used to sit when I was a little girl, smoothing my hair off my forehead as the movement lulled me to sleep. Now, though, she peered down at me. "I'm proud of the woman you're becoming, Gemma."

I felt my eyes grow huge in my head, knowing for certain that this was it. She knew what I was planning. She could see right through me. But the tenderness didn't ebb from her vision, and she looked more nostalgic than anything, and guilt quickly replaced the fear. This wasn't a lie itself, sneaking out, but it was deception at its highest point.

"It's all because of you and Dad," I murmured, but my voice came out small.

She kissed my forehead before wishing me goodnight, and though I knew I needed to get moving, I lay still for a long moment, watching my ceiling fan go around in lazy circles. Since Mom had flipped off my light switch, it powered down the fan as well, and it gradually slowed. *You have a good life,* my thoughts told me. *What's so wrong with it? What's so wrong with keeping your head down and your mouth shut?*

This life I had—it *was* a good one. There was a roof over my head and food on the table. My older brother cared for me, and my parents made sure I was always safe.

But they also dictated what I did in my free time, who I spent my time with, and the dreams I could dream.

It was a good life, but the only problem was that it wasn't mine.

My fan slowly ground to a halt, and that was when I threw the covers off. I knew the answer.

I grabbed the skirt off the sewing machine and quickly snagged a thick sweater from my closet, and with my collection, I tiptoed down the hallway. The living room light was off, no longer leaking into the corridor. Landon's door was shut, hinting that he was already tucked in for the night, and I made sure to move slowly past it, afraid he'd hear the floors creak.

All the while, my heart raced to a drumbeat from a heavy metal band, so hard that I wondered if I'd pass out before I even made it to the bathroom.

I eased the door shut behind me and quickly got dressed. As I pulled the skirt on, I had to swallow a little laugh at how strange the hemline tickling my thigh felt. I tucked my head into the oversized sweater next, and Rosie, once again, had been right. With my legs exposed,

I looked less like a girl styled by her mother and more like a girl who styled herself.

I looked pretty.

The cold, mid-September night air hit me as soon as I opened the window, and I didn't even look at how far the drop was before I hooked my legs over the sill, knowing that if I was going to do this, I couldn't waste any time.

Sucking in a breath, I fell the five feet onto the ground without making a sound. My feet slammed on impact, and it jarred up my legs, but it felt good. Once I reached up to slide the window down, leaving a one-inch gap for me to push open later, a rushing feeling swept through me.

I was out.

I couldn't help it—I laughed. I had to clamp a hand over my mouth to silence the sound, but the happiness still welled within, adrenaline hot on its heels.

I darted across the lawn, carefully letting myself out the back garden gate, and then I was at the sidewalk. *I was free.*

My sneakers slapped against the road in a sort of anthem to my happiness, and even though the wind was cold against my bare legs, I welcomed it as it tugged on my hair, pulling the black locks backward. My legs began burning, because flat-out running like this was new for me, but I couldn't stop. Not even if I wanted to.

I must've looked ridiculous, running down the middle of the road a little after nine o'clock at night, but I didn't care. For once in my life, I didn't have a single care in the world. It made me laugh again.

When I turned the corner from Huntington Avenue onto Willow Street, I heard him. Another note in the anthem in my head, as clear as day. "Gem!"

I whirled around, the world tilting with the sharp movement, and found Derrick's car on the opposite side of the street corner. The passenger side door was open, and Hudson stood beside it, palm resting on the roof. My tilting world shuddered for a moment, the dark street totally ebbing away as I focused on him. His eyes were wide, lips parted, almost like my suddenness shocked him speechless.

I bit down on my lower lip, chest expanding. "I thought you said left onto Willow."

His expression was hard to read even though the streetlamp directly overhead illuminated it clearly. "I did," Hudson said as I came closer. His eyes took a quick glimpse at my legs before darting up to my eyes. "Derrick parked on the wrong side."

"My bad," Derrick called from the driver's seat, ducking down to peer at me under the roof of the car. "Dang, look at all that hair you have. You could've saved some for me, you know." He ghosted a hand across his buzzed head.

My hair was wavy from being tied into a braid all day, and now that it was freed, the locks fell to my hips. I grinned at Derrick as I tucked a chunk behind my ear, knocking my knees together. Even though I'd been in love with the length back in the bathroom, it felt weird for so much of my skin to be on display for others to see. "So, what are we doing tonight?"

Hudson opened the backseat door for me. When I rounded the side of it, his lips stretched as he regarded me. I could see myself in the reflection of his eyes, all wide-eyed and wild-haired. In my chest, my heart gave a hiccupping gasp, like it short-circuited for a second before it began racing faster. "We," he began, voice a low murmur, "are going to have a fun night."

CHAPTER 17

Though the euphoric feeling ebbed a little the longer I sat in the backseat of Derrick's car, it didn't dissipate completely over the drive. Soft rock pumped through the speakers, a song I didn't recognize, but enjoyable all the same. Derrick drove into Jefferson and then out the other side, tapping his fingers against the steering wheel. His window was down, and his elbow stuck out the side, letting in the cool night air.

I had my face practically pressed against the window, staring at the rows of corn that we passed, ones that looked a little more ominous in the moonlight. "Where are we going?" I asked, raising my voice to be heard over the shout of the wind.

Derrick leaned his head toward the middle of the seats. "We're almost there."

I had no idea where "there" was, but I didn't mind it, either. I was so used to Mom having control over where "there" was, but putting it in the hands of Hudson and Derrick felt less like I was relinquishing my control, but more so trusting them with it. Trusting Hudson with it.

It was a strange feeling.

I didn't have to wait long to find out where our destination was. Without much warning, Derrick twisted the wheel sharply to the left, cutting into a path that'd been cleanly made through the corn. The dirt road was filled with potholes that rattled the car, and with how many times Derrick hit them hard, I was surprised nothing underneath the cab fell loose.

It was then that I found out how Betsy had come to sound the way she did.

Hudson turned around in his seat to face me, and the glow of the dashboard lights backlit the blond wisps of his hair. "We have a friend who lives out here. Their name's Tee. They're having a bonfire tonight."

"We're throwing it for you," Derrick interjected, grinning. "It's your first time sneaking out, so we're throwing a celebratory bonfire. You're our guest of honor."

"Me?"

"It's nothing major," Hudson hurried to say, as if sensing my growing anxiety. His blue eyes held mine tightly. "It's going to be us three and two others. We usually roast marshmallows—"

"Simon reads some of his god-awful poetry," Derrick piped in.

"—and hang out," Hudson finished, not even blinking in Derrick's direction. "For an hour or so. How does that sound?"

I pressed my palm to the bare skin of my knee, squeezing. The car still rocked back and forth with each pothole, almost like Derrick was seeing how many he could hit, but my attention had been captured by Hudson. "Can we stay longer than an hour?"

He chuckled. "For a girl who normally goes to bed at nine-thirty, can you *last* longer than an hour?"

I had the biggest urge to stick my tongue out at him, but that would've probably aided in his "toddler" argument.

Derrick interjected between us. "We can leave when you want. Ol' Betsy is your chariot tonight. And there's not even a chauffeur fee."

The corn on either side of us dispersed enough for a house at the end of the dirt driveway to come into view. It was taller than it was wide, with a giant wraparound porch like a house from a movie. Derrick didn't slow as he drove past it, leaving the dirt road and thumping along onto a two-tire track lane that sliced into the grass.

Hudson grabbed the handle above his head. "You could slow down, you know."

"Oh, I'm sorry, do *you* want to drive?"

"You know Mouse likes to dart out from the field. If you hit her, Tee would skin you alive."

Derrick huffed, but I felt the car decelerate a little. "Cats have nine lives, don't they?"

Derrick didn't drive much farther before a flickering fire came into view, one that trickled glowing embers into the sky. It also mostly obscured the two huddled figures who stood with their hands out. I could only see that one was shorter and one was taller.

"Hey, losers!" Derrick called as soon as he popped

open his door, pulling himself out into the night. "Who's got the marshmallows?"

I looked around the clearing as Hudson and I climbed out. Aside from the roiling fire contained by a metal ring, there wasn't much to look at besides trees and corn, both at a safe distance away from the flames, and a large wooden barn that was mostly swamped with shadow. I wrapped my arms around myself, because even though the trees nearby blocked off some of the wind, my sweater was still a pitiful barrier.

And then—warmth. Warmth accompanied by the heavy scent of citrus. Hudson draped his jacket over my shoulders, the heaviness of the jean material weighing me down. As gently as he could, he eased all of my hair out from underneath the collar. A shiver slipped down my spine. "That's okay," I began, but Hudson shook his head.

"The sweater I have on is much thicker than yours," he said, curling the collar against my throat. "And your legs are bare. Plus, I always run hot."

I didn't look away from him. Even though I knew there was a softer side to Hudson, it always surprised me when it slipped through, startling me speechless for a second. "Are you sure?"

"Take the jacket, Gem." Then, careful not to get my hair caught in the zipper, Hudson zipped the jacket up to my chin, bundling me in.

I touched the zipper when he turned away toward his friends, not sure why my heart was beating so fast.

Derrick, who'd nestled up beside the tallest of the two strangers, rushed to make introductions. "Gemma, this is Tee Bryant. Tee's a junior at Jefferson, lives on this lovely property right here, and if you're ever in the need for jelly snacks, come to them."

"Jeez, give her my star sign while you're at it," Tee muttered to him, but their expression cleared into something friendlier when they looked up at me. Their hair was cut into jagged points near their jawline, though they'd tucked most of it behind their ears. The hooked piercing on their eyebrow glinted as they quirked it up. "Hudson said you looked prudish, but I don't really see it."

"I said she was *voted* that," Hudson quickly interjected, shooting them a look. "Not that she *was*."

"I think *I* was the one to say she looked it," Derrick whispered back, and then grinned at me. "But don't worry, Milady, we accept all sorts around here."

Tee elbowed him in the ribs. "Anyway, nice to meet you. I've been needing someone to break up the monotony of testosterone."

Derrick responded by throwing his arm over their shoulders. "You love it."

I let my gaze shift past Tee and Derrick to the shorter shadow beyond the fire. "I'm Simon," he said as soon as our eyes met, and even from here, I could see his wide, braces-covered smile. "I go to Jefferson, too."

I recognized both of them from the gas station last Saturday, the four of them all laughing as they walked the aisles. Back then, I'd wanted so badly to be a part of that group, to laugh along with them, so being in front of them now felt surreal. "Nice to meet you. Both of you."

Either Simon or Tee had laid a quilt on the ground, and on top of that was a plethora of marshmallows and graham crackers waiting to be snacked on. Derrick ripped open one of the packages and began launching the white puffs at Simon, and Hudson began trailing after him to pick them off the ground. "Stop wasting the food!" he shouted, sounding very much like a parent chastising their kids.

"Please tell me you've had a s'more," Tee said as they crouched beside me, breaking open a container of graham crackers. "I know this is your first time sneaking out, but please tell me it's not your first bonfire."

Did I really give off that much of a "sheltered" vibe? "Not my first. I went to a camp this summer, so I've had plenty of s'mores." I took the roasting stick they offered to me, gaze landing on their fingertips. "Wow, I love your polish."

It was a sort of iridescent purple that seemed to glow in the firelight, and though it was chipping—to the point that my mother would've taken it off my nails herself—it was beautiful. Tee wiggled their fingers. "Want me to paint yours? The stuff's up in my room back at the house."

I imagined saying yes. What would the iridescent color look like on my nails? Beautiful, of course. I probably wouldn't have been able to stop looking at it, much in the way I was doing with Tee's nails. That *was* on my rebellion list, painting my nails. But Mom would demand to know where I got the polish from, and it would open a whole can of worms. "Maybe next time."

"I'm surprised Hudson brought you, you know." Tee speared their marshmallow and turned toward the fire, sticking their feet out to warm the soles of their shoes. "That's not, like, a knock against you or anything. Hudson has a hard time making friends."

I sat down beside them, tucking my legs underneath me. The glow of the flames warmed my cheeks, but I looked beyond them, to where Hudson now helped Simon shove a marshmallow onto a stick. "We were kind of forced together."

It was the plot twist of the century, me being here. Last week this time, I would've died if someone told me I'd be hanging out with the Grim Reaper and his friends after curfew. If someone told me that I'd sneak out of my bathroom window on a school night, I would've confessed it to Mom long before it could've happened.

And the guilt was still there, of course, but for now, it was easy enough to put it on the backburner.

As we roasted marshmallows—or in Derrick's case, lit them on fire until they were charred—a light, warm feeling spread from my chest to the rest of my body, chasing away the chill I'd felt the moment I stepped from the car. For the first time in a long time, I felt a happiness so unfiltered that it made me dizzy. Maybe it was the fact that Derrick was a loose cannon and could make everyone laugh, or maybe it was Simon's truly cheesy poetry, or even Tee's mellow temperament. The group around the fire truly felt like a band of misfits, and with me added to the mix, it made for a perfect night.

It made me wonder if it was indeed possible to get

drunk off of laughter. It was a sensation I'd always link to the word *freedom*.

"So, Gemma," Simon piped up from the other side of the fire. He had his legs folded in front of him, his hands on his knees. "What made you want to hang around Hudson? No one really does."

"Thanks," Hudson replied from where he sat beside me, loading another marshmallow onto a stick.

"Oh, you know what I mean. Everyone at school runs for the hills from *the Grim Reaper*. No offense, Gemma, but from what everyone's said, this sounds out of character for you."

"He's not as bad as everyone makes him out to be," I said as if Hudson wasn't right beside me. "Not all the time, anyway."

He rolled his eyes at me, but I caught a glimpse of a smile. His attention lingered on me for a moment. "Hold this," he instructed, passing me the stick. "I'll be right back."

I twirled the stick between my fingers, watching as he hurried off toward the car.

"We're protective of him," Tee said, drawing my gaze to them. Derrick and Tee sat on a separate blanket on the other side of the bonfire, illuminated by the flames. "He's got a lot on his plate, and it's not like anyone's willing to help him out."

Derrick nudged Tee's arm. "Except for Gemma. She's mentoring him, remember?"

Tee's gaze didn't soften from its firm stare, looking at me as if they could see *through* me. It wasn't necessarily unkind, but it wasn't overly friendly, either. "Is it for his benefit, though? Or is it more for yours?"

That sucked the air right out of me, but I understood where they were coming from. It was clear it was coming from a protective friend's perspective, and quite honestly, I was glad Hudson had one of those. After seeing how people literally backed away from him at school, I was glad he had his own friend group. "I want to be there for him," I said eventually, looking over to see Hudson's shadow coming back. "Like you're there for him."

Tee narrowed their eyes a bit before giving a satisfied nod, a hint of a relenting smile on their lips. "Good answer."

Suddenly, something soft draped across my bare legs, taking away a bit of the biting chill of the breeze. Hudson readjusted the blanket so it covered me, fully focused on the task. "I should've told you it was outdoors," he said, taking the marshmallow stick from me. His eyes met mine. "But I do like the skirt."

And suddenly I was very, very warm.

Hudson made a few more s'mores for everyone, but I'd filled up on them quickly, rubbing my hands together to get rid of their stickiness. Simon migrated his way over to sit beside me since that was where the chocolate was. Derrick walked his fingers up Tee's sweatpants-clad leg. Instead of swatting him off, though, Tee ignored him with a bored expression on their face until Derrick's fingers were on top of their knee. And then they leaned down and tried to bite him.

"Don't mind those two," Simon whispered to me,

unwrapping another chocolate bar. "They've been in love with each other since, like, the fifth grade."

"*Derrick's* been in love with Tee since the fifth grade," Hudson corrected, tightening his hold on his stick. He was on his last marshmallow, and he expertly turned it so it wouldn't catch on fire. "Tee only just stopped cussing him out when he touched them."

"And who knows how long that'll last," Tee muttered, but over the flames, I caught their smile.

I rested my arms on my knees and dropped my chin on them. The jean material smelled so much like Hudson, beyond the citric scent of his cologne. The blanket, too, smelled of citrus, and it was warm in the way a hug was. There was something else intoxicating there, and it caused everything in me to swim. As discreetly as I could, I watched him.

Hudson's profile was lit up by the orange glow, blond hair appearing darker in the night. He was balanced expertly on his toes, focused on the marshmallow and making sure it wouldn't burn. I was aware of every little thing about him, from the way his sweater caught on the tops of his jeans in the back to the way he tilted his head ever so slightly to the side as he worked. It was like my brain couldn't stop soaking him up.

He looked over his shoulder, raising his eyebrows as he caught me staring. "Can you help me assemble it?"

"Y-Yeah." I scrambled to pull the graham cracker out from the packaging and broke it in half, holding it steady as he maneuvered his marshmallow onto it. The concentration on his face was clear, teeth grazing his bottom lip.

He slid a piece of chocolate underneath one side of the graham cracker, and sandwiched the marshmallow between.

"You want it?" he asked, glancing at the little sandwich. "Last s'more of the night?"

"You can," I insisted, offering it out to him. I was so stuffed with all the sugar that I wasn't sure I could eat it.

"Suit yourself." He popped it into his mouth and chewed, closing his eyes as if it tasted like the best s'more in the world. He brought the pad of his finger up to his lips, licking off the chocolate that'd melted onto his skin. It was like the flames had moved from the logs onto my skin, watching his mouth wrap around his finger in a quick moment. He still had his mouth full when he said, "You missed out."

"I may have the bedtime of a toddler, but you *eat* like one," I said out with a little chuckle, pointing at my own mouth. "You have chocolate. Right here."

Hudson rubbed the back of his hand along his mouth. "Did I get it?"

"No, it's—right *here*." I pointed again at the corner of my mouth.

He leaned forward over the graham crackers and the open pack of marshmallows and brought his face close to mine. He had his contacts in tonight, so his eyes were such a vibrant blue even in the dark. The flames definitely only added to their magical appearance. "Get it for me," he said, tipping his face toward me.

Suddenly, I wasn't looking at the chocolate on Hudson's lips but at the lips themselves. He had a sort of downturned tilt to them even with his resting face, the corners pointing down ever so slightly. There was a dent in his bottom lip that I wondered if I'd be able to feel if I touched it. And, of course, the smear of chocolate.

With a shaky hand, I reached out and swiped my thumb along the corner of Hudson's mouth, feeling the seam where the top and bottom lip met, wiping the chocolate off. His mouth tensed at the touch—in fact, all of him stiffened, but he didn't pull away. I dusted my fingers together, gripping my hands to hide the shaking. "There you go."

Hudson's eyes were wide, filled with surprise. Between us, he raised his hand, showcasing something caught between his fingers. "I meant with the napkin, Gem."

I looked down at the napkin square in his hand, the *duh* realization washing over me like ice water. *Of course he didn't mean touch his mouth!* I sucked in a sharp breath as my body cringed with embarrassment, and I turned my face away, pressing a hand to my beet red cheeks. *Dear God, why would he ask you to rub your fingers against his mouth? Why was that the first thing you thought of? Why did you do it?*

I was going to die of embarrassment.

Risking a peek at Hudson between my fingertips, I found the corner of his lip curling up into a smile filled with something like amusement, something like...*curiosity*.

The corner of the lip I just felt up.

I hid my face again.

"Okay," Derrick said suddenly, pushing up from the ground. "I think it's time."

For one dizzying, horrifying moment, I thought Derrick was talking about Hudson and me—that something between us was time—but when I turned, he was already hurrying off in the direction of the dark barn behind us. It didn't seem like anyone else caught what'd happened, thank God. I wasn't sure I could live that down if multiple people witnessed.

I cleared my throat, refusing to look at Hudson. "Time for what?"

Simon got to his feet too, an excited expression flashing across his face. "Hudson planned this. Have you ever ridden an ATV?"

An ATV? Was it bad that I didn't exactly know what that was? "Never."

"Well, you will tonight." And with that, Simon hurried off toward the shed too.

Only Tee and Hudson remained, the former leaning forward to warm their hands on the fire, the latter catching my eye. "We race up and down the driveway sometimes. When the corn's harvested, we go through the fields, too."

"ATVs," I echoed, trying to picture it in my mind and coming up empty.

It took a few minutes for Derrick and Simon to persuade the two beasts of machinery from the barn, the engines letting out a low, purring rumble as they rode them out. They looked like four-wheelers—was there a difference?—and as Derrick rode his closer, I could see there were flames painted on the sides.

"Well, what do you think, Gemma?" he asked, stretching his arms wide. "Beautiful, right? Hudson and I fixed these up a couple of summers ago."

Hudson leaned close to me and dropped his voice. "When he says 'Hudson and I,' he means he was the one who handed me the wrenches."

"You like to do that then, huh?" I asked him. "Fix stuff up? You said you were helping your cousin fix up a van."

"My friends appreciate the free labor."

I laughed lightly, watching as Simon flicked on his headlights and Derrick followed suit. It was true I'd never been on an ATV before. We lived in the middle of the city, so it made no sense for us to get one, and I'd never even met someone who owned one. My curiosity was piqued as I eyed the thing, though, and I found myself climbing to my feet to get a better look.

Simon hopped off his seat and told Hudson he could have the first turn, which the Grim Reaper took. And in that moment, with the moonlight shining down and the bonfire casting an orange tint over him, the nickname suited him. He looked like a grim reaper on his steed, features in their relaxed, stoic mask.

He stretched one hand out to me, palm up. "You riding with me?"

I stared at him like an idiot. Ride with him. With Hudson. Joining the Grim Reaper on the ATV and riding around in the night. No, that wasn't what my brain snagged on—it was the fact that I would be squeezed in that small sliver of the seat behind him. Pressed up close. The idea of it made my mouth run dry.

"I'm not really wearing the right bottoms for it," I said, but even still, I took one step forward.

"I won't look."

Feeling magnetized toward him, I took another step forward toward the machine, toward him. "Live a little, right?"

Hudson tipped his head playfully. "Only if you want to."

"Hey, maybe she wants to ride with me," Derrick said, revving his engine a little and waggling his eyebrows.

"She's with me," Hudson replied without missing a beat, gaze intensifying. "Right, Gem?"

As our gazes met, I realized another thing—it wasn't the word *freedom* that would be etched on my heart forever when I thought of this night. Another word would be there as well. A name. *Hudson.* I'd always link the feeling from tonight to the word *freedom* and the name *Hudson.*

And it was then that another truth hit me. I thought I only liked the way Hudson made me *feel.* Now, though, with the way my heart was racing fast, I wondered if I liked something else.

Always, I thought to Hudson, wondering if it showed on my face, wondering why I didn't care whether or not it did. In the end, I placed my hand in Hudson's, letting him help me on.

He was true to his word and didn't look as I climbed on behind him. He kept his face toward the front as I hitched a leg over the bike and then tucked the fabric underneath my thigh so it hugged tighter to me. Though the cold air flushed my skin, if someone would've told me that it was the middle of July with my pale knees near Hudson's hips, I would've believed them.

"What made you think about doing this?" I asked him, leaning close to be heard around the engine.

"I feel like any rebellion list needs something like 'ride a motorcycle' or 'ride a dirt bike,'" he replied, speaking over his shoulder. "We don't have motorcycles or dirt bikes, but we do have ATVs."

It was a good substitute. It would've taken a whole lot more coercion to get me on the back of a motorcycle.

I rested my hands hesitantly at his sides, lightly enough that I couldn't really feel anything behind the thick material of Hudson's sweater. His head tilted down, and a second later, his hands wrapped around my own, their warmth stealing the chill that'd formed across my knuckles. He tugged my arms around his waist completely, drawing them like a buckle around him, tugging me flush to his body. "You'll have to hold on tight," he said without a trace of hesitancy. "If we hit a pothole, you don't want to fall off."

"Right," I said with a voice as quivering as could be, clearing my throat as if it'd make it any less obvious.

Derrick shot a look at Tee that I barely caught, one that included a little smirk and another wiggle of his eyebrows. It made my face flame hotter. "You ready?" he asked Hudson, pulling his ATV up beside us. Our head-lights mingled to illuminate the path before us, giving a clear view of the shadowy potholes and dips. He revved his engine again. "First to the end of the driveway and back wins?"

"Deal," Hudson agreed, leaning forward over the handlebars. My heart kicked up faster in my chest. "You holding on tight, Gem?"

I nodded, my chin brushing against his back.

"Three," Derrick called over the noise, grinning.

"Two," Hudson said, the one word reverberating in his chest.

"One," Derrick said, but as soon as he spoke, Hudson pressed something handlebars, propelling us forward in a sharp, jarring movement. Without thinking, I clutched him tighter, pressing my hands against the muscles that I could feel even through his sweater.

And we were off. The headlights were dull on the four-wheeler, and a bit foggy from disuse, but they still illuminated where each pothole was, and Hudson swerved around them skillfully. The air tore at my hair and pulled it behind me like a wave, and it'd probably be a tangled mess later—a tangled mess Mom would no doubt ream me out for—but now, I couldn't think beyond this moment.

Hudson jerked the handlebars to the right, swerving away from a pothole before the tire could fall into it, and I squeezed tighter to him. As hesitant as ever, I leaned my head against Hudson's back, my cheek fitting perfectly between his shoulder blades. His sweater was soft against my face, smelling like him and traces of the bonfire, and I inhaled deeply.

Derrick was hot on our heels, though when I turned back, I found his headlights bouncing from slamming into the potholes, not bothering to maneuver around them.

This was by far the most fun thing I'd ever done. More fun than seeing the scary movie and watching Hudson jump at the scares, and more fun than shouting a curse word in the counselor's office. It wasn't even something that was on my rebellion list, riding an ATV, but I instantly knew it should've been. And he knew. Hudson just knew.

"You good?" Hudson shouted as we sped toward the bonfire, the corn passing by us in a haze.

I risked reaching up to rub my eye, scrubbing away the wetness that blurred my vision, and nodded against his back. "Yeah," I called, settling deeper against him, allowing myself to smile. "I'm great."

CHAPTER 18

The ride back to Willow Street was a sleepy sort of quiet, accented with the heavy breathing of Simon in the seat beside me. His head was propped up against the window, and his eyes were open, but every few seconds, they'd droop low like he was fighting to stay awake. Derrick had the radio on, but it was playing a slow jazz song, one with lyrics that could've doubled as a lullaby.

I, however, was wide awake, the sugar in the marshmallows and the adrenaline of the night hitting me all at once.

Hudson had won the first ATV race, and the friend group spent turns going back and forth for at least another hour, racing with laughter echoing in the night. I felt warm and fuzzy on the inside with the sounds still lingering in my ears. The happy realization that I got to be in those moments with these people was nothing short of a gift.

It was a gift, but one that felt like it was really a loan. The experience was like a trailer of a movie, seeing all the good snippets, getting reeled in, but never able to watch the whole film. I could only have this moment by sneaking around, by lying, by rebelling, and for some reason now, it *hurt*. It was like something had wedged underneath my ribcage. I wished that I could've had both —my parents' approval and these moments of rebellion and excitement. But that wasn't reality. It wouldn't ever be.

A moment to enjoy for now, but not forever.

Derrick's brakes cried out as he eased Betsy to the side of Willow Street, flipping off his headlights in the process. "Thank you for the ride," I told him, touching the shoulder of his seat. "And thank you guys for letting me hang out with you tonight."

I gave the passenger seat headrest one last glance, chest tingling. I climbed from the car, smiling at Simon, who had peacefully succumbed to sleep.

But I wasn't the only one who climbed out. Hudson pulled himself from the car, ducking his head in. "I'll walk her to her house and then come back."

"Oh, you don't have to—"

"It's almost midnight," he replied, shutting the door. Just like that, it was the two of us. "And it's not far. I don't mind."

We walked along the sidewalk, where the dim streetlights only illuminated a small sliver. They mostly covered the road, and with the trees lining the boulevards, light only streamed through in small splotches. With each step we took, our hands swung to and fro from each other. I could feel the miniscule breeze his created brush the back of my palm, hinting at how close we were to touching.

It was the electricity from the night, surely, that sparked the thought of me pushing my hand an inch closer to him. I could almost imagine it—reaching out and trailing my fingers along the backs of his. Would he jerk away? Would he weave our fingers together? Probably not.

But what if he did?

The idea freaked me out, but almost in a good way.

"You know, the next thing on my list is to pull an all-nighter," I told him in a bright voice, wrapping my arms around my waist. "We should do one tonight."

"Trust me, school is already going to be rough tomorrow staying up this late. You'll regret this in the morning."

"I won't." My voice came out strong. It was forceful enough that he looked down at me again, eyebrows raised. "I won't regret it."

Sometimes, when I looked into Hudson's eyes, it was like time sort of...slowed. It didn't stop, but it was enough of a hiccup that had my brain reeling. Because looking into his eyes left me feeling off-balanced in a way I'd never felt before, like my feet were slipping on uneven ground. It felt like he saw me, deeply, and vice versa, I wanted to see him.

Severing the connection, I continued walking.

Hudson followed me to the garden gate that I'd escaped through mere hours before, and we both took a moment to look at my dark house. All of the lights were off, and I breathed out a sigh of relief at the confirmation. If my parents noticed I was gone, every light would be on. There'd probably even be police cars in the driveway.

"You know what I'm surprised about?" he asked before we stepped into my yard, lingering in the shadows. The wind swept past us, stirring his hair. "You have this whole rebellion list, but there isn't a single relationship one on there. I would have at least expected 'have my first kiss' would be on there."

"I've already had my first kiss."

If I'd known Hudson's expression would be so comical, I would've tried to have taken a picture on my junky phone. His eyebrows flew up on his forehead, and his jaw even dropped. "You already had yours?"

I laughed quietly as I recalled it. "We were at a birthday party for Jaden's mom in the eighth grade and Morgan dared me to kiss him while no one was looking. Maybe that's why he's always around now."

"You should've broadcasted it, then. I doubt you'd have gotten your prude label if people knew."

True. I hadn't thought about that. I wondered if people would be as shocked as Hudson was if they found out. Something else occurred to me, though. "But, hey, I'm trying really hard not to be offended that you're so shocked. When was *your* first kiss?"

Hudson stared at the siding of my house, almost pointedly so.

"No way. *No way.* You haven't had your first kiss?" I gasped when he didn't deny it. "Hudson Bishop, I'm seriously convinced your entire life is a lie!"

He ducked his head, and a small smile curled over his lips, one that looked more uncomfortable than anything else. "I know, I know. I'm an embarrassment to bad boys everywhere."

My amusement sobered a little as I thought about why Hudson might not have had his first kiss. Ever since his freshman year, he'd been an outcast, someone that no one got to know. Even students from other schools knew of the illustrious Grim Reaper. Of course he wouldn't have had his first kiss. He hadn't had a chance.

Hudson suddenly leaned down to bring his face level with mine, close enough that I could see each of his individual lashes, even in the darkness. When he blinked, they brushed against the tops of his cheekbones, against the scar on his cheek. "I could have mine now," he said.

"Your what?"

"My first kiss."

I sucked in a breath at how casually he dropped the words, how calm his expression was. *I could have mine—* once I understood exactly what he meant, my heart stopped and then kicked into overdrive, spurred on by something teasing.

"Think about it, how much more rebellious can you get?" His voice dropped to a low murmur as he leaned in, eyes sparking. "Kissing the bad boy?"

A thrill darted down my spine, causing goosebumps to rise on my skin. Back on the sidewalk, when I'd thought about holding his hand—had he been thinking about it too? When I wiped the chocolate off his mouth— had he been thinking about kissing me then? With the way he was staring at me now, I couldn't tell. "You wouldn't kiss me."

Hudson leaned closer, body slipping deeper into my personal space. The scent of him was everywhere, dizzying me further. "You sure about that?"

I could see where his scar was cut into his cheek, a little divot of where the skin stitched itself together. Much like before, I wanted to reach out and trace my finger along the seam. "Yes."

His lips stretched into a half-smile, but it wasn't the usual mocking one I'd become accustomed to from him. It was much more boyish and slanted in a way that magnetized my eyes to them, noting how full his lower lip was, wondering what it'd feel like. "How about now?"

I was embarrassingly aware of how loud my breath was, and I could fight to play it cool all that I wanted, but nothing stopped my knees from shaking. *He wouldn't kiss me,* I thought unsteadily, unable to pull away. It was like the ice in his blue eyes froze me. *He wouldn't kiss me, he wouldn't kiss me.*

Hudson reached up and pressed the pad of his thumb to the corner of my mouth, exactly as I'd done earlier in the night. The second he touched me, my lips parted a sliver on their own accord, a tiny gasp escaping me at the whisper of contact. The suffocating tension of that moment resurfaced easily now, and my mind was already playing the scene out with startling clarity, imagining what it'd be like if he replaced his thumb with his mouth.

He wouldn't kiss me.

And then a new voice, as clear as day. *But you want him to.*

His fingers slid from my lips to curve against my throat. "Wow, feel that heartbeat. Nervous, Gemma?"

I held perfectly still, hyper-focused on his closeness, waiting for him to lean in.

"Now you know how I felt when you touched my mouth." Hudson trailed his fingers through the hair above my ear now, threading the locks in a way that made me shiver. "You're lucky the others were around then. I probably would've kissed you if they hadn't been."

"Not now?" I asked stupidly, the strange desire over-taking obvious rational thought. I'd made myself fully transparent with two simple words.

He tucked my hair over my shoulder, eyes following the movement before they slid up to mine. "Not now," he repeated, pulling away from me entirely. The wind tugged at his hair, trying to push it into his eyes, trying to push him back to me. "Now, it's time for you to go inside."

Hudson looked toward my house, which gave me a moment to snap my jaw shut and force the heat from my cheeks. My heart was decelerating into normal territory, but my thoughts were still spinning, still caught in my imagination. *Why not now?* I wanted to ask him, but I'd had enough embarrassing moments for one night. I didn't need him to explain the reasoning behind the rejection.

"How are you getting back in?" Hudson asked, resting his hand on the metal gate.

"See that window right there? The one that's cracked? I'm going in through that."

"Are you going to jump the five feet to get to the sill, then?"

His words came like a pin to a balloon, popping it and releasing the shock. My stomach flipped as I spotted the fatal flaw in my plan much too late.

The way Hudson laughed cut into my momentary lapse in judgement, and then, so effortlessly, he did exactly what I'd been imagining the entire walk home. He reached down and plucked my hand up from my side, the coolness of his fingers enveloping the heat of mine, and he drew me through the gate. "C'mon, I'll be your stepladder."

Having Hudson Bishop this close to my house was bound to give me a panic attack, but I let him escort me to the window anyway, if only to memorize how his fingers felt against mine. His were very fine, much thinner than mine, but they weren't delicate. His knuckles were a bit knobby, but I liked them. I liked everything about his hands.

Which made it hard when he let go to link his fingers together, gesturing me to step into them. "I'll hoist you up."

I raised an eyebrow at him. "I'm wearing a skirt."

Hudson tipped his head at me. "I'm not going to look, Gem."

Without a word, I stuck my pinky out to him, narrowing my eyes.

Hudson unlinked his fingers to wrap his littlest finger

around mine, giving it a squeeze. But then he didn't let go, and neither did I, and we stared at each other with our fingers entwined. We were back to the moment from minutes ago, teetering on the edge of *something*.

"This weekend," Hudson said softly. "This weekend, we could pull the all-nighter. If you wanted."

I tried hard not to react, either in excitement or terror. "Are you sure *you* won't regret it?"

Hudson took a step closer to me, huddling deeper in the shadows that the house provided from the moonlight. He was close enough that I could hear the air tug between his teeth as he smiled. "Trust me," he said, his pinky still around mine. "I'm having more fun with you than I've had in a while."

A stupid grin crossed my face, and I lifted my shoulder, leaning my head toward it. "So, you're happy that you agreed to our friendship?"

"More like I was forced into our friendship, since *someone* wouldn't leave me alone, but yeah." He glanced down at our hands, something splitting across his gaze. "I am happy."

Was this...flirting? The back and forth, the way we spoke, the way he'd touched me moments ago... The realization came in a swift stab to my stomach. It *was*. I was flirting with Hudson Bishop, and Hudson Bishop was flirting *back*.

A startled laugh burst from me, one that had his eyes widening. I dropped his pinky, and he linked his own fingers together again, crouching once more. "Keep your promise," I whispered, and he squeezed his eyes shut. His lashes fanned across his cheekbones like little wisps, and I imagined brushing my fingertip across them, wondering how they'd feel.

Instead of acting on my weird thoughts, I put my sneaker into his hands and grabbed ahold of his shoulders to steady myself. The denim of his jacket was cool, but his shoulders were firm, reassuring. "Thank you," I whispered. "For tonight. For letting me have fun with you."

His expression softened, despite his eyes remaining shut, warming the cold night. "Thank *you*."

There was no struggle as Hudson lifted me up to the window, and though my awkward crawl inside might not have been that graceful—but thankfully not noisy—I couldn't help but grin as I looked down at him, feeling a bit like Juliet looking down at Romeo. He had his eyes shut still until I spoke. "Goodnight, Hudson."

"Goodnight, Gem," he whispered back, lifting his hand in a small wave. He couldn't linger—he couldn't risk getting caught by my parents or a nosy neighbor—but I found myself wishing that he could've. That I could've leaned out this window all night talking to him. Just listening to his voice.

But he turned around and crossed the lawn quickly, hesitating at the gate. He was too far for me to make out his expression, but my heart squeezed anyway as I gave another last wave.

I wasn't the sort of person who kept a diary, but for the first time, I wished that I did. I wanted nothing more than to record this night and keep it forever, to take it out once in a while and relive it all over again. Instead, I recorded the night in my heart as I padded to my bedroom, easing the door open with what had to be a euphoric smile on my face.

I'd shut it behind me before I noticed I wasn't alone. A figure sat on the floor beside my bed, leaning against the mattress. "Well, well," he said, sighing. "This is a surprise, isn't it?"

Landon.

CHAPTER 19

My brain, rapid-fire, took in the details of my room as if desperate to find myself a way out. Landon sat on the floor beside my bed with his legs stretched before him, still in his jeans. He had his sneakers on, tightly laced. Even though he was slouched, he seemed wide awake, as if, like me, he hadn't gone to bed early like Mom said.

His words *well, well* rang like alarm bells in my ears. There truly was no escape.

"I'll admit," Landon began in a soft voice, holding my gaze. "I feel very much like a parent in an after-school special right now, but be glad it's me that found out you were gone and not Mom."

"What—what are you doing in here?" I whispered, gripping the edge of my skirt so tightly that my knuckles had to be white.

"What am I doing?" Landon pushed himself up from the floor and rose to his full height, which towered over me. He seemed too large in the space, but his whispering took the edge off. "What are *you* doing? And what are you wearing? God, you *reek*, Gemma. Is that smoke?"

Confrontation made my mouth dry, especially when there was nothing *to* say. Not when the answers to his questions would bury me six feet under. My heart slammed in my chest as if desperate to escape the situation.

Landon suddenly let out a sharp breath, pressing a hand over his eyes as he leaned back. "Hang on, hang on. I sound like Mom and Dad. I don't want to." His hand slipped from his eyes to rest on the side of his neck, squeezing a little. "I won't tell them, Gemma. But...you should tell me where you were."

"I was out with friends."

"*Friends?*" It was as if the concept was foreign to him. "Who? Morgan?"

If I said yes, Landon would surely ask her tomorrow at school, and the Landon-lover that she was, no way would she lie to him. "No."

"Jaden?"

"No! Of course not."

He looked down at his tied shoes, turning his foot onto the side. The longer he stared at them, the stranger their appearance was to me.

Not a lie, but only a half-truth. I thought of Tee. "They go to Jefferson."

It was clear he was unsatisfied with the answer, the way he stared at me to continue, but my pulse was so loud that I could barely think. I didn't trust myself to say anything else, to dig myself deeper into the grave I'd already dug.

What if I had told Landon the truth? *I snuck out with Hudson Bishop to go to a bonfire.* He surely would've gone back on his promise. He would've stormed from the room to wake Mom and Dad, and then that would be the end of that. Goodbye rebellion list, goodbye public school, and goodbye Hudson Bishop.

"I thought we agreed not to listen to the Most Likely Tos," Landon said eventually. "That you wouldn't get all rebellious because of it."

"What about you?" I fired back at him, voice rising in pitch. "Did you go out and get a girlfriend because of the list? Is that why you're dating *Lacey?*"

Landon closed his eyes, wallowing in his annoyance. "Did you look at Babble?"

"Landon, even *Mom* asked me if you'd gotten a girl-friend. If you're trying to keep it a secret, you're doing a pretty sucky job of it."

"I'm not," he said, but he wouldn't look at me. "It's not a secret."

"Then why didn't you tell me?"

It wasn't like Landon and I were particularly close, but I had thought we were on the same page about this stuff. A sort of comradery. Sure, we never really talked about our love lives, but I would've thought he'd tell me if he actually got a girlfriend.

Then again, it wasn't like he was the only one who held a dirty little secret.

"I'm happy for you, you know," I said when his

cloudy expression didn't clear. "I mean, if it's for the right reasons, that is. You deserve to be happy, and if someone makes you happy, that's great. But you should introduce her to Mom and Dad."

A bitter smile twisted at his lips, and he ducked his head as if to hide it. "Maybe one day. You know how they can be."

"She's not like Madison?"

"Not even close." He laughed, but it was a tired sound. "I'm not dating her because of the list, Gemma."

"And the Most Likely Tos aren't why I snuck out." It was my own rebellion list. I lifted my chin, forcing myself to hold his gaze with as much confidence as possible. "My friends were having a bonfire, and I wanted to go."

Landon's face scrunched. "You had to *sneak out*, though, Gemma. On a school night. That's not you at all."

I wanted to tell him that it was obviously me, that I did those things. Gemma Settler was the one who opened the bathroom window, who ran down the street. The weird thing was that it *felt* like me doing those things. Sure, it was definitely out of the character our parents cultivated, but it wasn't as if I felt like a whole other person. If anything, I felt more me than I ever had.

Landon must've sensed that the conversation was going nowhere, because he sighed again. "Leave your clothes outside your door and I'll put them in my laundry. Mom won't suspect if it's my clothes that smell."

I squeezed the edges of my skirt tighter, still too frozen to move as he walked past me. As he did, I could've sworn he smelled strangely himself. Not like bonfire smoke, but something still easy to place —*perfume*. I wanted to ask him why he smelled like that —why he was still in his day clothes, as if *he* snuck out, too—but I didn't think he'd tell me.

"Be careful," Landon said once he made it to my door, lingering with his hand on the knob. He gestured at me, at the loose hair that hung around me. "Nothing good will come of this if Mom finds out, Gemma. And I'm sure you know it."

What am I supposed to do, then? I wanted to demand. *Sit back and obey? Be the doll that they want me to be?*

I didn't say that though, because as quickly as the thought came, it vanished as soon as Landon opened my bedroom door. The hallway light spilled inside for a split second before Landon slipped through the crack, leaving me and my thoughts alone.

For a moment, I stood in the middle of my bedroom, basking in the blueish glow from the moonlight, processing. I combed my fingers into my hair, wincing at the knots that had formed from tearing in the wind of the ATV ride.

If I had to be caught, I was glad it was by Landon, but the seed of doubt had started to sprout, spreading vines throughout my body. But the question was whether or not I'd heed his warning. *Nothing good will come of this if Mom finds out, Gemma. And I'm sure you know it.*

Hudson had been right. School *was* rough running on five and a half hours of sleep, and when I was finally done with the school day, certain that everything that I learned all day, I'd absorbed none of it.

I followed Morgan to her locker first, shuffling into the crowd of people. "Are you feeling any better?" she asked as she grabbed her lock, giving it a twist.

I groaned by way of an answer, rubbing my eyes, wishing the fuzziness would go away.

"How's everything been with the Settlers, anyway? The leash still tight?"

I quirked my lips to the side, thinking about what I'd gotten away with last night. In that regard, the leash *so* wasn't tight, but then again, did it really count since they didn't know about it? "Mom's not picking out my school outfits anymore."

"I wondered." Morgan appraised my appearance. I still wore a long skirt today since my closet was limited, but I'd taken Rosie's advice and gone for a shirt that was a little tighter, and even tied it into a knot at my waist. "You're starting to dress with a *smidge* more style. I'm proud of you."

Her backhanded compliment made me roll my eyes. "Thanks."

"How about the whole mentor thing? Are they seriously still cool with that?"

"You know..." I drew my lower lip into my mouth as the words danced in my head, unsure whether or not I should say them. "Hudson. He's not as bad as people say he is."

I wanted her to believe me. I wanted her to be on my side, not the side of gossip. I wanted her to trust my judgement, to listen as I unpacked all the craziness that'd happened over the past few weeks. I wanted her to be one of the ones who knew the truth about Hudson. I wasn't sure *why* I wanted her to believe me, but I was almost desperate with it.

Morgan's eyes narrowed on me. "What do you mean?"

"He's nice." The words came out lame, almost like I was embarrassed to be giving him compliments, but I forced myself to go on. "He's not like all the rumors that go around."

"I kind of figured, since you haven't gone running for the hills yet." But her expression was uneasy, and even though her eyebrows were hidden by her bangs, I knew they were drawn together. "But...don't tell me he's brainwashed you or *compelled* you or whatever vampires do."

"Morgan, he's *not* a vampire—"

"I think it's important to remember the obvious about him." She fully turned away from her locker. "He may have nice moments, Gemma, but don't forget why he's called the Grim Reaper in the first place."

I glanced around the hallway, grateful that even though there were a few students still collecting their things, Jaden wasn't around. "We don't know what happened in the fight with my brother."

"We know that he split Landon's lip and nearly broke Ashton's arm."

I hadn't heard that about Ashton, but I still shook my head. "That was three years ago, Morgan—"

Before I had a chance to say anything, Morgan went on. "I'm just saying, you can't forget that, okay? I get it, though. You've never made decisions on your own, so you don't see how naïve you're being."

The condescension dripping from her words was unsettling for a second, and I stared at her almost like I was looking at a stranger. "You're mad when I listen to my parents, you're mad when I make decisions for myself." My hands shook as I drew in a breath, fingers curling into fists. "What, should I let *you* make my decisions for me?"

She threw her hands up. "If trusting the Grim Reaper is one of your decisions, then maybe!"

I gave her the darkest look that I could. "Stop calling him that."

Morgan shook her head in a way that hinted she was fed up with the conversation, even though I was still boiling on the inside. "You're already starting to *glare* like him, you realize that?"

Squaring my jaw, I walked past her toward the S section of the sophomore lockers. I was fed up too.

Of course, though, she picked up her pace to join me at my side. "I'm worried about you—"

"Why? Because I'm not acting like my normal, prudish self just because I'm spending time with a boy?"

"It isn't the fact that he's a boy," she insisted. "It's *who* he is."

Almost as if our conversation summoned him, I

spotted Hudson farther down the hallway. He stood beside the vending machine with all the good snacks, rummaging around in his backpack as if he was looking for something. My steps faltered at the sight of him, and I forced myself not to recall the night before. At least I tried.

You're lucky the others were around then. I probably would've kissed you if they hadn't been.

Even now, I could practically feel his thumb against my lips.

And then I faltered for another reason. A girl stood beside him, with blonde hair and brown roots, her heeled booties bringing her to his height. She leaned up to him, red lips pulling into a grin like they were sharing a secret. I didn't recognize her, but I was instantly curious who she might've been. Someone who was brave enough to enter the personal space of the Grim Reaper. Was this the girl he was waiting for during lunch the other day?

She also looked weirdly familiar, but I couldn't place the face.

Morgan's gaze found where mine had settled, and she narrowed her eyes on Hudson. "Speak of the devil."

I stepped up to my locker and focused on the combination. "Let's change the subject."

"But I'm not finished."

"I am." I yanked on my lock, unable to fight my groan of frustration this time when it didn't open.

"Look who it is," a new voice drawled, instantly raising goosebumps. "It's the Settler sister."

When I turned around, I found the two seniors who'd

picked on Morgan and me last time, plus another new girl. I didn't know either of the girls' names. Wes looked as massive as he had that day, with biceps that had to be as big around as my head.

Wes smiled broadly, stopping directly in front of me. "You know," he went on, gaze sliding to me. "I thought after our first greeting in the hall, you'd have stuck your brother on me. At the very least, would've tattled to Principal Ollie-pop."

"You don't mean that much," I told him with a strange buzzing in my ears. My leftover anger with Morgan fueled my boldness now, because Wes was the last thing I wanted to deal with. Aside from that, something about the situation felt different than last time, but I couldn't place what it was. "Not enough to waste my breath on."

Morgan's eyes bugged wide, no doubt thinking I was crazy.

Wes snorted a little, turning to the girls. "I'm not, huh? Then what made Bishop step in that day?"

Instinctively, I glanced at the vending machines to find Hudson and the red-lipped girl staring at our group with intense eyes. He looked to me, and I gave my head the smallest of shakes. Him coming over here might've saved us last time Wes and his bundle chose to pick a fight, but now, for some reason, it felt like adding fuel to a fire.

"He acts like he's so much better than everyone else. Better than us. So what made the Grim Reaper so intrigued by *you*?" He reached out and nudged my shoulder with a shove that was a little too hard to be friendly, but not rough enough to make me knock back a step. "Virgin sacrifice, maybe?"

That was when the blood, which sang furiously in my veins, burned hotter underneath my skin. I curled my hands into fists. "Leave us alone."

"Or maybe," he went on as if I didn't speak, "it's revenge. For what your brother did to him freshman year. Now, *that's* a movie I'd watch."

I thought I heard him wrong. I heard "brother" and "freshman year," and my brain filled in the gaps neatly. Landon's swollen eye. His split lip. Landon, sobbing at the kitchen counter. But then my world hiccupped, the *real* meaning of his words sinking in. "What *my brother* did?"

But again, it was like I didn't speak. Maybe I hadn't. Maybe my whirling thoughts only sounded so loud in my head.

"But if Bishop is interested in you, then there must be something I'm not seeing." His eyes raked up and down my frame, taking in every inch of me like I was on display for him. "I've been thinking about that day a lot since then. How you and I have unfinished business." He reached down and slid his hand over my hand, and I jerked away from the icky caress. "I think I'm going to follow through on my promise last time. Let's see if we can fit you into that locker, huh?"

Wes wrapped his meaty hand around my shoulder, and it was almost alarming how large it was. We'd been in a stance much like this before, him threatening the exact same thing. Before, I'd followed my old adage. Keep my head down, keep my mouth shut.

Sometimes it's better not to fight back, I'd told Hudson back then, when he'd stepped in the first time. *Better to turn the other cheek.*

His response rang in my ear now, a voiceover to the sight of Jaden's head bouncing against the lockers and Morgan flinching from the girls. *Remember what I said about a backbone?*

Staring into Wes's ugly eyes, I did what I wanted to do last time.

I brought my knee up, slamming it between his legs.

Wes went down with a screech of pain, like a building toppling over, and that was when all hell broke loose.

Morgan pressed both of her hands to her mouth as she gasped, which made her an easy target for the girls to grab. They latched onto Morgan's backpack strap and jerked it, causing her to lose her footing. She cried out when she hit the ground, rolling away from one of the girls' boots as they kicked out.

Wes climbed to his feet much quicker than I thought he would've and latched onto me before I had a chance to react. Both of his hands closed over my upper arms this time, and with as much force as he could, he pushed me into the lockers, hard enough for my head to knock against the metal with a painful, metallic *thud.*

And then suddenly his hands were ripped from me, before he had a chance to fold me into an origami pancake—or see if I actually could've fit inside a locker.

Hudson appeared without a sound, but he moved almost faster than my eyes could keep track of. He grabbed Wes's wrist and twisted the jerk's arm behind his back, shoving him face-first into the metal doors beside me.

Hudson didn't even look like he struggled. "Picking on girls again, Wes?" he demanded, voice a lazy, bored drawl. "Come on."

Wes tried to shove against Hudson, but Hudson only twisted his wrist further, causing the guy to wilt against the locker in pain. "Let go."

The girls who'd been kicking Morgan halted for a second in their assault. "Stay out of this, Hudson," one of them said.

Hudson looked down at Morgan before cutting his gaze to me. "Looks like I'm already in it."

The girl who'd been standing with Hudson near the vending machines chose then to saunter over as well, her heeled boots clicking against the linoleum. She slung her arm over the mean girl's shoulders, squeezing. Her dark gaze found mine, and for a moment, I thought she was going to join in on Wes's side. "Why don't you guys pick on someone your own size?"

Wes glanced over. "You offering, Churchill?"

"You couldn't handle me," she retorted, barely even batting an eye. "But next time, if you want to sound tough, don't say it while someone has you pinned against a locker."

Showcasing his muscle, Wes burst free from Hudson's hold and staggered away from the metal doors. Hudson moved to position himself between Wes and me, his back close enough to me that my nose nearly grazed his T-shirt. I held my breath until my lungs began to ache, but the tension was too hard to breathe around.

Wes glanced at his friends, letting them bolster him. "Either join in or get out. Otherwise, this doesn't involve you."

"I know you're missing a few brain cells, but I'll try to be clearer." Hudson stepped into Wes's personal space. Though Wes was way more muscular, Hudson easily had four inches on him, looming like an imposing figure. Like the Grim Reaper. "You touch her, and you deal with me."

I went from focusing on Wes to staring at Hudson's head, lips parting. Everyone in the circle turned to look at the little sophomore hiding over Hudson's shoulder, but I couldn't look away. His blond hair fell over the collar of his black jacket, his shoulders straight without a hint of bending. The declaration made me freeze, and the low, threatening way he'd said it, but there was no ignoring the tingle that bloomed in my chest.

"Now, you tell me," Hudson went on, tilting his head once more. "Is it worth it?"

The red-lipped girl shoved past the two Wes minions and offered a hand down to Morgan, who took it with a heavy dose of hesitation. Once she got Morgan to her feet, she dusted her hand down Morgan's bag, swiping away the grit from the ground.

"You know what I don't really get?" Wes asked with a slow drawl, raising his eyebrows. There was something skin-crawling about the way he did it, totally unlike how Hudson looked with that expression. "Why you're over here. You hate underclassmen as much as any other senior. In fact, you hate *everyone*. So, what's different about sister Settler?"

"This little reason called none of your business."

It was the same line he'd given me once upon a time, and I would've smiled if the atmosphere of the hallway wasn't so icy. By then, other students had begun to gather around the fringe of the lockers, waiting to see what would happen next.

"I'm trying to figure out why a freak like you is hanging around a girl like her." Wes lifted his hands level with his shoulders. "Why risk pissing off that family *again*? You really want to get expelled this time?"

Hudson still didn't react. "And I'm just trying to figure out why you're still standing here, Wes."

"Maybe she wants a taste of the wild side, huh?" Wes leaned in closer to Hudson, but his gaze slid back to me, raking up from my shoes. "And you want to give it to her? You trying to get up that long skirt of hers, is that it? I don't blame you. Girls like her are fun to screw around with, aren't they?"

The tension Hudson had kept tightly wound snapped. Hudson grabbed Wes's collar with his left hand and pulled back his right, but before he could land the punch, two things happened. I grabbed ahold of his elbow with a death grip, squeezing hard enough to no doubt bruise his skin. And then, almost like she'd been expecting it too, the red-lipped girl stepped between Wes and Hudson, pressing a hand on each of their chests.

Wes, all the while, simply grinned.

"Don't," I whispered to Hudson, coming close enough to press my chest against his back. It was much how we'd been last night on the ATV, except the mood of everything had shifted. My heart didn't flutter now; it thrashed about like a butterfly trapped in a jar.

I tightened my grip on his arm, staring at the fist that seemed to take forever to loosen. I knew what would happen if it didn't. That thin ice Principal Oliphant said he stood on would shatter.

The red-lipped girl pried Hudson's fingers off of Wes's collar and shoved Wes back a step. He stumbled over his shoes, slamming into one of his friends. "Now, *you* tell *me*, Bishop," Wes said as he straightened, raising a challenging eyebrow. "When her parents find out, will *she* be worth it?"

Hudson lowered his arm, which I still hadn't let go of, and I could feel the muscles loosen beneath my fingers.

With his last line uttered, Wes stalked away without a backward glance, triumphant expression on his face, leaving his minions to follow.

For a moment, no one moved. Morgan's face was pale, staring at Hudson as if *he* was the one who'd started everything. The wariness was as clear as day. I could hear a flutter of phone cameras, no doubt catching in full glory how I held the Grim Reaper.

I took a step back, letting my hands fall to my sides. I could still feel Hudson's muscles like a lingering ghost touch, my desperation making my knuckles tingle.

"Well, that was dramatic," the girl muttered, reaching up to tear her fingers through her hair. Then she glared at

Hudson. "You're an idiot, you know that? Are you *trying* to get expelled?"

I opened my mouth, but my voice still didn't want to work. Hudson turned around to face me, his eyes dragging up and down in a way that was drastically different from Wes's slimy gaze. The tension in his eyes was impossible to miss, as was the tightness around his mouth. "Are you okay?"

My head ached from where it'd ricocheted off the lockers, and my upper arms still throbbed from where Wes grabbed, but I nodded. "Perfectly fine."

He turned to where Morgan and the red-lipped girl stood next. The girl had wrapped her arm around Morgan's waist, a supportive touch. "How about you, Morgan?"

Morgan blinked at the use of her name, her pale cheeks all at once filling with color. She pressed her hand against her side, and even from where I stood, I could see it shake. "What's a bruised rib or two?" she teased, but her voice still shook.

"You should go to tell Principal Oliphant," Hudson went on, clenching his hand into a fist and then releasing it. He looked at me. "Report what happened."

"But maybe leave Hudson's name out of it," the girl interjected, glancing between all of us. "He's on thin ice."

So the red-lipped girl knew about the thin ice, too? For some reason, that made my throat ache, like I couldn't swallow properly. Hudson passed her a look that I couldn't read, but as he shifted his attention, his focus caught on the students still surveying the scene.

The group of people who'd gathered was small, and only three of them had their phones out. Hudson seemed to look every single one of them in the eye, and before they had time to scatter, he took a step toward them. "Delete whatever videos and photos you have," he ordered in a voice so drastically different than the concerned one he'd used a second ago, and the under-classmen reacted to it as he wanted. "Or I'll personally make your life a living hell. Trust me, I've got a good memory." He walked up to a boy and grabbed his back-pack from where it hung off his hip, peering at the black canvas. "An *L4D* sticker, huh? Unique. You play?"

The intimidation worked wonders. Those who still had their phones out scrambled to open their photo apps and delete what was necessary, and those who'd already tucked their cells away pulled them back out to do the same. And then they all bolted, fleeing like mice set free from a cage.

When Hudson turned to us, the hallway was empty. "Well," he said, dusting his hand down his jacket sleeve. "I'd say that was effective."

Morgan moved over to me and away from the red-lipped girl. "He's right," she said to me. "We should tell Principal Oliphant. We should've told her the first time."

I agreed, even though Principal Oliphant would have to tell Mom. Despite wanting to keep all of this a secret for my sake, it wasn't fair to Morgan. I nodded at her, taking her backpack from her. "Thank you," I told both Hudson and the red-lipped girl, and even though I knew

I should've asked for her name, I couldn't bring myself to do so.

"Keep up the good leg work," she said with an appreciative smile, popping her knee.

Despite burning with curiosity over how she knew Hudson, a returning smile naturally sprung to my lips.

"Fine, I'll admit," Morgan said as we walked away from them and made our way to the office, rubbing her ribs. "He *is* kind of hot. Did you see the way he pried Wes off you? Like...*whoa*."

A startled laugh burst out of me, and I drew my lower lip between my teeth to fight a stupid grin. I glanced over my shoulder, stealing one last look of the blond boy as we both walked in opposite directions. Almost like he sensed it, he looked around and met my gaze, and suddenly it wasn't the Grim Reaper looking but Bridge Boy staring back, his open expression and half-smile on his lips. Whoa, indeed.

CHAPTER 20

One of the requirements in the Settler household was that everyone had to be present and accounted for at football games. No ifs, ands, or buts about it—if you weren't on the field, your butt was on a bleacher. The same held true for other seasons, of course. Since Landon played almost every sport Brentwood had to offer, a Friday night never went by without the Settlers at some sort of game.

And tonight was no exception.

The game went by with a little more resistance than last week's, the Ravens fighting as hard as they could against the Bobcats. In the end, though, it didn't amount to much—we still had a good lead. It didn't stop Mom and Dad from their usual scolding. Every time Landon made a bad pass or leaned too far into his throw, they were on him, relentless. I was just thankful they weren't yelling at any other players yet.

I was also thankful I'd never really gotten into sports, and that they never pushed them on me. I couldn't really imagine being in Landon's shoes, knowing that they were always looking at him with their judging eyes.

Jaden sat on the other side of me, elbows on his knees. "Whenever I watch football, I realize how happy I am that I don't play," he said, reaching up to rub his head. "I'd be snapped like a twig by the size of some of those guys."

"You're perfect for basketball, Jaden," Mom insisted, glancing over with a smile. "It's exciting that you'll be on the varsity team with Landon."

"Definitely an honor."

I fought the urge to groan.

When I focused on the field, Landon was in position for the beginning of the play, time suspended for a moment as every player leaned forward. His royal blue jersey—number 10—was smeared with grass stains that Mom would have me fight to get out later.

Landon called the play, and everyone moved into action. I watched him pull back with the ball and search for an opening, standing on the balls of his feet. A Raven had slid between the defenses, slamming into Landon's midsection with a clashing sound I could hear from here, like two boulders colliding.

"Come on, Landon!" Mom shouted, surprise springing her to her feet. Dad managed to ease her into her seat, but it began the cycle once again, berating Landon for not making the pass, for not paying more attention, for not running when he had the chance.

"He's got such a bad habit of hanging onto the ball too long," Mom said now, going back to that conversation.

"He spends too much time thinking about a decision before he makes it. This is football, not cricket."

"He needs to be careful, too," Dad added, frowning. "One bad tackle, and the team's in a world of hurt. He can't get injured, not a week before homecoming."

Sometimes I was surprised Mom didn't record the plays for them to review after the fact, like Nathan Tulane's mom did. But it was also something that required no effort from me. There'd been game nights that'd gone by where I never even spoke a word. I was there for looks, to keep up appearances, not for actual conversation.

Mom reached over and pressed her palm against my skirt. I wore a heavy corduroy one tonight, and even with my jacket zipped up, I still shivered. "You okay?"

"Hmm?" I straightened from my slouched posture, blinking at the field. "Oh. Yeah."

Mom wasn't easily brushed off, eyeing me. "You know, you've been much quieter lately."

Dad didn't turn his head, but he did lean sideways a little to make it known he was talking to us. "Is it about yesterday?"

Immediately, I stiffened. After telling Principal Oliphant what happened, I'd been right—she *had* called my mom and Mrs. Davies. When recounting the story, Morgan completely left Hudson out of it, so I followed her lead.

Hudson *and* that girl. *Churchill.* I assumed it was a last name, but I didn't recognize it.

"I still can't believe kids like that go to Brentwood,"

Mom muttered in a way that was clear she wasn't trying to keep her voice down.

"It's a public school, Mom. Anyone can go here."

"But it's a *good* public school." She scrunched her nose. "It's not like Chesterville or Jefferson."

A parent from behind us leaned forward and pressed her hand on Mom's shoulder. I couldn't tell for sure, but I thought it was one of the cheerleaders' moms. "I completely agree with you, Naomi. Kids like that who bully and cause trouble don't belong with kids who are actually there to learn."

A man who sat beside her folded his arms with a huff. "I still can't believe you didn't expel that Bishop kid when he picked a fight all those years ago. Cut your boy's face up and everything. You should've pressed charges."

Mom only hummed at that, no longer interested in the conversation. She made a show of shaking her coffee tumbler, focusing on the field.

I fisted my hands together in my lap, wishing everyone would mind their own business. But what that man said did spark something in my mind, and Wes's words rang like a warning bell in my ear. *Maybe it's revenge for what your brother did to him freshman year.*

Even now, it didn't make sense. Landon was the one with the bruised face—why would *Hudson* need revenge?

Dad let out a grumbled sigh then, tuning back in to the game as well. "Oh, come on! Let's be faster on our feet, Bobcats!"

Even though everyone's attention was successfully reeled back in by the game, the conversation left a bad taste in my mouth. *Maybe they're not all bad kids*, I wanted to argue, and had to bite down on my tongue to stop myself. *Maybe you're not giving them enough chances.*

I would've gotten weird looks for sure.

"I can't believe it's a week before homecoming," Jaden said, picking up the topic mentioned by Dad. "Have you, uh... Well, have you gotten a dress yet?"

From the corner of my eye, I could see Mom swivel a little more toward us, and I could see Jaden lean in. I refused to fully look at either of them. "Yeah, I have."

"What color is it?"

I squeezed my mittens in my lap. "Why?"

Mom reached over and patted my knee. "Gemma."

I fought an inward groan, finally looking at Jaden. The tips of his cheeks were pink. "It's burgundy."

Once more, Landon called the play, and the Bobcats shot forward into their designated spots. I watched as Connor pushed into the formation of the Ravens' defense, lingering near the thirty-yard line with his hands up. Landon drew his arm back to throw the ball, but before it could leave his hand, a Raven broke through the offensive line and slammed into Landon's midsection, taking him down. "I think I have burgundy ties."

The collective groan from the Bobcats' bleachers was nearly drowned out by my parents' reactions. "Come on, Landon!" Mom shouted, more angry than encouraging.

Dad grumbled along with her. "Our blockers need to be doing a better job, too. Come on, Bobcats, let's go!"

For me, it was hard to breathe until Landon managed

to get to his feet, and I watched him shake his hand as if he landed on it wrong. It seemed that we each had our own things to worry about: Mom worried about how Landon performed, Dad worried about how the team performed, and I worried about whether or not Landon got injured.

"So, any plans after the game?" Jaden asked, rubbing his palms over his knees. "I'm probably going to go home and sleep. It's felt like the longest week ever, hasn't it?"

"Same here," I replied, thinking of everything that'd happened in the past week. Monday, I'd gone to Hudson's house and nearly got hit by a car. Wednesday night, I went to the bonfire at Tee's house, running my thumb across Hudson's mouth. Yesterday, I nearly got shoved in a locker. And tonight...tonight my plans didn't even seem real. "Such a long week."

The clock ticked down slowly, and despite the Bobcats not making it to the final touchdown, the game ended with Brentwood winning by fourteen, securing the hope for a no-loss season. Mom and Dad packed up their portable folding bleacher seats, talking with the other parents as they did so.

Jaden lingered at my side, leaning closer. "You know," he whispered, his voice nearly taken out by the post-game chatter. "Morgan told me what happened yesterday. About Hudson."

I stiffened, glancing over, but my parents were both absorbed in conversation. "Jaden, *shh*."

"Sorry, sorry." He held his hands up innocently. He hunched his shoulders, ducking his ears closer to his collar. "I was just going to say…it sounds like you were right. About not judging someone if you don't know them."

I stared at Jaden for a long moment because his words were exactly the ones I'd wanted to hear from *someone*. Yesterday, I'd been wanting Morgan to agree with me so badly, wanted *somebody* to agree, and even though Jaden didn't know the whole depth to Hudson, he agreed. The relief I felt was strange, mostly because I couldn't figure out *why* I was relieved. Because someone else had faith in Hudson? Because someone believed me?

Because I had an opinion and someone didn't brush it off?

Whatever it was, it had the tension in my shoulders seeping away as I looked at Jaden.

"Jaden," Mom said as she turned toward us. She put her hand on my shoulder, fingers curling in. That should've been my sign that I wouldn't like what she said next, but I was still too caught up in Jaden agreeing with me. "Since we brought up homecoming earlier, it has me curious. Do you have a date to the homecoming dance yet?" She gave a laugh that was much louder than it needed to be, drawing the attention of some people. "I got to thinking, and I wondered if you hadn't asked Gemma yet because of our 'no dating' rule. But you do know you've got *special permission*, right?"

"Mom!" I whirled on her with a horror that I was sure lit up my entire face, but she wasn't looking at me. She was too busy ogling the boy over my shoulder. "Oh my gosh, leave him—"

"I *did* wonder how you'd react if I asked Gemma." Jaden's smile was stiff, going from his nonchalant self to nervous in a nanosecond, and his eyes bounced between my parents quickly. "I figured...well, I figured I wouldn't ask, but just go with her in a group."

"Going in a group isn't as fun." Mom waved her hand flippantly, scaring the idea away. "We, well—we already bought a tie last weekend that would match Gemma's dress perfectly. It's got your name on it."

I grabbed her arm and dug my fingers into her coat sleeve, startling her enough that her gaze locked onto mine. "*Stop*," I begged.

The drunk excitement flashed like a light flickering, letting darkness creep in for a split second. Even though it was a blip of blackness in Mom's eyes, my stomach flipped at the sight of it. I dropped her arm like it burned, ducking my head like I was going to be scolded then and there. Of course, I wouldn't be. Not in front of so many prying eyes.

"I'd love to take her to the dance," Jaden said then, sealing my fate for me. It was like I was inside of a box, hearing voices outside of it, unable to engage in discussion with them. *Keep your head down,* my old mantra echoed, creeping in. *And keep your mouth shut.*

And in my silence, my date was finalized.

We came down off the bleachers, and Jaden said goodnight before Mom turned on me.

"Now, Gemma," she began in an eerie tone, one I'd never heard her use before. "Care to explain why *you* were reprimanding *me* back there?"

I curled my fingers into a tight fist, the pressure in my knuckles building as my skin pulled taut. I focused on that sensation, trying *not* to notice how my stomach cramped up with something like dread. "I didn't mean to."

"Didn't mean to," she echoed, looking off in a different direction. "I would say you grabbing my arm was pretty intentional."

Dad smoothed a hand down her back. "Let's save this for later, Naomi."

"Maybe she needs the embarrassment of being scolded by her mother in front of all her classmates," Mom snapped back, folding her arms over her chest. "Tell me, Gemma. *Was* that accidental?"

"I just wanted you to stop," I murmured, glaring down at the grass. "I didn't mean to be disrespectful. Please...please don't be mad."

"Stop what?"

"Prying." The word slipped free like a breeze slipping through an open door, and I cringed at the coldness of it, quickly locking down. "I mean, I was just embarrassed. My mom getting me a date for homecoming. In front of everyone."

Mom reached out, and for some reason, I flinched like I expected her to hit me. Instead, she reached around and brought my braid over my shoulder, brushing it against my neck. The touch was gentle, contrasting with her attitude from a second ago. "You heard him. He wouldn't have asked you if I hadn't intervened."

Tell her that you didn't ask her to, my thoughts rooted,

encouraging the door to open up. *Tell her that you didn't want her to. Tell her! Stand up for yourself! Grow a backbone!*

But I physically couldn't. The anger from a moment ago had been enough of a gut punch that I couldn't imagine saying one more word that could've evoked more. And besides, it wasn't a battle I should pick tonight. There was a line I shouldn't cross.

I lifted my chin and faced my mother. "You're right," I said with a soft breath out my nose, swallowing the words and the sick feeling that stirred in my chest. "And it's a mom's job to embarrass their kid sometimes, right?"

It was the perfect thing to say. The creases by her brow smoothed over almost instantly, and Mom rubbed my shoulder with affection now, pleased by the submission she'd backed her daughter into. "Right."

We waited for Landon's coach to finish their post-game huddle, like we always did. With his shoulder pads hanging from his fingers, he stood a few feet away from us, trying to keep his football stench as far as possible. He listened as Mom and Dad advised him of plays he could've performed better, following their routine, and he nodded along obediently.

Once we got to the end of our song and dance, Landon lifted his head. "I'm going to crash at Reed's tonight," he said, flexing his free hand in a way that almost looked nervous. "If that's okay, I mean."

"Oh, more than okay," Dad said quickly, nodding. "Reed's a good kid. Tell him we miss seeing him on the field."

"I will, I will." Landon nodded his chin at me. "Don't go through my room while I'm gone."

Little did he know... "I won't," I promised.

The car ride to the house was quiet, and not even Mom or Dad spoke the whole time. I leaned my head against the glass of the window and shut my eyes, relishing in the coldness of the glass, trying to slow my breathing. For the whole drive, I didn't open my eyes. I listened to the finance podcast Dad had playing over the speakers.

I didn't open my eyes when we pulled into the driveway, and I didn't open them when Dad shut the car off. With my hands in my lap and my breaths even, I held perfectly still. "Oh, she's fast asleep," Dad said, in the way one might when they notice a cat napping.

"It *is* late for her," Mom replied, and I could hear the seat move as she turned around. Her voice sounded nearer. "Gemma, sweetie. Gemma? We're home."

Pretending to be asleep was easier than I thought it'd be, but pretending to wake up was tough. I made a show of blinking my eyes and drawing in a deep breath, blinking between Mom and Dad blurrily. "Already?"

Was that believable?

"You must be so tired," Mom said, unbuckling her seatbelt. "Maybe that's why you were a bit snappish earlier."

"Maybe," I agreed, even though the word settled oddly on my tongue. However, she gave me the opening I'd been waiting for. "I think I'm going to sleep in a little bit tomorrow. With everything that happened yesterday... I've just been feeling more tired than usual."

Bingo. Their sympathetic expressions were the exact ones I'd hoped for. Planned for. In a way, I guess I could've said I was grateful to Wes for picking such a fight. He cleared a perfect path for my Friday night plans.

Because little did anyone know that I wasn't staying home tonight.

It was eleven when I emerged from my bedroom, still dressed in my day clothes, my hair loose from its braid. It was wavy down my back, and I tiptoed to the bathroom, making a beeline for my escape route.

This time, my heart wasn't racing nearly as fast as it'd been before. The adrenaline was there, the excitement, but there was no doubt this time. Not after Mom deciding my homecoming date. Not after everything that'd been accumulating to this moment. I was going to live my life for me, and I wasn't going to regret it.

Slipping out of the bathroom window, I hurried through the backyard and down the street, spotting the car promised to be waiting for me in the exact spot it was supposed to be.

I couldn't ignore how happy I felt now with how far we'd come in a month's time.

How far *I'd* come.

And I couldn't wait to see where it would go from here.

CHAPTER 21

"**A**dmit it," Tee said as they pulled out onto the open road, one that I recognized as the main route to Jefferson. "You were surprised to see me, weren't you?"

"I was," I agreed, settling deeper into the passenger's seat. Tee's car was considerably nicer than Derrick's, without all the clutter along the footboards, too. As we picked up speed, the wind began to howl as it wove itself through each of the open windows, chilling off the interior. "But pleasantly surprised. Where are we going?"

"My house again," Tee said over the noise, casting me a look that glowed with the dashboard lights. "We're not like the outcasts that hang out behind dumpsters at night. Is that cool?"

I spread my fingers out along my skirt, smoothing out a wrinkle. "Beyond cool." Anywhere was cool, as long as it wasn't my house. It was my first Friday night in a very, very long time that I'd be doing something other than staring up at my ceiling.

Tee's hair flicked around mildly in the wind, tugged

this way and that, and it looked like they barely noticed. I smoothed as many of my flyaways behind my ears as possible, keeping the majority of it trapped behind my shoulder blades. "The boys are already there, playing whatever zombie game they could steal from my little brother," they said, and a corner of their mouth quirked up a little.

"So, Hudson *will* be there? Here I thought he was bailing on pulling an all-nighter in favor of his beauty sleep."

"He needs it, doesn't he?" They snorted, tapping their painted nails against the steering wheel. "Yeah, he'll be there. Simon wanted him to play a campaign with him, and I like driving at night."

I nodded lightly, tucking my hair back again.

"I stopped by the store on my way over," they said after a moment of silence, gesturing a hand toward the backseat. "Hopefully there's something you like. Hudson said you're pulling an all-nighter, so I got a few energy drinks."

"I've never had one before," I said, twisting around and grabbing the plastic bag from the floor. It was heavy, and the straps felt like they'd give out before I dropped it into my lap. "My mom won't even let me have coffee."

"Coffee's overhyped," Tee said. "Energy drinks are where it's at."

I pulled out a brightly colored can and turned it over, feeling my eyes bug when I looked at how much sugar it contained.

"Yeah, you're not supposed to read the labels. And

don't drink it all. You definitely don't need that big of a caffeine rush your first time."

My parents would freak if they found out I drank such a thing—then again, this probably would've fallen at the bottom of their list of worries.

"*So*," I dragged the word out, as if making the single syllable longer would make my question sound more natural. "I have a weird question. There's this girl at school who hangs around Hudson. She's about my height, brownish-blonde hair—"

"You mean Lacey Churchill?" Tee glanced over, checking my expression. "With a nose ring? Usually has red lipstick on? Yeah, I know her. She's Hudson's cousin."

Cousin. That was the cousin he always mentioned? The one fixing up the van? Oh my gosh, had I really been jealous of his *cousin*? *No, not jealous*, my thoughts scoffed. *We're not jealous.*

Then a new realization hit me. "Did you say Lacey?"

"Yep. Lacey."

Wait, wait, wait. Lacey...like the Lacey my brother was dating? My brother's girlfriend, Lacey? Could that really be? I balked at the idea. Not that Lacey wasn't pretty, because she was, but she was so different than who I'd expected Landon to be with. Her leather jacket looked like a hand-me-down, well-worn and well-loved, and the tights underneath her denim shorts were ripped high up on her thigh.

A complete opposite of Madison, who I always thought he'd been crushing on.

And plus, my brother, dating Hudson Bishop's

cousin? Did Landon know? I spiraled silently, and Tee was waiting for a reply, so I mumbled, "I didn't realize that's who that was."

"They weren't really that close, at least not before this past summer when she moved in. Something went down with her mom, I guess, so they took her in." A smirk formed on their lips. "Why? Were you jealous, thinking she was a girl interested in him?"

"No," I rushed to say, though it sounded like a lie. "I just think...I think she's dating my brother."

Tee looked over with their eyebrows raised, chuckling as they readjusted their grip on the wheel. "The plot thickens. Man, I guess it was fate that made you a part of our pack, huh?"

Fate. Was it fate that Hudson was the one who stumbled upon me that day on the bridge? Was it fate that had Hudson crashing into me in the hallway? Fate that Principal Oliphant paired us together for the buddy program? Surely I'd never have met Tee or Simon or Derrick without Hudson. I would've been stuck at my own lunch table, listening to conversations and never joining in on them. Maybe it *was* fate.

We drove the rest of the way to their house in a comfortable quiet, filled with the noise of the wind and stereo. Even in the dark, Tee knew exactly how to swerve and when to avoid the massive potholes in their driveway, and they took the route much slower than Derrick's high speed last time.

"Thank you for letting me come tonight," I said softly, my voice barely audible over the music. "I've never really had friends that I could hang out with like this, so it means a lot."

I thought Tee didn't hear me at first, since their silence stretched out. "Hudson's never really gotten close with anyone besides us. So it kind of feels like, really, I should be thanking *you*."

I clutched the plastic bag tightly, watching the corn pass by in a blur.

"Hudson is very touchy," Tee went on. "He's had more hurt in his lifetime than anyone should. Losing his mom so young, not growing up with many friends. He's used to pushing people away. He'll push you, too, if you let him."

"I told him he's stuck with me." Tee's words echoed in my head, though. He'd mentioned that his mother died, and then there was the rumor about what happened over the summer, but I didn't know too much about his past.

Derrick sat on the porch steps when Tee pulled up in front of the house, the headlights blinding him, but he stared into them as if it were a challenge. He was barefoot, elbows digging into his knees, chin propped up by his fists. "Took you long enough," he said glumly when we got out.

Tee rolled their keys around a finger. "Sorry to give you separation anxiety."

"You don't sound sorry."

"It's called sarcasm."

Tee joined Derrick on the porch, and he slung his arm over their shoulders, tucking Tee close. Their height difference seemed close to the one Hudson and I shared, and that thought had my heart skipping. I was jittery, unable to stand still, almost as if I'd already drunk the energy drinks from the bag.

Derrick led me down into the basement after Tee ran upstairs to grab something from their room. As we descended the creaky steps, I could hear the sound of gunfire get louder and louder, along with Simon's voice. "Get into a corner, get into a corner!"

"They're playing a video game," Derrick said before I could ask, and then gave a sad sigh. "It's a two-player game. We take turns every campaign."

"No wonder you were waiting for Tee to get back."

"And you," he added, looking over his shoulder. In the dark stairwell, his grin was bright. "You're another person to talk to."

Tee's basement wasn't that wide, but it was deep. It was only half-finished, with the drywall up but the ceiling left exposing the beams and air ducts. Despite that, it was cozy, with mismatched rugs and a sectional in the farthest corner of the room. Simon lounged along the L part of the sofa, and Hudson sat in the middle seat of the other section, both of their attention focused on the giant TV screen in front of them.

"Dude, *dodge the freaking cars!*" Simon's voice rose an octave. "How many times do we have to play this game for you to realize that if you hit the car, it alerts the horde?"

"That was so not me," Hudson said defensively, clicking the controller rapidly. "I swear it was the CPU."

"Dude, it says right there on the screen, 'Bishop-Boy1463 alerted the horde.'"

Hudson shook his head but leaned forward, squinting at the screen. Derrick and I hung out of their peripheral, watching the TV as the zombies surrounded both of their characters, blood spattering on the screen with each gunshot. It was quickly easy to figure out which side of the split screen was which boy—Hudson's health dropped into the danger zone while Simon's still remained in the green.

In the end, though, the zombie horde won, and both of the screens flashed red as the scene faded to black. "And we died." Simon threw his hands up in disgust, dropping the controller into his lap. "You suck at this game."

"Yeah, dude," Derrick piped up, taking a step forward. "You didn't even last one level."

Simon looked over, and his scowl disappeared. "Gemma! You're here!"

When Hudson looked up, my fingers instinctively clutched the bag tighter. He had his glasses on and his cotton candy sweatshirt, the same one he'd worn that day on the bridge. He had his hair tucked behind his ears, giving a perfect view of the expression that crossed his face. "You made it," he said in a voice that came out soft.

My heart swelled almost uncomfortably at the sight of him, and in each beat it thumped, it whispered, *I like this version of him best.* "I did," I said. "All in one piece."

"*And* she and Tee brought the goods." Derrick jerked

the plastic bag from my arms and carried it over to the coffee table, leaving me to trail behind.

While Hudson watched Derrick unload the bag, I still couldn't turn my attention away. He had his sweatshirt sleeves rolled up to his elbows, exposing his forearms that rested on his sweatpants-clad legs. It felt weird, seeing him like this, like we were at some sort of sleepover. Which, in a way, it kind of was—if the sleepover meant no sleep at all.

Hudson looked up and caught me studying him, and if it weren't for the lowlight of the basement, my blush would've been painfully obvious.

"You want to play, Gemma?" Simon asked, saving me from trying to blabber out an excuse for my staring problem. "It's not that hard. I can switch the mode to easy."

Hudson patted the empty space between him and the arm of the couch. "You can take my controller. Simon's probably ready for a break from me."

"I am," Simon said with a nod. "And plus, I'll be able to protect her a whole lot better than you. You shot me more than you hit the zombies."

I rounded the coffee table and sat down on the plush sofa, my knees knocking together underneath my skirt. The black controller was warm as I held it, replacing the same spots Hudson's hands had been holding before. I stared at the multi-colored buttons and the little joysticks. He scooted closer to me to point at the controls, explaining. "This one is to reload," Hudson said, pointing at the red button. "The green is to jump, and the joysticks move you around."

"Got it," I said, giving the joystick a little swirl.

"This button—" His hand came around on the other side of mine and pressed down against my fingers, causing me to click a button on the backside of the controller. "—is to shoot."

I drew my lower lip between my teeth as I gave a nod, holding perfectly still underneath his touch. His fingers were soft and warm. "Got it." My voice was considerably less strong. "I'm going to crush your high score."

Derrick coughed. "Won't be hard."

We quickly found out that I sucked at shooting zombies, even more than Hudson did. I had a few things I could blame my absolute failure on. I'd never played a videogame in my life. The assault of all the colors and movements on my senses was even scarier than the idea of a zombie attack. Another excuse could've been because Simon moved *fast* through the level, too fast for me to keep up with.

The last reason? The one I'd never admit aloud? When Hudson leaned against the sofa to watch us play, his shoulder pressed into mine, and there was no stopping the torrent of thoughts that came with the small touch. *Is he doing this on purpose? Is he really not aware of me? Should I move away? Should I lean closer?*

It was no wonder that I died, screen flashing red with defeat.

Hudson leaned closer. "Harder than it looks, huh?"

"It looked pretty hard," I returned, giving the joysticks a sad roll.

Tee came around the side of the sofa and knelt in

front of me, beginning to unload their supplies onto the coffee table. It was a nailfile, a buffer, and a bottle of mauve-colored polish—at least it looked mauve in the low light. "Give me your hand," Tee said, holding theirs out and waiting for me to offer mine. "It's on whatever list you have, isn't it?" Tee glanced at Hudson. "At least, he said it was."

Had Hudson memorized my rebellion list? Painting my nails seemed bland in comparison to pulling an all-nighter, and it'd disappeared into the back of my brain. Hudson, though...he'd remembered.

"I give the best manicures around," they assured me, taking my hand and laying it flat on my knee. "And we can take it off before you leave if you want. But we should check it off your list."

"Yeah," I said finally, wiggling my fingers, giving Tee the perfect angle to file them however they wished. "That sounds good."

"And then, a little later, we've got a scary movie to watch," Derrick added as he took the controller from me, plopping down on the other side of Hudson. "I know we already checked it off, but we should make Hudson squirm again, yeah?"

When I'd made the rebellion list, I never would've dreamed I'd have so many people to check things off with. After spending so much of my time keeping to myself, keeping my head down, the thought of experiencing all this with others made me feel so *light*.

Hudson leaned against the couch once more, and instead of letting his shoulder brush mine again, he maneuvered so his arm lined the back of the sofa, an action that seemed totally nonchalant and innocent, but one that ultimately brought him closer. It made me think of how Derrick and Tee stood on the porch, his arm slung around them.

I found myself smiling at the scene in front of me. Simon and Derrick beginning their zombie campaign, already nagging each other about which weapon to choose. Tee, shaking the bottle of polish and uncapping it. Hudson at my side, there for me no matter what. In that moment, I thought Tee was right—it *was* fate.

CHAPTER 22

I underestimated how hard it was to pull an all-nighter.

On the rare occasions I got to stay the night at Morgan's, we were in bed before midnight. We were mostly likely *out* before midnight, drooling and every-thing. Hudson and his friends were definitely not like that, so spending the majority of the night with them was a good choice.

After they tired of playing videogames—and losing repeatedly to the zombie hordes—Tee rolled out their karaoke system, and I got to learn how truly terrible Derrick was at singing. Cosmically bad. Hudson refused the mic, of course, but booed along heartily when Derrick tried to serenade him. After karaoke came out a card game that my mother definitely wouldn't have approved of, filled with dirty jokes and innuendos that mostly went over my head, but I still laughed along with everyone.

Now, though, somewhere in the back of my head, I knew it was a bad thing that I fell asleep, but there was no keeping my eyes from shutting the longer the hours stretched on. Especially not when Derrick popped in *Evil Killer Babies* and I had my eyes closed most of the time because of the amount of fake blood there was. Jump scares I could take, but apparently not fake blood. I'd curled myself up enough on the couch to rest my head on the arm, and after a few tries of dodging the gore and the demonic little baby that ran around, my eyes didn't reopen.

Until now. At first, even though I'd woken up, I just lay there with my eyes closed.

"I'm telling you," I could hear Derrick say, but it was faint, as if he was on the other side of the room. "They probably barely spent anything on making that movie. That budget had to be microscopic."

"That's a big word for you," Simon teased in reply.

I didn't hear Tee or Hudson, but they must've been over there too, rehashing the movie that must've ended. I tucked my nose deeper into the warm blanket—which I didn't have when I fell asleep. That confusion was what had me opening my eyes.

Hudson was the first thing that I saw over my hip. Tee might've been over there engaging in the *Evil Killer Babies* talk, but Hudson hadn't moved from his position at my side. His attention was captured by his phone, and the blanket wasn't only over me, but over *us*. The yellow, soft fabric was strewn across his lap in a haphazard way that couldn't have kept him warm.

Hudson looked over, expression going from neutral to happy in a second. The blanket instantly felt warmer. "Welcome back."

Hudson's smile was lazy, as if *he* was the one growing sleepy. For some reason, that caused something sharp to go through me—something like alarm. "You should've woken me. This was supposed to be an all-nighter."

"It's only three. Plenty of time to do fun things." Hudson laid his arm on top of my blanket, on the side of my calf. I tried my best not to react, even though my heart skipped. "Speaking of, they're all going to crash. Tee's already up in bed."

I sat up enough to peer over the back of the couch. Derrick sat on the bottom step of the staircase with Simon leaning against the wall beside him. They did both look tired, especially Simon, whose blinks were getting slower and slower. "We should leave then, shouldn't we?"

"Don't worry," he said, patting my leg. "We'll do something fun. We've got a few more hours until sunrise."

Our eyes met. A few hours. It sounded like a long time. It was seven hours of staying awake, but it was also seven hours of hanging out with Hudson, doing whatever we thought up. The longest time I'd spend with him ever.

Being on the couch now, though...I didn't mind it. It was against the spirit of pulling an all-nighter, but I wouldn't have minded if Hudson wanted to stay here for the rest of the night. Lying on my side with him to peer up at, I could've stayed here until the sun rose.

"Derrick?" Hudson called, pushing to his feet. "You still okay with me borrowing the car?"

"Knock yourself out, kid," he replied, digging into his pocket and pulling out his keys. From across the room, he tossed them to Hudson, who caught them easily. "Don't wreck her even more than she is."

"I don't think that's possible," Hudson muttered, collecting the energy drinks.

We said our goodbyes quickly, and Hudson led me out to Derrick's car. It'd cooled off considerably since earlier, and I shivered in the passenger seat while the heat struggled to kick on. Hudson put it on full blast, but even then, it was a sad chug.

"So, want to go for a drive?" Hudson asked me, drawing his seatbelt across his chest. "We could drive out to the beach, kill some time. I'm sure the stars would be easy to see out there."

The beach at night would be pretty—I could practically imagine it now.

We were quiet for the first little bit. Hudson left me to sift through the songs on his playlist. I smiled at a few artists I recognized before ultimately settling on a slow acoustic song, smiling as it coasted from the speakers. Betsy might've been rough around the edges, but she had a good sound system.

As Hudson merged onto the highway, I thought about my parents and my brother, and how they were fast asleep by now. No doubt they all assumed I was, too.

Instead, I was with Hudson, driving into the night like we were running away.

"Did your parents flip over what happened in the hallway yesterday?" Hudson asked once we reached speed, leaning back into the seat. There weren't any other cars on the road, so it was only Betsy's headlights illuminating the way. There was something eerie about the scene, like in a world that is usually busy and bright, Hudson and I were the only ones left. "With Wes, I mean."

"I wouldn't say *flip*. They chewed Principal Oliphant out, though, for, and I quote, 'letting riffraff in the district.'"

"Perfect word for him." Hudson smiled, but then it faltered as something else occurred to him. He propped his elbow on the console between us, letting his hand dangle. "You shouldn't have kneed Wes yesterday, you know. You could've gotten in trouble."

"*You* shouldn't have stepped in," I returned. "*You* could've gotten in trouble."

"That's why you shook your head? Because you were worried about me?"

"Hey, if I have to be shoved into a locker to keep you from being expelled, I'll do it."

I'd meant the words to be teasing, but Hudson's expression didn't lighten at all. If anything, the corners of his lips just turned down more as he glanced over. "Gemma."

"Don't give me that face," I ordered, cutting him off. "You should make up your mind, you know. You want me to grow a backbone, you don't..."

"I want you to be *safe*. Backbone or no backbone."

I looked at where Hudson's hand dangled near the gearshift. His fingers were completely relaxed, and like before, I imagined what it'd look like if I curled my fingers around his. I was at that stage of tiredness where my brain tried to coax me into reaching over. If he jerked away, I could pretend our hands just bumped on accident. If he wrapped his fingers around mine, then...well, then...

I curled my fingers into fists, fighting the urge. "Speaking of, don't take this the wrong way, okay?"

"I hesitantly say 'okay.'"

I shifted so I could face him a bit more fully in the seat, my belt straining against my neck. "Why was Wes so intimidated by you? I mean, you pulled a whole self-defense move on him—which Morgan thought was bad...*butt*, by the way—otherwise, he easily has twenty pounds of muscle over you."

"Let's not exaggerate." Hudson chuckled once, but his expression relaxed into something more resigned. "It's kind of like the whole Grim Reaper thing. The rumors. People don't know what's true, so they avoid me anyway. I guess Wes listens to gossip."

I studied his profile. The sharp lines of his face looked even sharper with the shadows, and the flat expression on his face was the one I was used to. It reminded me a bit of the flowery smiles Mom put on for her friends, or the practiced expression Principal Oliphant always wore. For Hudson, his mask wasn't a smile. It was a carefully crafted look of boredom, of barely-there animosity, warning off anyone who dared to come close. "I don't think you're scary."

"It's because you can't see as clearly in the dark."

"That's not it."

"The glasses, then," he suggested.

I reached out and nudged his arm on the console. "You're not scary. I wish you'd stop acting like you are." His serious expression didn't change, eyes on the road. He looked wide awake for three in the morning, like he did this often. "The Grim Reaper thing. That was the role you felt forced into, right?"

Our conversation from the bridge felt like forever ago. Before, when I'd asked a similar question, he'd refused to answer. Somewhere along the way, his convictions about it all changed. Silently, he gave one nod.

"Why didn't you fight until something changed?"

His fingers flexed around the steering wheel, shoulders rising and falling with a deep breath. "Everyone at school started calling me that after the fight with your brother and his friends. I tried to ignore it, at first, but gossip had already spread. With how I looked, everyone had made up their mind about me. It's hard to change someone's mind when it's already made up."

I studied him a bit closer. "How you looked?"

He pointed to his cheek, right above where his scar was.

My stomach turned uneasily. "Wait, wait—you got that from the fight?"

"I fell into the brick wall by the school. Cut it on the top. Seven stitches."

Now my stomach flipped over, thinking about Hudson hitting one of the bricks, thinking of all the blood that must've come from the fall. I swallowed hard, trying to push the image away, but it left me feeling sick. "Why did you do it?"

"Do what?"

"Pick the fight." I tried to see his gaze, but the thick arm of his glasses obscured it. "Why would you go against three people?"

Hudson's hand grasped the steering wheel tighter. I couldn't see his eyes, but I could see his mouth, and it tightened before pinching into a rueful smile. "It doesn't matter," he said. "It really doesn't matter."

His response lacked the warmth his voice had held moments before, hinting that we had reached the end of the rope for the conversation. My curiosity was hard to crush, though—we'd come so close to talking about what happened, something that'd been weighing on my mind for days now, but none of my questions were answered. But I knew one thing for sure—bringing up the subject was hard for him. He might've worn a pinched smile, but his body was absorbed in tension, gaze too firmly fixed on the road. I thought of the way he tensed up when he saw Ashton in the hallway, the way his breathing shook after the encounter. Like he'd been afraid.

"You must've been lonely," I said after a moment, watching for his reaction. "No one deserves to be outcasted. For any reason."

This time, Hudson didn't respond. When he drew in another breath, this one seemed to shake.

I reached out and cupped my hand over his, giving the backs of his fingers a squeeze. "You have me now," I said brightly, waiting for him to look over at me. "So I hope you won't be lonely anymore."

I knew this was a night I'd remember for the rest of

my life, even if I only ever remembered this moment. Even if it was just remembering the way Hudson's eyes softened. All of the defenses behind his normally carefully guarded glare lowered, and though I'd caught glimpses of it before, I watched as the shield dropped entirely. Maybe it was the glasses. Maybe it was the darkness of the cab. Maybe it was the fact that it was three in the morning and he was overly tired.

Whatever it was, it felt like, right then and there, something just *clicked*.

As confident as could be, Hudson twisted his hand in my grip and threaded his fingers through mine. My breath stalled in my chest as I stared at our hands, at the way the dashboard lights lit them up.

"I hope," Hudson began, but stopped to clear his throat. "I hope you won't be lonely anymore, either."

I curled my fingers tighter around his, thinking about the rest of the night ahead of us. With the music filtering from the stereo, with Hudson's hand in mine, I couldn't imagine anything more perfect.

CHAPTER 23

We ended up staying at the beach for only a little while, since the breeze off the water was so cold. After chatting a bit in the car, we took the long way to Brentwood. The spot we picked to watch the sunrise was definitely fitting, since it was the first place we met.

Lookout Ledge was beautiful in the dark. Though almost all of the houses in its view had their lights off, I could still see the few high-rises of Brentwood beyond the trees. They looked magical, even with the light pollution they gave off. We were far enough away from it all, though, to have a clearer view of the stars, and for a while, Hudson and I tried in vain to find any constellations we knew.

Once that had taken up our attention—and once my eyes had started getting sleepy—we broke out a can of energy drink each.

Hudson had laid out a blanket from Derrick's car over the stone ledge so our butts wouldn't freeze, and we faced each other. He crossed his legs and leaned an elbow on his knee now, thinking. "Never have I ever painted my nails."

I smiled down at my nail polish. Tee had given me a bottle of polish remover before I left, since I wouldn't be able to have it tomorrow—Mom would no doubt notice and demand to know when I'd had the time to paint my nails. The mauve polish clung to my nails, and I savored every angle that I could. "That was boring," I said, taking a drink from my can, smacking my lips at the overly sweet taste. "Never have I ever...punched someone."

Hudson tipped his can back. "Never have I ever kneed someone."

Smirking, I drank. Despite an energy drinks, Hudson's blinks were getting slower and slower as he looked at me, and my heart did a strange flutter. "You can lie down if you want," I told him. "An all-nighter is written on my list, not yours."

"You don't know that. I could've written it down."

I leaned closer to him. "I *don't* know. You haven't told me any on yours. I don't even know if you have a list or not."

He tilted his head, and for a moment, I thought he was going to confess one of them to me. It was like seeing inside his house—pulling back the curtain, finding out what stirred around in his head. What he wanted to do but hadn't done yet.

"What's next on yours?" he asked instead of answering.

"Try coffee, which I feel like I'll let an energy drink

count." I tipped my can. "And then I think after that, it's skip a class and...cut my hair."

Hudson's gaze trailed along my hair slowly. "Do you think you'll do that? Cut your hair?"

I reached around and threaded my fingers through my loose locks, feeling the small tangles and the waves in it. The weight of it, even loose, was still enough to pull on my scalp uncomfortably. The fine line I'd walked all along would have a hole blown into it if I did the last one. *Cut my hair.* "I don't know."

"There's no time limit on this, you know. No one said you have to do all the tasks in two weeks."

"Our deal," I reminded him. "We agreed to be friends for a month. You could decide to drop boring ol' Gemma Settler at the end of the month, and I'll have no one to check things off with."

I said it with enough sarcasm that it made Hudson roll his eyes, but I didn't really believe that, though. It wasn't that I had a set amount of time, but once I got started, I hadn't wanted to stop. I'd gotten a taste of that freedom, that new feeling, and I kept wanting more. And besides, they were excuses to spend time outside my house, with new friends. With Hudson.

I thought back to two weeks ago, the first time I bumped into him in the hallway. "Do you think I've grown it?" I asked, swiveling to drape my legs over the stone ledge. "My backbone, I mean."

"Is that why you're doing all this?" Hudson regarded me with a curious but quiet expression, trying to decipher what I meant before I said it. "Sneaking out, pulling an all-nighter—the whole rebellion list. Is it because of the Most Likely To list, or…is it because of what I said?"

"I wouldn't say it's *because* of either one of those things." I stared beyond the ledge, at the tops of the trees that waved in the wind. The sight was a lot more ominous than it had been on my birthday, the last time I sat here. Except with Hudson at my side, I didn't mind the dark at all. "At least, not exclusively. It's more like they were each a part of the catalyst."

Hudson turned too, which brought his body closer to mine. Our hands were nearly touching on the blanket.

"Landon and I, our whole lives, have lived under my parents' thumbs. He gets more freedom than I do. Maybe it's because he's older, maybe it's because he's a boy, but I think…I think they think I'm easier than him. Quieter. More…moldable." I bit my lip, picturing my parents' expressions. "I'm sixteen years old, and I don't really know who I am. That's kind of sad, isn't it?"

Hudson let out a breath. "I don't think so. Does anyone ever really know who they are?"

I turned toward him, studying his profile. "I've never had the chance to find out. Until now."

"As long as you're doing this for *you*. Not because of what anyone else says. Especially not me."

I chuckled a little as I nodded. "It is for me. I promise."

We stayed suspended like that, regarding each other in the dull light. The sky had begun to turn a strange gray color, and I wondered if that meant the sunrise would soon be on the horizon. I bit my lip in anticipation, wondering what the colors would look like as they star-bursted into the trees.

"Can I ask you a personal question?" I asked eventually.

"I guess so."

I waffled back and forth on saying anything. At first, it was because I didn't know how to bring it up tactfully. Then it was because I was afraid to hear his answer. "Principal Oliphant said that you were arrested this summer. Is that true?"

It was almost as if he'd been expecting this question. He didn't seem shocked at all. "I was," Hudson said, leveling his gaze with mine. "I wondered why you hadn't asked earlier."

"It's none of my business—"

"You're out in a secluded location with someone potentially dangerous." Hudson leaned away from me, as if his own words alarmed him. "It is your business."

"You're not dangerous." *But...* Both Landon and Principal Oliphant had warned me off of Hudson like he was the plague. Bad news. They'd both told me he'd been arrested, but only Principal Oliphant alluded to what it could've been. *Assault.* It was an ugly word, a scary word, but one I couldn't associate with Hudson no matter how hard I tried. "Tell me what happened, then. And then I'll make the decision whether or not to run for the hills."

Hudson looked down at the rings on his fingers and studied them, using the pad of his thumb to spin them around. The nervous fidget had me turning toward the ledge, wanting to give him as much privacy as he needed.

"It was this past summer," he said after a second. "I got into a fight with someone outside of Allen's Alley," he said eventually, voice heavy. "He called the police, and they cuffed me."

I tried to imagine Hudson striking someone. Even as he'd stood before Wes yesterday, I couldn't imagine it. Pulling his arm back, curling his hand into a fist, landing a punch with precision. "Did he bowl a higher score than you did?"

Hudson snorted at my attempt at humor. "He's dating my aunt, and he's a terrible person. Worse than Wes. We were leaving the alley and he saw us and came up to harass my cousin. It escalated, and...well. He's the kind of guy who'll provoke a wild animal and then shoot it when it bites him."

I tried to imagine the scenario, and something tight coiled in my stomach. "He plays the victim."

"Exactly." He let out a sharp breath, spinning the ring on his index finger around. "Which is why, despite him hitting my cousin, I was the one arrested for it. That was what he wanted, though. For us to get in trouble. I get it now."

So that was the situation behind the rumors. Because some adult thought it was a good idea to try to hit a minor, Hudson was the one who got busted for it when he was doing nothing but standing up for someone. "Your cousin...do you mean Lacey?"

"Yeah. Lacey. She's been living with us since it happened." He glanced over. "She was the one who was with me yesterday."

It wasn't even just a minor that guy had been messing with, but a girl, too? I kind of didn't know what he was thinking—though nice, Lacey was definitely intimidating. Like the Grim Reaper side of Hudson, but without all the ice.

"Is she who's dating Landon?"

Hudson arched an eyebrow at me. "You didn't know that?"

"He's been keeping it a secret from my parents, which means he's been keeping it a secret from me."

"That's a weird match, isn't it?"

"Kind of." I looked at him closer. "Do you approve? After everything that happened?"

"I think your brother is a good person," Hudson said, surprising me further. He shook his head a little. "I think if I were to regret anything about that day in ninth grade, it would've been hitting him. I shouldn't have done it." The side note dulled back as we returned to the subject at hand, both of us quieting for a moment. Hudson stared at his splayed fingers, looking at them with an intensity that was a contrast with his slow, sleepy blinks earlier. "And I shouldn't have hit my aunt's boyfriend, either. It didn't help my case any. People...once they decide who I am, they'll take anything and make it fit their narrative. Punching someone outside of a family-friendly bowling alley must mean that I'm a danger to society. Wearing all black must mean I'm messed up in the head. Getting into one fistfight freshman year must mean I'm a lost cause."

I took Hudson in all at once. His shoulders were curved as he slouched over his folded legs, still staring at his hands. His expression was the same sort of bare it'd been earlier, with eyes so clear that it was like I could finally see through them. His head was ducked now, making it harder to see, but the sincerity was painted across his face in a clear swipe. There was no missing the bone-weariness there, nor the sadness that lingered by the downturned corners of his lips.

I reached over and slid my hand into one of his, feeling the coolness of his rings press against my skin. I curled my fingers around his hand, hoping the warmth of mine would swallow the leftover cold of his. "You're not a lost cause."

"I was okay with being one." Hudson brought our hands up in front of him, and his other came to trace the backs of my knuckles. "With just ghosting through the halls until graduation. Letting people avoid me, not getting attached. Keeping my head down."

A flare of heat surged inside me, my familiar mantra popping into my mind. *Keep your head down and keep your mouth shut.*

"Until you, you know. Until you decided you weren't going to stay in the mold others put you in. And I started wondering if I could be the same way."

I watched him watch our hands, feeling as though my heart was about to burst from my chest. "What people say about you isn't your fault," I returned steadily, being as firm with him now as he'd been with me earlier. "I know we joke about it, but you're *not* the Grim Reaper. You're not some terrifying, horrible senior to steer clear of. You're human, and you might mess up, but that doesn't mean you're not good enough. That doesn't mean that I can't hold your hand."

"Gemma—"

"That doesn't mean I can't like you." The words came out as a confident declaration, words I'd never have said if the sun was up. Hudson's lips parted from the shock of the words, but I pushed ahead. "And...I *do* like you, Hudson. A good idea or a bad idea, I don't know, but it's too late to figure it out now."

Hudson held perfectly still as I leaned closer to him, and I could feel his fingers instinctively tighten around mine, squeezing lightning into my veins. It brought us close, only a scant few inches between his face and mine —his mouth and mine—and my body was hyperaware of it.

"I told you that I didn't know who I was," I whispered, because now that he was closer, my words felt too loud. Too present. "But these past few weeks, I've felt more like myself than I have my entire life."

I thought he'd say something, but he didn't. Hudson's fingers eased a lock of hair behind my ear. His fingertips lingered by the skin there, almost as if memorizing the touch.

As gracefully as I could, I inched closer, forward. I looked past his glasses and into his eyes, at the little flecks of gray and blue that made up their color. They were latched onto mine like they'd never move. And then, giving into the urge that'd risen time and time again, I swiped the pad of my thumb along the scar on his cheek. The divot was easy to feel, but so was the softness of his cheek, the warmth that pooled there just underneath his skin, almost as if he was blushing. Something in me tightened.

Hudson shivered.

My fingers trailed down to his pulse "Wow," I murmured with a little gasp, looking up at him with amusement. "Your heart's beating fast."

"I want to kiss you," he said suddenly, without pause or hesitation, the clarity hitting me with the force of a truck.

I almost dropped my hand. "Why don't you?"

"Because," he said, voice gently caressing the words, "I want you to want it, too."

I do, I thought a little unsteadily. *I do, I do, I do.*

"This entire time, you've been the one holding the reins," he said, reaching past me to thread his fingers through my hair. "Everything's been your choice. I want this to be, too."

I leaned forward and kissed the scar on his cheek. Even though it was a short moment, my heart raced with the tenderness of it, dizziness enveloping me as I pulled back. "There," I murmured, breathless. "I made my choice—"

The words were barely out of my mouth before Hudson reached up and took my face in both of his hands, kissing me back with absolutely zero hesitation.

I fell into the yielding softness of the kiss, of the way his lips molded to mine. I could taste the grape sweetness of his energy drink, and he had to taste the passion fruit flavor of mine. His thumbs smoothed across my cheeks in a lulling swipe, and I reached around to rest my hand on the nape of his neck, holding him to me, chest expanding.

It was our first kiss, but it didn't feel like a first—the way he let me lead, matched me kiss for kiss, it felt like we'd done this before. Like it was a dance we'd been practicing for weeks, finally getting to perform. There was something earnest about it, unrelenting, open. My heart had to be on the brink of exploding in my chest. I was Hudson's first kiss—the first one he got to experience *this* with—and the knowledge of it made me smile against his mouth. Hudson dropped one hand to cup my waist, fingers pressing into my hip, a light squeeze. I slipped my hands up his shoulders, grasping the fabric of his jacket, letting the world spin and tilt, as long as I had him to hold onto.

This hadn't been on my rebellion list, but man, oh man, it should've been.

We both pulled away at the same time, lingering in the closeness while our hearts slowed. Hudson let out a shaky breath, and I reached up and traced the edge of his bottom lip, causing his eyes to flare again. "Now you know the hype around kissing," I whispered to him.

"It's a *lot* better than I thought it'd be."

"Only because you had a really good partner."

Hudson laughed, and as carefully as he could since we were still on the ledge, he pulled me into him. I rested my head on his shoulder, listening to his chuckle reverberate. Hearing Hudson's musical laugh, I had the shocking, out-of-body realization of how much my life had changed. I didn't feel different, though. It didn't feel like I was playing a role in a musical, or that I was pretending to be someone that I wasn't.

Instead, what I'd told Hudson had been truthful—I'd never felt more like *me*. Gemma Settler, finally free of the mold she'd been stuck into. Finally free to be who she wanted.

"Don't regret this later," he murmured, smoothing his hand in lulling circles against my sweatshirt.

Beyond his shoulder, the sky began to lighten into a dull grayish-blue, the first glimpse of daylight on the horizon. The sunrise was coming, and I had a gut feeling it would be beautiful. "Trust me," I whispered, melting in deeper as his arms tightened around my waist. "I won't."

CHAPTER 24

consequence of staying up all night I considered—but didn't put enough weight into —was the fact that I'd be dead tired that following Saturday. I didn't realize that tiredness would extend into Sunday, though. In the back of my head, I knew I'd be tired, but I hadn't anticipated *how* tired. It left me foggy all weekend, time flying by in a blur. Mom, convinced I was sick, thankfully let me "sleep it off" most of the weekend.

I did not, however, escape Sunday tea.

I sat sandwiched between Madison Oliphant and Mrs. Morris, both of whom were listening intently as my mom spoke about the upcoming homecoming festivities. Leading up to the big game this Friday, Brentwood High was going all out in terms of being celebratory. Mom had organized a committee to go around the city to "dress it up" by hanging flyers and spreading as much gold and blue spirit as possible.

"We've convinced almost all the shops on Main Street to paint pawprints on their windows for the big game," Mom said excitedly, looking around the circular table with wide eyes. She looked a bit like a storyteller surrounded by children, trying to be as animated as possible. "A lot of people are hanging ribbons on their doors. If you don't have one, stop by my car after tea, and I'll get you one. I've got plenty to go around."

I picked up my teacup and took the world's smallest sip from the super-floral, super-sweet concoction. No matter how many of the teas I went to, I wasn't sure I'd ever acquire the taste.

"Don't forget, Center Inspire is hosting their Brentwood High art show, as well," Mom went on, flipping a bit of her red hair over her shoulder. "I talked things over with Lila Matthews, and the way they're organizing everything is going to look so lovely."

"Madison dropped some of the artwork off the other day, and she said it's going to be great." Principal Oliphant looked at her daughter with a warm smile. It was funny how the two of them looked alike. If Principal Oliphant was a few years younger, they could've looked like sisters. "We'll be there for the show, of course, supporting the gallery and the school."

The table ran like clockwork. Mom was the ringleader, always leading the conversations, while everyone else had turns here and there. Except for Madison and me, of course. Madison was much better at listening than I was, but as I watched her today, I wondered if she *was* listening. Her eyes were bouncing around the table as people spoke, but they looked distant.

So, while Mrs. Morris engaged Mom, I leaned over. "Have you gotten your dress yet?"

Madison looked over at me and smiled automatically, and I was right—she *was* distracted. "Dress?"

"For homecoming."

"Oh." She drew in a breath and then nodded. "I have. I'm on homecoming court, so I had to get it early."

"Custom made," Principal Oliphant interjected, patting her daughter's shoulder. "She's going to look so lovely in it."

I was sure Madison would look lovely in anything she wore. Even as I eyed her now, in a simple pink sundress, I was envious of how effortless she looked. Her makeup was subtle but flawless. Her blonde hair was coiled into perfect curls, ones she wore up in a ponytail. Everything about her seemed perfect. Then again, I would've expected nothing less from one of the leaders in the Top Tier.

Our topic had snagged Mom's attention, and I saw her turn from Mrs. Morris. "Madison, you're walking with Landon, aren't you? Since he's on homecoming court, too? I've already got his suit picked out and everything. We should make sure we get a tie that matches your dress."

Madison nodded as she took a sip of her tea. "I actually picked up a tie when we bought the dress. I'll be sure to give that to him at school."

"Talia, isn't this perfect? Madison and Landon on homecoming court together? I couldn't have planned it more perfectly myself!" Mom leaned across her place setting eagerly, and all of the ladies at the table leaned in too, just as curious to hear what she'd say next. "Has he asked you to the dance yet?"

"Me?" Madison's pink lips parted in surprise. "Oh, he wouldn't ask me."

"Why not?" Mom demanded, confused. "It's perfect."

If it were Morgan, I would've stomped on her foot. If it were Jaden, I would've nudged his arm. But it was Madison, and I could do nothing but plead with eyes she never looked over to meet. "I'm sure he'll ask his girl-friend," Madison said innocently, and then the table exploded.

"Girlfriend?" Mrs. Morris all but gasped, at the same time Mrs. Gunther exclaimed, "So the rumor *was* true!"

"Landon has a girlfriend?" Principal Oliphant asked her daughter, and Madison frantically looked around the table, unsure who to settle on. Ultimately, she looked down at me.

I gave her a grimace that could've passed as a smile.

For a person who liked everything planned out, I wondered what Mom was thinking. Nothing showed on her expression. Not shock, not surprise, not anger, not happiness. It was a little scary. "Do you know her name, dear?"

This time, Madison glanced at me before she spoke. "Um, you know, I can't remember."

"It's Lacey," Mrs. Gunther said, leaning her elbow onto the table. "I remember it from the Babble article.

How interesting that it was true! I can't believe you didn't know, Naomi."

"I thought you said it was a rumor, Gemma."

All of the attention turned to me in a way that maximized my discomfort. I clutched my teacup tightly, frantically trying to think of what to say to downplay it all. "I've...never met her."

Technically a lie, but I didn't know who she was when I did meet her, so did it count?

"Well, this is just..." Mom trailed off, but I knew her well enough to know how she was going to finish that sentence. *Disappointing.*

The whole table started buzzing with the new gossip, and I reached for another cucumber finger sandwich, thinking about how my brother had one heck of a story to spin when we got home. That, or finally come clean. Even though I hadn't been the one to spill the beans, I felt guilty. I wouldn't want to be him, forced to explain something he'd been keeping to himself for so long.

How would I fare if I was in his shoes? If I had to come clean to Mom about Hudson?

Maybe that would be worse, though. It wasn't like Lacey had bad history with our family.

Thinking about Hudson had me thinking of everything that'd come with Friday night's all-nighter. From the confessions to the kiss. It was hard to imagine anyone *not* liking Hudson, but it was like he said. People couldn't get past first impressions.

And I hoped, for my brother's sake, that Mom

wouldn't automatically veto Lacey simply because she wasn't Madison.

I slid my cell out of my jacket pocket and slid open the keypad, thankful for the tiny keyboard so I could send Landon a text without looking.

GEMMA

soo, someone spilled the beans about Lacey to Mom. Wasn't me. Wanted to warn you.

While the rest of the time everyone gossiped about my brother, I took a page from Madison's book. I looked around, nodded when necessary, but I thought about Hudson for the rest of the time. If I concentrated, I could practically feel how his pulse hammered underneath my fingers, and I could remember the way his fingers felt on my cheeks. And, of course, his *lips*.

It was then that I decided that no matter what happened, I was going to hold onto him for a good and long while.

"I can't believe it's homecoming week," Jaden said as we waited at the bus stop Monday morning, huddling deeper in his jacket. He'd broken out a thicker one as the mornings grew colder, and I found myself shivering, wishing I'd done the same. "Nice pajamas, by the way. Ducklings are super awesome."

It was Spirit Week to celebrate homecoming, and

today was Pajama Day. I looked down at my pants, the ones I'd gotten approved by Mom and Dad before wearing them out. I didn't normally wear pants to bed—normally, I opted for a nightgown—but I wanted to be a little spirited this week. They were still much comfier than jeans.

I didn't have the heart to tell Jaden that they were chicks, not ducks. "Thanks. I like your... Are those Canadian flags?"

"Yep. I got them when we went to Toronto last fall. Cool, right?" Jaden stuck his leg out, allowing me to get a closer look. The red color was a little faded from the wash, but...sure. Pretty cool. "Anything fun happen this weekend?"

I smiled a little as I recalled it all, but there was no chance I'd ever tell Jaden the truth. "Mom found out about Landon's secret girlfriend."

"Oh!" He stepped closer, like we were about to delve into a gossip session. "What happened with that?"

"Mom was actually pretty calm about it. She just came home and told Landon that she didn't appreciate other people knowing before her, and he promised to bring her over. Which, of course, will be the event of the century."

"Have you met her? Landon's girlfriend?"

I nodded. "Briefly. She seems nice, though." I just didn't know how Mom would react once she found out she was related to Hudson. Probably not well.

Jaden let out a breath that fogged in the air, bundling deeper underneath his jacket. "The mornings are cooling off. I'm not looking forward to waiting out here when there's snow."

"Me either," I said, looking at the empty roadway.

"Are your parents not letting you get your permit?"

I looked up at Jaden quickly, forehead creasing. "What?"

"You haven't talked about it. I know that was something you were looking forward to on your birthday. I've been waiting for you to bring it up."

"You knew that?"

Jaden chuckled. "Yeah, Gemma. I know *you*. I mean, you'd always talk about it with Morgan. I meant to bring it up earlier, but..." He laughed again, though this time it was much more awkward-sounding. "You've been a little different lately. Quieter."

I placed my sneaker on a crack in the sidewalk, trying to act as nonchalant as possible. "I didn't notice."

He shifted his weight on his feet. "That's kind of what I mean, Gemma. Even now. I feel like you look at me less."

I forced myself to shift my attention up. "I look at you."

"Not like you used to."

The air was cold, much colder than it'd been when I first stepped out of the house. With us standing here waiting for the bus, regarding each other solemnly, it felt like the beginning of an end. I knew it was a tie I needed to cut, but I was too afraid of the side effects. This would be the end to the era of calmness, because once I said what I needed to, everything would be thrown into a tailspin.

"Things feel different," I conceded finally, curling my hands into little fists at my sides. "I don't know how to explain it."

Jaden leaned forward. "You don't like me anymore, do you?"

I wanted to tell him that I wasn't sure I liked him in the first place. I should've at least had the decency to look up at him when I said it, but like he'd focused on my chicks, I focused on his Canadian flags. "I like you as a friend. I just don't think I...*like*-like you."

I could practically hear my house of cards *whoosh* as it began to topple. I could hear Mom's voice now, demanding to know why I'd turned down such a boy, a boy they'd tried to plan my future with. She and Mrs. Morris talked about it in the way moms do, with tittering quips and whispered teases. Living with that had been another version of keeping my head down and keeping my mouth shut. Letting it happen because the flipside was too hard.

Jaden's lips stretched into a smile, one that then morphed into a wide grin, and then he laughed. He actually laughed. "Gemma," he began, shaking his head. "I don't *like*-like you either."

I blinked, waiting, but he didn't follow up with anything else. The words lingered in the air between us like the condensation of an exhale. "You...don't?"

Jaden stuffed his hands into his pajama pants pockets, rocking on his heels. "I like you as a friend, too. I always have. I know our parents really pushed for the opposite, and I guess for a while I thought you wanted that, too. I—well, I was never really that bothered, and it wasn't like I had anyone else or anything, and you're a good friend to talk to and stuff, but I—"

"You *don't* like me?"

Jaden gave a nervous chuckle, glancing around as if this were a trick question. "Not like that, no."

I curled my arms tighter around myself, as if that could help me through my confusion. "But—you kissed me. In the eighth grade."

"You can kiss someone and not feel anything for them," he said, like *duh*.

"You walk me to the bus every day."

"Your mom asked me to do that. And I have to ride the bus anyway, so it works out." He laughed. "Our parents really wanted us to be together, I guess. Both of our parents. I think they liked the idea of having control."

It was almost startling how much he hit the nail on the head with that, at least with my parents. There was no risk with Jaden.

My brain seriously couldn't wrap around the fact for a long, long moment. Not because I thought I was hot stuff or anything like that, but because I'd never even *thought* to wonder whether or not Jaden liked me romantically. From how hard our parents pushed us together, and for how attentive he always was, it never even crossed my mind that he'd been in the same boat as I'd been, with his decisions made for him.

"Can we keep this a secret from our parents?" I

asked, hoping he wouldn't think my request was weird. "For a little while?"

Jaden mimed zipping his lips shut. "Don't worry, I'm looking forward to setting them straight about as much as you are."

"So not at all?"

"Bingo."

Mrs. Savion rumbled up with Bus 32 at that moment, stopping beside Jaden and me at the curb. Like always, Jaden let me walk on first, and he sat down beside me on the seat. "I always wondered how awkward this conversation would be, eventually." He nudged my leg. "Turns out, not that bad."

"I can't…" I shook my head, but the bewilderment still didn't clear. "Morgan's going to freak, you know."

"You can tell her."

"Uh-uh." I elbowed him in the side. "You can."

Jaden swayed from side to side beside me, ultimately leaning in. "Do you think I should ask her to homecoming?"

I shoved him again, unable to keep a shocked laugh from escaping. "I can only handle so much shock in one day, okay? *Ask Morgan…*" The bus bounced with a pothole that jostled us together, and I ultimately sighed. "She'd probably say yes. If you asked her."

He grinned at that, which caused me to scoff again. This *was* a day for shock, apparently. I wasn't sure how to look at Jaden now that I knew he didn't have feelings for me, and I definitely didn't know how to look at him if he had feelings for Morgan. Too, too weird.

Mrs. Savion stopped at a street that picked up a few boys, and Jaden looked up at them as they passed. "If it's okay with you," he began tentatively, "I'm going to go sit with Trevor and the guys."

I wasn't overly sure who "Trevor and the guys" were, but I nodded. "See you at lunch?"

"See you then," he said, and then he hurried into the bus's aisle, trying to get into a seat before Mrs. Savion picked up speed. I turned around to watch him maneuver toward the back, feeling like with every step, a weight rolled off my chest.

Of all the things to happen that Monday, that was one of the best things. My house of cards didn't tumble. Instead, it was an amicable way of tearing down the awkward wall between Jaden and me, one that opened new doors. I liked the idea of him not being tied to my parents, tucked in their pocket—it was almost like I could look at him with new eyes now.

Mrs. Savion pulled up to Vista Villas, letting Hudson climb aboard. My heart rushed into high gear at the sight of him, tousled blond hair and sleepy-looking eyes. Seeing him caused everything that happened Friday night to rush back, especially him reaching out and clasping my cheeks, drawing my lips to his.

His eyes fell on the empty space beside me now, but even though I patted the seat, he still sat in the one across from me. "What are you doing?" I asked.

"I thought we needed to hide it from your friends."

"Jaden's in the back." I patted the seat again, giving him my best impression of puppy-dog eyes. "I won't bite."

I never would've guessed the puppy eyes would've worked on him, but then again, it wasn't true that his heart was made of ice. The Grim Reaper's, maybe, but not Hudson Bishop's. He collected his things with an sigh, and as quickly as he could, he slipped across the aisle and into the space beside me. His shoulder brushed mine, and then his thigh did as he shoved his backpack down by his feet. "I think this is the first time I'm seeing you in pants," he said, taking in my chicks. "It's different."

"Where are *your* pjs, Mr. Ripped Jeans?" I asked, reaching out and brushing my fingertip across the tear that flared over his knee.

"I'm more comfortable like this."

"It's not scary enough for the Grim Reaper to wear pajamas to school?"

The corner of his mouth twitched. "Not really."

His hands were in his lap, and mine were still awkwardly wrapped around my backpack, and no one would've even guessed we'd kissed Friday night. Everything that'd happened on Friday happened under the cover of night, when inhibitions were low, or whatever. However, that did leave me wondering, with a little seed of panic, whether or not he regretted it.

Hudson cleared his throat. "You know, I realized over the weekend—I don't even have your number. I couldn't even text to see if you were a total zombie."

"I definitely was," I said, and then I pulled out my phone. "Here, let me put your number into my phone."

We rode the rest of the bus route with my headphones plugged into my MP3 player, one earbud in my ear, the other in Hudson's. He mostly skipped through the songs and commented on ones he knew—"oh, you listen to Untapped Potential, too?"—but it was a simple interaction that started the Monday morning beautifully.

Mrs. Savion pulled into the lot and the bus rocked as all the students climbed to their feet. Through the dirty window, I could see Superintendent Filmore standing by the doors that led into the school like he always did, smiling at everyone who walked in. He looked like such a happy old man that it was hard to see him as the guy who was trying to sink Hudson's ship and take him down.

Hudson shifted into the aisle first, and I edged into the aisle right behind him before the other students could stampede past.

"Slow down, Mr. Kessinger," Mrs. Savion scolded as I passed her, and she glared off behind me. "You boys have too much energy for the morning, I swear—"

I pulled my backpack around the front of me to shove my MP3 player inside the small front pocket, and I'd just taken the step off the bus toward the sidewalk when a student shoved into my back.

It pitched me forward unevenly, and my ankle twisted where it landed on the sidewalk, pain shooting up the tendon. My backpack hit the ground, contents spilling everywhere, my palms jarring against the concrete.

People were shouting around me, but the words were all masked by the ringing in my ears. For a long moment, I sat there, braced against the cold concrete, feeling the strongest sense of déjà vu.

A large hand curved around my upper shoulder, and then I tipped my chin up, meeting Hudson's vivid blue eyes. "You okay?"

"I think I twisted my ankle," I said through my teeth, and even though I didn't put any pressure on my foot, it throbbed along with my racing heart.

Mrs. Savion was berating Mr. Kessinger in the background, no doubt who'd bulldozed into me, and Jaden dropped down beside me to help collect a few of the contents from my bag. My MP3 player was among them, and I didn't have hopes that it survived the kamikaze.

Hudson glanced around, too, to see if there was anything he needed to pick up, when he stiffened.

Pencils, erasers, and a few coins had fallen out, but following Hudson's gaze, I saw what his attention fell on.

A purple pocketknife shined like a beacon on the concrete. In the fall, the button must've gotten pushed, because the shiny, iridescent blade glimmered in full view.

Hudson's pocketknife. The one I never took out of my bag.

CHAPTER 25

For a moment, no one moved. Time stopped. My heart stopped. Everyone around me turned to see me fall, but their eyes slid past my crouched figure to find the knife, open by my side. Technically a weapon on school grounds.

And of course the blade popped free.

I sucked in a gasp as Hudson reached for the handle, no doubt attempting to snatch it up—even though it was way too late. "Put your hands up, Hudson!" Mrs. Savion's shout came like a bullhorn behind me, and if I thought she'd been yelling at the boy who shoved me, she was definitely yelling now. "Drop the knife, *now!*"

Hudson never even had a chance to pick it up, though. He raised his palms like she pointed a gun at him, and he sighed, shutting his eyes as he did so.

At the word "knife," the crowd around us started buzzing with their chatter swelling in my ears.

Superintendent Filmore, who'd been greeting students cheerfully at the door, turned into a bull as he charged his way over. With a rough jerk, he hauled

Hudson to his feet. "You brought a knife onto school grounds? I knew you were thick in the head, but I guess I didn't realize *how* thick," he said, giving Hudson a hard shake.

From the way he was angled, it was impossible to see Hudson's expression. I could hear his voice, though, and it was as nonchalant as ever. "I've never really been known for my good decisions, have I?"

Superintendent Filmore's expression grew angrier, cheeks turning red. "Let's go."

"Wait!" I'd tried standing up, too, but I'd shifted my weight onto my leg, the pain sending me crashing back to the ground. I sucked in a sharp breath as if that would satiate the fiery bolt that shot up my ankle. When I looked up, the superintendent's back was starting to merge into the crowd. "Mr. Filmore, I—"

"Are you hurt, Gemma?" Mrs. Savion ducked down beside me, plucking the knife up and shutting it with a *click*. Her wrinkled face was filled with concern and worry lines, but for the wrong reasons. "Is it your ankle?"

"It's not Hudson's knife," I said, once again trying to scramble to my feet. Mr. Filmore had drawn Hudson away at that point; I couldn't see his blond head in the crowd. "I have to tell him that, I have to tell them—"

"You need to go to the nurse's office," Mrs. Savion said, the calm quality in her voice clearly indicating that she hadn't picked up on the intensity of mine. She looked up at people who were still lingering and staring. "Who can help Gemma to the nurse?"

I wanted to scream.

Two junior girls I didn't recognize helped me to my feet. One wrapped their arm around my waist to hold me up and the other carried my backpack, and despite my protests, they took me to the nurse, not to Principal Oliphant. When I told Mrs. Wells, the school nurse, that I needed to go to the office, her response had been immediate. "You can go after we check out your ankle."

And so, despite practically fidgeting out of my skin on the cot, I let Mrs. Wells do her job.

"It's a small sprain," Mrs. Wells, said as she finished wrapping my ankle up. Her royal blue scrub top matched Brentwood High's colors, and so did her golden yellow scrub bottoms. "We'll keep some ice on it and keep it wrapped, and the swelling should go down."

I shifted my position on the firm cot, looking down at where Mrs. Wells had propped my foot on a little yoga block. I couldn't necessarily see that it was swollen, but it *felt* like it, like several bees had stung up along my ankle. "Can I walk on it?"

"Ah, I'd recommend against that," she replied, and gave a little laugh. "It's not a bad sprain, so you could put some weight on it after twenty-four hours. I would recommend forty-eight, though, to be on the safe side. I'll give you a crutch you can borrow for the next few days."

A sprained ankle. All because some junior was eager to get off the bus. The dread that reared its ugly head in waves came out in full force as I recalled the events that'd followed like I was watching a horror movie.

"Got the ice!" Rosie stormed through the open door of the nurse's office with a plastic bag of ice, waving it like a trophy. "Sorry it took me so long. I got lost on my way to the cafeteria. Apparently, you *don't* memorize the layout of a school after two weeks."

"Thank you, Rosie." Mrs. Wells took the bag from her and carefully laid it on the top of my ankle, letting the excess ice flow over to cover the sides of my foot. "Let's let that sit for a while. Your mom should be here shortly."

My world tilted. "My mom?"

"Principal Oliphant called her for the incident, since she's the president of the school board. Something to do with a school safety issue."

I couldn't even believe how fast things were devolving, like I was in a plane that was nosediving toward the ground. Impact was coming.

Mrs. Wells walked into the front of the office, leaving me mid-spiral. Rosie sat down on the stool the nurse had occupied, smoothing down her black silky pajama top. During all of this, I was still sitting in my pjs. What was quickly becoming the worst day of my life, and I was in my pajamas for it.

"Rosie," I said, pushing the cot to sit up straighter. "Did you see Principal Oliphant in the hallway?"

Rosie glanced over her shoulder at the open door before propelling herself closer to me, the stool's wheels squeaking a little. "I didn't get lost," she whispered conspiratorially. "But I did stop by the office to 'ask for directions.'"

I could've hugged her. "What's going on in there?"

"There wasn't anyone in the office's waiting area, but it sounded like there was a party in Principal Oliphant's room." Rosie gestured wildly with her hands at the next part. "So many people talking at once. I didn't hear Principal Oliphant's voice, though, but a lot of male voices."

Was one of those voices Hudson's dad? The thought of Principal Oliphant calling his dad made me feel sick, because that meant things were serious. Which of course they were—there was an open knife on campus—but it wasn't Hudson's fault. It'd fallen out of *my* bag. I needed to tell them that.

"And there was..." She trailed off, frowning.

"What?"

"There was a police officer sitting in one of the chairs."

Police. No, no, no. "I have to get to the office," I told her, frantically looking around the room. "Where's the crutch Mrs. Wells said I could borrow? Can you get it for me?"

Thankfully, instead of insisting I stay in the nurse's office, Rosie rushed to grab the crutch from the next room. Mrs. Wells frowned at us both when we emerged from the room, and she stood up from her desk. "Gemma, I really think you should wait until your mom—"

I didn't give her time to finish, and I shoved out of the infirmary with Rosie right behind me. "What are you going to say?" she asked, keeping up with my hobbling pace. The crutch was too short for me, and it scraped against my side with every step. "Storming in there like this might not be the best plan of attack."

She was probably right, but I really only had one plan —not to let Hudson face this alone. None of this was his fault, anyway. Hudson was in there facing the firing squad while I was the one sitting in silence with ice on my leg. He didn't deserve to be in there—*I* did.

I hadn't remembered that the knife was in my backpack, but now, I could remember it with perfect clarity. Hudson passing me the knife. Me holding it in the backseat of Derrick's car for a moment before slipping it into my backpack pocket, where I'd completely forgotten about it. It was a wonder I hadn't discovered it earlier, but with pencils and erasers and other random things stuffed into that pocket, I must've missed it.

My mind fell into the worst-case scenario—suspension, expulsion, permanent records—and there was no thinking beyond it.

"Why were you in the infirmary, anyway?" I asked Rosie, casting her a sidelong glance. "Are you sick?"

"I help Mrs. Wells with paperwork and everything for first period. It's technically counted as an extracurricular." She shrugged a little. "It's a solution I worked out with Principal Oliphant since I'm late waiting for my siblings' bus sometimes. It's easier to come in and help Mrs. Wells rather than interrupt a history lesson or something."

My eyebrows shot up in surprise. "That's allowed?"

"I mean, I don't know if it's something they do for everyone, but, yeah."

Her situation sounded awfully similar to Hudson's, but instead of being punished for it, she was given an option to make things easier. How was *that* fair?

It's hard to change someone's mind when it's already

made up, and Principal Oliphant had talked about the school board's vendetta. Just because they didn't like Hudson, they weren't going to help him like they'd help others.

Since classes were currently in session, there was no one in the halls to witness us hurry through, or hurrying as much as I could with my throbbing ankle. We turned down the main hallway, and the office door was in sight. Just a few more steps—

The door swung inward, and I stumbled to a halt when the person who stepped out into the hall turned to face us.

Mom.

Mom was dressed in her work clothes, with a pretty top covered by a thick cardigan, her red curls pinned up out of her face. It exposed every single inch of the anger that tightened her features, the tendons in her neck sticking out as she drew in a deep breath. I'd never seen her so upset.

I crumpled under Mom's stare, a muted sort of panic making my skin feel hot and cold all over. A wave of dizziness struck me, one so strong that I nearly toppled on my unsteady crutch. I hobbled forward, the crutch the only noise that pierced the air. Black spots popped up at the corner of my vision, and suddenly actually falling into Rosie seemed like a very real possibility.

Mom met me halfway, standing in front of the school's bulletin board. "Before I say anything," she began, voice eerily calm. Calmer than her expression hinted at. "Are you okay?"

I looked down at my ankle, the vise around my throat tightening. I nodded.

"In that case, it seems as though you have had an eventful morning. Or, should I say, eventful past few weeks?"

Panic fluttered like a caged bird in my chest, thrashing against my ribs uncomfortably, stirring nausea. I never fully thought this moment through—the idea of Mom finding out about *anything* that'd happened over these past few weeks was scary, but I never knew how truly terrifying it was.

This was my house of cards, exploding into the air.

"Can you give us a moment?" Mom asked Rosie, not even sparing her a glance. I nearly reached out and grabbed Rosie's wrist, refusing to let her leave us, but I couldn't move. Rosie only hesitated a second before she turned around, her footsteps a quiet retreat. "Care to tell me anything, Gemma?"

I hated the question, because it left me to guess what she was the most upset about, left me to guess what she knew exactly. Was she talking about the buddy program? About the knife? About Hudson in general? My voice came out in a broken whisper to her heels. "Please don't be mad at me."

"Don't be mad?" Mom repeated, taking a step closer to me. "Don't be *mad*, Gemma? Tell me how I should be feeling, finding out my daughter's lied to me about every-thing she's been doing since school has started?"

I sucked in a short, trembling breath, blinking to try and clear my hazy vision. My brain felt like it was shutting down, cowering away from the confrontation, and I could do nothing but stand still.

"I specifically remember you telling me that your buddy was a girl. A girl that you *went to the movies with.*" Her voice dipped into a hiss. "Did Morgan even go with you that day?"

The breath I let out shook, doing nothing to alleviate the ache in my chest. "No."

She scoffed, glancing around the hall as if she wanted to convene with someone about how insane her daughter was. "Why on earth would you let Talia talk you into this, Gemma? What made you not tell me? Why on earth did you think that was even a remotely good idea?"

Please, I thought, and I wasn't sure why I thought it, but it was a word that blazed its way across my mind. *Please, please, please, please.* "Please don't be mad."

Mom got fed up with me staring at her shoes, because suddenly her fingers were underneath my chin, lifting my head up. My vision swam. "I can't even understand you," she said, the exasperation in her tone clear. "I've never been more disappointed in my life. And I know your father will be disappointed too when we tell him. We raised you better than this, didn't we? *I* raised you better!"

She slapped the disappointment card down with no mercy. I hated how much it made me shrink into myself, cold darkness pooling around me. I was once more in the cardboard box, but this time, I wasn't banging on the sides. I cowered in the corner, hoping the shadows could hide me, swallow me whole.

When I was little, I learned what it meant to be a Settler. We were a founding family, one of the most popular families of Brentwood. We had an image to maintain. The Settlers, the Dyers, the Oliphants, the Brays—we were the families that people in town knew. People would call Mom and invite her to their parties, or people would call Dad and invite him for a barbeque. Landon was picked first on all the teams, and even landed quarterback.

My entire life, we'd been in the spotlight. We were meant to keep our heads down, to be above reproach. And I'd been perfectly okay with it all, never thinking twice.

Until I wasn't. Until I woke up.

Never in my life had I so desperately wished I'd still been asleep.

"Please don't be mad at me," I repeated, drawing my lower lip between my teeth and biting down, trying hard to stifle the increasing pressure in my chest. *Please, please, please.*

"Do you know what people will say about *you* if word gets out? Sneaking around with—with—*Gemma.* What were you thinking?"

I thought I'd be able to handle the consequences of my parents finding out. I thought I'd be able to handle whatever they threw at me, and that I'd be a whole new person who didn't care what her parents thought. I thought I'd found my footing in the new me, but the truth was that I'd only been playing a new kind of role, and the curtains were pulling to a close.

Mom being upset over this hurt more than I thought it would. I knew it would sting, but it did more than just that—it *crippled* me, to the point that I just wanted to fall at her feet and beg for her forgiveness. I didn't want her to think less of me, to be disappointed with me. In that moment, all I wanted to do was go back in time, to never do anything that would risk her getting angry in the first place.

Did you fight against it, or did you just give in to it? I'd asked Hudson that first day on the bridge.

And Hudson had tipped his head down, a smile on his face. *Is there a point to fighting it if nothing will change?*

"I'm sorry, Mom," I whispered, something desperate holding my lungs hostage, refusing to let me draw in a deep breath. The throbbing in my ankle was definitely getting worse, but even worse was the pain splintering in my chest, spiraling me into an ocean of misery. All the years of following my mantra and doing what I was told had me not knowing how bad disobeying made me feel. I never knew how heavy Mom's disappointment really was.

In the midst of finding myself, I felt worthless in a matter of seconds.

Grow a backbone. The words were a faint whisper in my head, drowned out by the voices that screamed of defeat.

And, like before, I yielded. I forgot Hudson was in the office, still in the mess I was the one to throw him in. I forgot about the knife, forgot about the buddy program, and forgot everything. I backed down. Gave in to her. Gave up entirely.

"I'm really, really sorry," I murmured again, and the sob that'd been building and building finally burst free, and once I started to cry, it was a long time before I stopped.

CHAPTER 26

I laid limp underneath my duvet, the warm air I breathed out making it hard to breathe in. It was absolutely dark underneath the covers, but I blinked into the black, unable to close my eyes. Hours had passed since Mom drove me home from school, but her words still lingered in my ears.

"You broke my trust in you," she'd said, not bothering to look at my tear-soaked cheeks. *"You should've told me as soon as Principal Oliphant came to you. Are you trying to cause trouble, Gemma? Stir rumors? I didn't raise you to be so irresponsible!"*

She hadn't pulled any punches, almost like she enjoyed saying things to hurt me.

I drew in a trembling breath thinking about it now, about the wide-eyed, fuming way she looked at me. She hadn't even given me a chance to explain—not that there was much to explain. I went against her. I lied to her.

The panic from earlier in the high school hallway had left an emptiness behind that was suffocating itself, and I felt like a zombie—not dead, but not fully alive either.

And the situation with Mom—and with Dad, as soon as he popped his head into my room to give me a round of his disappointment—wasn't the only thing weighing on my mind.

Even though it was pitch black under my blankets, I turned my cell phone over in my hand, picturing the silver thing, heart giving a slow *thump-thump* as I waited for it to buzz. My parents were so unused to groundings that she forgot to take it away from me, which I knew I should be grateful for. I didn't feel anything, though. I waited for my phone to buzz. Any second.

GEMMA

Hudson, it's Gemma…I'm so sorry for everything. What happened in the office? Did you tell everyone it was in my bag?

No response.

GEMMA

Hudson?

Morgan and Jaden texted me, so I knew my phone was working. Hudson just wasn't replying.

GEMMA

I totally understand if you're mad at me

Morgan and Jaden asked about what happened, which made me think that the gossip mill hadn't been spreading around too much. I wondered, briefly, if it was a big enough deal to get onto Babble.

I think it was safe to say I remedied my Stay A Prude label.

GEMMA

You're not in trouble, are you?

One of the many cons of having a phone from the dinosaur era meant that I couldn't even see if Hudson read the message or not. Without his reply, I was left in a dark sea of waiting, one that caused the pit in my stomach to open wider and wider. It was dread mixing with panic, an ugly concoction that choked me.

GEMMA

I'm really, really sorry

It soon went from noon to four o'clock, and then from four to seven. Nothing. Not a single reply.

I was freefalling during those hours, spinning through the air without a parachute. I hated the sensation, but I was more afraid of what it'd feel like to hit the ground.

If I'd told my parents about Hudson from the beginning, none of this would've happened. I would've had the one encounter with him in Principal Oliphant's office, but that would've been it. Life would've been so much different if we would've left it there.

But you wouldn't have gotten to taste freedom, my thoughts whispered, like reassuring words falling on hard-of-hearing ears. *You wouldn't have fallen for Hudson.*

Yeah, the other side of my brain replied, *and look where that got you.*

Everything in me ached, like I was constantly on the edge of bursting into tears.

A soft knock sounded at my door, and then a second later, it opened. I stashed my cell underneath my pillows and poked my head out from underneath my duvet, spotting my brother at the door. "Hey," he said tentatively, and when he lifted his hands, I saw he had a plate in one and a bowl in the other. "Hungry?"

It was past dinnertime, but I'd given in to the fact that Mom wasn't going to call me to supper. I wondered if she would eventually deliver food, but my stomach felt as if it'd shriveled up like a deflated balloon. The idea of eating almost made me nauseous, but I still sat up. "What is it?" I asked, voice croaking as he came closer.

Landon offered the bowl to me when I sat up, setting the plate on my bedspread. "Stew. We had a few cans of it in the pantry. I warmed myself up one."

I stirred my spoon through the thick, sludge-looking food, and despite my growling stomach, my appetite waned. "Thanks."

Landon sat down on the stool beside my desk, and it groaned beneath his weight. He looked a bit like Dad in that moment, serious expression bearing down on me. "How's the ankle?"

I broke open the roll and dunked it into the soup, taking a big bite. It was lukewarm. "Ouchy."

"Missing a step off the bus will do that."

I lifted my head. "Did Mom tell you what happened?"

"No, but I heard her talking to Dad. And I heard what everyone's been saying around school." Landon rubbed his hands over his knees, sighing at the same time. "So what happened?"

I didn't want to tell him. I didn't want to rehash the situation and have him tell me that he didn't recognize me, either. Despite not wanting to tell him, there was no point in keeping the secrets any longer. "I fell off the bus and I dropped my bag. I had a pocketknife in it, and it fell out. The superintendent thought it was Hudson Bishop's, and I'm not sure what happened after that. Principal Oliphant told Mom to take me home and that we'd talk tomorrow."

Landon sat silent through the brief story, and I waited for some sort of reaction at Hudson's name, but he didn't have one. "Why did you have a pocketknife?"

I had a feeling I'd be telling the same story many times over the next few days, and it made me exhausted thinking about it. "Hudson gave it to me." Landon still didn't react. I took a peek at his expression, but it wasn't even surprised. "You're not going to ask me why he gave me a knife?"

"I know he's your mentee."

My spoon clattered in my bowl when it slipped from my fingers, little bits of stew splattering onto my hand. Had he heard Mom say that? Or was *that* the gossip going around school, too?

"Gemma, you were running around with the school's

bad boy, and you didn't think anyone would tell me?" he asked, giving me a look. "My girlfriend's *cousin*, at that. Principal Oliphant, who paired you two together, is Madison's mom, and Madison tells me everything. Did you really think I wouldn't find out?"

Okay, when he said it like that, I felt stupid.

"So, you've known this whole time?" I liked to think I knew my brother pretty well, but his reaction wasn't one I'd expected. He was way, way too calm. "Why didn't you say anything? Why didn't you tell Mom?"

"It would've been a nuclear meltdown if Mom found out. Which, I'm sure, you know. Why did *you* let yourself be paired up with him?"

"He's not who everyone says he is." I looked down into the murky depths of my stew, unsure if I could even take another bite. I was so desperate for someone to believe me. "He's not dangerous. He's a good guy. I don't care what you or Mom or anyone else says—"

"Gemma." Landon's eyebrows rose expectantly at me. "I agree."

For the second time, I froze at my brother's words, sure I misunderstood. "Agree...with what?"

"That Hudson isn't dangerous."

All this time, I'd been desperate for someone to take my side in it, and *my brother* was going to be that person? "I thought you'd think the opposite," I stammered, totally lost. "After ninth grade."

Landon tugged his hand through his red locks, gaze drifting away from mine to stare at my nightstand. He was serious in a way I hadn't seen him before, eyes growing transparent. "I never told you what happened in that fight. Mom told me not to ever talk about it again. But...it didn't happen how everyone thought."

I set the stew on my nightstand and sat up straighter, skin prickling with the undercurrent of his words. "What happened?"

"It was Ashton, Kyle, and me—we were walking to the store after school when we saw Hudson walking down the sidewalk. He was walking home, I guess. I thought we were going to pass him, but for some reason, Kyle stopped and...started picking on him." Landon's voice thickened with something that sounded like nerves, and he rubbed his shoulder. "Hudson was a really small kid then. Skinny. Glasses. Made an easy target for Ashton and Kyle to mess with. I don't know. It started off...fine. Ashton shoved him around a little, but nothing crazy. And then things...escalated."

Anticipation for what he said next stirred sickly in my stomach. "Escalated how?"

"It wasn't until Hudson pushed Ashton back that Ashton punched him, and then Kyle punched him, and I—"

My jaw dropped. "*You* hit him?"

"No!" Landon let out a sharp breath and pressed his palms to his eyes. I could hear the soft gasps his breath came in, and even from here, I could see his fingers shake. "I—I stood there like an idiot, with blood pounding so loud in my ears. I should've stopped it, but I couldn't...I couldn't stop staring. I wanted to run. I've never wanted to run away so badly in my life, and I wasn't even the one being punched."

The image Landon painted almost had me certain I was going to throw up the measly bites of stew. Three boys against one. Against Hudson. "Your face," I said after a moment, my voice shaking. I wasn't sure with what emotion, but it tasted a lot like anger. "How did it get that way?"

"After a few good punches, it was like a switch flipped. Like Hudson went into survival mode. He must've had self-defense training at some point or something, because in a second, he had Kyle flung into the brick wall by the school and Ashton's arm behind his back. From how loud Ashton yelled, I thought Hudson was going to snap it. I—I tried grabbing him, to pull him off Ashton, but he kicked my feet out from under me. He punched me a few times, but I didn't even try to stop him. I deserved it."

From the way Landon's voice quivered as he spoke, it was clear that he was still heavily affected by what happened that day. It reminded me a little of Hudson in the first few seconds that he saw Ashton in the hallway— freezing, body locking up as it recalled the fight. "And then what happened?" I asked Landon.

"Ashton shoved Hudson into the brick wall, but his face—" Landon squeezed his eyes shut, grimacing. "Hudson's face cut open on one of the bricks. There was *so much blood.* He still didn't stay down, though. For a kid so scrawny, he looked *terrifying.* Ashton said he looked like a zombie. Even with his cheek cut up, he kept at Kyle and Ashton until we all bolted."

"That's where the nickname came from," I murmured distantly, pressing my hand to my stomach. "The Grim Reaper."

My sickness was reflected on Landon's face, because even he looked filled with dread at recounting the story. Throughout the years, it never occurred to me that Landon could've lied about what happened. I never would've guessed that Landon had it in him to lie about that. But then again, he didn't lie exactly, since he never said what happened—he just never contradicted the rumors others spread. Thinking back to the day he'd come home with a split lip and a quickly swelling eye, he'd been sobbing so hard. Too hard to speak. Like he'd been beaten up...or like he'd been a part of something bad. "Why are you still friends with them? Ashton and Kyle?"

"You know how much Mom loves Ashton's mom. We were all on the junior varsity football team together, our parents were friends, they made us do everything together... I could never get away from them."

"Why didn't you turn them in?" I demanded. "Why didn't you tell anyone the truth of what happened?"

Landon looked at me with a slight downturn to his lips. His eyes were bright, and from here, they looked a little red. "Mom was the one who told me to not tell anyone," he said. "She was the one who told me she'd take care of it. And the next time I went to school, I found out that everyone thought it was Hudson who started the fight. That was what Ashton and Kyle were going around saying. That was what Mom had told the school board."

I blinked once, twice, but the words still swam in the air like alphabet soup, mushing around, not making sense. My voice was almost a whisper. "*Mom?*"

"I went to her, telling her that wasn't what happened, and she said—" Landon cleared his throat. "She said 'what's done is done, and we're not going to talk about it again.' It was the next few days after that where the 'no bullying' policy came out. Mom had been planning to make stronger consequences for it the whole time, and she couldn't have it getting out that her son was a bully himself, now could she?"

I almost felt like I needed to lie down with how hard it all hit me. I tried to picture Mom doing that—saying any of that—throwing Hudson under the bus. Could she really have been the one to sweep everything under the rug? The woman who taught me to do the right thing my entire life...could she really do something like that? "W-Why didn't you say anything anyway? Why did you let her say those things?"

Even after I asked, I knew Landon's answer. I knew it before he even opened his mouth. Because we were cut from the same cloth, with parents we were raised to never let down. "It was Mom. I never thought to doubt her before. But I should've told the truth. I should've said something when they gave Hudson that stupid nickname. I was so, so afraid of making her angry or disappointed, Gemma. I was so afraid of messing things up for her."

The Settlers have always been in the spotlight, especially Landon. Landon, the golden child, always praised for his athletics and cooed over for his shyness. He'd been in the popular crowd since middle school, and Mom and Dad celebrated him for it. Encouraged him for it. I never even considered Landon suffering under the pressure placed on him, but this was a clear example of him giving in to that stress. Backing down and falling in line. During his freshman year, he was exactly where I was now.

"There was a time that Ashton saw Hudson in the hallway," I said, recalling the event with perfect clarity. "He grabbed Hudson's backpack. And then later, Connor said something about telling you about it. Why *you?*"

"Hudson's off-limits." Landon didn't even hesitate, didn't seem the slightest bit confused. His voice was steady. "I made it clear that if anyone messes with him, I'm not standing down this time. People might've made that choice for me then, keeping quiet about the whole fight, but I'm not going to sit back again. I told them that I'd kick them out of the stupid Top Tier. I'd get them cut from the team. I'd use the Settler status to do whatever I needed to."

For some reason, his words made my throat sting, almost like my tears wanted to make a reappearance. I repositioned my ankle on the pillow, swallowing hard. "I guess that's one way to try to compensate for everything that happened."

"I'll regret that fight for the rest of my life," Landon said, pushing to his feet and towering in the center of my room. "But I sure as hell am not going to let it happen again."

Me either. The thought trickled through my mind, faint but there, but everything in me braced as if the sentence was a scary one. As if it was an impossible one. Landon had been exactly where I was, except he vowed never to let it happen again. He made a promise to himself that he'd fight whoever he needed to for Hudson. Could I say the same?

Mom's face flashed across my mind, angry and disappointed. The image nearly had tears springing to my eyes again. "I have to find out if Hudson's in trouble," I whispered, shaking my head a little. "If he's in trouble..."

"I'll find out tomorrow," Landon promised, and kicked his foot out to lightly nudge my bed. "Try not to let your thoughts spiral, okay? We'll make sure everything works out the way it should."

Landon left me alone after that. Everything felt all jumbled, like all the puzzle pieces were still in a box being shaken around, not putting together a picture yet. Knowing the truth about the fight left me feeling even worse, especially now, knowing that Mom had a hand in painting Hudson as the monster instead of Ashton and Kyle. It was like history was repeating itself.

If Mom did something now, said something, painted Hudson as the bad guy for the knife situation—I wasn't sure how I would react. Worse, though, I wasn't sure if I'd be brave enough to fight her on it. The idea of standing up to her, going under her fire again, made me want to duck underneath my covers, never to emerge.

I looked down at my ankle sadly, hating that it twisted, hating that I had to stay off my feet, hating that I wasn't going to school tomorrow. When I needed to face Hudson the most was when I was separated from him, and of course, that was when he decided not to text me back. Because even now, my cell still sat silent underneath my pillows, all my texts unanswered.

CHAPTER 27

Mom barely spoke to me in the morning. She didn't braid my hair like she always did, since I had nowhere to go. She knocked once on my door to tell me that she was leaving, but never poked her head in.

Which was probably a good thing. I wasn't sure I could face her anyway, not after everything that happened yesterday, and after everything I found out. My sadness and hollowness had been replaced with hot frustration toward her. The fact that she was the one who got Hudson into the position he was in his freshman year —that it was her fault he was labeled as the Grim Reaper —was too much to confront right now. And sooner or later, she'd forgive me for acting out. She put her prized doll down now, but she'd pick me up again one day when she wanted me to attend Landon's games or to take me to her Sunday teas, or just to flaunt us as a family. If I kept my head down, the old family atmosphere could be salvageable.

The problem was that I couldn't keep my head down and date Hudson at the same time.

When my thoughts traveled down that path, everything in me ached. More than my ankle. It didn't make any sense, the idea that three weeks could've changed me so much, but it had. The taste of freedom was one that lingered in my soul, and there'd be no getting rid of it, even though I wasn't sure I wanted to taste it anymore.

Was that the part of me that my parents had fostered from years of training, years of pressure to behave in exactly the way they wanted? The part that only knew how to keep her head down and how to keep her mouth shut. The other part of me couldn't even imagine changing anything.

Well, I would've taken the knife out of my backpack.

I texted Morgan throughout the entire school day, but she had no concrete answers for me in terms of Hudson. Apparently, there were so many rumors going around that it was too hard to figure what was the truth, which for someone so obsessed with gossip, it was saying something that Morgan couldn't get to the bottom of it.

I sat on the couch now, staring at the front door as if I could will Landon to walk through it. It was four-twenty-one, which meant that he should be home any moment. Any second. He would've seen Lacey at some point today, and he'd have answers for me, answers that would no doubt soothe the dread and anxiety that'd been swirling inside me like a storm. He'd tell me everything was going to be okay. If he ever got home from stupid football practice.

The door opened, but it wasn't Landon—it was Dad.

"Hey, kid," he said with a bit of tiredness in his voice, like seeing me exhausted him a little. "What are you doing out of your room?"

The sentence didn't sound hostile—I took it as a white flag. "Stretching my ankle."

"Be careful on it. Sprains can get bad if you push the healing process too fast."

I looked down at my still-wrapped ankle where I had it propped on the ottoman before me. The ache today wasn't as bad as it'd been yesterday, but it still throbbed each time I put pressure on it. "I'm being careful."

Dad started toward the archway that led into the kitchen, pausing a little. "Gemma," he began, readjusting his hold on his briefcase. "When your mother told me the truth about your buddy program, I was surprised."

"Because you didn't think your little girl would lie to you?"

"I didn't think you'd ever put yourself through something like that. Especially with *him*."

I clenched my jaw and dropped my gaze to my ankle again, staring at it bitterly. "Sorry to disappoint you."

"I'm not disappointed," he said. "Not in the slightest."

I lifted my chin, but he was already walking through the archway, leaving his words lingering in the air. Before I had the chance to go after him, Landon came through the front door much less gracefully than Dad, bumping his shoulder pads on the frame and stifling a curse in the process. All thoughts of Dad and his cryptic sentence were forgotten, and so was my ankle, because I shot to my feet. "So?" I demanded, ignoring the twinge of pain. "What's going on?"

"Give—me—" Landon shuffled into the house and kicked the door shut behind him a little too hard, causing it to slam. "—a second."

"Landon."

He kicked his sneakers off, tripping over one of them as he tried to step forward. "Just let me get through the door, Gemma—"

"*Landon!*"

With a huff, Landon dropped everything—his shoulder pads, his backpack, his jacket—and it piled at his feet with a loud *thud*. Dad called from the kitchen asking if everything was okay. "Everything's fine, Dad," Landon said, giving me an exasperated look. "Just all my stuff."

"I don't know why you bring that home with you every day," Dad called back, but even from here, his grumble was clear. "Stinks up your whole room!"

I shook my head, forcing him to the topic at hand. "So? What's going on with Hudson?"

"The rumors going around school are kind of all over the place," he said, moving to sit on the chair nearest the door. It was normally the chair Mom sat in, and he looked like a giant in it. "Some people are saying Hudson pulled the knife on you, on the bus driver, on the superintendent himself—other people are saying that someone threw the knife down by Hudson just to get him in trouble."

"But is he?" I knotted my fingers together, squeezing. "In trouble?"

Landon let out a breath, but finally, he nodded. "Lacey said that Superintendent Filmore gave him an option of withdrawing from Brentwood on his own accord or being expelled—which would obviously look a lot worse on his transcripts. She said it wasn't really a choice."

I let out a breath as if it'd been punched from me, reeling for several seconds, unable to inhale. "He dropped out?"

"Lacey said he told them that it was his knife out of his pocket," Landon told me. "Not that it came out of your bag. He said he was the one who dropped it."

The disbelief snapped in an instant, transforming from shock and horror to *anger*. It burned hot underneath my skin, and I was almost surprised with how quickly it'd come on, and how fierce it'd been. Of course he'd lie about it. Of course he would. Hudson and I were one and the same at times, weren't we? Both of us backing down when faced with opposition. Both of us playing the part of the role we were forced into.

But I wasn't going to let it fly.

After dinner—which was delivered to me in my room once again, because Mom was still pursuing the silent treatment and only giving me messages through Landon —I knew what I was going to do. The previous night, Mom and Dad left me alone in my room, never once poking their heads in. I wasn't sure if that would still be the case tonight, but I didn't have a choice. I couldn't sit back.

GEMMA

> I'm going to the bridge at Lookout Ledge tonight at 8.

> Please come meet me.

> I'm going to wait there until you show up.

The ledge of the bridge was much colder than it'd been Saturday when I'd sat at this very spot with Hudson, and I shivered with each gust of late September wind that brushed through the tops of the trees. The sun was setting in the sky, looking much like it had on my birthday, with beautiful colors comforting me when nothing else could. The pinks and purples and yellows blended together beautifully, even when everything else was falling apart.

He'll come, I thought to myself, clutching the edge of the bridge. My nails scraped on the rough surface. *He'll come, he'll come. He will.*

My body shook, but it wasn't just from the cold. The pressure building in my body had me trembling like I would soon explode.

I probably shouldn't have been sitting so close to the edge with as shaky as I was, but I wasn't going to move. I wasn't going to move until Hudson showed. As I waited for him, I practiced all the things I could say, knowing that I needed to at least try and keep my cool, but I wasn't sure how possible it was going to be. The idea of being calm in the mess I found myself in was almost laughable.

The pink sky faded to purple, the temperature dropping. He'd come.

Sooner or later, Mom and Dad would discover I was missing. The old rebellious side of me reared its head, hoping it would be sooner. That part wanted Mom to walk into my room and discover the open window. It wanted Mom to realize that despite the shame she'd tried pouring into me, I was still going to make my own choices.

The other part, though, deeply hoped I could make it home before she found my empty room.

The purple sky bled into indigo.

I looked down the direction of the bridge he'd come in, but there was nothing. No one walking toward me, not even a shadow of a person. Nothing.

The current racing down my skin zapped, and I swung my legs over the edge of the bridge, landing in the roadway. Fine. If he wasn't going to come to me, I'd go to him. Did he think I wouldn't? To hell with getting back before Mom found me gone—if that's what would happen, so be it. I wasn't going to let him ignore me.

Right as I set off in the direction of where Vista Villas was—even though it was easily a forty-five-minute walk— headlights swept over the bridge. I edged onto the shoulder, but the vehicle slowed as it approached me. It was a van I didn't recognize, one that was a faded, peeling blue color that probably looked gorgeous in its heyday. Despite its dated appearance, the tires looked brand new, and the bumper was bright and shiny, as if it'd been recently replaced.

And the headlights were mega bright, enough that I had to lift my hand to shield the glare as it blared directly into my eyes.

Before I had a chance to be thoroughly freaked out, the driver's side door popped open, and out stepped Hudson.

I'd been expecting Bridge Boy, with his cotton candy-colored sweatshirt and his glasses. That wasn't what I got, though. The boy in front of me was in his full Grim Reaper glory. He had on his leather jacket and ripped black pants, his combat boots loosely laced. And the expression—it was so different from what I'd grown to expect. It wasn't cold, but it was distant, as if there were worlds between us instead of a few feet.

"Hi," I said, but it was such a quiet whisper that I wasn't sure he heard it.

Hudson's expression didn't change. "Get in. I'll take you home."

Flat. Emotionless. A bad sign. "I'm not going home until we talk." My voice was firmer now, enough that I wanted to pat myself on the back for it.

"About what?"

"About—" I blinked in disbelief. "About the fact that you got yourself expelled, Hudson!"

He closed his eyes with annoyance painted on his face, visible even in the dark. "Just drop it, Gem. What's done is done."

"How could you not tell them I was the one who had the knife?"

Hudson folded his arms across his chest, leaning against the side of the van. "You think they'd believe that? That prim and proper Gemma Settler brought a pocketknife to school? One with *my* initials on it?"

I winced a bit at the *prim and proper* line, but I couldn't tell if he'd intended for the blow to hit home. It was hard to fully see his expression with the glare of the headlights. "It's the truth."

"If it wasn't going to be the knife, it was going to be something else they'd expel me for, Gemma. That's how they work."

"But that's not how they're *supposed* to work! They should be giving you options; they should be on your side—"

"If this school has taught me anything, it's that the only person you can count on is yourself."

Now *that* felt like an intended blow. Of course he was jaded by everyone else, but I couldn't help but feel lumped with everyone else. I had to swallow past the thickness in my throat, digging my nails into the stone of the bridge once more. "Why didn't you tell me that you didn't start the fight freshman year?" I asked him. "Why didn't you tell me that *they* were the ones who targeted *you*?"

"Would it have made a difference?" he demanded, voice a snap. "Would it have made a difference if you knew that they threw the first punch? You wanted me to tell you that? You want me to tell you that there was so much blood in my mouth that I choked on it? You want me to tell you that I carried that knife in my pocket because I was so afraid that something like that would happen again? What would it have changed, Gemma?"

He was in his full scary mode, with his glowering gaze and sharp tongue, but this time, it didn't make me cower —it made me *angry* right back. "You think I would've sat by if I knew the truth?"

"I don't know. Would you have?"

"Of course not! I could've said something to my mom, to *someone*. I could've stuck up for you."

Hudson turned and leaned against the van, tipping his head to peer at me. "You *could've*. But *would* you have?"

"What?"

"Would you have stood up to your mom about that? About me?" The cold wind tugged through the gap between us, punctuating the iciness in his words. When he sighed, it almost sounded as if it shook a little. "I don't want to turn you against your family, Gemma. And it's all right. I'm not upset about it, okay? I'm not upset about taking the blame for the knife. I was the one who gave it to you, after all."

He might not have been upset about taking the blame, but I was. I was more upset by the finality to his voice, too, the way it clung to his voice like words unsaid. Suddenly, all of my unanswered texts weighed heavy in my pocket, like my phone had instantly turned into a stone.

Tee's words from the night I'd stayed out with

Hudson came back to me in an echoing clarity, even though that felt like a lifetime ago rather than a few days. *He's used to pushing people away. He'll push you, too, if you let him.*

"I—I can fight it with you," I said, voice losing some of its confidence. "The—the school board, my mom, whoever—"

"Why?" The glare of the headlights was still bright, but even from here, I could see the muscle in his jaw clench. "What's the point? What's the point of fighting, Gemma?"

My heart squeezed so tightly that I thought it was going to burst, hearing the defeated tone to his voice. It weighed his words down like they'd been left out in the rain, dripping and cold.

"Just...get in the car. I'll take you home, and we'll forget about this."

About us, he didn't say, but I heard the words anyway.

We both stared at each other, unmoving. The temperature on the bridge had dropped several degrees since he'd shown up, but my shivering had turned inward, rattling my core. *What's the point of fighting?* The words rang from when he'd said them the very first day we met. *What's the point of fighting if nothing will change?*

These past few weeks had been a dream. We'd both gone through the days naively. Working our way through the rebellion list had been fun, exciting, but eventually, we'd get to the last one. Life wasn't going to stay in that perfect, secret world forever, but neither of us were prepared for it to end this way.

I took a step toward him, wincing when I put weight onto my ankle, but fighting to not let it show on my face. The closer I got, the more I could see that the blue depths of his eyes glimmered as if there was fire behind them. Fire, or something else that was shiny. "I get why you didn't try to fight your role over the years," I murmured, voice thickening. "It's easier to be feared than afraid. To keep who your true self is hidden so no one can judge you. Hurt you. You don't like the dirt," I added, bringing up our previous conversation the day I went to his house. "You only like how comfortable it is."

"Like you," he returned dully. "You like how comfortable it is."

He was right, of course. Before the rose-colored glasses came off, I enjoyed it all. Them making decisions for me made things easier at times. There were never any complications. Life had been simple, easy. Comfortable. And there I was, ready to fall back into it.

He was also right about this—I couldn't fight for him if he wasn't ready to fight, either. I couldn't force him into a choice, like how my parents always forced me. I couldn't change his mind for him. The revelation settled like a boulder on my chest, crushing out the air. "Maybe... maybe we both need to grow a backbone," I said, the pressure behind my eyes building. Hudson's image turned wavy. "And see where we end up."

Hudson didn't reply, but I didn't really expect him to, either. Like we stood at the edge of the bridge now, we'd come to a ledge of our own. We could go through a rebellion list all we wanted, but now we'd have to face the truth. Life was much easier when you could pretend you were someone else, but we'd come as far as we could as these versions of us. Hudson was right, prim and proper Gemma Settler couldn't date the Grim Reaper.

It was time for both of us to walk away or jump.

I turned around and started down the road, leaving Hudson standing beside the van he'd driven. I didn't turn around to look either. My walk home wasn't far, but I took my time, limping and thinking. I couldn't be upset with Hudson for not fighting his role when I barely fought mine. I said I could've stood up for him, but Hudson was right—*would* I have? Would I have stood up to my mother, thrown my brother under the bus, to clear Hudson's name? A few weeks ago, I wouldn't have. Now...

Now, could I really put this all behind me? Could I really put all these memories in a box and pretend they never happened? Life would've been easier that way. I got my taste of rebellion, and I got the taste of the consequences.

But then again, after tasing the sweetness of freedom, after waking up from the storybook world I'd been in, could I really, *really* go back?

These past few weeks with Hudson were both blurry and vivid, like blips of a dream that weaved in and out of focus. If I were to let him go, it *would* fade into more fuzzy than clear. Ten years down the line, I'd remember the bad boy Hudson Bishop, but would I remember everything that came with him? Would I remember Bridge Boy with his glasses and cotton candy-colored sweatshirt? Would I remember the way Hudson smiled at me? The way my stomach flipped whenever he did?

Ten years down the line, would I be living the life I wanted? Or would I be living the life my parents wanted?

I got to my house before I realized it, and from the street, I could see my bedroom window still cracked open. My curtains swayed with the wind, beckoning me back, and the light was still off. From how quiet and sleepy the house looked, no one had found out that I was gone.

I stared at the window. It'd be tough to pull myself back in, but I could do it. I could slip in and no one would know.

I turned at the sound of an engine down the road and caught a flash of taillights sweep down Willow Street—as if a certain someone had made sure I'd gotten home safe.

Walk away from the edge or jump off.

My feet carried me forward, up the sidewalk path, to the front door. And then, making my decision with a peaceful weight settling over my chest, I lifted my fist and knocked.

Jump off, it is.

CHAPTER 28

When I was in the third grade, almost everyone in my class had short hair. At least, shorter than mine. At that age, my hair hung down past my waist, ending in little wisps that were always tangled and knotted. Despite the pain, I loved Mom brushing them out every night, listening to her hum as she did so. But that was until little Gemma had a realization of her own. The other girls in class wore their hair in different styles every day—buns, ponytails, curls. And I wanted that. I didn't want a long braid every day. I wanted my hair to look how I wanted it to, so I cut it off.

I don't remember actually cutting my hair, almost like that had been deleted from my memory, but the aftermath was crystal clear, like someone preserved the moment in time on video. Mom came into my bedroom and found me with the craft scissors, found the hair spread all over my floor. I remember feeling happy—so incredibly happy at the uneven bob-length cut I'd given myself—until I saw Mom's face. I'd never seen it look like that, pinched and twisted in a way that looked ugly.

And then she started crying. Screaming at me and crying. I couldn't even remember what she said, but the pitch of her voice as she spoke still rang in my ears, like a song on my MP3 player.

My response also rang clearly in my memory. *Please don't be mad at me, please, please, please.*

All of that buzzed in my head now as I waited for the door to open.

It took several moments after my knock for the deadbolt to flip over, and another second of hesitation before the wooden door swung inward, revealing Dad, dressed in sweatpants and a well-worn T-shirt.

He blinked at me standing on the welcome mat, looking like he was dreaming. "Gemma?"

"Hi," I said, and my voice sounded odd to my own ears, almost like I was speaking underwater. "Can I come in?"

Mom moved into view over Dad's shoulder, standing with her robe tied tightly around her. For the first time in two days, I could look her straight in the face, and the bags under her eyes were clear as day. She must've been feeling the same amount of stress as I was. "Gemma Marie Settler," she began, words more confused than outraged. "Do you know what time it is?"

I didn't. I didn't know how long I'd been sitting at the bridge, waiting for Hudson to show. Given how dark the sky was, I guessed a while.

"Where have you been?" Dad asked, and he sounded equally confused as Mom. "How did you get out of your room?"

"The window," I replied.

Mom gasped. *"The window!"*

I didn't know what would've summoned Landon from the other side of the house—we weren't being that loud—but in the next moment, he was there rubbing his fingers through his hair. "What's going—Gemma?"

Apparently, everyone in the Settler household needed a turn to say my name.

"Jeez, let her in, Dad, she must be freezing."

It was almost like the thought hadn't occurred to Dad. He blinked again, practically springing to the side to give me room to pass. Everyone stared at me as if I'd grown two heads.

Mom was the first to speak, looking at me with something like betrayal. "I have absolutely no idea what's gotten into you. This rebellious streak of yours, Gemma, I'll have nothing of it! Do we need to crack down, is that what we need to do? Say no phones, no friends, no school? Homeschooling isn't off the table!"

My lips twitched even though her words were anything but funny. She'd isolate me just like she isolated Hudson, and she wouldn't even think twice about it. Because it *was* her fault he was outcasted. All her fault. I couldn't remember what Mom had been like during Landon's freshman year. Then again, I *could* picture Mom doing that, throwing someone under the bus to preserve her own family image. With how easily she cut Mrs. Davies from her life for daring to vote against her, I could see Mom doing that with ease.

"It's only rebellious because it's not me doing what

you want," I murmured under my breath, but Mom still caught it.

"Yes, Gemma, defying your parents is rebellion!"

"It makes me a normal teenager!" I fired back, shocked by my own sudden harshness, at the anger that burst from the humming sound in my head. "I want to be a *normal teenager* who dresses how she wants and has whatever friends she wants and talks to whatever boys she wants. A normal teenager who goes to see a horror movie, who paints her nails, who pulls all-nighters. A normal teenager who *drives!*"

Landon's eyes were wide as he surveyed the scene, looking around our trio like he was ready to bolt between us.

Mom shook her head. "We're back to that?" Some of her fury faltered, like a split in the surface, cracking to reveal something unsettled. "I don't see how that has anything to do with you showing up so late."

"You don't know the first thing about me," I said, looking between her and Dad with my heart pumping so hard that I thought I was about to topple over. "You don't know my favorite color, or whether or not I wanted to go with Jaden to homecoming. Whether or not I wanted a date in the first place. You didn't know that the only thing I wanted for my birthday was to get my learner's permit. You don't know that I want to cut my hair. Or," I went on, nodding, "maybe you do, and maybe you don't care."

Dad took a step toward me, concerned. "Did something happen, Gemma?"

"Everything happened." The one guy who made me

feel like myself took the blame for something that was my fault and now wouldn't see me anymore. The freedom I'd felt these past few weeks went up in smoke. And possibly the worst yet was the fact that I'd found out who I truly was deep down only to lose myself again—but I made my choice. *Jump.* "You never gave me the chance to tell you the truth, but it's not Hudson's fault about the knife. It was in *my* backpack. No matter what he said otherwise—"

"It doesn't matter where it was, Gemma," Mom interjected, face growing flushed. "He took the blame for it, end of story. Trying to change the narrative now will just turn you into a liar. And I won't have you making up excuses to protect the likes of him!"

Landon did take a step forward now, raising his palms like he was approaching two rabid dogs. "You know, it's late, maybe we should talk about this in the—"

"He was a normal boy, too, before all of this," I told her, holding her gaze with a ferocity of my own. "Before Landon's loser friends attacked him and before you made sure the truth was covered up. You lied about who picked the fight, and you ruined his life. He was just a normal boy whose mom just died, and you were the one to turn him into an outcast. Into a villain. You were the one to take his name and drag it through the mud, all to protect our image. *Your image.* Look around, Mom—the only villain here is *you.*"

Mom physically recoiled, bumping into the edge of the sofa with the backs of her legs. My chest rose and fell hard with the severity of the storm inside me, one that started to dissipate upon seeing Mom's faltering expression, brow creasing and knitting together.

"If you want someone to blame, blame yourself for agreeing to the mentoring thing for me. You never asked me. You never asked if I'd be comfortable meeting with someone alone, or if I would even want to *mentor* someone. You didn't care what I thought." I cleared my throat. "Tomorrow, I'm going to Principal Oliphant, or Superintendent Filmore, or whoever the hell I need to, and I'm telling them the truth about the knife. I'll take whatever punishment they give me, but I'm not letting Hudson take it for me."

How I was going to change the school board's judgment about Hudson, I had no idea. With Mom as president, they'd probably all take her side still, right? Would they believe me if I told them the truth about the fight Landon's freshman year? But that would be the next issue to tackle. I needed to come clean first.

"It's my decision," I went on. "I'm choosing to do the right thing." Even though my insides quivered, the old fear and nervousness creeping in, I held her gaze. Her beautiful, fiery gaze. I wanted that fire to burn brightly inside of me instead of flickering. "And I won't let you make my decisions for me. Not anymore."

Silence fell over the living room like someone had muted the entire space. There wasn't a single sound besides the ringing in my ears. No one moved, and no one breathed for a long time. My hands shook in the fists they'd formed at my sides, bracing for an impact. I didn't back down, though. I wouldn't.

Dad, surprisingly, was the first to move. He reached out and placed his hand on my shoulder, its weight pressing me to the floor. "Let's take a break for the night," he told all of us. "We'll talk more about this tomorrow, when we've all had time to cool off."

I wanted to tell him that I felt cool—and *he* sounded cool—but Mom didn't look it. Her anger had subsided, though, sloughed off into a pinched and twisted expression. The same one that'd been on her face the day I cut my hair off, seconds before she started crying.

Mom didn't cry now. Instead, without another word, she turned and walked toward her bedroom, and a moment after she disappeared down the hallway, I heard her door click shut.

I let out a huge breath then, like I was finally given the okay to breathe. With her gone, my heart kicked up its pace, as if recognizing the danger only after it passed. Dad took his hand off my shoulder and followed after Mom. "Make sure the door is locked," he said, but didn't look at me when he said it.

He left Landon and me in the living room alone, standing in the darkness since no one had turned a light on. I stood by the door watching him, waiting for his reaction, waiting for him to tell me that I'd gone too far. That I shouldn't have yelled at Mom. That I should've just resorted to being the good little girl they expected from me.

Instead, Landon chuckled once. "Badass, Gemma," he said appreciatively, nodding. "Badass."

CHAPTER 29

The next morning, Mom did not come into my room to make sure I was awake, like she always did. She did not wait for me in the bathroom to braid my hair, like she always did. She did not stand with me in the doorway to send me off to school, like she always did.

"She left early today," Dad told me when I came out into the living room.

I'd brushed through my hair on my own, getting all the knots out, looking at myself in the mirror as I did it. I didn't look any different after standing up for myself, but I *felt* different. The change was so fundamental inside me that I would've sworn that it'd make an outward appearance, but no.

However, brushing my hair with no one around, I had the biggest, biggest urge to take the scissors out of the drawer and chop it all off.

"How's your ankle feel?" Landon asked as he braked for a stop sign, glancing over at me.

I looked down at the footwell of his car, at my ballet

flat that was visible, as well as the inches of exposed skin from my skirt. I'd picked the one that I'd cut up the day I went to the bonfire at Tee's, the skirt that gave me a connection to him. "It still hurts a little, but it's not that bad. I was able to take the binding off today."

"You practice what you're going to say?"

Even the mention of the confrontation that was about to go down spurred a whole new wave of butterflies. Landon offered to drive me to school this morning so I could talk to Principal Oliphant early. "Not really," I confessed, shifting uneasily. "But I'm going to tell the truth. I shouldn't have to practice the truth, right?"

Landon nodded. "Are you sure you don't want me to come with you? To come clean about the fight?"

Landon had been insistent about coming with me, telling his truth too, but every time, I shook my head. "We'll tackle one issue at a time," I said now, picking at my hemline. "But I'll let you know if it comes up."

I tucked my hair behind my ear, thinking about Hudson and what he was doing. Was he awake? Had he already started the transfer process to another school? I hoped not. I hoped that I could get to Principal Oliphant and Superintendent Filmore in time to reverse everything.

And they'd believe me. They'd have to.

The Brentwood High parking lot was pretty empty when Landon pulled into it, since it was still almost forty-five minutes until school started. He cut the engine, turning to look at me. "Whatever happens with Mom and Dad, I've got your back, you know." He reached out and thumped my arm with his fingers. "You can always trust me."

"How come *you* didn't trust *me*?" I asked, and when he raised his eyebrows, I added, "With Lacey."

"Lacey's...special," he admitted, a corner of his mouth tugging up. "When things are special, they need to be handled with care."

Though I wasn't totally sure what he meant by that for his situation, his words made me think of Hudson. *Yeah*, I thought. *They do.*

Landon and I parted ways inside the school, with him going toward the gym and me heading toward the offices. It still seemed crazy to me how different things were now. A few weeks ago, I'd been marching behind Principal Oliphant as she led me to her office, where Hudson Bishop sat slouched in a chair. I'd been so afraid to even sit beside him. Now, as I made that same march to her office, I realized that her buddy program had been a success.

Only one of the whispering secretaries was at her desk when I walked into the office, sipping from a coffee mug, blinking at me with surprise. I was fully prepared to tell her that I demanded to speak with the principal, but she got her words out first. "Gemma. Your mother's in talking with Principal Oliphant now."

I sucked in a sharp breath because that was the *last* thing I expected her to say. "My mother?" I echoed, but without waiting for a response, I darted to Principal Oliphant's door and latched onto the handle when I heard Mom's voice filter through.

"—my resignation as the school board president, effective immediately."

I froze. I stared at the frosted glass of Principal Oliphant's door, unable to make out anything but a blur of shapes beyond. That was definitely my mom's voice, but there was no way that was what she just said.

"Naomi, what on earth?" The voice wasn't Principal Oliphant's—it was definitely male, deep. It took me until he spoke again to realize it was Superintendent Filmore. "You can't be serious. Just because of all this?"

"'All this' is a completely valid excuse to resign," Mom replied, her voice calm, collected. "And there's no time like the present."

All this—all of what? I tightened my grip on the handle.

"Who's outside the door?" Principal Oliphant demanded, and then there was a shuffle. "Ms. June, if you're eavesdropping again—"

The door tugged open out of my grip, revealing a bright room filled with serious faces.

Principal Oliphant took a step away from the threshold, blinking at me in surprise, but she wasn't the one I focused on. The next person my eyes found was Superintendent Filmore sitting stonily in his chair, a far cry from the normally cheery expression he wore when greeting students each morning.

"Gemma," Mom said, and for the first time, I really looked at her. She didn't have any makeup on, and her hair was only pulled back by a hair clip, not styled in its usual way. She wore a sweater and jeans, which wasn't her usual work attire. Her voice sounded tired. "You're here early."

"Uh...yeah." I glanced around at everyone, trying to find information on *someone's* face that I could latch on to. Everyone looked at me, though, like they had no idea why I'd be showing up. Well, Principal Oliphant and Mom looked at me that way—Superintendent Filmore refused to meet my eyes. "What's going on?"

Principal Oliphant and Mom exchanged a look, one that Superintendent Filmore didn't seem inclined to join in on. "We were just discussing the incident with Hudson," Principal Oliphant eventually answered for the group, and she ventured toward her desk, easing into her seat. "And how it was you who had the knife, not Hudson, as Superintendent Filmore initially assumed."

"He was reaching for it, "Superintendent Filmore insisted. "And it *did* have his initials on it."

"That wasn't an excuse for yanking him around by his collar," I retorted, half shocked by the tone of my voice. Aside from using it on Mom last night, I'd never spoken to an adult like that before. Especially not someone as important as the superintendent. "Hudson's not a bad student. He's just so used to people not giving him chances. So used to people judging him. To *you* not giving him a chance."

"Gemma," Principal Oliphant began.

"The school board's sabotaged him this entire time, didn't look to see how they could *help*, only how they could get rid of a problem." This time, I turned toward Mom, latching on to her gaze. "And it's not right."

"You're right," Principal Oliphant said, cutting into my heated speech not unkindly. "You're right, Hudson *is* used to people judging him. To not getting chances. As a school, we should be horrified—" She shot the superintendent a look. "—to learn that a student would feel this way within our walls."

Superintendent Filmore coughed an agreement, nothing about his expression hinting at how horrified he was supposed to feel.

"I heard what you said," I said to Mom, shifting on my feet. The confrontation from last night still lingered between us, creating an awkward tension. "You're resigning?"

Mom lifted her chin. "I am."

"Why?"

She pressed her lips together, and I thought she was going to ignore me entirely, but she ended up turning to Principal Oliphant. "Talia, can you excuse me a minute to talk to Gemma?"

Principal Oliphant nodded. "Go ahead. I've got a feeling that we'll be here a while."

Superintendent Filmore let out a sigh, settling deeper into his seat.

I followed Mom out into the main office, walking past the secretary and out into the hallway. It was still deserted since it was so early, not a single student in sight. I shifted my weight onto my good ankle, fumbling for something to say, to pick one of the many questions in my head.

"Talia's doing a good job at holding Gene accountable for everything he's done. For jumping the gun." Mom reached up and pushed some of her loose curls out of her face. "She's very persuasive. I can see how she got you to agree to mentoring Hudson."

"She knows how to guilt trip," I agreed, but felt too far from smiling. "Mom—"

"You know, when Landon was a freshman, that was my first year on the school board," she said, cutting me off. She didn't quite look at me either—she looked just over my shoulder. Like she *couldn't* quite look at me. "I've always been quite the social butterfly in town, but this took it to a whole new level. I didn't quite realize how *public* I'd be."

I frowned a little, not seeing where she was going with what she was saying.

"There's a lot of pressure in any sort of position, but I was ready for it. At least, I thought I was." She blinked a few times, almost like she was fighting a wave of tears. Her eyes, though, seemed dry. "The first thing I thought I'd do was introduce a stricter no-bullying policy. Brentwood was rampant with altercations when I was elected. They had quite the social caste system, and you wouldn't know it looking at the school now, but there used to be phone calls to police because the peer violence could be so bad."

There *had* been rumors that Brentwood had been a lot different just four years ago. That was why Mom had been praised so much for the zero-tolerance policy. People said she cleaned up Brentwood, straightened the students' acts. I wouldn't say she got rid of any social caste system—hello, Top Tier and the Most Likely Tos—but aside from Wes and his friends, there *wasn't* much bullying. Not the blatant, just-for-fun kind.

"Days before it went into effect, everything with your brother went down." Mom shook her head a little. "It was...bad timing."

"So what?" I demanded, drawing in a breath. "So you let someone else take the heat for it? You blamed an innocent kid after he was *attacked*?"

"You won't understand me," she said, voice thin. "Superintendent Filmore—Kyle's father—was already putting things in motion. Spreading that rumor. Kaia Shaw joined in. I weighed my options—contradict them during my first few months of my elected term or agree with them and try to move past it. I didn't realize that boy would suffer from that choice."

I spoke through gritted teeth. "Hudson."

She nodded. "Hudson. I didn't realize Hudson would suffer. I didn't think there would be long-lasting consequences. I put my son—myself—before another student, and it's so far from okay. And that, Gemma, is why I'm resigning."

I still didn't quite understand. "Why now?"

"Because I thought about it all night, and I don't want to be the villain in anyone's stories." Mom's eyes softened for the first time in the whole conversation, and this time, I could see the little gleam to them. "Especially not yours."

I drew in a breath to brace myself, but for some reason, her words still hit my chest hard all the same.

Mom glanced around the high school hallway. "When you were growing up, we were close, you and me. I loved listening to the stories you came up with, seeing what clothes you put on your dolls, drawing with you. You used to love it when I braided your hair before bed. You'd beg me to use the strawberry-scented detangler, do you remember that? Not the watermelon—only strawberry. And I loved that section of life together. Raising you and your brother—it was the best. And I just wanted it to stay that way forever."

My throat swelled like I needed to cough, my own eyes beginning to sting. I looked down at my feet, at my ankle that still looked a little swollen, swallowing hard. "It's not supposed to be that way forever."

Mom chuckled a little sadly. "I see that now. I didn't realize I wasn't letting you grow up, Gemma. I didn't realize I was treating you like a little girl instead of a normal teenager. I *should've* known. I knew you wanted your learner's permit. I knew you wanted a bit more independence. I was so used to having you by my side, having you there to talk to. I didn't want to let you go." Mom gave me a sad smile. "But you've got your wings now. You aren't old enough to fly out of the nest completely, of course, but you...you should have the chance to test fly them once in a while, without caring what anyone thinks."

Now it was my turn to have tears spring to my eyes, because this was the response I'd been longing for, desperate for. Even back to that day where I sat on the bridge, driver's permit application in my hand, that was all I wanted to hear her say. Morgan and Hudson were right. She was strict. But despite how strict she was, of course I loved my mom. I didn't *want* to fight with her, just like I didn't want her upset with me. I didn't want to do things against her, but I also knew that I couldn't go back to the way things were.

And here she was, telling me that the way things were now could work toward becoming our new normal.

"I'm sorry that I made your decisions for you, that we got to this point," she went on, taking a big sniff and swiping her fingers along the corners of her eyes. Water glistened there, but she was quick to mop it up. "I promise to be better about asking for your opinion on things, letting you make your own choices."

"Like cut my hair."

She pulled in a breath, the instant regret crossing her features. But then it cleared, and I could see her actively work through the response. "It'll be hard," she admitted, looking at my loose locks all around me. "But yes. Even cut your hair, if that's what you want. As long as I can go with you to the appointment."

I gave Mom a watery smile, nodding. "Deal."

Without another word, Mom wrapped her arms around my frame, and I settled into her embrace as I slowly returned the hug. It might've been embarrassing that we were having this conversation in the high school hallway, where anyone could turn the corner and see me hugging my mom, but I couldn't have cared less in that moment. The steps we took in the right direction were huge, and it was a big difference from the place we'd been at forty-eight hours ago.

Mom squeezed me tighter, almost like she didn't want to let me go. She reached up and smoothed her hand down my back. "I'll..." She cleared her throat. "I'll make sure Hudson gets cleared, okay? As my last act as school board president, I'll make sure of it."

"Thank you," I whispered back, sniffing. I didn't realize how much it was a relief to have her on my side until she said it, and I let out a little sigh, relaxing even deeper in her embrace.

"You might be facing some consequences, though." Mom pulled away to peer at my expression. "Bringing a weapon on school grounds—however unintentionally—there will need to be some consequences for you as well."

"I don't care," I said immediately, shaking my head. "I'll take whatever it is. Just as long as Hudson isn't in trouble."

She reached up and swiped her fingers against my cheeks, knocking the tears away. "I'll make sure he's okay. I promise. It seems...it seems I really misjudged him. You really like him?"

"More than anything," I said confidently, but my heart squeezed. Because even though I finally won Mom over to my side, I knew where I'd left things with Hudson, and even with his name cleared, it didn't change anything about *us*.

"I'll look into making an appointment for your driver's permit," she went on. "I should've seen how badly you wanted it."

A part of me felt half afraid to hope, but the bigger part—the part that'd been so excited to wake up on my birthday—smiled now, feeling weightless. "But you see now."

"I do." Mom slipped my hair over my shoulder, tucking it over my ear to expose my full expression. I was so used to her always pulling my braid over my shoulder, saying that I looked prettier that way, that I held perfectly still as she took in every drop of emotion in my eyes. "That I do."

Yesterday, I'd been so afraid that we'd never come to this position. Because just like Mom felt, *I* was used to always having *her* at my side, too. I was used to having her to rely on. But she was also right—I had grown my wings. It was time to do some flying.

This time, though, I had her permission. I had her support. And that meant more than anything in the world.

CHAPTER 30

I stood at the bus stop Wednesday morning with my backpack high on my shoulders, letting out a breath that fogged in the air. Jaden didn't stand beside me this morning—Mom texted his mom last night that they wouldn't need him walking me to the bus stop anymore. That I would be walking myself.

It was small, me walking the block on my own, but it left me feeling wide awake despite the early time.

Then again, I had a few things that made me feel like I'd had two entire energy drinks.

Wind brushed past me, tickling my neck where it was exposed above the collar of my jacket. I reached up and readjusted the fabric, and as I did so, my knuckles brushed against the feathery ends of my hair.

Yesterday, after school—or, more specifically, after I got out of detention—I went straight to Serious Style and made a walk-in appointment with Kim, Mom's hairdresser. She had a client coming in twenty minutes from when Mom and I stepped into the salon, but her expression when I told her what I wanted was like a kid on Christmas, lighting up with as much excitement as I'd ever seen on an adult.

"You want your hair cut!" she had exclaimed, winding her arm around my waist and ushering me toward the chair. "Oh, I've been waiting for this day! Big step for us, huh, Mom?"

Mom had clutched her purse tightly against her side, almost like she was using it for emotional support as she watched us. "Big step," she had agreed.

As Kim had draped the black cape over me, I thought back to the day I'd been in here with Mom. There had been a little girl getting her hair cut then, with her mother tearfully watching. In that moment, I'd been so angry. I was angry that I couldn't have that, that Mom would never get to a place to let me have that.

But there she was, standing behind me, watching as Kim had sectioned off my hair. She had looked like crying, for sure—and she did end up letting the water-works loose—but she never stepped in, never interrupted. She had let Kim snip away.

Big steps, indeed.

I threaded my fingers through my shoulder-length hair now, still in awe every time I touched it at how light it felt. Waking up and not needing to have it braided was almost like a dream. It had a little wave to it from how I slept, but it was so pretty.

It was so me.

Bus 32 pulled up to the curb right on time, and Mrs.

Savion started smiling even before she opened the door. "Good morning, Gemma. No Jaden today?"

"I think his parents are driving him," I replied, climbing on with a little hop to my step. My hair swished with the movement, tickling my skin.

"Oh, your hair!" Mrs. Savion followed my movement in her large rearview mirror, finding my gaze. "You look so mature. I bet it feels so much lighter."

I beamed at her, reaching up and touching the ends once more.

When we turned into the Vista Villas lot, I kept my face practically plastered against the dusty glass, breath fogging up the reflection. I checked in with Principal Oliphant after school yesterday and before detention, and she said that she contacted Hudson's dad and told him that the truth about the situation came to light, and that Hudson was allowed to return to school. Mrs. Savion turning down Vista Villas proved that she'd spoken the truth, because we were on our way to Hudson's bus stop.

I closed my eyes a little, mentally preparing myself for seeing him. We hadn't left each other in the best place, and I had no idea how he'd react upon seeing me. Seeing my hair. I'd taken the jump off the edge, but I knew I needed to wait for him to make his choice. Just like how he wanted me to kiss him first, he had to want to fight for himself.

And I really, really wanted him to.

But as Mrs. Savion pulled up to the designated bus stop, my heart fell. Hudson was nowhere in sight, and the cable box he usually leaned against was empty. Mrs.

Savion glanced around as if waiting for Hudson to suddenly appear, but he never did. After a moment of waiting, she shut the doors and eased off the brake, letting the bus roll forward, kicking up dust in its wake.

Did he already go through the process of enrolling in another school? Did he say to hell with Brentwood and all the problems that were in its walls? Maybe he was just sick today. Maybe he'd be waiting at the bus stop tomorrow. Maybe it wasn't fully over.

I pulled out my cell, but the last text that sat between Hudson and me was the one where I told him I'd be going to the bridge. It read like the final page in a book, a last line that left the reader feeling bittersweet.

I pocketed my phone, swallowing hard.

Superintendent Filmore stood greeting the students like he normally did, but he didn't even look at me, almost like I wasn't there. Which was fine—I was totally content with pretending he didn't exist either. I shuffled inside with the flow of students, keeping my head down, looking at my leggings. They were a deep maroon print with faint abstract shapes, and it went perfectly with my cream-colored oversized sweater. Rosie would be proud of the outfit, I thought—I knew I was. It was strange not wearing a skirt, weird to feel fabric touching my skin so tightly, but for one of the first times in my life, I felt *fashionable.*

I felt like *me.*

I'd gotten a little ways down the sophomore hallway before I lifted my gaze, stumbling to a halt.

A boy sat on the ground in front of my locker with his

legs bent at the knees in front of him. The denim was a light wash, not a tear in sight, and his sneakers were navy Converse, not a boot. The cotton candy-colored sweatshirt he wore had the sleeves pushed up to his elbows, exposing his forearms where he rested them on his knees. And when I got to his face, I found blond hair tucked over the boy's ears, exposing the black arm of thick glasses frames.

As if sensing me, he turned his head and met my gaping gaze, and for a long moment, neither of us moved. Students passed by me, but I barely registered anyone but him.

Bridge Boy.

Hudson Bishop.

He hurried to get to his feet as I forced my feet to move toward him, and he dusted his palms along his jeans, straightening his sweatshirt. No one paid any attention to him in the hallway, not looking close enough to realize he was the Grim Reaper, not caring about the boy in the light-colored sweatshirt. I cared, though. So much.

"Your hair," Hudson said when I got close, eyes widening at the blunt ends. He gave a disbelieving blink. "It's short."

I smiled a little at the obvious statement, reaching up and fanning my fingers through it. "It's been a pretty crazy past twenty-four hours." I raised my eyebrows at him. "This guy I really like made me realize how much I needed to fight for what I want."

Hudson's lips twitched, too, but in a way that made him look more uncertain. "How'd he do that?"

"I knew I couldn't be with him unless I *did* fight for it. The choice was easy."

He dropped his gaze to the floor for a moment, nudging his glasses up his nose with a knuckle. "When she called yesterday, Principal Oliphant said that you took the blame for the knife."

"Because it's my fault. I'd do it again."

"Even though I told you I didn't mind doing it."

"My entire life, everyone's made my decisions for me." My voice was level, firm, even though my pulse fluttered unevenly in my throat. It was easy to bask in the confidence of the choice now, and the relief that came hot on its heels. "I wasn't going to let you make this choice for me."

His lips turned up at the corners more, but the smile looked more sheepish than anything. Students were beginning to gather more now, and I had to step out of someone's way as they asked to get into their locker.

"Come with me," I told him, and without waiting for him to reply, I reached out and grabbed ahold of his hand, fitting our palms together and winding his fingers with mine. I almost expected him to pull away, but he didn't. He didn't squeeze my hand back, but he did let me pull him through the hall.

It was strange, walking hand-in-hand down the hallway with Hudson Bishop. No one even looked twice. It made me realize then how identifiable Hudson had been by his dark clothes. That people would see him from the corner of their eye but never really look closely. It was how I'd been that very first day on the bridge—he'd looked *like* someone I knew more than like the Grim Reaper himself. And now, no one really looked twice.

Ms. Murphy was in her office when I knocked on her open door, and she looked up from her desk. "Do you mind if we talk in here for a second?" I asked her, refusing to let Hudson's hand go.

"Oh, sure, sure!" She got to her feet and picked up something from her desk. "I need to make copies of something anyway. So...take your time."

I could've hugged her for how easily she gave us space, no questions asked. Maybe she knew the entire situation and knew how much we needed to hash everything out. At least, hash out as much as we could before first period started in ten minutes.

Hudson moved into the seat on the opposite side of Ms. Murphy's desk, but I didn't sit in the open space beside him. "What happened Monday in the office?" I asked him, leaning on the edge of Ms. Murphy's desk. "Did they say you were the one who had the knife?"

"Not right away." Hudson tipped his head to the side, grimacing as he recalled. "I actually had to wait in Principal Oliphant's office until my dad came, like I was arrested and I needed a lawyer before I could talk. Superintendent Filmore was in there, fuming in the way he does, but no one really said anything until my dad walked in...with your mom."

"My mom?" I tried to picture it. "She came in with your dad?"

"I think they saw each other in the parking lot." He scrubbed a hand over his face before threading it through his hair, tugging through the blond locks. "I don't know. But as soon as she was in there, that's when Filmore started telling her and my dad everything. He talked about the buddy program that Principal Oliphant kept secret, talked about how I must've brainwashed you, how I pulled out a knife."

As Hudson went on, my frustration built anew, and I wished I could see Superintendent Filmore and his stupid smile one more time so I could hit it off his face.

Hudson cleared his throat as he went on, shifting how he sat in the chair. "Principal Oliphant said that I have a clean slate now. That everything that happened in the past—the tardies, the absences, the arrest—they're going to wipe it from my record. Treat me like I'm a whole new student. Which is...hard to wrap my head around."

About time, I wanted to say, but I still held my breath.

"She said she had a solution for the days I might be tardy because of Paisley's bus. That I'd have a flexible first period." Hudson met my eye. "She said that you reminded her of that being a possibility for me."

"I told you that I'd fight for you," I said without hesitation, making my voice as firm as possible. "I meant it."

He reached up and traced his fingertip along the arm of his glasses. "I was wrong. Fighting for what you want isn't pointless."

"Speaking of." I lowered my chin to catch his eye.

"Landon's ready to go to the principal about the fight freshman year, too. To tell the truth."

Hudson's eyebrows drew together in a small frown, and he surprised me by shaking his head. "It's funny, I never really thought of exposing the truth to that. Not really. And now, I just want to put that behind me. I know the truth. My family knows the truth. You know the truth." His gray-blue gaze locked onto mine. "That's enough for me."

I opened my mouth to argue him on that—how could he not want to throw Kyle and Ashton rightfully under the bus?—but the words ended up dying on my tongue. The fight, the aftermath—it was all attached to the Grim Reaper. He wanted to put the title and all it encompassed behind him. Besides, there wasn't really any guarantee of justice anyway—not with Kyle's dad as superintendent. "We know the truth," I agreed, nodding. "And if that's enough for you, it's enough for me."

Hudson reached into his sweatshirt pocket and pulled out a folded piece of paper. It was wrinkled, as if it'd been crumped once upon a time, but Hudson smoothed the paper flat. "You know how you asked me if I ever made a list, too?" He cleared his throat. "It's not a rebellion list, though. And there are only two things on it."

"I came up with eight and you came up with *two*?"

"Well, there were only two things I wanted."

Anticipation caused my chest to tickle. "Do I get to see?"

The way he looked at me hinted that he almost

wasn't going to hand it over, that there was still a part of him holding back. But then he stretched his hand out, and I got a full view of what the paper read.

In black ink, the letters were bold.

MOST LIKELY TO: STAY A PRUDE

Gemma Settler

Recognition flared instantly. "Was this the paper taped to my locker?"

Hudson nodded.

I wanted to laugh at the thought of him keeping it. As I took the sheet, I realized the Most Likely To label wasn't the only thing written on it. Just underneath the letters, written in smudged graphite pencil, it read:

HELP GEMMA FIND OUT WHO SHE WANTS
TO BE
FIGHT MY ROLE

"Laugh at my incredible cheesiness," Hudson said in a deadpan voice, totally unaware that I'd stopped breathing. "But this...this was what I had written down."

I traced my fingertips over the letters, over his boyish handwriting, trying to imagine him sitting down and writing this. Was it that same day he'd told me to write a rebellion list? Out of all the things he could've wanted, he just picked these two? One to do with him, and one to do with me.

As for him, it was always him and me.

"I'm not used to people fighting for me." His voice carried a soft, solemn quality, and the sound caused all the nerves and the frustration that'd built over the past few days to *hush*. Like his voice alone just took the volume and turned it down to low. "And I'm not used to fighting for what matters to me."

I swallowed. "And now?"

Hudson looked down at his sweatshirt for a brief second before turning to me, the expression in his eyes so easy to read. I couldn't remember the last time he'd looked at me so unguardedly. He drew in a breath as he got to his feet, and with how small Ms. Murphy's office was, he was only an arm's reach away. "I'm ready to wash the dirt off," he murmured, lips twitching like an almost smile. "To grow a backbone and be who I really want to be. With you."

So many times, anticipation built when I was with Hudson, feeling like I was at the tippy top of a roller-coaster ride, seconds before the drop. His words, though, finally tipped the car over the edge, sending a flood of warmth rushing through my veins.

I had to clear my throat before I spoke, folding the paper back up. I was definitely keeping it. "That was a really good answer."

Hudson stretched his hand into the distance between us, offering it out to me. "I'm Hudson Bishop," he said.

Instead of shaking his hand, I wove underneath his hand and slipped my pinky around his, giving it a firm squeeze. It was the smallest action, but called back so much between us, and it felt *right*. "I'm Gemma," I told him, lips stretching into a grin. "With a G."

And then, with my pinky still firmly wrapped around his, I leaned forward and kissed him.

His response was immediate, almost like it'd been on his mind too. Hudson tugged our hands closer, taking a step forward and closing the gap. With his free hand, he reached up and threaded his fingers into my hair, gathering it in his palm. I leaned into him, sinking into the way he felt, the way he tasted, my lips curving over his.

It felt like a lifetime had passed since our first kiss, and in a way, it had. We'd both had different outlooks that night, because even though we'd been together, it felt more like a stolen moment in time. There was always that lingering fear that at any moment, everything would crash down around us. That fear was gone now, cut off like long hair, discarded like old clothes. There was nothing to shy away from, but still everything to fight for.

We both pulled away at the same time, and Ms. Murphy's room veered into focus even though I didn't want it to. I wanted to stay in the warmth of Hudson's embrace, to linger as long as possible in the electric zap of his touch.

Above us, the five-minute warning bell rang out, dashing those dreams of mine to the ground.

"We should get going," Hudson whispered, drawing his fingertips along the edge of my jaw, directly at odds with his words. "It'll look bad if I get a tardy on the first day my slate's wiped clean."

"Speaking of clean slates," I said, drawing in a breath to calm the furious rhythm of my heart. "I finished everything on my rebellion list. *And* before homecoming."

"We'll have to make a new list, then," Hudson said, wrapping his arms around me, pulling me close. I could hear his pulse racing just as fast as mine as I pressed my cheek to his chest, and he rested his chin on the top of my head. "Together."

Together. I really, really liked the sound of that.

EPILOGUE

The Thursday before homecoming, Landon decided it was time to introduce Lacey to Mom and Dad. She was going to swing by here before they went to one of the pre-homecoming parties a guy from the team was throwing. Landon came home after practice and showered, dressing in a shirt that was way too formal for the occasion, and paced around his room until it was time for Lacey to show. Even from my bedroom, I could hear his footfalls wearing a path in his carpet, and I gave up trying to sew the hemline on one of my skirts and went next door.

"Landon," I said as I stepped into the doorway, and sure enough, the boy was standing in the middle of his room. He had his hands cupped in front of him, lost in thought until I interrupted. "Take a chill pill."

"I shouldn't be so nervous," he said with a slight chuckle. "It's not a big deal."

I arched an eyebrow. "The girlfriend meeting the parents isn't a big deal?"

Landon swallowed hard. "It is a big deal, isn't it? It's a

big deal. Especially for Mom and Dad. Especially since Mom's been wanting me to date Madison my entire life."

"Hey, I'll be here as a buffer to curb any Madison conversation," I told him, leaning my elbow against the doorway. "But I don't think Mom will bring her up. From what she's told me, she's excited to meet Lacey."

This was Mom practicing with Landon what she was learning with me—letting him make his choices. I had thought she seemed disappointed about Landon having a girlfriend who wasn't Madison the other day, but when she got home from work, the first thing she asked me to help her with was tidying up the kitchen. "I want to make a good first impression," she'd said.

And it was also the same time she told me she'd made the appointment for the DMV—next Monday, four o'clock. I smiled even now, thinking about the way every-thing worked out.

I looked at my brother now, whose thoughts were still obviously running a mile a minute, judging by the fact that his eyes never settled on any one place for long. "Don't be nervous."

Landon drew in a breath and held it.

"And breathe," I reminded him.

It was just as he let out a harsh breath that there was a knock at the front door, causing both of us to react. Mom must've been waiting close by the door, because her voice came only a few seconds after the knock, warm and happy. "You must be Lacey."

"Go greet your girlfriend," I told Landon, stepping out of the way for him to barrel through his bedroom door. I followed closely behind him, stepping into the living room and hanging back, assessing the scene.

Mom was shutting the door behind Lacey, who stood just over the threshold. She had her brown and blonde hair pulled up by a claw clip with a few strands framing her face, and she had on a pink sweater and jeans. Her lips were painted red just like they'd been that day I met her in the hallway, and they were pulled into a wide smile.

She looked up at Landon as he approached, and if possible, her grin stretched wider. "Hi."

Landon reacted immediately by reaching for her hand, pulling her closer. "Hi," he returned, and the quality of his voice almost made me laugh. Gone were the nerves and the anxiety—the way he spoke to Lacey was soft and gentle, in such a way I'd never heard from him before. *Smitten,* I thought with a small grin of my own, biting my lip to keep it to myself. *Totally smitten.*

Landon went through the introductions of Mom, who stood beside them eagerly, and Dad, who hovered in the doorway of the kitchen, before he turned to me. "This is Gemma," he said, gesturing toward me. "I think— you've met her before, right?"

"Yeah," I said, nodding. "She helped me out during the whole situation in the hallway with Morgan."

"It's nice to properly meet you," she told me, her voice light. She reached up and rubbed her hand affectionately along Landon's arm. "Landon's sister *and* Hudson's girlfriend. I knew you had to be pretty great."

Despite vouching for Hudson a few days ago, Mom still reacted to his name, blinking. "You know Hudson?"

"He's my cousin," Lacey replied. "On my mom's side. It's funny, because we don't have the same last name, but they're both church-related. Hudson *Bishop*, Lacey *Churchill*. Talk about ironic. Speaking of." Lacey turned toward me. "He's actually waiting outside, if you wanted to go say hi. He's on his way to Tee's."

"Can I go with him?" I asked Mom, pouring as much pleading into the puppy-dog gaze I gave her as I could, even going as far as batting my eyelashes. "I'll be home by eight, I promise."

The look Landon gave me was pure betrayal, and it was after the fact that I remembered I'd promised to play buffer. But he had to realize he had nothing to worry about. The way Mom reacted toward Lacey should've clued him into the fact that all of his nerves had been for nothing—it was clear that Mom was already drawn in.

"Take your phone," she told me, but she couldn't keep all the uneasiness from her expression, even though it was clear she tried. "And text me when you get there, okay?"

"I will," I told her, and then rushed to shove my feet into my sneakers. When I got close enough, I placed a hand on Lacey's shoulder. "It was really nice to meet you. Hopefully we can chat again soon sometime?"

"Definitely," she agreed. "We can secret swap about the boys."

Landon sucked in a breath. "Totally not necessary—"

"Deal," I cut him off, quickly waving at Mom and Dad as I opened the door.

Even as I shut the door behind me, I could hear Mom's voice carry through the crack, as chipper as could be. "Well, come in, come in! Are you hungry? I made a few sandwiches..."

And then I shut the door, whirling around to find a blue van parked at the curb, a boy sitting patiently behind the wheel.

It was the same van Hudson had shown up in Tuesday night, but in the daylight, the blue paint on the metal was much prettier. He was still wearing the same clothes he'd been wearing this morning at school—the cotton candy sweatshirt with his glasses firmly in place on his nose—and he tilted his head when he saw me, happy expression crossing his features.

The sight of it had my bones feeling two sizes too big for my body, and I crossed the distance between the house and the van quickly. "News travels fast, huh?" I asked him as I hauled the door open, raising my eyebrows expectantly at him. "You already told your cousin that I was your girlfriend when we just made up this morning?"

"We never officially broke up," he pointed out.

"We never officially said we were *together*, either."

It was Hudson's turn to raise his eyebrows at me. "Oh, so you just go around kissing anyone?"

That startled a laugh out of me, one that made Hudson join in.

The van was a bit higher than the average car, and I had to hop a little to get into the seat. There was an air freshener clipped to one of the air vents, radiating the clean Fresh Car Smell scent. "Is this it, then?" I asked him, turning around to peer at the backseat. "The van you and your cousin are fixing up?"

Except it wasn't the fixer-upper I'd been expecting. It almost looked fully completed. They'd converted it into a little living quarter, with a small platform bed built in the half where the back doors opened. A yellow sunflower comforter was draped over the bed, with two yellow pillows popping in the space. Since the bed was made, I could see the storage underneath. On one side of the van was a small counter with a mini fridge and even a sink, and the other had a wooden piece hanging from the wall, like it popped out and formed a table.

"It's really, really close to its final form," Hudson said, turning to peer at the space along with me. "Pretty cool, huh?"

"Does that faucet actually work?"

"Yeah, there's a small water tank underneath the sink. The mini fridge is powered by a battery, too. It's kind of crazy everything Lacey's tricked out in this thing. She really thought it through." Even though his words were positive, a strange note clung to them, almost like the sight of the van unnerved him a bit. He quickly shook it off, smiling at me. "Makes quite the vehicle to travel around in."

"Is this hers, then?"

"Yep. Or, it will be. It's technically a graduation-slash-birthday present."

I still didn't think that the van life was for me, but I

could appreciate it for Lacey. I had to admit, something about her seemed to fit that sort of free lifestyle. I hadn't gotten a chance to *really* talk to her yet, but from what I'd seen of her so far, she seemed bubbly, brave, and badass. I was glad Landon was dating a girl like her, especially since it meant I'd be able to get to know her more.

I raised an eyebrow at him. "Wait, you're driving her graduation present?"

"It's just a loan." Hudson propped his elbow on the steering wheel and peered at me, and I could've closed my eyes to bask in the warmth on his face. There wasn't a trace of the Grim Reaper mask he'd been wearing, no flatness, no malice. Just *him*. "I was right, you know."

"About what?"

Hudson reached out and coasted the palm of his hand down the back of my head, gently caressing until he came to the ends of my hair. "Long hair or short, you *are* still pretty. Still beautiful."

The words woke up the butterflies in my stomach, and I had to turn my head away so he didn't get to see my blushing cheeks full-on.

He must've caught enough of a glimpse, though, because he laughed. "Did I get lucky and I get to bring you with me to Tee's?"

I fell into the passenger seat and clicked my seatbelt into place, turning to look at him. "As long as we're not watching *Evil Killer Babies* 2 or something."

"Or playing zombie games. Even though I'm sure Simon will try to convince you."

"You'd have to show me the controls again." I thought

of the way his hand curved around mine when he'd shown me the first time, and I could remember the exact feeling that'd surfaced then, too.

Hudson must've been thinking the same thing. "You just want to hold my hand, don't you?"

"No," I said, letting my gaze roam over his face. "I just want to do this." And I leaned across the middle console and kissed him.

Hudson's lips immediately curved underneath mine, and the little smile that I kissed caused my heart to thump harder in my chest. The seatbelt cut into my neck, but I didn't care, pressing as close as I possibly could in the small cab. Hudson laid his hand on the side of my neck, his cool hand pressing against my hot skin. The entire world faded out except for the two of us, our pulses racing, our lips pressed together in the world's most perfect moment.

When we broke apart, Hudson leaned up and pressed one last kiss against my forehead, the tender touch causing my eyes to slip closed. "I think you're pretty great, Gemma with a G."

"And I think you're pretty perfect, Hudson with an H."

The boyish smile on his face was one I'd think about for the rest of my life. Lopsided, but miles away from the smirk he used to give as the Grim Reaper. This was Hudson with no guard up, no barbed wire keeping people out, and he was beautiful.

I cleared my throat as he started the car up, willing

my cheeks to cool down. "But seriously, you'll have to show me the controls again if I play that game."

Hudson put the car into gear before looking at me once more. "If you wanted to hold my hand," he said, reaching over, winding his fingers through mine where they rested on my leg, "you should've just asked."

I held Hudson's hand between both of mine as we made the journey to Tee's, excited to see them again, and excited that it was with permission this time. When I'd met them all for the first time, disappointment had been so heavy at the thought of never getting to *this* moment. Of being able to go to a friend's house without having to sneak out, of getting to sit beside Hudson without any negativity hanging over us. It wasn't rebellious to be beside him anymore, but I still felt electric with the excitement of it. Of finding my own friends, of finding myself, of finally getting to call Hudson Bishop something other than the Grim Reaper and Bridge Boy.

I finally got to call him mine.

Thank you so much for reading!
Order Book 4 in the Most Likely To series, *Fake Dating the Football Player*, today and read Lacey and Landon's story!

Flip the page to see a bonus scene from Hudson's point of view!

HUDSON'S POV

"I told you—the *left* side of the street."

"And I told you I didn't know which direction you meant we were coming from!"

I let out a disparaging sigh and slumped lower in the passenger seat of Derrick's car, kicking the soda cans and old receipts as I did so. There was more trash in the footwell than normal, because before we left my house to park at Willow, I made sure to collect whatever was in the backseat and put it up front.

Derrick's gaze flicked to my feet. "I don't think Milady would mind a few pop bottles at her feet, you know."

My knee bounced up and down. "You could've cleaned up a *little*."

"Hey, you never cared before." I didn't miss the smirk that tugged at his mouth. "But bring a pretty girl into the picture—"

I smacked him in the shoulder with the back of my hand, refusing to acknowledge him after that. Ever since we went to the movies, he'd been relentless. In hindsight,

I never should've invited him to the theater in the first place. It was an impulsive move, one born from two big brown eyes looking up at me and asking if I had any ideas on how we'd get a ride. All rational thought had dissolved into each of the flecks in her eyes, in the nervousness that coursed there—nervousness mixed with excitement.

So, of course I had to figure out a solution to the problem. Too bad my solution had a big mouth.

"She should be coming soon, huh?" Derrick asked, slapping his palm on top of his dash, causing the time to blink back into focus. "Unless she bailed."

It was a possibility, but one I didn't put too much weight on. "She'll come."

"You think this is a good idea, bro?" His voice turned serious, causing me to look over at him directly for the first time. He had an uncharacteristically solemn expression on his face, his dark eyebrows brought together. "Milady seems great—she really does—but what if her parents realize she snuck out? What if they find out she was with *you*?"

I'd be lying if I said that hadn't crossed my mind. The feelings that surged when I thought of Gemma's family were strange, mostly because they were so contradictory. The thought of her mother caused a scowl to spring to my face, unbidden, impossible to shake. Her mother was one of the reasons I carried the feared title I did—and so was Gemma's brother. One side of me wanted them to pay for all the issues and setbacks and trouble. The other part of me, though, couldn't separate them from Gemma. They were Gemma's family—the ones she loved—and I couldn't do anything that would hurt her in the end, too.

"We'll cross that bridge when we come to it," I said eventually, looking down the street. Gemma lived on the street perpendicular to this one, and I waited for her figure to pop up. It was two minutes past our agreed-upon time. "The benefits outweigh the risks, I guess."

"What are *you* benefitting from this? Sneaking her out and everything?"

I thought about the list I'd created—not quite a rebellion list like Gemma's, but one that held the two things that'd popped into my mind when I sat down to make it. *Help Gemma find herself. Fight my role.* Spending time with Gemma...I was doing just that. Both of those things. Two birds with one stone.

Derrick would've made fun of me to no end if I told him that, though. Might as well let him tease me about something he already knew. "It's like you said." My lips twitched into a half smile. "We get to be around a pretty girl."

This time, it was Derrick who thumped me on the arm, and my grin just widened at the way he cooed at me. I swatted him away, kicking the garbage at my feet again.

It was five minutes past our meeting time when I cursed myself for not giving her my number earlier. I had no way to check in with her to see if she was still coming, or if she'd gotten caught. Hopefully it wasn't the latter. Picturing Gemma in trouble because of me...it made my stomach turn.

Just when I started believing the idea that she wasn't coming, I saw her.

At first, I was almost convinced it wasn't her. Her legs were long and pale in the night, taking long strides as she came up the street. I'd never seen so much of her skin before, and the sight of it caused my chest to tighten. The nearer she drew, I realized that the blackness trailing behind her wasn't just the night—her long, dark hair was loose, much like it'd been the day she showed up at my house after school. The wind was tearing its fingers through it in a way I was jealous of, cascading it back and exposing her expression.

And *that* was what really had the air in my lungs freezing, crystalizing to a point that was painful. Gemma was grinning like she'd just gotten away with the world's biggest heist, and I'd never seen an expression so beautiful.

I knew it immediately then, accepting the fact without faltering. Whatever happened with us now from here on out, it would all be worth it for this moment. To see her so thrilled as she ran down the street, looking like she was laughing as she did so. To know that I was able to make her feel this way, even just once. A hint of this realization had come when we went to the movies, when I'd looked over at her and found her snorting at the scary movie that literally gave me nightmares. But now, I knew it for a fact. Someone write it on a stone tablet. Whatever Gemma Settler wanted, I was in it for the long haul. And whatever would happen, it would be worth it. Just for this moment.

Derrick slapped me again. "Dude, she's going the wrong direction."

I blinked to clear my head, spotting Gemma running down the street in front of us. "That's because someone —" I fumbled to unclasp my seatbelt "—parked on the *wrong side.*"

"I told you—" Derrick began, but I'd already thrown my door open, climbing out into the night.

"Gem!"

And Gemma whirled around, her hair spinning out, her skirt following the movement, and the grin she'd been wearing deepened at the sight of me. Dazzling. Beautiful.

Worth it, I thought as she bit down on her lip, swallowing a wide grin of my own. *Whatever happens, it's all worth it.*

www.ingramcontent.com/pod-product-compliance
Lightning Source LLC
Chambersburg PA
CBHW050955210726
48287CB00004B/1241